THE OFFICERS' CLUB

Forge Books by Ralph Peters

The War After Armageddon
The Officers' Club

THE
OFFICERS' CLUB

Ralph Peters

A Tom Doherty Associates Book  New York

THE OFFICERS' CLUB

Copyright © 2010 by Ralph Peters

A Forge Book
Published by Tom Doherty Associates, LLC
175 Fifth Avenue
New York, NY 10010

www.tor-forge.com

Forge® is a registered trademark of Tom Doherty Associates, LLC.

Library of Congress Cataloging-in-Publication Data

Peters, Ralph, 1952–
     The officers' club / Ralph Peters. — 1st ed.
        p.   cm.
     "A Tom Doherty Associates book"
     ISBN 978-0-7653-2680-5 (alk. paper)
     1. United States. Army—Fiction.   2. Women soldiers—Crimes against—Fiction.   I. Title.
PS3566.E7559O37   2011
813'.54—dc22

                                                    2010036252

First Edition: January 2011

Printed in the United States of America

0   9   8   7   6   5   4   3   2   1

To my beloved old black-boot Army

'Tis one thing to be tempted, Escalus,
Another thing to fall.
—Shakespeare, *Measure for Measure*

THE OFFICERS' CLUB

1

The guy flashing the badge at my door that morning looked like a Mormon missionary. His double-knit sport coat was a sweat machine, his cheap tie a noose. He glanced at the can of Tecate in my hand: wanton violation of the Sabbath.

We were off to a bad start.

"Special Agent Tompkins. CID. I'd like to ask you a few questions."

"Sure." I pushed open the screen door. He had the look of an NCO eager to be mistaken for an officer. "Want a beer?"

I couldn't help teasing him. I was screwed, anyway. A fitting end to the affair. Now that Nikki was gone, after reducing my heart to shit, somebody must have gone running to the chain of command, whining about a violation of the Uniform Code of Military Justice: *adultery*, a cold word for a conflagration. Probably her husband, whining from afar.

"Have a seat."

Tompkins sat on the couch, ignoring the stains. He glanced around, in search of evidence. Nikki was everywhere. But nowhere he could see.

His eyes settled on the unread Sunday paper. An Abscam conviction shared headline space with the Fed's 14 percent interest rate.

I leaned against the wall. Varnished knotty pine met bare flesh. The air conditioner grumped at the desert heat.

"Would you mind turning off the music?"

I flipped up the tonearm and stopped the record. Steve Winwood. *Arc of a Diver*. Not my life's usual soundtrack. One of Nikki's favorites. My self-flagellation.

"Did you just take a shower?" Tompkins asked. It wasn't great sleuthing: My hair was wet, and I wore nothing but a pair of cut-off jeans.

"Dropped the towel when you rang the bell."

"*Why* did you take a shower just now?"

I made a *what the fuck?* face. I'd been on a long suicidal run out in the proving grounds. Me against the Arizona sun. Stupidity, vanity and heartbreak, calves, thighs and lungs. I liked to jump the wire and run forbidden trails, just me and the rattlesnakes. The adjudicating authority could add that to the score.

"I stank."

"From what?"

"I was out running."

"How long were you gone?"

I shrugged. "About an hour. What's this all about?"

"Where were you were last night? Start at six in the evening and talk me forward."

I didn't see what my lonesome Saturday night had to do with Nikki and a conduct-unbecoming charge. Although it had everything to do with Nikki.

"I was here. All evening. All night."

"Alone?"

"Yes. Alone."

"That doesn't sound like you. The way people describe you." Then he added, "Lieutenant."

"Look, would you tell me what this is about?" I was no longer so sure that I knew. "And aren't you supposed to read me my rights or something?"

"Do you want me to read you your rights? Are you guilty of something?"

"You tell me."

"Do you consider yourself a suspect?"

"A suspect for what?"

"Where were you last night, Lieutenant Banks? Let's narrow it down. Where were you between midnight and six A.M.?"

"Here. I told you. I was in bed by midnight."

"Asleep?"

"I don't know when I fell asleep. But I was in bed."

"Were you alone?"

"I told you that, too." Alone. And sick at heart. Unable to read. Unable to bear any music I had played when we were together. Unable to jerk off without feeling puking sick at the thought of her gone.

"But you have no witnesses?"

"How could I have witnesses? I was alone."

He canted his head toward the wall behind him. Cinder block, painted white, on that side of the room. My apartment sat in the middle of a building that looked like a one-story motel bypassed by a new highway. Junk decorated the yards across the street; an abandoned Airstream lurked behind the back fence. Huachuca City, USA, model desert slum.

"Neighbors?"

"They might've heard me. I don't know. I didn't have the stereo on very long."

"So . . . you have no proof that you were where you say you were between midnight and six A.M.? Are you sure you didn't have any visitors? A female? Are you protecting someone's reputation? As a gentleman?"

I hadn't felt very gentlemanly of late. I didn't answer, didn't need to.

"What about your civilian friend from Bisbee, the homosexual?"

He spoke the last word as if fearing infection.

"He wasn't here. No female, either. For Christ's sake. Can't you tell me what this is all about?"

It couldn't be about Nikki. Even though everything in my life was about her now. Casual sex exploded into a wrecking passion. I fell in love with a slut as worthless as I was. Then watched, helplessly, as she walked away.

"Describe your relationship with First Lieutenant Jessica Lamoureaux."

The penny dropped. Partway. Jessie Lamoureaux was born for trouble. This was all about *her*. Nikki was just plain gone. Not even the CID was going to bring her back to me.

"I don't know what to call it, exactly. Not really friendship. Acquaintances? We've been on the outs."

"Did you ever have sexual relations with Lieutenant Lamoureaux?"

"No."

"You're certain of that?"

"I'd remember."

Was she the one facing charges? There was plenty of sleep-around, emotional bloodshed to raise a stink about. And the jealous wives to do it. Then there was the darker stuff. Much darker.

"Could you pass a polygraph on that? Swearing that you never had sexual relations with First Lieutenant Jessica Lamoureaux?"

"If the polygraph works. Yeah."

"Did you ever *attempt* to have sexual relations with her?"

"Jessie isn't my type."

He looked at me skeptically. To the average male observer, Jessie was everybody's type. "She never rebuffed you?"

I couldn't help smirking. I remembered Jessie naked, wet and cold, a gorgeous serpent, coiling around me. Waist-deep in the Sea of Cortez at two A.M. In one of the few wise actions of my life, I had broken her grip and waded back to the beach. That had been the beginning, not the end, of our relationship.

"She never 'rebuffed' me."

"Would you describe Lieutenant Lamoureaux as promiscuous?"

I killed the smile. "I'd describe her as socially energetic."

Then he slipped. An NCO, not an officer. "She was a very attractive woman, wouldn't you say?"

The chill hit me. It had nothing to do with the struggling air conditioner. "Has something happened to her?"

"Why do you say that?"

"You just used the past tense. You said she *was* an attractive woman."

That miffed him. He recalibrated his deadpan expression.

"Lieutenant Lamoureaux was murdered. Early this morning."

I sat down. On the floor. Right where I had been standing. I parked the empty beer can so clumsily that it fell on its side and rolled.

"Did you kill her?" Tompkins asked me.

I shook my head. Then I raised my hand: *Wait a minute, give me a minute.*

Dinwiddie? Had she driven the poor bastard crazy? Crazy enough to kill her? Or Jerry? He had the skills. And, in his mind, the reason. Gene? Earnest, silly Pete? The Kraut? Another broken lover, or his spouse? Jessie left plenty of casualties in her wake. Or had it been one of her murky Tucson pals? Or the Mexicans? Jessie played with so many different kinds of fire that getting burned was inevitable. But she never seemed the kind who wound up at the stake. Jessie got away with things, with everything. She might end up scorched, but not dead.

I thought of her shocking, reptilian beauty. Blue black hair and perfect skin that gleamed pale through a tan. Full lips and ruthless cheekbones. Arctic eyes so blue, they were almost gray. Torso slightly too long, legs faintly too short, but who cared? She could have been the damsel of a Deep South trailer court, or born to the best suite in a Geneva hotel. We had buried pasts in common.

"How did she die?" I asked.

Tompkins had been looking at me hard.

"No tears, Lieutenant Banks?"

I shook my head again. "Jessie wasn't the kind of woman I'd cry over. She would've laughed, if she saw me crying. How was she . . . how did it happen?"

"Are you sure you can't shed some light on that?"

I lost it. Scrambling to my feet. Knocking over a shelf of books and records. Barking. Snarling. Shouting.

"What the fuck, man? Read me my rights. Or stop playing asshole games. Just tell me how she died, for Christ's sake. Just tell me how she died."

He looked at me. Impassive. The master, after all. The bureaucrats always win, in the end.

"If you don't know how she died," he told me, "you don't want to know."

Exhibitionists pose for others, but narcissists pose for themselves. I was minding my own business. Alone with a half-empty can of beer, doing my existentialist riff on a Mex beach after midnight. It was March and the nights got cold, but I was the coolest living thing under that full moon. I sat on my ass on the sand and watched the water.

Puerto Peñasco was just a run-down fishing ville in those days, with one rathole motel that had rooms for roisterers down from Arizona for the weekend. At night, the town slept. If you hadn't brought along anybody to fuck, there was nothing to do.

I was soloing that weekend. I'd loaned my car to my current bed-filler so she could drive up to Scottsdale to visit her husband's family. Neither of us wanted them popping up at Fort Huachuca to see the sights.

So I was the odd man out in the little cabal we mockingly called the Officers' Club, our answer to the impossibly dreary O-club on the fort. To which we were forced to pay dues to keep the bar open for the walking dead who lived above the parade field.

I had come down to the beach to get away from the sexual vandalism in the next room. Jerry was banging his DD-cup date against the wall. To needle me. She made barnyard sounds. I could picture him grinning. Nor did I want to think about the scene between the other two officers who'd tagged along.

When I stretched out my hand, the sand felt startlingly cold. My denim shirt didn't keep me warm. But I was Mr. Zen, telling myself the chill was an illusion.

I didn't even want the beer, really. It was just part of the role.

The world refused to respond to my profundity. The moonlit sea just stayed the same, no matter how long you stared at it. I shifted from pondering infinity to think about the girl who'd borrowed my car. Tight little lieutenant, married to her ROTC sweetheart right after graduation. We could've made some noise, had she come along. Although that was all she was good for. Nicole Weaver, second lieutenant, United States Army. I didn't even know her maiden name. Didn't want to.

I stopped thinking about her, too.

I didn't hear Jessie Lamoureaux's approach. She could've been watching me for an hour. Although Jessie wasn't the kind of girl to wait that long for anything.

Bare feet, bare calves. Pale on the pale sand.

"I could've robbed you," she said. "I could've murdered you."

I shrugged. She sat down beside me. We stared at the *so what?* sea.

"It's beautiful," she said. "Isn't it? And so quiet."

"It was. Quiet."

She laughed. Jessie put more of a southern accent into her laugh than into her speech. And her speech was theatrical enough.

"Got another beer there, Mr. Serious?"

"Nope."

I couldn't really see her. But I'm sure she shook her head.

"Where I come from, no self-respecting gentleman would go wandering off from his friends in the dead of night with less than a six-pack. You Yankees aren't drinking men, are you?"

"We try not to puke on our dates."

"That girl you've been seeing's a terrible little slut. You must know that."

"Here. You can have what's left. It's warm."

She took the can. "I'm just sorry you and I haven't been able to have a heart-to-heart before this."

"Are we having a heart-to-heart?"

She drained the can and flung it. That was within the Mex rules. The poor bugger with whom she'd come down—a permanent-party major who wasn't supposed to be sneaking off with transient junior officers—had cut his foot on broken glass on the beach early in the evening. Before anybody had downed enough beer and tequila to have an excuse for bleeding.

"Where's the major?"

"How would I know? Asleep, I suppose."

"I thought you were together? That was the impression he gave. When he thrust himself on Jerry and me. His big date."

"We're just friends. Separate rooms—I'm surprised you didn't notice, Mr. Intelligence Officer. Oh, he's nice enough, I suppose. But not my type at all."

That explained why Major Leon Dinwiddie, a balding character battling a weight problem, had drunk more than a lacerated foot excused. Back at the fort, his nickname was Major Dim-witted. Even his fellow staff officers called him that. The U.S. Army Intelligence Center and School was a small town: Peyton Place without the moral restraint.

"So we're both alone," Jessie added. "You and me."

"I'm spoken for, ma'am."

She snickered. "You're fucking another officer's wife."

"That's putting it bluntly."

"I don't mind shocking people. When they need it."

"And I need it?"

"I think so. You're just playing at life. I've been watching you. For a while now. You don't have any future with that little tramp."

"Maybe I'm not looking for a future."

"Then why do you always walk around looking so serious when you're in uniform? And acting so hush-hush about that project they've got you on?"

The project *was* "hush-hush." In a doesn't-really-matter Fort Huachuca kind of way.

"What else have you found out, Inspector?"

"That you've got more walls around you than Parchman Farm."

"Keeps the little girls intrigued. Case in point. Watch out for the scorpions, by the way. They sneak up on you."

"The way I did? On you?" She granted me another stage laugh. "I should have been born a Scorpio. But I'm just a poor little Capricorn. What's your sign, Roy?"

It was the first time she'd used my name.

" 'Dead end.' "

"See what I mean? Well, I've done a little research into Second Lieutenant Roy Banks, I'll have you know."

"And?"

"You're twenty-eight years old. That's old, for a second lieutenant. Even for a first lieutenant."

"I'm former-enlisted."

"I know that, too. Four years."

"Major Dinwiddie show you my personnel file? Shame on him."

"He didn't do any such thing. The poor man. But you're flattered. Aren't you? That I went to so much trouble?"

"Depends on why." Two gulls strafed the moon.

"I've got my reasons."

"So now you know all there is to know. Case closed."

She kept her silence for a moment, picking up a fistful of sand to strew across the darkness.

"Southern girls do the math," she told me. "You're twenty-eight. Allow a year for OCS and the course you just finished out here, and that gets us down to twenty-seven. Subtract four years enlisted time. That brings us down to twenty-three. You didn't join the Army until you were twenty-three. Either that's pathetic and you were a complete failure at something else . . . or you've got something to hide."

"Maybe I'm hiding my failure?"

"Where *were* you between college and the day you joined the Army?"

"This an interrogation? Am I a prisoner?"

"I could make you my prisoner. If I wanted. Tell me about those missing years, Man of Mystery."

"I was a riverboat gambler. And a carnival barker. Then I did a short stint as an astronaut. After which I became a Zen monk." I turned my torso, examining her profile: 1940s Hollywood, back when women *had* profiles. Unpinned, her River Styx hair graced confident shoulders. "How about you, Miss Scarlett? I hear you came in from the National Guard for training, then convinced the Army to shift you to active duty. That takes some serious powers of persuasion. Or string-pulling of the first order . . ."

"What else do you think you know about me?"

"Only that you've already burned a hole in one marriage on post. The Kraut."

We called the *Bundeswehr* liaison officer "Hitler without the Charm."

"Colonel Faulenzer? He was just a pest. Just a poor, pesky old man. There was never anything between us."

"Enough for his wife to go crying to the commandant."

"And nothing came of it. Not one thing. Because nothing happened. Except that the creep would show up at my quarters in the middle of the night. What was I supposed to do?"

"Promote cordial international relations, I suppose. The point I was getting to is that you're not the world's youngest lieutenant, either."

"A gentleman never asks a lady about her age."

"That statement contains two possibly unjustified assumptions."

"I was enlisted myself. For a while."

"Naw. You don't have the enlisted gene. And I can do math, too. Basic arithmetic, anyway. I peg you for . . . say, twenty-six. Make that twenty-seven. Where were *you* all these years, Blanche? Shambling about the rooms of the old plantation?"

Jessie stood up. "We're wasting all this beautiful moonlight. I'm going for a swim."

She dropped her shorts and pulled her T-shirt over her head, tossing back her darker-than-darkness hair. I expected her to stop at her bra and panties. She didn't.

"You'll freeze," I told her. "And watch out for the glass."

"Sissy!" she yelled. With a laugh.

She ran for the water.

I did what I was conditioned to do. I stripped down and ran after her.

The water was shockingly cold. Splashing upward. Biting. I kept moving. Stones bruised my feet. She was tougher than I was.

When I caught up with Jessie, in waist-deep water, she turned to face me. Moonlight washed the left side of her face. I could not see the least hint of emotion.

Shock of skin-on-skin. One-size-fits-all, she *applied* herself to me. Wet flesh. Cold flesh. Warm flesh. Hair. Muscles.

"You were right," she said. "It's freezing." Her face reached up. A wet paw on the back of my neck pulled me down.

Our lips met.

Her tongue could have been a viper's.

I've never been able to put a name to what I felt, to that instant of un-categorizable revulsion. That single time in my life my instincts saved me.

I broke her grip. Roughly. And marched toward the shore.

It made no sense. None of it made sense. Why on earth was I walking away—running away—from a gorgeous, naked, aggressively willing woman? I felt her ghost against me.

I left the water in a rage. Behind me, I heard laughter.

. . .

When I strolled into the diner that Sunday morning, Jerry was already sprawled in our regular booth, grinning. After giving me a few more seconds of his cat-that-ate-the-whole-cage-of-canaries look, he called out to the waitress.

"*Rosalita, mi corazón! Una cerveza por mi amigo! Ándale! Es una emergencia!*"

"I don't want a beer," I told him, dropping into the booth facing him.

Jerry shrugged. "I'll drink it. Don't worry about it. Hey, you look tired, man. I'm the one's supposed to be tired. I almost came over to get you in the middle of the night, you know that? I needed some help, brother. She was definitely out of control."

He'd upgraded to a lonesome captain for the weekend. Lot of pent-up energy. She was plump for my tastes, but Jerry was an equal-opportunity fornicator.

"And where is the good captain, pray tell?"

Jerry grinned. "Good? She was *great*. More cushion for the pushin'. Just don't bring her back for a rematch in ten years. I never sleep with women I can't bench-press."

Rosalita, who had proved trainable over the months, didn't bring me a beer. She delivered hot water and a jar of Nescafé. It was as good as the local coffee got. A young, rotund Indian, she seemed to think we were funny, doubtless thought we were stupid, flirted with me and adored Jerry. All women adored Jerry. Even the ones who thought they hated him, the sort who derided him as an ass to each other, then screwed his brains out when their girlfriends weren't around.

I suppose I adored him, too. He'd been Special Forces as an enlisted man and looked the part. Handsome, the Marlboro Man's kid brother, he had massive biceps, an incandescent smile, and hilarious war stories from his time in Central America playing hide-and-seek with the Sandinistas. He was the soldier I wanted to be.

Rosalita hovered.

"Huevos rancheros," I told her. *"Por favor."*

Her meaningless smile didn't change. *"No hay huevos. Camarones?"*

"Sure. *Camarones.*" The joint, La Cita, couldn't be called fly-specked. Flies had more pride. But it was the only place to eat within an hour's drive. Toast might not be available and eggs were always iffy, but the fishing fleet docked down the street and shrimp were a mainstay.

"Camarones coke-tell?" Spanish wasn't her first language, either.

"Sure. *Sí. Camarones* coke-tell. My favorite breakfast. *Gracias.*"

Jerry's grin was unkillable. "I wonder if Major Dim-witted got more than he bargained for? Should we go out looking for his body?"

"I'm not sure he had the weekend he expected."

Jerry cocked an eyebrow. "Oh? And what am I to make of that, *mi amigo*? Don't tell me you were on the night shift, after all?"

Before I could answer, Jessie Lamoureaux paraded down the dirt street, khaki shorts, white blouse, and glam-girl sunglasses. She spotted us behind the window and waved. Fingers doing a ballet flutter.

"Man, I'd have to go into training . . . ," Jerry said.

I expected her to keep her distance after my flight—a retreat I already regretted, telling myself that I was king of the chimps for not nailing her on the beach in an X-rated version of the surf scene in *From Here to Eternity*. She was a stunning woman, all good dirt. What had I been thinking?

Jessie *wasn't* aloof. She smiled as if we were mad about each other, then slipped into the booth beside me, rubbing close, playful.

"Sorry if I frightened you last night," she told me. For Jerry's benefit.

He bit. "Is this true love . . . or merely lust, my children?"

"You'll never know," Jessie said. "Is that all they have? Nescafé?"

"You can have a beer," I said. "Where's the major?"

"Now, how would I know that?" She smiled at Jerry. "What I wouldn't give for a cup of French Market coffee right now."

"I thought you were from Mississippi," I said.

"Mississippi's where we go to church. N'Awlins is where we go to the devil." She took possession of my cup. "Pass the sugar?"

Major Dinwiddie limped in, bandaged foot wedged into a sandal. His face was absinthe green.

He misread the scene in front of him. As Jessie intended.

Jerry's captain didn't show up for breakfast. She'd come down with a morning-after case of Montezuma's revenge. It was hard to get her out of the motel.

The ride back to Fort Huachuca wasn't much fun.

2

I found Nikki on my couch, studying. Dressed in one of my T-shirts and curled up beside the lamp. She looked tiny. Tomboy haircut, with blond strands tucked behind her ears in her work mode. She began to rise, then made a face that erased her lopsided smile.

"I can smell you from here."

"Long story. Not worth telling."

On the way home, we had stopped a dozen times for Jerry's date to empty her guts by the roadside. She was dizzy and terrified at the thought of rattlesnakes in the ditches. I had expected Jessie to help her, but Jessie didn't do sisterly solidarity. She waited in the car in the heat, impatient. Major Dinwiddie offered advice, but the captain's distress mortified him.

By the final stretch, Jerry and I were both supporting the captain, whose name was Janet, as she shit brown water. She kept muttering, "I'm so ashamed. . . ." We ran out of tissues and then out of handkerchiefs. Janet threw up on me in the car. At the border crossing, the customs agent got one whiff of the vehicle's interior and waved us through fast.

Nikki came into the bathroom while I showered. Sitting down on the toilet lid, she raised her voice against the cascade. "Roy? I need you to explain something to me. We've got this IPB quiz tomorrow. And I don't get it, I don't get the difference between High Priority Targets and High Value Targets. They sound the same to me."

The school was going through its early Intelligence Preparation of the Battlefield phase, an attempt to systematize the dynamic chaos of war. I was skeptical. All I saw were clumsy overlays that made it impossible to read the map beneath them.

I turned off the water and reached for the towel. "An HPT is a target you need to hit fast, either because it influences the current fight, or because it presents a fleeting opportunity. An HVT is just about anything that would screw up the enemy, if he loses it."

"Why can't they just say that? In the manual?"

"Doctrine writers get paid by the syllable. Don't you think you have an excessive amount of clothing on?"

"Be serious. Just for a minute."

"I *am* serious."

She looked at me. "Just help me for a minute, okay? Please, Roy. If a High Priority Target influences things, the way you say, why isn't that the same as a High Value Target?"

"It's not a perfect system. Somebody just thought up the terms, and everybody else went along. Think of it like this: The person you want to spend the weekend with is a High Priority Target. The person you might marry is a High Value Target. Sometimes, a High Priority Target turns out to be a High Value Target. But for testing purposes, I'm an HPT. Your husband's an HVT. Date tactically; marry strategically. How were the in-laws?"

"The subject's off-limits."

"Then how was your weekend?"

"A month of boredom crammed into two days. How was yours? Fun in the sun?"

"Bland in the sand. I wish you'd been with me."

"Me, too." She stood up and took off the T-shirt.

"I love it so much," she said. Voice breaking. "*God,* I love it so much." It was what she'd said the first time she felt me inside her. On the way back from Nogales. Pulled off on the side of the road in the middle of the afternoon. Not giving a damn who saw what. It was what she always said.

"I'm still not your type?" she asked.

We needed to be sleeping. The duty day came early. Instead, we lay in our sweat. With the air charged between us.

"No."

"No blondes."

"That's right."

"Because blondes have no souls."

"Right."

"But I'm an exception. For equal-opportunity purposes."

"Right again."

"I'm a dirty blonde, anyway."

I chuckled. "In more ways than one."

On time delay, she asked, "Should I take that as a compliment?"

"Under the circumstances."

"And we're just fuck-buddies. And that's all we'll ever be."

"Right."

"And we're not getting emotionally involved."

"What is this, a catechism?"

"I'm looking out for you, Roy. I need to be sure *you* understand the rules."

"All clubs, no hearts. When you leave Fort Huachuca, it's over. Got it."

"And we're just using each other."

"Purely for recreational purposes."

"You're not going to make me fall in love with you, you know. I really need you to understand that. I'm being honest with you. So don't make this some macho ego thing, all right?"

"I'm not going to fall in love with you, either, kiddo."

"I'm glad."

"Me, too."

"I need to wash before we go to sleep."

I reached out in the dark and found her wrist. "Don't."

"I need to wash you out of me."

"Don't."

She didn't answer, just turned on her side. I held her until she fell asleep, then kept on holding her.

"Pussy!" Jerry said.

I struggled with the weight. Grunting. Arching my back the way they told you not to.

"Come on. You can do it. Don't be a twat."

But I couldn't. I felt myself losing it. Arms quivering.

"Help me."

After a torturous, teasing few seconds, he did. He yanked the bar up and settled it in the cradle. I had tried to bench 230, but couldn't make the ten-pound jump. I was a runner, not a lifter.

I sat up. Half-sick from the effort. Still a little dehydrated from too much alcohol and too little *agua* in Mexico.

Major Dinwiddie limped into the gym. Our uniforms back then looked like green janitor's outfits. The major's blouse was too tight across the middle. He scanned the room, spotted us, then made his way through the lunchtime crowd.

"Lieutenant Banks? Lieutenant Purvis?"

In Mexico, it had been *Roy* and *Jerry*. We were back on duty now.

I rose. "Yes, sir?"

"May I speak to you two men?"

We mumbled and shrugged.

"Outside, I mean."

We followed him out past the front desk. Two months late, the attendant was mounting a framed photo of President Reagan in the entryway, at the top of the chain of command rogue's gallery. Carter lay discarded on the floor. I wasn't sure about the former actor in the White House, but I liked the rumors of a big pay raise.

Warm sun, crisp breeze, pure sky. Beyond a fringe of military buildings, rugged mountains rose from the high desert. God made Arizona after he'd had a lot of practice.

The major cleared his throat. In a badly scripted movie. The brim of his green baseball cap shadowed his small eyes.

"I just . . . wanted to be certain that we all understand each other. Not everybody understands . . . the spirit of off-duty fellowship. Some people are very rank conscious, you know. I wouldn't want anyone to get the wrong idea. About this weekend . . ."

"What happens inside the Officers' Club is off the record, sir," Jerry assured him. "You were never even there."

Major Dinwiddie nodded. "And you both understand that nothing untoward—nothing inappropriate—happened between myself and Lieutenant Lamoureaux. We're simply friends. I've been trying to mentor her."

"Yes, sir," I said. "Got it."

"She's misunderstood, you see. She's been the victim of unjust innuendo. Lieutenant Lamoureaux actually maintains a high moral standard. She was afraid you boys might misunderstand."

"Did she ask you to talk to us?" I said.

"No, no. I inferred that. We all have to be wary of a young female officer getting an undeserved reputation. I just wanted to be sure we all understood each other."

"Yes, sir," Jerry said. "No problem. You weren't there; she wasn't there. Not sure I'd recognize her, if she walked past me this minute."

Dinwiddie caught the sarcasm. It wasn't elusive.

"No need to carry things to extremes, Lieutenant. I'm just glad we all understand each other." He summoned a staff officer's smile, then limped away. We both saluted. He didn't look back.

Jerry and I turned back to the gym.

"Well, she didn't give him any, that's for sure," Jerry said. "Poor old Dim-witted."

The men's locker room was a humid crypt. At least one hidden body was in an advanced state of decomposition.

Jerry toweled himself and preened. He could be so insufferable, it made me shake my head and laugh.

"Hey, I told you," he said as I slipped on my watch. "Get rid of that piece of junk, get yourself a *real* Rolex, not the training wheels version." My watch showed only the time and date. Jerry wore one of those monster Rolexes equipped for a trip to Mars. Special Forces types liked big watches, big breasts, and big engines in their cars. Jerry drove a Corvette. Struggling with the payments.

"It's got sentimental value," I told him.

"Yeah, yeah, yeah. Truth is, you're just cheap-ass. That wreck you drive."

"It's going to be a classic."

"It isn't going to last that long. It's going to disintegrate. I can see it now. You and your tomboy Lolita stranded on I-10, halfway to Tucson. I'm sure a trucker will give her a lift, but you'll be food for the coyotes." He cackled. "I don't know what any woman sees in you, *compadre.*"

"You're all booked up. So they settle for second-best." I stood up with a jerk. And regretted it. "Shit. I think I pulled something."

"Man, you are *such* an MI weenie."

"You're an MI weenie, too, now. Remember?"

Jerry grunted. "Not for long, pardner. I'll be back in SF before you know it. Why do you think I'm still here on casual status? Wheels are turning, pal. Meanwhile, you're still a wimp."

"Like the last time we ran up the canyon? A pregnant woman could double-time circles around your ass."

"Want me to come over for a beer after work?"

"I might be working late."

He pulled up his zipper and rolled his eyes. "You're such a lifer. Nobody takes anything to do with the training department seriously. It's not like this is Fort Benning or something. And your buddy Massetto doesn't have a clue." He glanced at his massive watch. "Old Gene can lock my heels, but I'm going to duck over to the clinic to check on Janet."

"They kept her in?"

"Dehydration, man. To be expected. But stay away. She'll never want to see you again, after all you saw back in *México lindo*." Jerry shrugged. "Fact is, I don't want to see her, either. I mean, yuck. One more of life's little mistakes. But what can you do?"

Captain Gene Massetto stood with folded arms in front of the cluttered maps covering the walls. He had let himself into the room at the back of the secure facility where I was working on "the project."

"Don't stretch the lunch hours out too long," he told me.

"I was working out. I plan to stay late."

He nodded. It wasn't a harsh admonition. But Gene took everything about the Army seriously. He had ended up being my boss back at Fort Hood and had recommended me for Officer Candidate School. In spite of the traditions of military decorum, we had become friends across the ranks.

Of the two pals I felt I had at Fort Huachuca, it would have been hard to achieve a greater contrast. Jerry Purvis was the guy you wanted to go catting with or to have on your side in a bar fight. Gene Massetto was the one you would trust with the thing that you loved the most. Jerry was a wild man. Gene had a little brush he used to clean under his fingernails, a habit he said he developed as an enlisted man in Vietnam. Jerry rarely stuck with a woman for more than a few weeks. Gene had a classic presentation wife, Marilyn. Gene adored her almost as much as Marilyn adored him.

Gene could have been an Italian prince, the sort who plays polo, while Marilyn looked like an updated Rita Hayworth. In reality, he was a surfer from Huntington Beach who'd been drafted, served in Nam, then got a commission through ROTC. Marilyn was a flame-haired Midwestern gal who never finished college. Utterly out of step with the times, she just wanted to be a wife. They were unfashionably happy. She cooked dinners that belonged on *The Donna Reed Show,* and Gene ate them without paying much attention. I never heard her utter an obscenity, and Gene never raised his voice inside his home.

He wore Brut cologne, and she wore Shalimar in excess, as if someone deep in her past had told her that girls smell.

"Impressive," Gene said, looking over my work. He picked up a stack of spot reports I was drafting. They fed students the information, bit by bit, that they'd need to analyze the scenario laid out on the maps. "How close are you?"

"A month. Maybe five weeks."

"Make it a month. Maximum. I want time to take Colonel Jacoby through it from start to finish and have plenty of space to make any changes he wants. And he'll want changes, trust me. He can't help himself. He's old white-glove-on-the-footlocker Army."

"It's going to be a difficult exercise, sir." Although we used first names off duty, I always threw in the occasional *sir* when we were in uniform. Even when it was only the two of us. The world just worked better that way. "I mean, really tough."

"Jacoby wants it tough. He was furious when he found out the captains in the Advanced Course were doing the same final exercise as the lieutenants."

The scenario I'd designed laid out a Soviet breakthrough effort in the Meiningen Gap in Germany. In most of the map exercises the Intelligence officers faced in their course work, the problems were elementary and unrealistic. A Soviet tank regiment in an assembly area was plotted at a single grid, while the real thing would've sprawled over a dozen square kilometers or more. For the attack phase, I factored in fuel consumption, resupply problems, communications challenges, and vehicle breakdowns that threw off the textbook numbers of moving target indicators. I even created distinct personalities and behavior patterns for the Soviet commanders, something I had never seen done in a war game. I'd been given the mission of creating the most realistic training exercise possible. I took it seriously.

The one condition was that no one could know I was doing it. Gene had the only other key to the room, which had been a supply closet. Back at Fort Hood, he had hauled me up to the brigade Intel shop from a line battalion after recognizing that I was covering for an alkie deuce. Now he was using a new lieutenant, held over at Fort Huachuca, to design the end-of-course training exercise for captains. If the captains found out, it was a prescription for a mutiny.

"What's this?" Gene asked, pointing to an odd symbol on the map.

"PRTB. Mobile rocket technical base. See that go active, and you need to get ready for nukes, bugs, or gas."

"The captains are going to hate whoever designed this."

"They'll figure it was you, sir."

Gene nodded. "Well, blaming another captain's bad enough. Let one word of this slip, and I'll Article Fifteen your butt from here to the unemployment line. How late were you planning on working?"

"Depends. Seven, maybe."

"Knock off at six. Come over to the house. Marilyn's making meat loaf. There'll be plenty. And make sure you're drinking enough water in this sweatbox."

"Can I bring a six-pack? Jug of dago red?"

He waved the offer away. "By the way, Roy . . ."

I met his eyes.

"People notice. Nobody's saying anything. Yet. About that married lieutenant. Be a little discreet, huh? Big taboo. And regulations are regulations."

I had been home just long enough to hit the head and put Ornette Coleman on the turntable when the doorbell rang. Sometimes the bell worked; sometimes it didn't. It was my unlucky night.

Jessie Lamoureaux. Jeans and a sweatshirt, not a seduction outfit. I hadn't heard her pull in, but she drove a beat-up Maverick and generally tried to park it out of sight. It was the kind of detail I believed an Intelligence officer should notice. I should have paid attention to more important things.

"May I come in?"

"If you promise to keep your clothes on."

She smiled, not displeased, and brushed past me. Inside, she kicked off her tennis shoes.

"That okay? Or do you find feet erotic? I never understood that."

I didn't find feet erotic.

"Beer?"

"Have any wine?" She dropped onto the sofa. In Nikki's usual spot. Near the lamp, but not too near.

"Just mountain zin. Jug stuff."

"I'll take that. Please. Where's your little cheerleader reject?"

"No need to be catty."

I poured her a glass of wine. I wasn't drinking.

"I just didn't want to interrupt anything. Am I interrupting anything?"

"No. But it's a work night."

"I'll drink my glass and go. You're not much of a host."

"I like to know what a guest has in mind."

"We can have a truce. I come to you in peace. All right?"

"And I'm a Quaker."

She looked absolutely stunning in repose. In her sweatshirt and jeans. It was *not* a prescription for a truce. She pulled her feet up under her. "Obviously not feeling your oats . . ."

"I thought we had a truce?"

"We do. But I need a period of adjustment. I never had a man turn me down like that. Wounds a girl's vanity."

"What's this about, Jessie?"

"We never finished our conversation. On the beach. Where were you? Between college and the day you joined the Army?"

"Why?"

"I've been telling myself it might explain something. The girl who broke your heart. Did she look like me? Was that it?"

"Nobody looks like you."

"A compliment, Lieutenant Banks?"

"A fact."

"Are we changing our mind?"

"No."

"Your little blondie's an awful tramp, you know. And she's not even that pretty. Just mildly cute, if you ask me."

"I didn't. Ask you."

"If it wasn't you, it'd be whoever showed up."

"Claws out, Lieutenant Lamoureaux?"

"And she has a boy's ass. Does that turn you on?"

A fist hammered on the doorframe. Jerry. He knew the bell was unreliable.

I let him in. He looked at me, at Jessie. He was wobbling drunk. And crying. Jerry didn't cry.

"What's the matter, man?"

"I hit a curb. Down the street. Hit the curb. I think . . . I think I bent the wheel."

"Come on, for Christ's sake. It's not that big a deal. You probably just knocked it out of alignment."

"Stupid bitch. Stupid fucking bitch."

"You're coming in broken, brother. Say again entire transmission."

"Stupid motherfucking bitch."

"Who? The Vette?"

"Janet. Fatso. Fat ass. Her."

"I thought she was in the hospital?"

"They let her out. She went back to the BOQ. And hanged herself. She fucking hanged herself, man. Because she was fucking embarrassed. I mean, what the fuck, man? What the fuck?"

He kicked over my coffee table. Books flew. Jessie leapt out of the way.

Jerry sat down on a chair too small for him, burying his face in big hands. It was a side of him I'd never seen, never imagined.

"It's not your fault, Jerry. Christ. She ate something and got sick. She couldn't help it. We just tried to help her. It can't have been just that . . ."

"I *hate* this place," Jerry said. "I *hate* it. Fort goddamned We-gotcha. It just screws people up, I swear. I wish I was back in SF. But I just had to be a fucking officer. . . ."

"When did you hear about it?"

He raised a tormented face. "I found her."

Jessie put a hand on his shoulder. I recall the ghost of a smile, but I might be creating that memory.

"Come on," she told Jerry. "I'll drive you home."

Two days later, after our lunchtime workout, Jerry asked me, "Did Jessie tell you she visited Janet in the hospital?"

I pulled on my right sock. "No." I pondered it for a moment. "Jessie doesn't strike me as the bedside manner type. She wasn't much use on the drive back."

Jerry nodded. "But she helped Janet check out. And drove her back to her BOQ room. Life's a funny thing."

"You do her? The other night?"

"Jessie? Sure. It was almost worth banging up the Corvette." He tucked one leg of his starched fatigues into a combat boot. "Speaking of which . . . could you loan me three hundred bucks until I get my income tax refund?"

3

My mother had me on the phone. Mom stuff. She was the only woman of German descent in Cincinnati who had kept her figure over forty, but she couldn't escape the *Hausfrau* taint entirely. I recalled visiting her parents, Oma and Opa, as a child. They refused to leave Over-the-Rhine, even though it was already a ghetto. Born on the banks of the Ohio River in the first decade of the twentieth century, they still had faint German accents.

My mother's voice was pure suburbs.

"Oh, I almost forgot the reason I called," she said.

"Another reason?"

"Don't you be a smarty-pants. A letter came for you. From one of your foreign friends."

"I don't have any foreign friends."

"I can never read their writing, but it looks like the first name is Al. Is he the one who wrote to you before?"

"Just throw it away."

"That's rude. And you know it. I didn't raise you to be rude. If someone takes the trouble to write to you, you should at least read the letter, show that much courtesy."

"I don't want to read any letters. You know that."

She sighed. The eternal mom sigh. "I wish you'd tell me what happened over there, Roy. It's been almost five years. Or has it been longer? I lose track since we lost your father. You could talk to me. I'm your mother."

"Nothing happened. So there's nothing to talk about."

"I can put the letter in another envelope."

"Don't. Please, Mom. Just toss it."

She gave up. And moved on. "I ran into Ingrid Schaeffer the other day. I always warned you she'd get heavy before she was thirty. You should see her, she's the size of a house."

One result of my mother keeping her figure was that she loved to see other women get fat. Especially younger ones. A friend's overweight daughter was cause for celebration. Mom wasn't mean. Just human. And she didn't have a lot else to delight in since my father's death. He'd been a political-machine man who dreamed of running the machine himself, but never rose above middling city offices. The official story was that he died of a heart attack in a booth at his favorite coffee shop, but rumor had it he was visiting an apartment in Over-the-Rhine. And not hunting for the last traces of my mother's German heritage.

When I dropped the phone back in its cradle, Nikki pressed against me and said, "What was all that stuff about your foreign friends? I could hear everything, you know."

"My mother has a rich fantasy life," I told her.

"Were drugs involved?"

I stood at parade rest, rigidly, in front of Colonel Jacoby's desk. With the office door shut.

I opened my mouth to speak. He cut me off.

"Think before you answer, Lieutenant."

Even sitting, Jacoby projected ferocity. The shaven head was the least of it. He was a big man, all gristle and bone. The colonel was built for football without shoulder pads, but his waist would've been the envy of any southern belle. When he lit a fresh cigarette—a Camel—it looked like a toothpick in his big, smashed paw. But all of that was pure marshmallow compared to the expression he wore in perpetuity.

"Sir, to the best of my knowledge—"

He lifted a hand, cutting me off again. "Don't use qualifying phrases. Fuck me to bloodred tears. I am going to break all of you of your MI on-the-other-hand, cover-your-ass bullshit. Speak like a man. Directly. Were drugs involved?"

"No, sir. I have no reason to—"

"Didn't you hear a word I said? 'Yes, sir,' or 'No, sir.' That's all I want to hear."

"No, sir."

"Better."

He leaned back in his chair. Taking a hit off the Camel. In contrast to most up-the-chain-of-command offices, Jacoby's was a monk's cell. He hadn't covered the walls with plaques, awards, and citations or littered the standard-issue bookcase with military knickknacks. There was just a red and white pennant from 2/7 Cav and a couple of photos from his unit in Vietnam.

"How well did you know Captain Flanagan?"

"Sir, I saw her around post. But I never spoke to her before she got in the car last weekend."

"So you didn't know her? Anything about her?"

"No, sir. Just her rank and her name."

"I suppose the name Colonel John Flanagan doesn't mean anything to you?"

"No, sir."

"Went down in a Huey north of Bong San. Janet Flanagan was his daughter. Only child." He looked down at his desk, but caught himself after an instant. "Not made of the same stuff as John, apparently. Why do you think she hanged herself, Lieutenant Banks?"

"Sir, on our drive home—"

"Spare me the story about her embarrassment for crapping herself. I've already heard that one from Lieutenant Purvis." He sat back again. The chair's springs bitched. "Captain Flanagan was extremely religious. Catholic, of course. Not that you would've known that. Or cared. Why do you think she agreed to go on a weekend jaunt to Mexico with a lieutenant she hardly knew?"

"Sir, Jerry Purvis draws women like flies. He's very—"

"You are a no-go at this station. She received her final decree of divorce last week. She didn't mention it?"

"No, sir. Not to me."

"And neither you nor Purvis would've cared, anyway. Am I right?"

"Yes, sir."

He leaned forward, planting his elbows on the glass plate that covered his desk. "Look, Banks. I don't expect lieutenants to be angels. God knows I wasn't. But keep it in limits. Stop once in a while to consider the consequences." He grunted. "I'm not one of these goddamned Holy Rollers. I don't care what any of you do in your private lives. Until you bring it on post and it interferes with the mission. Don't interfere with the mission, Banks. Understand me?"

"Yes, sir."

"I doubt it." He shook his head. Slowly. As if the muscles in his neck resisted. "Do you *know* what it takes to rebuild an army? To take an organization that's been gutted and shit on, and to thump, hammer, and beat it back into health? I wish you—you and your buddy Purvis—could've experienced the Army I served in as a lieutenant. Before Vietnam. It wasn't perfect, but it was a thing of fucking beauty. High and tight, six days a week, and no excuses. Think you would've lasted in that Army, Banks?"

"I don't know, sir."

"No. You don't fucking know. All right, stand at ease. Unless you have something else to tell me about the late Captain Flanagan?"

41

I relaxed my posture. But not much.

"How's our project going? You going to put the Advanced Course through the wringer for me?"

"Sir, Captain Massetto thinks—"

He slammed his palm down on his desktop. The landscape rattled. "Jesus Christ, what does it take? Did I ask you what Captain Massetto thinks?"

"No, sir."

"I am going to make men of you yet, I fucking swear. I am sick and tired of MI officers equivocating and fucking tap dancing and ducking behind the opinions of others when anybody asks them a question. So let's try again, Lieutenant: How's our special project going?"

"It's going well, sir."

"And it's going to be tough? I want them to hate it while they're going through it. But I want them prepared for what it's really like out there. I don't want them standing in front of their division commander and giving him baby talk history lessons."

"It's going to be tough, sir."

He almost smiled. "Well, Captain Massetto thinks so, too. He's worried it might be too tough, that they'll all be whining by the end of the first day. If they do, that's fine with me. One last thing, Banks."

"Yes, sir."

"I want you to do something for me. Confidentially. It's personal. A request, not an order. But you will not breathe a word of this to another living thing, whether you agree to help me or not."

"No, sir."

"If you sense that Major Dinwiddie's about to get himself in trouble . . . trouble of *any* kind . . . I want you to let me know *mach* fucking *schnell*." His face hardened. "I'm well aware of the views some people on this post have of him. Suffice it to say, there's more to the man. But that's none of your business. You just need to know that I take a personal interest in Major Dinwiddie. Who's been going through a nasty divorce of his own, by the way. Come see me . . . or call me . . . if you think he might do something foolish. Will you agree to do that?"

"Yes, sir."

"For the record: I'm not asking you to be some sneaking little spy. No CI crap. I'm just interested in helping a man who may need help. A man who's earned it. I need somebody to shoot the red star cluster, if it comes to that."

"Yes, sir."

"Dismissed."

I cracked the heels of my Corcorans together. The sound would've passed muster with Frederick the Great. When I saluted, I brought my hand up fast, shaving an imaginary millimeter of lint off my uniform.

Jacoby snapped a field salute back at me, then took up a stack of papers. I pivoted and marched for the door.

"Lieutenant Banks?" he called. Just before I exited.

"Yes, sir?"

"I'm told you have the makings of a competent officer. Don't fuck it up."

"You always hang around the men's underwear section?" I asked Jessie Lamoureaux.

Her smile would have seduced legions. "Not regularly. I just saw you and came over. There's something I need to tell you." The smile never wavered.

We stood in the ratty PX. Jockey shorts were about the only thing worth buying. Maybe athletic socks, too. Civilians imagined the post exchange as a treasure house, but it was a junk shop stocked with last year's unsold merchandise from down-market chain stores.

Jessie stood out in those shabby aisles. To say the least. Her beauty was such that men and women alike could not walk by without staring at her.

She glanced at the plastic-wrapped underwear in my hand, reading the size. "Aren't men's underwear dull, though? I couldn't stand it, if I were a man."

"You had something to tell me?"

"You need to help your girlfriend. With her studies. She's flunking her course work."

"And how would you happen to know that?"

"Roy, do you think they have me sitting in the faculty offices just for decoration? I've been grading exams all day. And I'm only telling you this—I really shouldn't tell you—because I trust you. And you need to know. She's flunking out."

I shrugged. "If they recycle her to the next class, I'll just have her around longer. Nikki's nice to have around."

The response jolted her. As if she hadn't thought things through.

"You're an absolute monster," she said. Without conviction.

"Any news on your clearance?" Jessie had wangled an assignment to a specialized course that prepared officers to manage the analysis of highly classified imagery. The catch was that she needed a top secret clearance for the program. And there'd been a hold up on the Defense Investigative Service end. In the meantime, the academic department had parked her in admin support. Apparently, they trusted her to grade papers. Among God knew what other office missions.

"Oh, it'll be here any day. There's a *terrible* backlog of investigations. The agents here on post are very apologetic." She stepped closer, lowering her voice. Even in uniform, she wore an evening perfume. "The truth is, Roy, my daddy was involved in what people down our way call 'checkered financial affairs.'" She sighed, a belle watching from the plantation porch as her gray-clad beau rides off to war. "Poor Daddy always means well, but he's just too genteel to make a good businessman."

On the other side of the underwear rack, an overweight Army wife wheeled a shopping cart past us. The cart corralled a fat little yard ape, and the woman's smile spit poison. Jessie would never be just one of the girls.

"I hear that you and Jerry are an item," I said. "Congratulations."

"Now, did he say that?" She shook her head, briefly widening those blue gray eyes. "Isn't that sweet?" She put on an expression meant to express concern. "I hope I didn't lead him on."

I was still too polite to roll my eyes. "That's between you and Jerry. Gotta go, sweetheart."

She summoned her smile again. "Roy, I just *adore* it when you try to be manly in your speech. It's charming, in its silly way. . . ."

"Then I'll see you around, toots."

"Not this weekend. I'm invited to a party in Tucson."

"All weekend?"

"It's a *very* interesting party."

"And you expect me to relay the message to Jerry? Is that the point?"

"Only if you want to, Roy. I wouldn't want him wasting his time looking all over for me."

"Jessie, you are a work of art."

She smiled wonderfully. "It's nice to be appreciated." She turned away before I could pivot myself.

All I wanted to do was to pay for my three-pack of underwear, drive back out the North Gate road to Huachuca City, and leave the duty day behind. But I got a tap on the shoulder before I could head for the line of cash registers.

"Hi, Roy! Is she your girl now? She's really beautiful. I guess she's what people call a classic beauty. Wouldn't you say?"

It was my fellow lieutenant, Pete Paulson, who was assigned to the care and feeding of the enlisted students. Pete was short, with a crew cut and an underdeveloped nose. He was supposed to set an example for the enlisted kids, but his uniform always managed to go awry, with a gigline by Picasso. He couldn't shine his boots properly, either.

Pete had taken it as his personal mission to bring me back to Jesus.

"No, she isn't my girl."

"She sure is beautiful, though. Is she new around here?"

"Jessie? She's been around for months. Come on, Pete. You must've noticed her. Jessie Lamoureaux's kind of hard to miss."

He shook his head. Squeezing an excess of honesty into his facial features. "I guess I've had other things on my mind. But she sure is a head-turner."

"Pete, for your own good, file that woman under 'Delilah.' Or 'Jezebel.' Okay?"

"Whatever you say, Roy." He had a glee club smile and freckles. "You know, you never came to our Wednesday-night prayer meeting. After you promised me."

I flared. "Pete, I *never* promised I'd come. *Never*. I said I'd *think* about it."

"And did you? Think about it?"

"Yes. I actually did think about it. And I decided I'd just resent being there. Being cornered into it. All right?"

"I didn't mean to make you feel cornered. But the battle to save souls is unconditional warfare."

"Oh, Jesus Christ. Did you make that up yourself, Pete? Or is the church newly militant?"

"Don't worry, Roy. I'm not going to criticize you for taking the Lord's name in vain. I realize it's just a casual expression to you. We're not intolerant. But you really should come to one of our prayer meetings. You'd be surprised how many officers come. Enlisted men, too. We're all brothers in Christ, you know. And the ladies of the church provide free sandwiches, and coffee and cookies. We have a good time together."

"Pete . . . why are you so convinced that I don't believe in the message of Jesus Christ?"

"Because you sin. And glory in it."

I weighed the proposition. "Yup. I sin. That is a fact, Pete." I folded my arms, clutching the packet of Jockey shorts under an armpit. "Not sure I glory in it, though. Anyway, we're all sinners, aren't we?"

"Yes, Roy. That's true. We're all sinners. But only those who seek redemption will be forgiven when he returns to judge the living and the dead."

"Well, I'll find my own path to salvation, all right? Thanks, Pete." I began, yet again, to head for the checkout line.

He tapped my forearm, demanding further attention. "That's the sin of Pride talking. I don't mind if you laugh at me, Roy. I really don't. I know you're a good person. Underneath everything. I can see it."

"Tell it to Colonel Jacoby. Listen, Pete. I really have to be getting along."

"Sure. I understand. But, please . . ."

To my dismay, he got down on his knees. Between the dangling two-for-one packs of socks and the T-shirts. The guy was a true believer, I'll say that for him. Martyrdom always sounded easy to me. It's glamorous. But embarrassing yourself in the post exchange takes a serious commitment.

"Pete, get up. For fuck's sake, man."

"I want you to promise me something, Roy. Just one small thing."

"What?"

"Tonight . . . I want you to read Galatians. Just the first chapter. I'm not even asking you to pray. Just read it. Tonight."

"I'll read it. All right. Get up. Okay?"

"You promise?"

"I promise."

The bloated wife with the chubby ankle-biter was on her return trip. She clucked her tongue. Loud enough to be heard over on the rifle range.

Pete got up. Grinning.

"May I go now?" I asked.

"Sure, Roy. Of course. I'll walk out with you." He straightened his uniform, leaving it more askew. "That girl you were talking to really was a beauty, I have to say. What was her name again?"

I stopped. In front of a display of Russell Stover candies.

"Don't try to save her soul, Pete. I'm not sure she has one."

He touched my forearm again. As a girl might.

"But what was her *name*?"

Nikki called out my name. It shocked me. Nikki never used names during sex. I figured she was afraid she'd get them confused.

It excited me. Unreasonably. She called my name again.

Sex strips down a voice to its essence. We hear things, or imagine we do, that go unsaid in the milder moments we share.

Afterwards, as we lay in the lamplight, I asked her, "Why did you get married?"

"The subject's off-limits."

I didn't ask again. The tonearm reached the center of the record.

"Any requests?"

"It seemed like a good idea at the time."

"What?"

"Getting married. I love Jimmy, anyway. You probably think that's funny."

"No, I don't. Choice of music, *madame*?"

"I don't want to hear anything else. Turn it off, please. Jimmy has a house picked out for us. At Fort Lewis. I'm going to make it work."

"All right."

"I'm a slut. I know it. I can't keep my skirt down. But I'm going to get better."

"Don't start yet. Okay?"

"I wonder what you really think of me."

"I think you're physically spectacular."

"Even though I'm blond?"

"Even though you're blond. My bigotry has been unfounded."

"Can we be serious? For a minute."

"Sure." I was being serious. As serious as I could stomach.

"We have to stick to the deal."

"Fuck buddies. Got it."

She rolled against me. "I wish we didn't ever have to talk. I hate talking."

And she hated reading anything that wasn't required. She hated jazz. Maybe she hated me a little. Apart from being Army officers, we had nothing in common but flesh.

Later, before she drifted off to sleep, I asked her if she needed help with her studies.

"Why?"

"You asked me about High Value Targets. Remember? I just thought you might need help. But didn't want to bother me."

She waited to respond, thinking things through, then said, "That'd be great. I don't want to let Jimmy down. He's expecting me."

"I'll help you," I told her.

In the morning of a bright early-April Friday, Nikki slumped behind her coffee mug.

"What's wrong?"

She tried to construct her crooked smile, but the scaffolding collapsed. She didn't answer me.

"Come on. What's the matter, Nix?"

She blew up her cheeks, pretended to glare at me, then exhaled with a clown noise. "Come on. We need to get going."

I looked at my watch. "Plenty of time. What's weighing on heart and soul in this garden of beauty?"

"I was just thinking."

"More coffee? I'm going to turn it off. What were you thinking about?"

"Last night. I noticed something."

"And?"

"You were reading your Bible. Before I came over. Weren't you? It was out on the table."

"Long story. Not worth telling. Just keeping a promise."

"To your mother?"

I laughed. "I guarantee you, my mother would not suggest specific readings from the Bible. Neither New Testament nor Old."

Nikki finished her juice and wiped her mouth with the back of her hand. Like a little kid. "I wish I could believe in God. The way I did when I was younger. I always think that, if only I could believe, everything would be all right. That I'd behave. But I can't. Believe. Or behave. It's all crazy, if you think about it. None of it makes sense. Religion, I mean." She stood up. Even in her drab fatigue uniform, she made me want her. "Okay if we leave the dishes?"

"This once," I told her.

"Christ, Jerry. You ought to clean this place up."

He waved down my advice. "Brings out the mothering instinct in them. No matter what the women's-libbers say, they love cleaning up after a guy."

I looked around the inside of his trailer. I was on the side of the feminists.

Jerry's rental was in a small court on the south side of Sierra Vista, the parasite town that began at the fort's front gate. The other residents looked as though they were struggling to summon the energy to hitch a ride to the pawnshop. But they did have the sense not to mess with the Corvette.

Jerry had his own views on interior decoration. Dirty dishes filled the sink and counters, along with takeout cartons from a global food tour. Discarded clothes had failed to make it to the bedroom and lay on the floor of the narrow living room. A vile bedsheet covered part of the sofa, and the lampshade hung at an after-the-fistfight cant. The trailer smelled of deep-fried Chinese food, spilled beer, and stubborn drains.

"Anyway, I don't give a shit," he said. "She can go to Tucson. I don't have any papers on her, and she doesn't have any papers on me. It was just a one-night stand." He paused, thought, smiled. "Hell of a good one, though. The little bitch."

"Look, I gotta go."

"Hey, I thought we could go over to the gym, work out for an hour, then hit the bars. Declare a formal meeting of the Officers' Club. It's Friday night, brother."

"I'm seeing Nikki."

He grimaced. "Man, you are so pussy-whipped. By a dumb-as-a-rock, barely five-foot lieutenant who should be back home waiting tables. Equal-opportunity, my ass. It's a plot to destroy the military."

"Nikki's trying. She's just a kid, a little confused . . ."

"And you're going to straighten her out? Good luck."

"It's a self-help universe. But I give bonus points to people who try. And she's trying. Okay?"

He flopped onto the sofa. A hidden animal groaned. "Speaking of universal truths . . . you get that fucking Pete Paulson off my case, or I'm going to knock his teeth so far down his throat, he'll shit molars. Know what he did to me? Right there in line at Burger King?"

"Get down on his knees?"

"He did it to you, too?"

"It worked."

"Not on me. I just went to McDonald's instead. If there's anything I hate worse than preaching, it's preaching from somebody who's not even a preacher. I guess you wouldn't want me crashing on your couch tonight?"

"It's a small apartment . . . maybe a little privacy? What's wrong with the palace here?"

He made a disgusted face. "I ran out of propane again. Gets kind of raw at night."

"Hey, Mr. Special Forces. I thought you were impervious and imperturbable?"

"I did my time in Panama and Central America. Never froze my ass off once. I ever tell you about the Sandinista chick and the furniture truck?"

"No."

"Craziest thing. Damnedest thing. Don't know why it popped into my head this afternoon. We hit this Sandinista safe house, the local boys and three of us along as 'advisers.' For what that turned out to be worth. Whatever their other faults, the local *hombres* don't dick around, I'll say that for them. *Bang-bang,* you're dead, no regrets, no paperwork. Not a lot of finesse, but there's a certain finality to it. Well, after the shooting stops, this babe comes out of nowhere with her hands up. 'Don't shoot, I'm innocent.' You know?" He twisted up one end of his mouth. "She gives us this big story about how she was kidnapped and blindfolded and stuffed in the back of a furniture truck and brought to the house. And this local guy we're supposed to be advising, Tony Valenzuela, he just pulls out his 9 mike-mike and gives it to her between the eyes. I mean, right between them. We were shocked. Brains all over the walls, blood everywhere, real Jackson Pollock stuff. And she really was good looking, too. Long brown hair, big brown eyes. Man, she hit the floor like a sack of shit, all lumpy and dead and *adios, muchachos.* Captain Bittman's an SF lifer, but he just about crapped in his pants. 'Why'd you do that? Christ, Tony?' And fucking Tony—he's a major on paper, but you never really know with those guys—he spits on Mystery Girl, looks at us, and says, 'If she was blindfolded, how did she know it was a furniture truck?' Man, we were babes in the woods compared to those guys." Jerry snorted. "They weren't much on combined arms and advanced tactics, but they didn't play Freddie Fuckaround."

"On that cheerful note . . ." I turned toward the tin door, then turned back again. "You okay, man? Been a tough week."

Jerry put on his screw-it-all grin. "At least the Corvette wasn't as bad as I thought. Got to keep things in perspective. Hey, can you believe they gave that De Niro wimp a fucking Oscar for playing a prizefighter? That pussy? I mean, I still can't believe it."

"Stale news, bro. Time to move on."

Suddenly, his grin collapsed. For a look-away moment, he seemed about to cry. "Hanging herself, man. That was . . . unnecessary, you know? *Nothing's* that important."

"She tell you about her divorce?"

"Yeah. Yeah, she told me. I blew it off. I mean, in SF, you're not fully A-team qualified until you've got at least one ex."

"Not your fault, Jerry."

He jumped up from the couch, the master blaster again. Grinning like he'd just inherited a harem.

"Ever read Nietzsche?" he asked me.

4

I wasn't interested in going beyond good and evil. Just in beating my own best time running the canyon. But after two miles, as I reached the stretch where the fire road narrows into a trail, I knew it wasn't my day to qualify for the Olympics. I slowed my pace, letting my heartbeat even out, and just enjoyed myself. If I couldn't go for time, I'd go for distance.

I was into pop Zen, a mush of Alan Watts and various roshis with book contracts, to which I added equal parts Krishnamurti and Gurdjieff to confound things utterly. Some of it worked, though. As I ran, I paid attention to my body, trying to feel each muscle, to "be at one with the mechanics of life." The runner's high, which kicked in early, tuned me in to the morning's brilliance, to nature's unerring beauty: new leaves, the first spring color, diamonds down where the creek ran. I blew through shadowed glades that were downright cold, emerging into patches of sun that instantly warmed my back.

"Be one with the trail," I told myself. My appetite for bullshit was enormous.

There was also a downside to meditative oneness with the universe. During an earlier run, I had transcended reality sufficiently to overlook a rattlesnake stretched across the trail. I didn't realize I had company until I had a heel beyond him and a toe dragging behind. The rattler must've been contemplating his own infinity, though, since he was as surprised as I was. He shot off into the brush. The adrenaline boost I got injected rocket fuel.

I turned onto a steep firebreak, scrambling into the sunshine. Letting my thighs ache. Grabbing air to fill my lungs. Slipping as eroding dirt gave way, I slowed to a jogger's trudge, but kept going up.

As I crested the spur, the landscape down below spread vast and fine. Beyond the shrunken buildings of the fort and the town beyond, the high desert stretched to a faint line of cottonwoods tracing the San Pedro River. Clusters of violet mountains fixed the horizon. In an hour, those mountains would go flat brown and the desert would become an unkempt scrubland. But the moment was all.

To my right and a howitzer shot away lay Mexico. That file of cottonwoods traced Coronado's path. Fort Huachuca had been established to discipline the Apaches, who played games with the border. The site had been chosen for its water supply. Beauty had come along free as part of the package.

A plume of smoke from the copper smelter hidden behind the mountains was the only stain upon the world.

I jogged in place, wary of pausing. In that moment, I could not understand how anyone could fail to love being alive.

Restless, I had driven onto the post before the recorded bugle call. Nikki had a talent for sleeping late, so I left her to her intermittent snores. I was ambivalent about Huachuca in many ways, but I loved it unreservedly in the mornings, when the rising sun painted the mountains with shaman colors. My route along the North Gate road ran for miles up a slope so gentle, it seemed flat. Behind the low-slung government buildings, the mountains were all liquid shadows and peekaboo gleams. A coyote crossed the road in the smoky light, tightening my grip upon the wheel.

The south side of the fort, to the left, retained a clutter of World War II clapboard barracks, many derelict. The workaday installation centered on Riley Barracks now, a public-housing knockoff where seen-it-all sergeants tried to keep the enlisted trainees from committing outright felonies. I worked in the officers' training complex, where the post's newest buildings sought to fit into the landscape, but failed.

The part of the post that drew me was its Cavalry-era heart, the carefully tended enclave flanking the parade field below the canyon's mouth. Down the slope, rows of nineteenth-century barracks had housed the buffalo soldiers. Updated, they served as offices for doctrine writers and program managers. On the upper side of the field, in the shelter of Reservoir Hill, the houses along "colonels' row" recalled a different age, when military service at Fort Huachuca meant harsh isolation, not impulsive jaunts to Tucson. I romanticized that old Army and liked to think myself part of its traditions. But I wondered if I really had the stuff.

I was "Army" enough, though, to cast a cold eye on the fort's country club atmosphere. Few of any rank seemed able to march in step for a hundred yards. It was a lulling place, where few duties were onerous and training standards were low. I was hardly an old soldier, but my enlisted years at Fort Hood had given me an appreciation for what the line doggies went through. It annoyed me that the privileged young officers training at the fort—complaining, as all soldiers do, about their burdens—had no inkling of what it was like to break track in the humidity and mud left behind by an August boomer in Texas.

Of course, not all the officers were burning up the nights, as Jerry and I imagined ourselves to be doing. The two of us strutted at one extreme, while the born-again coven knelt and prayed at the other. The mass of lieutenants in between just plodded along, learning a new world's rules and mostly behaving. Now and then, a second lieutenant got hit with a letter of reprimand for drunken driving, but even that was rare. And the captains who returned for advanced training were in full career mode, married and determined to be dull.

Even as I played around at Huachuca, I missed the crispness down in the line units, the no-nonsense atmosphere of gunnery tables and field exercises. I even missed things I had bitched about, and forgot the duties I'd hated at Fort Hood.

Worn out when I trotted back into the grove where I'd parked, I pulled on a sweatshirt and opened my thermos of coffee. Inhaling the steam and scent like dope, I drank it black in the shade. Pacing, loosening up, pausing to stretch out my hamstrings. Then I sat down at a picnic table and cradled the cup in my hands. Water could wait. The world could wait. I picked burrs out of my socks, then poured another cup. For a few minutes, I pretended I was at peace.

I told myself I was letting Nikki sleep. But I craved a longer interval alone, just a few more minutes, before going back to the apartment. I even considered driving out through Sierra Vista to see if Jerry was okay. But I didn't want to see Jerry. I wanted to see Nikki.

That was the problem.

I had the top down. The wind noise gave us an excuse not to talk. We were each nettled enough by the other to sense the danger of a sudden argument. As the road twisted into the Mule Mountains, I played one of Nikki's tapes, the Little River Band. It added another layer of excuse for our silence.

After I returned from my run and showered, we'd spent an hour or so going over field manuals and training circulars. Lying beside Nikki on a junkyard rug, I tried to explain the map symbols and computational formulas. Surrounded by maps and foldout diagrams, she just seemed baffled. To be fair, my heart may not have been in the lesson, since I thought Intelligence Preparation of the Battlefield was a self-licking ice cream cone. I preferred the emphasis on thinking in the old FM 30-5, *Combat Intelligence*. But the generals hadn't asked for my opinion.

Nikki started off with a burst of enthusiasm, but soon her mind started wandering. I pulled her back into the task. Like a child, she made a show of paying attention. Only to drift away once more.

"Nix," I said at last. "It's not that *hard.*"

She looked at me as if I had slapped her.

"I'm trying," she told me. Half-wounded, half-resentful. "It's easy for you."

Maybe it was. And I knew she was trying, in her inept way. She dutifully spent hours of homework time staring at her books or attending group study sessions. But it didn't take. The truth was that she didn't care about being an MI officer or any other kind of officer. It wasn't a vocation for her. It was the obligation that followed a college education paid for by ROTC.

Nikki had majored in Spanish, but could not order a meal.

I was determined that she'd pass the course, though. It became a point of pride. From the start, our study sessions were about my vanity, not about her. And our personalities were not well matched for a teacher–pupil relationship. Nikki just hoped to squeak through. I wanted her to take things seriously.

After an abysmal attempt at diagramming a Soviet motorized rifle battalion on the approach march, she had the sense to call it quits for the day.

"I can't do any more. It's too nice out. You said we were going to Bisbee."

So we went to Bisbee, an old copper-mining town squeezed into barren canyons. On its deathbed by the 1960s, it had been revived by hippies who found it cheap, funky, and relaxed about law enforcement. By 1981, Bisbee was a counterculture haven with a couple of raw music joints that didn't rise to barroom status, a string of head shops and junk stores, a macrobiotic café, and an old-fashioned lunchroom.

I parked in the gulch below the Copper Queen Hotel, which dominated the town like a medieval castle. The sun's heat fought the wind's chill.

"Aren't you going to put the top up?" Nikki asked. She had been too young for the hippie era, and the residents all looked like derelicts to her. Some were.

"It's better with the top down. That way, they don't have to break a window to go through the glove compartment."

Nikki *liked* Bisbee. At least at night, when the music blasted. She could pogo-dance with the best of them. But midday social dissonance unsettled her. This was our first daylight foray to Bisbee together. She walked through it like a visitor at a zoo.

"It's just up the block," I told her. "Lunch is on me."

Nikki could eat, too. We burned up a lot of calories.

She tugged my arm: *Stop.* A window display of tie-dyed T-shirts had caught her eye.

"Who'd wear something like that?" she asked. "I mean, it's, like, for granddad or something."

I had owned a tie-dyed shirt or two.

"Bisbee's a time capsule."

Jessie Lamoureaux emerged from a recessed doorway just past the shop window. Lugging a big purse.

We held a who's-more-surprised? contest.

"I thought you were in Tucson? At Caligula's weekend party?"

She recovered fast. "The party starts tonight, actually."

"You never struck me as a Bisbee kind of girl."

"Just saying hi to somebody." She shifted her posture, from impatient to very impatient. "I really have to go, Roy. It's *hours* from here to Tucson. Bye, Nicole. We need to get together sometime."

And she marched away, shouldering the big purse like a rucksack.

"I hate her," Nikki muttered.

"I thought you didn't know her?"

"Have you ever slept with her?"

"No. I have not."

"But you're friends? You never told me."

"I wouldn't say that, either. She's a fascinating case study."

"If you're going to sleep with her, tell me. So I can clear out."

"Whoaa there, Annie Oakley! First of all, I have no intention—*none*—of having sex with Jessie Lamoureaux. Trust me on that one. Second, I assume you made love with your husband when you flew up to see him last month?"

"That's different."

"The point is I never asked you about it."

We were on the verge of an argument, after all.

"You can sleep with whoever you want. Go ahead, Roy. Fuck her."

I caught her arm. Not too hard. But hard enough.

"Nikki . . . I *am* sleeping with who I want."

To my astonishment, her eyes glistened.

"Keep it that way." She put on her tomboy scowl, laughed, then seized my arm.

"Don't want to get too affectionate in public," I told her. "Seems you never know who you'll run into."

She tightened her grip.

After lunch, we strolled up the main street, past the last commercial building, and into the maze of rotting gingerbread shacks. It began to feel seriously warm, and Nikki slowed down.

"You all right?"

She brushed off my concern. "It's just the heat. And all the french fries."

"And the beer," I added.

"And the beer."

"Want to find a place to sit down?"

"No. Can we go?"

"Sure. It's all downhill from here."

By the time we reached the gulch again, she seemed to have perked up. I asked her if she minded stopping at a used record store in one of the alleys. I'd recently been tipped off to its existence.

She didn't care.

I did. The immaculate little shop was hardly more than a corridor. But it was a treasure house. The guy behind the cash box—no register— looked up from his book when we came in, gave us the Bisbee nod, then went back to reading.

I was transported to Wonderland. The shop had a fabulous inventory, far better than any in Tucson. Each in a protective plastic sleeve, there were thousands of rare jazz recordings you would have had to work to track down in Manhattan. To say nothing of Cincinnati.

"There aren't any *new* records," Nikki whispered.

"It's a used-record store. It's okay, I won't be long."

I could have spent all afternoon going through the bins, whose contents progressed from old 78s up through electric Miles.

The shop was an important find, since I was slowly rebuilding my jazz collection. I had amassed a good one over the years, but during my stint at OCS, someone in the personal-property warehouse had sifted through my few possessions and stolen the only things I had of value—almost seven hundred jazz recordings, going back to the early bebop era. The Army reimbursement adjudicator's formula priced any record album more than two years old at fifty cents, with no exceptions, so it was going to be a long time before I could afford to replace what I'd lost. Knowing that the goods were available helped, though.

Nikki told me she was going to wait outside.

I could read the tea leaves. And didn't want anything to spoil the evening activities ahead.

Fearful of the answer, I carried my first-choice album up to the guy with the book and asked how much it cost. There were no price tags. Meant to mask the value of items from pilferers, I assumed.

He glanced at the album, then looked at me in surprise.

"Just a minute." Drawing a ledger from under the counter, he paged through it. "All right. Now *just* let me see." He had a fey accent. "Here we are . . . Charlie Parker and His Orchestra . . . with Gillespie and Monk . . . first cut, C-410-2, 'Bloomdido,' recorded New York City, June 8, 1950."

"You're tormenting me on purpose. Aren't you?"

He grinned. His teeth were mildly discolored. Premature gray laced shoulder-length black hair. Alert eyes shone.

"Guilty. You're from over at the fort?"

"No points for guessing. Given the haircut."

"It *suits* you. But never mind, I'm being nasty. It's just that . . . this is my magic shop. Customers are magically uninterested."

"It's an incredible shop."

His eyes scouted past me. "I suppose I'd better get down to business . . . since your lady friend's giving me the *wickedest* look through the window. She could almost be a boy, you know."

"Hadn't occurred to me."

"And now I must sound my own death knell: That particular album— which is in mint condition, by the way—is seventy-five dollars."

I responded as if punched. I wanted it so badly. But the month's budget didn't include so grand a purchase. Lieutenants weren't part of the gentry class financially.

"You're a serious Parker fan?" the proprietor asked me.

"Back to Jay McShann and His Orchestra."

"Me, too. God, it's marvelous to know that I'm not alone in the universe. You have *no* idea . . ."

"Don't bet on it. I'm surrounded by headbangers. Look, could you hold it for me? Please? Until the end of the month."

He laughed. "As if it wouldn't still be there? Here. Take it. I'll trust you to come back and pay for it. By the end of the first week in May."

I began to protest, but he said, "My good deed for the day. And for the week. And the year."

I held out my hand. "Roy Banks."

His grip was firm. "Eli Lemberger. Pleased to meet you. And I do hope to see more of you." A veil of self-awareness darkened his face. "I didn't mean that in an impertinent way. I meant as a fellow Charlie Parker fan."

"Understood." I took up a pen and pulled his notepad toward me.

"So I'll know where to send the collection agency?"

"If you're ever passing through Huachuca City, give me a call. I'll buy you a beer. And tell you my sad record-collection story."

"Huachuca City?" He lifted his eyes to heaven. "That is just too perfect. Bird would have understood. Really, it's perfect."

"It's a very Zen place," I said. "Perfection's our specialty."

"You'd better go. Your lady friend's melting the sidewalk."

"Well, thanks again."

I started for the door.

"Did you mean that?" he said. "About stopping by for a beer?"

"Yes."

"I'm adept at maintaining boundaries. Just so you know."

"I didn't ask."

I took my treasure out to Nikki's world, leaving behind the loneliest man in Arizona.

"I thought you were going to marry him," Nikki said.

"Now, now."

"He was hitting on you. I could tell it without hearing a word he said."

"No, he wasn't. For Christ's sake."

"He was. And it's disgusting. *They're* disgusting."

As wild as she could be behind closed doors, Nikki liked her social order orderly.

Outside my apartment, someone honked a car horn with the determination of a really bad kid who'd locked himself inside dad's Buick on purpose.

Sunday evening was as quiet as it got in Huachuca City. And I was trying to read, with Nikki back in her BOQ room studying and waiting for the weekly call from her husband. I stepped outside. Jeans, no shirt. Feet bare on the concrete and cold gravel.

Someone had pulled up beside my old convertible in a gleaming white 280ZX. Fresh off the lot, the sports car had temporary plates.

The honking stopped. Leaving a blaring Blondie tape to spoil the silence. "Rapture."

Jessie Lamoureaux emerged from the driver's side. She leaned over the hood, posing.

"Want to go for a ride, soldier boy?"

5

"Man, you embarrass me when you drive up in that wreck," Jerry said.
He stood in the doorway of the trailer and gestured at his surroundings.
"Even the Mexicans laugh at you."

"It's going to be a classic. Just wait."

"*Guatemalans* would laugh at you, man, the Hondurans . . . they'd be
howling in El Sal . . ." He put on his Speedy Gonzales–meets–Pancho
Villa accent. "Cheap-ass *gringo maricón* . . ."

Across the pitted entry road, a Hispanic woman pulled clothes off a
sagging line, face as unmoving as an Aztec mask. As she dumped her
armload into a basket, I noticed that her jeans could not be buttoned at
the waist. She wore them with the zipper half-down. It wasn't erotic.

"Come on in, man. I got your money. Don't worry." Jerry cackled.
"Payback's a mike-foxtrot, right? You been checking out the evening
news on TV?"

"How could I check out the TV, when I was in the car?"

"Right."

"What's happening?"

I followed him into his trailer. And stopped. Stunned.

It had been scoured clean and put in immaculate order. Even the screen of the portable TV had been polished until it reflected every particle of light in the room. An anchorman read unemployment statistics.

Jerry grinned. "Need a beer? This all too much for you?"

"I didn't think you had it in you."

"I don't, man. Like I told you. Women love to clean up after a man."

"You bang *la deliciosa* across the street there? Quid pro quo?"

"Hey, she's not so bad. . . ."

I shook my head. "Really, you pay a maid service or something? I hope it didn't come out of the three hundred bucks you owe me. My investment horizons just expanded."

His grin only widened. Jerry's insufferable grin.

"Naw. Jessie did it. Came by Monday night and went to work. Wouldn't let me lay a glove on her until it was all done."

"And you didn't assist, I take it?"

He shook his head. "I just got out of her way. I'm telling you, Roy-Boy, you're too respectful of women, you don't understand their many-layered psychological composition. Christ, she's a piece of work, though. Did you see the car?"

"Yeah. I saw the car."

"My American dream. Good-lookin' gal in a luxury sports car with economy-model morals."

I helped myself to a beer from the fridge. Other than a half-depleted six-pack, the shelves were empty. Nor had they been cleaned. And the kitchen faucet still dripped. Not everything had been repaired or refurbished.

The news ended and Jerry clicked off the TV.

"So what was the big story that got your attention?" I asked him with a nod toward the box. I took a stool by the breakfast bar that divided the kitchen from the sitting area.

Jerry dropped onto the newly sanitized sofa. "They had this special report on the embassy hostages. You know, in Tehran? What's it been, three months since Reagan talked and the prisoners walked? And they're just starting to let them tell the world what happened, what they went through. Heap bad juju, bro. I mean, they still look wasted, like something out of a Warren Zevon song. I would *love* to read those debriefings." He made his badass face. "Leave it up to me, and I'd nuke every raghead downrange. Payback." He shifted his butt on the cushions like a kid with pinworms. "The rags thought the Gipper was going to give it to them on Day One. No coincidence on the timing of that release, brother. *Adios,* Mr. Peanut."

He tossed his empty beer can across the tiny room. Arcing toward the trash bin, it sprayed its last contents on the wall and floor. The trailer wasn't going to stay clean long.

Before I could respond to his macho crap, he added, "He *should've* nuked them. Object lesson. Don't mess with the Land of the Big PX."

"You don't really believe that, man."

"Fuck I don't."

"Can we have a serious conversation?"

He sat up straight and brought his knees together, then placed his palms atop them.

"I'm listening, Father. Explain to me why we should not smite the unrighteous."

"It's not that *simple.* For Christ's sake, Jerry. It's not *all* the Iranians. Most of the poor sonsofbitches just bought into the whole freedom thing, they wanted to get rid of the shah, stick it to Daddy. Mr. Jefferson, meet Dr. Freud. They had no idea what they were in for. None. Zip. *Nada.* Okay?"

"No need to get wired up, bro. Stay cool, it's cool. Poor old Jerry had no idea that, in addition to being an expert on the Soviet Army and nubile women—as well as a founding member of the Officers' Club—you're a professor of Ragheadology." He smirked and made a peace sign.

"It's just not that simple. It just *isn't.* There were good people, too.

They got caught up in things they didn't understand. They were absolutely fucking clueless."

"I should phone CI. 'Agent of the ayatollah in our midst!' Take it easy, man. I really didn't know you were into all that Iran shit."

"I'm not." I let my shoulders slump and crimped my beer can. The aluminum popped partway back. "Not in the least. I don't even know what I'm talking about, I don't know what set me off. Bad day at the office."

"Massetto busting your chops? Or did Jacoby deign to visit?"

"Just a figure of speech. I need some chow."

"Want to go cruising for burgers? Got to take the Vette, though. I will no longer be seen or heard in a clunker Mustang with a faggot turquoise paint job."

"I'm headed over to Gene Massetto's for dinner. Home cooking. Ever heard of it?"

"What's it like over there? Really? Ward and June, without the Beaver? Or I guess that's you. Could I be Wally?" He flopped back and cackled. "Man, you and Massetto are two peas in a pod. Born lifers. I'd bang the wife, though. She's hot, in a retro sort of way."

"Well, she wouldn't bang you."

"Don't be too sure."

"You're on thin ice now." Said in a no-nonsense tone.

Jerry rolled his eyes. "The knight-errant defends milady's honor. You take things too seriously, Roy. I mean, Christ. Getting all fired up about Iran and shit. Who cares? I didn't know you were so big on the sanctity of marriage, either. You know what? You read too much. I'm going to have to post new rules for the club." He grinned and gestured under the coffee table. A copy of *Soldier of Fortune* lay atop an issue of *Hustler*. Somewhere deeper down in the stack of magazines would be at least a couple of issues of *Muscle & Fitness.* "That's all the intellectual stimulation I need."

"And Nietzsche. Last month it was Camus. And Kierkegaard before that."

"I never made it all the way through Kierkegaard, to tell you the truth. Some of the Really Big Things really don't matter. But Hegel, man, and Schopenhauer . . . that is some truly cool shit. 'The world as will and idea.' I get that. It's, like, Nietzsche before Nietzsche." He rolled his muscles. "Listen, I have a proposition for you. Regarding that three hundred bucks you loaned me?"

"No."

"Just let me—"

"The answer is no."

"Just listen a minute. Cut me some slack, huh? With the Vette repairs and all, I'm going to come up short this month."

"That's what I loaned you the money for. Jerry, you are such a con. You're driving a brand-new Corvette, I'm driving a thirteen-year-old Mustang with a patched roof—"

"Which is going to be a classic."

"—and you're trying to wriggle out of paying up."

"No *way*, bro. No friggin' way. I'm just trying to help you budget your money. So you won't blow it all at once. I'm like that David Stockman guy. Or the IG. I'm here to help you."

"What's the deal?"

"A hundred right now, a hundred at midmonth pay, and I wrap it up at the end of the month. Leaves me with some operating capital. I had to get the propane tank filled. I got to live, man."

"Show me the hundred."

He took out a fat, battered wallet and pulled five twenties. "Want me to set you up with *Señorita Bonita* across the driveway? *Muy caliente, compadre.* Don't let a little thing like missing teeth spoil the fun. . . ."

A car pulled in and parked close. Smooth engine. Headlights powered through the trailer's curtains. The engine and lights died.

Jessie knocked and let herself in. The duty day had been over for a couple of hours, but she still wore her uniform. She had unpinned her hair, though. Against regulations.

"Isn't this sweet?" she said. "I always think male friendships are so nice."

We were four at table. Gene and Marilyn, Major Dinwiddie and me. Marilyn clearly viewed Dinwiddie as a safer date than any girl I'd bring along.

Lasagna and a side salad of iceberg lettuce with ranch dressing. Jug Chianti Gene kept in the fridge. Marilyn never drank at dinner, but liked a single highball afterwards. She rarely spoke during a meal, letting the males jabber about the military. But I never sensed that she felt slighted. It was just the way things were supposed to be.

Few things are easier to mock than a happy marriage, especially if its rituals are mundane. As we all climbed out of the pit decade of the 1970s, it was reassuring to see that two human beings could love each other for longer than a television season. Although there was some of that Italian macho bullshit on Gene's side, there was also the proud-to-provide-for-my-family stuff, too. It worked for Marilyn. When her eyes settled on her husband, they were rarely less than pleased.

As for me, I avoided resting my eyes on Marilyn too often. I had nursed a light crush on her since Gene first introduced us. Beneath that Donna Reed TV-homemaker surface lurked the Donna Reed hooker in *From Here to Eternity*. Or so I imagined. No woman could be as rigorously nice as Marilyn without something nasty hidden deep down in a drawer.

But that was just my little fantasy. She and Gene had the ideal military marriage, right down to the mediocre furniture, the couple of awful heirlooms, and the knickknacks that scarred every military household: colored crystal wineglasses, heavy as baseball bats and rarely risked in use; a knockoff Persian rug chemically treated to shine like silk; and the inevitable pair of cheap tinted prints of German townscapes—Nuremberg and Rothenburg. Their worldly goods fit perfectly in their tiny cinder block quarters, a 1950s rectangle painted in one of the pastel colors designated for the streets sequestering company-grade officers and their families. Each house had a carport, a snug privacy-fenced grilling area, and a utility shed. The only visible differences between the domain of Gene and Marilyn and the realms of their neighbors were that the Massettos were compellingly attractive and didn't yet have the standard-issue ankle-biters expected of a captain and his wife.

The only dissension I ever detected between Marilyn and Gene lay in her desire for kids sooner rather than later. Gene was evading his duty to the pope. For all his professional dedication and discipline, a board-length of surfer dude broke the surface now and then.

There was nothing "Surf's up!" about Major Leon Dinwiddie. He wasn't the kind of man you actively disliked, just the sort you never could like very much. Officious, but it was evident that he meant well. Going paunchy, he sucked in his gut and puffed out his chest whenever he caught himself slouching. Balding, he overvalued the plastered-down strands that crossed his peeling scalp. And he talked too much, a fault he would abruptly recognize, only to seek to mend it with more talk.

"I'd have them executed, every one of them," Dinwiddie said. "I mean it, I really do. They should be executed. Legally, of course. But with no undue punctiliousness. Execute them, if they're found guilty. Everybody involved in this narcotics business. Executed. Without compunction, without regret. For that matter, I'd recommend exactly the same policy toward this fellow who just tried to kill the president. Wouldn't be surprised if he was on drugs himself. Probably higher than a kite. No, my friends, we have to be firm to protect our social fabric, tattered though it may be. Mercy misplaced is no mercy at all." He paused for breath, lifting a forkload of lasagna. Strands of cheese tethered it to his plate. He pulled at them with a thumb and middle finger. "Young people are so vulnerable, you know. We have to protect them. Within reasonable limits, of course. The law-abiding ones. Don't want to break their spirits, I don't mean that. But a society requires adequate safeguards. Events like this demand a forceful answer, they really do."

"Well, it's the most excitement southern Arizona's had since the Apaches surrendered," Gene said. "Sounds like it was quite a firefight."

"*The Arizona Daily Star* says they had military weapons," I put in.

"Journalists," Dinwiddie said, then swallowed. "Journalists don't always recognize what is or isn't a military weapon. Tanks, for instance. They call everything a tank. But then, I suppose no tanks were involved this time. . . ." He tendered the last line as a joke. Only he chuckled.

"The drug problem's out of control," Gene said. "I don't see how the border could get any worse."

"The situation requires a military solution," Dinwiddie told us. "That's the only way. Don't want to do it, of course. The Army, I mean. *Posse comitatus,* all that. Still, it *is* our international border. Really, I don't see any other answer. Terrible mission, though. Politics, it wouldn't be anything but politics, right and left. Hate to be in command of something like that, hate to be the officer responsible."

A drug-gang gunfight had started in Agua Prieta, Mexico, crossed the border into Douglas, hit a lull with assorted casualties down, then moved west to Bisbee, where an American citizen had been killed. The cops were having a bitch of a time, the Mexicans weren't interested in helping, and the reporters were having a ball.

"Anybody hear anything else about the dead guy in Bisbee?" I asked. "Any details?"

Abruptly, Marilyn spoke. Her only other comment of the evening had been that Prince Charles's betrothed looked like a beanpole.

"I don't know how people can live like that," she said in a scolding voice. "I went over to Bisbee last week with some of the girls. We'd heard there was a craft shop. And it was . . . I don't know . . . it was absolutely squalid. *Filthy.* I really don't know how people can live like that, it's unimaginable."

· · ·

The lime Jell-O held mandarin orange segments and button marshmallows in suspension. It looked like someone had chewed up the Irish flag, half digested it, puked it back up, and froze it.

We faced another duty day in the morning, so the after-dinner drinks were short and quick. Marilyn cleaned up while we sat and swapped tales of how bad things had been in the barracks in the 1970s. I offered the enlisted man's side, which always shocked officers who thought they knew the worst that had gone on. That got Gene and Dinwiddie deploring how discipline broke down in Vietnam.

We briefly mourned the death of Omar Bradley; then Dinwiddie made his excuses, praising Marilyn too long and too extravagantly. I moved to follow him out the door, but Gene caught me by the arm. It was a habit he had, not meant to be rude. He was just a physical guy.

"Hang back for a minute. Business talk."

I didn't know what couldn't wait for the morning, but we sat back down.

"Colonel Jacoby came by. After hours. He went through your stuff. In so much detail that I barely made it back here in time for dinner."

"And?"

"You're now officially the golden boy. Don't tarnish it."

"Gold doesn't tarnish. That's silver."

"Anyway, he's pleased with the way things are looking."

"But?"

"In the east, on the flank of the breakthrough? Where you positioned the *Volksarmee* division?"

I nodded.

"He wants you to have one of the East German regiments peel off on day three, when they're pushing south on the Coburg–Bamberg–Nuremberg axis. He wants them to head for Bayreuth."

I frowned. "That makes no military sense."

"He knows that. He wants to force the students to think cross-boundary

coordination. You can make it work. Just have the East German commander screw up. Or deflect him."

"It's going to mean a lot of reworking. Everything's so interconnected.
I'll need to write the exercise all the way to the Czech border, work up the
cross-boundary events, the traffic."

"Listen to me, Roy. I know Jacoby. You're getting off lightly. This is a
hug and a big wet kiss. I told you he'd have to change something. He always does. But this is small stuff. You should've heard him tearing Bate-
man a new bore evacuator the other day. Over a couple of typos in a
training-circular draft."

"Got it. Thanks for running interference."

Gene made his restrained umpire gesture: *Safe!* "No interference required. The work's solid. Just double-down and bring it home."

"Roger. Good copy."

"See you tomorrow."

Penetrating her veil of Shalimar, I gave Marilyn a good-bye kiss on
the cheek. She had skin from a cold cream ad.

"If Gene ever goes AWOL, give me a call, ma'am."

"Just a minute. I packaged up some lasagna for you. Since you liked it
so much."

I hadn't liked it, actually. My diet ran closer to chicken, vegetables,
and yogurt shakes with fruit and protein powder. Jerry was going to get
a meal on the house.

The food at Trattoria Massetto was never good. The draw was the in-
tact couple. I wanted to believe.

Major Dinwiddie waited by my car. "I had one of these," he told me
wistfully. "Hardtop, though. A '67. Bought it when I came back from
Vietnam the first time. It was red. I wish I'd kept it." He traced a finger
along the strip atop the driver's door. Gently. "She still run pretty well?"

"I need to put in a new radiator. Before the real heat hits. I'll have to root through every junkyard in Tucson."

He nodded, pondering the existential aspects of car ownership. "Let me make a call or two. You never know. I may be able to help." He turned his face toward me for the first time since acknowledging my approach. "She's a '68, right?"

"You know your Mustangs, sir."

He snorted. "Useless knowledge. We acquire no end of useless knowledge in life. I can rebuild an engine. But I'll never rebuild an engine. Never again, I mean. Why would I? I don't want to. And I don't need to—I'm not a lieutenant anymore. So what good does that knowledge do me?"

"Like you said, sir: 'You never know.' Maybe you'll end up as a vintage-car collector."

"Unlikely, Lieutenant Banks. Unlikely. Tell me something. If you don't mind. If you really don't mind, I mean. Your friend. That Purvis fellow. Would you say that he and Lieutenant Lamoureaux are . . . together? Romantically, I mean? Is that a fair assessment?"

"I'd say they're dating. More or less."

"Purvis seems unreliable. Between the two of us."

"He's just the way he is. A lot of it's the ex-SF bullshit, sir. He's just trying to figure things out. Like the rest of us. Jerry's just noisier about it."

"Yes. Yes, we're all trying to figure things out." A big, dark form, he drew in his stomach and expanded his chest. "A man never stops trying to figure things out. I can tell you that, voice of experience. No, there's always another mystery, always one more."

"Yes, sir." I wanted to go home, go to bed. Although it would be a solo flight, with Nikki in her BOQ room studying for a test on security precautions.

"You see, the thing is . . . ," Dinwiddie resumed, ". . . I'm concerned for Lieutenant Lamoureaux's welfare. Oh, I know she appears to have something of a hard shell. A carapace, you might even call it. But I fear she's really quite fragile, a bit on the delicate side. People mask their vulnerabilities, you know. We're always hiding something or other. Human condition, I suppose. I just . . . what I meant to say . . . is that I believe she has a good heart. She can be brusque. Oh, yes. Brusque, indeed. Have you experienced that side of her? But there's a good heart in there, don't you think? And we don't want to see her hurt too badly. Do we?"

I shrugged. "Sir, I really don't know her that well."

"She's drawn to you, though. A person can see that. I can't understand it myself." He straightened out of his paunchy slouch again. "I didn't mean that the way it sounded."

"No offense taken, sir. She just likes to talk to me. Maybe because I don't want anything from her. You know, a physically attractive woman—"

"A *beautiful* woman. We might as well say it. Striking. That raven hair, the widow's peak. We might as well admit it. Not that I'm suggesting anything, don't take me wrong. But she could talk to *me*. If she ever felt the need. I'd like her to know that." He shifted from one foot to the other, an indecisive child. "Of course, it wouldn't do for you to *tell* her that. She'd know we'd been discussing her. That really wouldn't do."

"No, sir."

He leaned toward me. Confiding. "If she ever needs help . . . if she should need a strong shoulder to lean on . . ."

"Yes, sir. I'll keep that in mind."

"Good. Thank you. I believe we understand each other. We can be her friends. In the background. Keep watch over her. Not prying, I don't mean that. But silent friends." He clapped his hands together. "Refreshing, to come to a meeting of the minds. Isn't it, Banks? Shall we consider ourselves silent partners, then?"

I wasn't sure Major Dinwiddie would ever be silent about anything. I really wanted to get in my car and go.

"Well, that's that," he concluded. "I'm so glad we had this talk. It could turn out to be quite important. You never know."

"No, sir."

He ran a hand back over his scalp. The night was cool, but I sensed he had been sweating.

"I'm holding you up, I suppose. Didn't mean to. Sometimes it's hard to talk man-to-man like this. Hard to get the words out, to say what you really mean." He corrected his posture again. "Well, off with you! Boots and saddles. To all a good night. Oh, by the way. I hear rumors that you're going to make us all proud!"

I was vain about how fit I was. It wasn't a weight-room day, so at lunch I pulled my usual stunt of running a six-mile loop out to the range road and back. It was the first authentically hot day of the year, April previewing July, but that wasn't why I ran without a shirt.

Looping around ranks of mothballed barracks, I ran a tough pace facing traffic, as pleased with myself as a human being could be. No Zen required.

Where the barracks ended, a bull-chested figure charged down a side road toward me. It was Colonel Jacoby.

Scars adorned his tree-trunk thighs. Shrapnel wounds.

Didn't slow him down, though. He fell in beside me.

"Mind if I join you, Lieutenant?" He was pushing hard. Panting like a bulldog.

"Road's free, sir."

"*Don't* you slow down for me, Banks. Keep up the pace. Pick it back up."

I accelerated. If he wanted a duel, he had one. We raced down the grade toward the line of ranges. No red flags were up. The only danger came from cars headed into town for lunch.

The colonel hadn't joined me for a conversation. Beyond the occasional grunt, he didn't speak. A good six-four and classically muscled, he wasn't an enemy you wanted in hand-to-hand combat. Gilded with sweat, he might have been Ulysses in *The Iliad*. Just paste on a beard and replace the nylon running shorts with Greek skivvies.

We turned right on the rim road. The grade turned up, gently at first. Bewildered at its broken spine, a snake twitched on the asphalt.

We ran. Hard. Then harder.

"Don't throttle back, Banks. Show me something."

Jacoby was breathing hard, though. The curve that swept up toward the clinic and housing area was a mother in the heat.

We needed water; both of us were idiots.

Soldiers. Being soldiers.

We reached the main-post plateau again. The grade still ran uphill, but much less steeply.

"Show me what you've got, Banks. Show me your stuff."

Jacoby seemed possessed. Not really dueling with me, but with himself, with the inexorable.

"Going to let . . . an old man . . . beat you?" He gasped, fighting aging lungs. Growling at the universe.

Water tower to the right. The rug rat school, its forlorn playground abandoned in the heat. The housing area waited beyond.

"You're not . . . showing me anything . . . Banks."

I lost it. Exactly the way he wanted me to lose it. *Kiss my ass, old man.* I punched up the pace mercilessly, running harder than I knew I could.

He kept up. For about a hundred yards.

Slapping a big paw over his chest, the colonel stopped cold. I pulled up and turned back toward him.

He tore the hand away from his chest, as if it had disgraced him. But he remained bent over, settling his palms above his knees.

"Sir, you all right?"

"You keep . . . *running* . . . damn you. . . ." His face had lost its color, but his shaven skull was the hue of cooked salmon.

The heat could kill. It *did* kill. We were both in violation of the post regulations on hot-weather exercise.

Jacoby tried to straighten up. Couldn't. He stared at me with some-

thing that looked like hatred, but felt different. There are places words
don't reach.

"I . . . said . . . keep running. Order . . ."

His face had exploded with sweat.

"Win, Lieutenant. *Go!"*

I went. Racing back toward the gym, a drink, a shower. Telling myself he was close enough to the post hospital, if it came to that.

He had been teaching me a lesson, but I got it wrong.

My first encounter with Colonel Jacoby had come early in my Basic
Course. With a zeal that soared beyond MI's instinct to classify the toilet
paper in the latrines, the training bureaucracy had rated a BBC news special SECRET. The hour-long program had been broadcast the year before
and had been seen by millions of viewers, but that was irrelevant to the security minded. *The Bull's-eye War* explained, in simplified terms, how the
electronic systems worked on a modern British warship. There was no information in the program you couldn't find in a magazine or a defense-
industry brochure. But someone had decided that the existence of radar
was still close-hold information after half a century. So we were warned
before and after we watched the film not to discuss anything we saw in it
outside of a secure facility.

I believe in good order and discipline when in uniform, but I cracked
up. The instructor asked me what was so funny. I told him. Bluntly. Then
Jerry Purvis, who had already been my partner-in-crime back in OCS,
chimed in. Even less politely. I think the quote of the day was, "Come on,
Captain Kopko. This is shit." A few of the ROTC students then joined
the mutiny, although our two West Pointers maintained an aloof silence.

By the end of the duty day, I was standing at attention in front of
Colonel Jacoby's desk.

He had dismissed the instructor, leaving us alone. With the door shut. Establishing a pattern: The door always seemed to be shut when I saw the colonel.

"Who in the hell do you think you are, Lieutenant? God's gift to MI? I don't give a good goddamn if you were an enlisted man since the Peloponnesian War, you don't humiliate my instructors in front of the other students, you don't shoot off your fucking butterbar mouth, and you sit down, shut up, and try to earn your goddamned pay by learning something. Got that, Lieutenant Banks?"

"Yes, sir. But there's no—"

He performed a magician's trick of leaping over his desk and hovering over me with a fiery sword without rising from his chair.

"*Did* I ask you for an opinion, Lieutenant?"

"No, sir."

"*Do* you think I failed to understand what you said while Captain Kopko was present?"

"No, sir."

"Then shut your ration trap. And pray that, for the rest of your time on this post, you never come to my attention again. Your year-group's over strength in MI lieutenants. Did you know that, Banks?"

I didn't like being bullied. No matter who was doing it. Past a point, even a colonel's eagle was nothing but cheap tin feathers.

"Is it over strength in *good* MI lieutenants, sir?"

Briefly—oh-so briefly—his mouth opened in astonishment.

Colonel Jacoby didn't speak. He growled. The way big cats do. He shook his head, then looked out the window. Belatedly, I realized he was fighting back a smile.

"Get out of here, Banks," he said, mastering himself. "And make it a point to stay out of my way."

When Nikki's class went through its Basic Course instruction, the film had been declassified and Captain Kopko was gone.

6

For once, I left work punctually at five. Barely out the door of the secure facility, I snapped to attention at the report of the blank howitzer round. As the bugle call echoed up the canyons, I saluted the flag I couldn't see. The last note faded and I double-timed to the Mustang.

I didn't detour home to change, but drove over to Bisbee in my fatigues. I wanted to reach the used-record shop before it closed. I didn't like owing anybody anything.

Eli Lemberger stopped sweeping and hooked his hair over an ear. He inspected me from a distance.

"Well, Lieutenant! This *is* a pleasant surprise."

"You know military ranks?"

"I know police ranks."

"I just wanted to pay you."

He lifted his eyebrows in mock disbelief. "I not only have a customer, I have a customer who collects old Charlie Parker albums and pays ahead of schedule. This could *almost* restore my faith in humanity."

I followed him to the back of the shop, where his little cash box waited.

"Your credit's good, Roy. If you'd like to take anything else along . . ."

"I don't like being in debt to the company store. I'll come back next payday." Then I reconsidered. "Dexter Gordon? *Our Man in Paris?*"

"What a charming request! I've always felt that was the most atmospheric of Dexter's early recordings—one smells the cigarette smoke in the air, the tart scent of cheap wine. I have three copies. Unless one's been requisitioned by the populace." After locking the tin box again, he came around the counter. "The one in top condition is seven dollars, if I remember correctly. Dexter isn't as in demand as Bird. And *Our Man in Paris* is fairly easy to come by." He led the way up the narrow aisle between the bins.

"I like his lyricism," I told Eli. "So he's not a Miles or a Trane. Genius wears me out sometimes. And I just want to hear something human. Really good, but not great. That make sense?"

He pulled the three albums from their sleeves in turn. Checking for scratches.

"Perfect sense," he agreed. "Genius *does* wear one out. To say nothing of the demands of self-declared geniuses. Here. This is the one you want."

"Only seven bucks?"

"I'll check the register. But really, I'm certain. Certain enough. Plus tax, of course." We walked back toward the cash box. "Enjoying the Charlie Parker?"

"I am. My girlfriend hates it."

"Ah."

"Six years between us, and there's a generation gap."

"It strikes me, Roy, that there may be more to it than six years." He folded his arms snugly and appraised me. "My vision of you—and I *do* have a crystal ball, acquired from the *perfect* gypsy—is that you read the Beat poets, but more for the image than for their quality." He smiled. "*A Ferlinghetti of the Mind,* you might say."

Prematurely graying hair makes it hard to peg a man's age, and time and the sun had eroded Eli's skin. I judged him to be in his late thirties, but couldn't be sure.

"Eli, what on earth possessed you—?"

"To follow my dream and open the Doomed Record Store?" He smiled. Teeth slightly off straight. "I suppose I should have set up in Tombstone, not Bisbee."

"That's not an answer. But, if I'm prying . . ."

He sighed. "It's dear of you to ask, really. Listen, Roy . . . would you care to join me for a beer? I've got some empanadas I'm going to heat up. Strictly as two stranded jazz fans, I mean. Nothing else implied."

"We already settled that. And yeah, I could use a beer. You and me and Dexter here."

He smiled. With the unfiltered delight of a child. "Oh, no. Save Mr. Gordon for your mansion in Huachuca City and your inamorata—I can understand her charm, by the way, despite any musical differences you two may have. There's something winningly androgynous about her."

"Trust me. Nikki's not androgynous."

"No, I suppose not. But before I sidetracked myself—I do that—I meant to say that we'll take a few recordings with us, shall we? I don't keep many at the house. There's quite a bit of breaking-and-entering, I'm afraid. The good people of Bisbee take a communal attitude toward property. Pick out anything you like, Roy. What would you like to listen to?"

"You pick. Impress me with my ignorance."

He smiled. "That's not my idea of fun. Really, it isn't. I'd rather impress you by how well I intuit your tastes."

He picked out two early Coltrane albums and a Swedish issue of the Miles Davis Quintet. "I'm playing it safe."

Eli had a miner's cottage up a side street. The porch wrapped around three sides of it, while the rear wall flirted intimately with the hillside. It was one of two recently painted houses on the street. A cat watched us from the porch railing as we went in.

The interior was a surprise, but shouldn't have been. I'd expected at least a bit of the camp stereotype, but Eli had filled his refuge with old mission furniture and lamps with milk glass shades. Handsomely worn Caucasian rugs and kilims padded varnished planks. His Santa Fe School prints looked like originals.

I was still in my discount-mart-existentialist, possessions-don't-matter mode, but I felt a twinge of jealousy.

Eli saw that I was impressed. It pleased him.

"Life as a private work of art," he told me. "And ever a work in progress." He unlocked a tall armoire, revealing an array of hand-built stereo components. "I dread the day when my neighbors grasp that old furniture isn't all junk. Meanwhile, I wouldn't dare put anything *new* in here. A face peers in the window now and then. I think we'll start with Miles, would that be all right?"

"Eli, how, in the name of Christ, did you end up here?"

He placed the album on his turntable with a lover's tenderness. "Christ wasn't involved. And I hope I haven't quite 'ended up.' Just one more station of the cross—oh, I hope I didn't offend you? I *always* slip into sacrilege, and it is *always* Christian iconography, and it is *always* unintentional. Religion may be shunned, but never mocked. And we Jews must step lightly."

"How did you *arrive* here, then?"

"How did you arrive in Huachuca City, Roy? Surely no man picks it as his first-choice destination?"

"I asked first."

"Yes. You did."

Miles's trumpet rose, zombie slow, over a nervous beat. I sat down in an armchair. Wishing I'd had time to change, to get my boots off. My feet were shrink-wrapped in damp socks.

"This is good," I said. "But I still want to hear the Saga of Eli Lemberger. Who knows police rank insignia."

"Ah. I knew you wouldn't let that slip by. Just let me heat the oven for the empanadas. Negro Modelo? Or would you prefer a Carta Blanca?"

"The latter, please."

He fiddled in the kitchen. I surveyed his universe from my chair, sensing that something was off. As perfect as the room appeared, something was absent that would have made it a genuine human abode.

Photographs. There were no pictures of friends or family, no vacation snapshots. Just the acutely chosen artwork on the walls.

It was a museum, not a home.

Eli came back with the beers. In antique German steins.

"Bavarian and Bohemian immigrants founded *all* of Mexico's breweries," he said. "So it only seems appropriate."

At the end of a hectic day, the beer tasted as lovely as Paradise before the Fall.

"So . . . what's the story, Eli? You're the illegitimate son of a Levantine spy and a refugee opera singer? Laundering ill-gotten fortunes through a record store in Bisbee, Arizona?"

His mouth tensed. "A word of caution, Roy. Don't ever speak of money-laundering while you're in Bisbee. People don't always understand an outsider's jokes."

"Which reminds me. Quite a gun battle you had earlier this week."

He nodded. "For a small town, Bisbee's got plenty of layers." He searched the far wall for words. "It's like one of those dreadful little Russian doll sets you pull apart, only to find each next doll uglier than the last."

He paused to do his conversational sums. I wanted to ask if that was Diz on trumpet, but decided not to interrupt his musings. The interrogator's rule was to let a subject have some leash, if he looked about to talk.

Eli downed an installment of beer, clapped the stein's lid shut, and asked, "Do you *really* want to hear my story?"

"I was a lawyer," he told me. "A very well paid lawyer, Roy. In L.A. I wasn't a celebrity lawyer like Mel Belli. I was a lawyer *for* celebrities.

Mel's goal is to get all the parties into court so he can perform for the whole, wide world. My style was to keep my clients as far from a jury as possible." He flipped his hair back behind his ear again. "I was a cleanup man, the best-rewarded janitor from Montecito to Palm Springs. I could handle messes that should have sent people whose names make the masses sigh to prison for very long stretches."

He leaned into his memories. "I don't care where you've been or what you've seen in your life . . . I guarantee you that you have never seen the depravity—worse, the callousness—generated by the combination of fame, power, easy money, out-of-control egos, sexual urges, and Southern California. I was the go-to guy when there was blood in the bedroom. Or something worse in the bathroom. And I was *good* at what I did."

He got up. "I'll put the empanadas in. Another beer?" The recording ended. "Would you be a dear and change that? I'm trusting you with my most-cherished remaining possession, by the way. The stereo's name is Edith. For Edith Cavell. Her story *always* gave me goose bumps."

He returned with two more beers and sat down again. I had put on Coltrane, the pre-transcendent stuff. Lovely, searching music.

"We'll have to keep an ear tuned to the timer," Eli told me. "Really, we should just listen to this *divine* music. Instead of chattering."

"I was enjoying the mea culpa."

A fly settled on the turban atop a lamp.

"Ah. The wicked Eli. Lightening his emotional load, instead of bearing it stoically. Well, I *was* awfully proud of myself. I even had a Ferrari, although there was no place to drive it properly. The freeway? Oh, please. But a certain element in my social life found the Ferrari irresistible. Not the best element, need I add? I felt so powerful in those days, godlike. You have no *idea.* All those famous faces mere mortals only see twenty feet wide on a screen or inviolate on a television set . . . I saw them terrified, shaking, begging . . . the men and women alike . . ." He looked beyond me, into a different world. "They never forgive you for seeing them like that. But they pay in full. And promptly. Because they don't want you telling anyone else how you saw them—on their hands and knees, because they'd finally gone much, much too far. They needed me then, no matter how studiously they avoided me later. I knew how to get rid of the bodies, you see. Literally, in two cases."

He sighed, but it didn't suggest nostalgia. "Meanwhile, I was simply *integral* to the social scene. The gay scene, to be explicit. And the 1970s in the Hollywood Hills made Sodom and Gomorrah seem like Salt Lake City. Those whips, those chains!" He conjured a weak smile. "Only kidding. But the horrible thing was that I went along with all of it, even though I despised it as I did it. I've never really believed that, just because others thought my needs immoral, I should *be* immoral to spite them. As *sauvage* as I could be in my professional life, I was just a little homebody at heart. Past a certain point, promiscuity becomes mere ostentation. I wanted my equivalent of domestic bliss in the suburbs. Or in Malibu, anyway." He looked at me with a new, unguarded earnestness. "I don't think you'll laugh at me. Will you, Roy? No man who loves Charlie Parker can plead ignorance of the devils in our lives. . . ."

"Go on," I said. "Please."

"I disgusted myself. Oh, not because I'm prudish. Although I do have a streak of that. But because I was doing things that left me feeling hollowed out . . . and, worse, absurd. I can bear horror, Roy, but not waste." He smirked at his remembered self. "Of course, I fell in love. I was just dying to. So I did. And L.A. is no place to fall in love, not ever. Especially not for those sick at heart in the seventies. There goes the buzzer! Let me just take them out so they can cool."

Coltrane provided a bizarrely perfect soundtrack to Eli's story. I turned the album over, then waited, nursing my beer. The baked-dough fragrance of the empanadas drew acid into my gut.

"Shall we give them ten minutes? We don't want to burn our tongues," Eli said. "Where was I in my sad story? Ah. A broken heart. There's always a broken heart in there somewhere. Isn't there?"

"Sometimes."

"Did anyone ever break your heart, Roy?"

"This is your hour on the stage."

"Ah. My lawyerly tactics are failing me. I rust unburnished, having declined to shine in use. Yes. Well. When Kurt left me, I was simply devastated. But I remain sufficiently Jewish to view work as the ultimate therapy. So I threw myself into ruining what was left of broken little lives so the big careless lives could decamp to Cannes or Portofino, or at least to Big Sur for the weekend, without legal restraint or the wrong kind of publicity. I had a unique flair for compartmentalization, you see. I yearned to live a moral life—at least, my version of one—in the private sphere. Professionally, I remained an amoral monster. No, that's not right. My monstrosity, my cruelty, worsened. And I delighted in it . . . a sin for which I shall never be forgiven." His shoulders slumped. "I sometimes think I was switched at birth, that I really belong to this tormented Catholic family . . . perhaps that's why I'm comfortable around Mexicans. . . ."

He glanced toward the kitchen and the empanadas. Longing to escape the confessional. But he decided to go on.

"Cue the violins now, Roy. As well as the violas, the entire string section. This is the part where self-pity shields the devil from self-awareness." He straightened his back, a witness on the stand. "On yet another nondescript afternoon . . . it's smoggy, but the day has no special character in the screen treatment . . . I find myself in a studio apartment on the wrong side of Sunset, threatening a kid who's never going to have children, who was treated to not one, not two, but three, count 'em, three venereal diseases by one of the nicest, kindest men on the television screen—who also knocked out her front teeth using his police-issue handcuffs as brass knuckles. Because she declined to fuck any more of his gathered friends. I'll spare you the details of her rectal hemorrhage."

His eyes retreated into his skull and he shoved his hair back forcefully. "There I am, God in a hand-sewn Italian suit, telling her how she's going to go to jail for slander, and two highly respected doctors will testify that she gave Mr. Nice-and-Kind the VD trifecta, not the other way around. And the kid's wailing in this hick Midwestern accent, 'I'll do anything you want, *anything*, Mr. Lemberger. I just don't want my mom and dad to know.' Of course, I had advised Mr. Oh-So-Nice not to pay her a cent, not to so much as cover her treatments, because a court might construe any such action as an admission of guilt. And Mr. Nice-and-Kind was only too glad to hear it, ladies and gentlemen, because he'd already saved a bundle by letting his mother die in a county home for the indigent—the old lady never said a word, she was so proud of her son."

His lips trembled. "You know what this kid from Outhouse, Iowa, does? You know what she does? She gets down on the carpet, down on her belly, then *crawls* over to me and starts kissing my shoes. *Kissing* them. Over and over. Is there something like that in the Christian religion, the New Testament? Where you kiss somebody's feet for forgiveness? Because that's what it's all about; she's slobbering on my very expensive shoes and begging *me* to forgive *her*. And not to tell Ma and Pa Kettle . . ."

After a wordless interval within our jazz cocoon, I said, "And?"

"Maybe there *is* a god, Roy. Maybe there's a stern, vengeful, wrathful god up there. Or over in Pasadena, among the Republicans. I was in perfect health, great shape. But suddenly, my heart's pounding like Buddy Rich on meth, the temperature in the room plummets and soars at the same time, and I'm immobilized, turned into a pillar of salt. And I'm terrified, sure I'm having a heart attack at the very least, even though I'm still on my feet. And this kid, she senses something's wrong, she gets up on her knees and looks at me from blow job level. This fresh-faced kid who's fucked over for life. And she asks me, 'Are you all right, Mr. Lemberger? Can I get you a glass of water?' "

He covered his mouth with his palm, calming his lips, before he spoke again. "Revelations happen, Roy. They're not myths. Even if there's no God, revelations are real. I had one that day."

"And what happened?"

"The empanadas are getting cold."

"I like them at room temperature."

He wiped his eyes with his fingers. Delicately. "I ran away. Literally *ran.* God knows what the poor thing thought. That evening, I phoned Mr. Oh-So-Nice at his ranch and told him that she was going to go public, and damn the consequences. My reputation was such that he didn't question me. America's beloved paterfamilias coughed up two hundred and fifty thousand dollars." He curled one side of his mouth. "Not much, really, for a ruined life. But I didn't want to push the numbers and have him call another lawyer for a second opinion." Eli closed his eyes. "And the kid. Bless her, the stupid little thing. She thought I'd done her the world's greatest favor. . . ."

"Great empanadas," I said.

"Well, I am *so* pleased. Having made them myself. Another beer?"

"Two's my limit when I'm driving. So how does all that connect you to Bisbee and a great record shop with no customers?"

"If you don't seize the last empanada, Roy, you'll be responsible for its tragic effect on my waistline."

"Let's split it."

"I'll bet you have at least three Art Pepper albums. Maybe four."

"I had five. But don't change the subject. Complete the Lemberger Odyssey, please."

"Coffee?"

"No, thanks."

"Ah. The Lemberger Odyssey. Not much more to tell. I did what my forebears did in the wastes of Judea: I went into the desert. Bisbee seemed the one spot where I'd never see a face or any other body part from Hollywood. Careful with that hot sauce, it operates on a time-delay. Thing of it is that, placed under the microscope, my life was terrifyingly empty. Kurt had wrecked the Ferrari, and I sold it as-is. The house was affordable only if I kept on crushing the little people for the giants their admission fees had created. I had a thousand acquaintances. And not one friend I would miss. Although I'll admit, I enjoyed the bitchy lunches. Anyway, the only thing in my life that I truly loved was jazz: Edith— built for me by one of the best engineers at Elektra, by the way—and my recordings. So I sold the house for more than any house should ever be worth and let a broker have the furnishings at a discount. I sent some anonymous checks out of guilt and vanity, then began life again. Here."

"Don't you get bored?"

"With all that music? And my books? I'm often lonely. But never bored. Anyway, the legal profession doesn't let a man go so easily. I still have all the superficial human interaction I can stomach."

"You have a practice?"

"Nothing that formal. I haven't put out a shingle, and don't expect I ever will again. Unless the times become *truly* desperate. But people find things out about you, God knows how. I'm a member of the Arizona bar, thanks to some old clients in Scottsdale, and I started getting inquiries. Minor drug cases, mostly. That's our excitement around here. Fried old hippies trying to grow a stash up in the rocks, or a none-too-tidy earth mother dealing a key or two to make her smoke. I can usually get them off." He shrugged, found his smile again. "If they hand over a first installment on what they owe me, they figure that shows sufficient good faith to cancel the rest of the debt. And some pay in-kind, which can get interesting. I've got some *terrifying* macramé wall hangings hidden in the cellar, and I'm entitled to free goat's milk until the day I die."

"You said 'mostly.' "

"Ah. I forget that I'm speaking with an Intelligence officer. Distinguished by his bravery in consuming Sally Peace Starlight's homemade hot sauce—which was, by the way, also a payment-in-kind. That was a divorce case. My client got to keep the hand-loom *and* the family horse."

" 'Mostly'?"

He grew jarringly serious. "I've handled a few more-complex drug cases. The sort that straddle the border. Nice supplement to my all-too-fixed income, but I'm not enamored of the work. Or of the people, to be honest. But I'm not sure turning down their cases would be wise." He attempted to lighten his expression again, but didn't quite pull it off. "There's a breed of *Homo sapiens* that likes to have its own way. I know, since I was one of the breed in my previous life. The members of that breed have difficulty comprehending a refusal."

"So Bisbee isn't the refuge you thought it would be?"

"On the contrary. It's as close to ideal as this flawed world has to offer." His smile grew genuine again, but wistful. "There's always a serpent in the garden, isn't there?"

We sat in the living room again. Full night had come and insects tapped at the windows. We were drinking coffee, after all.

"I'm afraid I've ruined the evening," Eli said. "We were supposed to listen to wonderful music and commune on an artistic plane."

"I'll take a rain check."

"But it won't rain for months."

"I pay early. I did tonight, didn't I? For the Parker album?"

"I *am* sorry—dreadfully sorry—if I bored you."

"You didn't. I think you know that."

"But one mustn't be too vain about it. At least not openly. And now it's your turn. Tell me everything, how you came to join the Army—no French Foreign Legion recruiting office in your hometown? Fair's fair. Tell all! How were you wounded?"

"I've never been wounded. I was never in a war."

I caught a ghost of the lawyer in his eyes. "Of course you're wounded. A blind man could see it. Regale me with the Life and Times of Roy Banks."

I looked at my watch. Too obviously. "It's late. The Army's day starts earlier than yours, Eli. I really have to go."

"Ah. And would this be what our men and women in uniform call 'escape and evasion,' by any chance?"

"The empanadas were terrific. As was the company."

"Really, Roy . . . are you sure you're not a lawyer yourself?" Instead of smiling, he grinned outright. It struck me that I had made a fellow human being happy. The willingness to listen bridges galaxies.

"Shall I have a rain check on the Roy Banks Story, too?" Eli asked.

"It won't rain for months," I said.

7

Gene Massetto knocked once and entered my sweatshop. I turned from correcting an overlay. Gene rarely interrupted me while I worked.

"Take a break," he said. He gestured toward the table that served as my desk. "Grab your shirt and your headgear."

"I'm in the middle of something."

Gene tightened his expression. It was captain to lieutenant now.

"I need you to come with me."

"Yes, sir."

Gene grimaced. "I don't know how you stand it in here. You drinking enough water?"

"*Quo vadis?*"

"Alvarado Hall. A computer demonstration. Colonel Jacoby wants you there."

I locked up my cell. "I don't know anything about computers."

"Maybe that's why he wants you there."

A major and a captain—wearing Class A's, not fatigues—had set up a line of screens that looked like the TV sets from *The Jetsons*. Electronics and shielded wires cluttered a series of tables and the floor. A few dozen faculty members had gathered, milling about in slow motion, waiting for Jacoby so the show could begin.

When the colonel finally came through the doors, a newbie called, *"Attention!"*

We all snapped to, assuming the USAICS commander was putting in a surprise appearance. But there were no stars approaching. Only Jacoby and his eagle.

"At ease," he barked. "For Christ's sake." Then he let it go, striding to the front of the group. He did an eyeball inspection of the technology pushers and said, "Execute, Major Dudley."

The major in dress greens invited the colonel and the rest of us to close in around him; then he sat down at a keyboard and started the show. He began by demonstrating how computers could help the Army with straightforward mathematical problems, beginning with march-table calculations, then brought it home to MI by sorting radio signals and frequencies. Prioritizing mock intercepts, he soared into physics-lab math.

The speed of the calculations was impressive, but we all knew computers could do that sort of thing. I could see useful applications, but the briefer kept claiming that, rather than being a helpmate, the computer was going to dominate the battlefield. On a larger screen, he produced complex decision matrices with weighted values, telling us that the computer would do the work of a commander in the future, but without human error. Finally, he shifted to the last setup and showed us how "artificial intelligence" could design stunningly detailed, constantly evolving graphics, with infinite variations.

Finished with the hands-on portion of his presentation, Major Dudley stood up and faced the colonel.

"Sir," he said, "*this* is the future. Computers are going to replace Fire Direction Center officers in the near-term and, in the not-too-distant future, battlefield commanders themselves. Computers will strip away the 'fog of war.' Emotional distortions will be removed from the decision-making process. We'll enter the realm of perfect decisions made instantaneously and based strictly upon empirical data. As for Military Intelligence . . . the applications are many and obvious. Ten years from now, we'll no longer need human analysts." He surveyed the pack of inferior human beings surrounding him. "*All* analysis will be done by the computer. By eliminating the unreliable human factor, we'll achieve performance levels never before attained in the history of warfare. This is the ultimate revolution in military affairs." He didn't just smile; he radiated. "Questions?"

Silence. Everyone waited for the colonel to give his verdict.

He turned to me.

"Lieutenant Banks? What do you make of all this?"

"Sir . . . there are clearly some practical applications. If the systems can be field-hardened so they're reliable in a combat environment. But I don't think any machine is going to replace human commanders on the battlefield. Or intelligence analysts. Human behavior isn't subject to mathematical formulas and—"

Jacoby began to glower. My answer was too long.

I squared my shoulders. "Sir, the claims are bullshit."

The ghost of a smile passed over his face before he turned to the briefer.

"Major Dudley, you've given us a very impressive demonstration. I do not doubt that the field of cybernetics has the potential to make powerful changes in the way the Army does business. You've made a convincing case for several sensible applications, for ways in which such devices may *assist* officers in the future. But, right now, I'm exercising all my willpower not to throw you and your fucking machines out into the dirt."

The other officers shrank back.

Jacoby grunted. He had a very authoritative grunt. "Major Dudley . . . judging by your uniform, I take it you didn't serve in Vietnam?"

"No, sir." The major looked like a rabbit cornered by a boa constrictor. "I was the recipient of a Rhodes Scholarship out of West Point. I'm afraid I missed the last action. To my regret, sir."

"Well, let me tell you something, Major. From a man who's heard one too many goddamned promises about how technology's going to fix everything and get us all home in time for lunch. Do you know what happens when the promises don't come true, when the shit doesn't work?"

"Sir, all advanced technologies are initially unstable. Naturally, an interval of inherent performance volatility is—"

Instead of raising his voice, the colonel lowered it. "Just stop now, Major. You're talking to an unreceptive audience. And I need to tell you why I'm unreceptive. Because when the promises made by the developers and the contractors and the acquisition officers and, not least, the members of Congress don't come true, soldiers die. They *die,* Major. They die because an ambitious someone or other exaggerated a little bit. Then, as various programs competed for Pentagon backing, the little exaggeration became a medium-sized lie. Then it got to the budget markup on the Hill. And the medium-sized lie became an enormous lie. And the enormous lie went to Vietnam with the miraculous new solution to all of warfare's problems. And it didn't fucking work. And soldiers died. And I never saw one die pretty."

Jacoby shook his head. "For once in my career, I agree with a lieutenant. Your claims are bullshit. Thank you for the demonstration, Major Dudley."

I gladly would have basked in the glow of Colonel Jacoby's praise. But Gene drifted off to confer with a pair of instructors, and Pete Paulson followed me into the men's latrine.

"I was hoping I'd see you, Roy."

"Jeez, Pete. Can't I take a piss?"

"Sure. Sure, Roy. I'll wait outside."

"Thank you."

As he walked away, I realized what the rodent had just done: By his calculation, I had just agreed to a conversation.

I considered not washing my hands and giving his paw a good, long shake.

Pete had positioned himself so that I couldn't escape. A spiritual kamikaze, he zoomed in.

"You were *wrong*, Roy! I just had to let you know that. I felt obliged."

I pushed open the exit door. The world waited out there. There was a chance a meteorite would hit Pete.

"About the computers? I just don't think they'll—"

"No, no. Not about the computers. I wouldn't know about that stuff. About Jessica Lamoureaux, Lieutenant Lamoureaux."

I stopped. Facing the sun. Shielding my eyes.

"She's a *good* person," Pete went on. "Children *love* her. I asked her, and she came to one of our meetings. She came on Wednesday, not Tuesday, though. And that's men's night, so we couldn't let her in on the actual prayer meeting. But everything worked out—she helped take care of the children a few of our members bring along. Some wives have to work, you know. Bearing the water from the well. In a manner of speaking."

"Jessie came to one of your church meetings?"

"She helped clean up afterwards, too. You were wrong about her, all wrong. I told her what you said, about her being Delilah or Jezebel. But you're not in trouble. She forgave you. She's a good Christian. She thought it was funny."

"Well, Jesus H. Christ. It sounds like she'd make an ideal wife for you, Pete."

He thought about it. "Oh, I don't really think so. Jessica could take her pick of anybody, she's so beautiful. 'Arrayed in glory,' I guess you could say." He refreshed his eager smile. "But, then, the Lord works in mysterious ways."

.   .   .

"Jessie, what the hell are you doing to Pete Paulson?"

I'd spotted her after work, in the parking lot, and followed her to her car. She posed beside it.

"Isn't Pete a darling? He'd do anything for you, wouldn't he? He *so* looks up to you, Roy. Did you know that?"

"I'm not interested in being the object of Pete's adoration. Which seems to be your department, anyway." I crossed my arms. Doing my Colonel Jacoby imitation. "Come on, Jessie. Don't you think it's just a little too heartless to tease the guy, to lead the poor kid on?"

She blinked those blue gray eyes. Below her cap, dark hair gleamed.

"Is that what I'm doing? Leading him on?"

"Knock off the poor-little-ole-me stuff, okay? Jerry's fair game, that's a gimme. Even Dinwiddie. He's a big boy. But Pete Paulson's a child trapped in a man's body. If not a particularly impressive one."

"Why, Roy Banks! I do believe you're jealous!"

"Trust me on this one. I'm not jealous. Pete's a pest, but the fact is I kind of admire the guy's faith. I mean, he lives it. Dreary as that may be."

"I'll tell him you said that, Roy. He'll be touched."

"Don't. Please, Jessie. Give the kid a break. How many scalps do you need?"

"Roy, have you ever considered that I may have my own religious beliefs? That I may have a deep spiritual side."

"It honestly never occurred to me."

"Now, why are you being so cruel?"

Two captains walked by. Jessie and I came to attention and saluted. Neither of the captains noticed me.

"Don't try to turn this around," I told her. "You're the one who's being cruel. You're being a downright bitch. The poor kid's in slobbering love with you. And you don't have the least shred of interest in him. And you know exactly what you're doing."

She smiled at me, but didn't answer.

"Come on, Jessie. Pick on someone your own size."

"All right," she said. Glancing around the lot. As if she intended to pull out a pistol and shoot me, but didn't want any witnesses.

Instead, she reached up and kissed me, quickly and hard, on the lips.

"Stop it, goddamn it."

" 'Fraidy-cat," she said. "Say hi to Lolita for me."

She slipped into her car.

Nikki waited until after we'd made love—more ferociously than usual—before speaking. Then she struggled to keep her tone casual.

"Someone saw you kissing Jessie Lamoureaux in the parking lot today."

I sat upright. Fast. "That is *not* true. She kissed me. And I didn't expect it. I told her to knock it off."

"What were you doing with her?"

I almost told Nikki that, given her marital status, I reserved the right to talk to anyone I wanted. But I thought better of it.

"First, I have no interest, none, in Jessie Lamoureaux. I'd rather go to bed with a rattlesnake. I think it bothers her, that's all. Second, I was talking to her because she's doing a number on Pete Paulson, this Jesus-freak lieutenant on the Born-Again posse."

"I know him. He's creepy. He asked me to make a date to go to church. Before I met you."

"Creepy or not, he's an emotional child. And Jessie's a snake. With more than her fair share of venom. She's been leading him on, and Pete's clueless and witless, and it isn't right."

"And it isn't any of your business. *And* she kissed you." Her voice made it clear that she had not yet surrendered to my explanation.

In my frustration, I almost told Nikki I loved her. We all say things we don't mean when we're upset.

. . .

"She's a lying goddamned bitch," Jerry said. "And I'm going to fucking kill her."

"Slow down, cowboy. Let's take this rodeo outside."

He scanned the area around our table. Yeah, some of the other customers had heard him. Impossible not to.

We sat in La Casita, a little Mex joint on the Sierra Vista strip, a mile from the main gate. During the wait for our lunchtime taco specials, Jerry had built up some hot sauce.

He lowered his voice, but his face remained as dark as thunderheads over the mountains. Leaning toward me, he said, "She does this on purpose. She likes to torture people."

"Doesn't strike me as hot-off-the-presses news. What did she do this time?"

"We had a date. We were supposed to go up to Tucson on Saturday. And party down. And she calls me. She can't go. Because she's going away for the weekend. And guess who's the lucky travel partner?"

"Please. Don't tell me it's Pete Paulson."

He looked bewildered. "Why would she be going anywhere with that jerk-off? It's Dim-witted. She's going off with that fat asshole. And, of course, the bitch made a point to tell me about it, because she 'doesn't want to hide anything from me' and she 'values our relationship.' I mean, what the fuck?"

"Jerry. Look at me, man. And keep it down, huh?"

Mad-eyed, he focused on me. Barely restraining himself from overturning tables and tearing up the restaurant.

"Jerry . . . brother . . . the woman is heap bad medicine, seriously bad juju. Enjoy the sweaty memories and move on. She's just playing you. She plays everybody. It doesn't take an Intelligence officer to figure it out."

Suddenly earnest, he asked, "Why, though? Why would she jerk me around like this? Because she's a sadist? Christ, Roy . . ."

"Don't let your ego team up with your dick. Maybe it's just about notches on her belt. But it's clear that she is not a good emotional investment. Okay, man?"

Our taco plates arrived. The refried beans were the color of baby shit. And steaming.

As the waitress waddled off, Jerry said, "Yeah. Yeah, man. But she's the best lay I've had in my entire life." He looked distraught. Drained. "You don't know, man. You just have no idea."

"I don't know why you want me," Nikki said. In the bedroom again, in the darkness. Where we belonged. "I mean, I'm not beautiful. I know that. You could have other girls."

The shadow of Jessie Lamoureaux was upon her.

I reached over and turned on the lamp. To look at her. Short golden hair, nose slightly upturned. The girl who didn't quite make the cheerleading team.

If Nikki's body was compact, her confidence hadn't been. Until now. If she wasn't photo-spread gorgeous, she enlivened the rooms she entered. An enticing lover, she was instinctive, surprising. *Unexpected.* And now she expected something from me, not just a textbook compliment, reassurance at a discount. But she wasn't sure exactly what that something was. Neither was I.

I gave it a shot. "Nix, we can never really explain why we want the people we want, the wiring's too convoluted. I mean, we can explain the initial attraction. To some extent. When I first saw you, I thought you looked impudent. Hands-on-the-hips cocky. And I liked that. Impudent, and sexy enough to scorch your unsuspecting victims. You weren't mass-market goods, straight off the rack." I laid a hand on the softness below her shoulder, on warm, faintly damp flesh. "Beyond the first attraction, though, it all just gets too complicated. The physical stuff seems obvious. But when we try to explain even that much, we turn to clichés. At least, I do. I mean, who really understands any of it? What matters is that you're here. And I want you to be here. And I want you to want to be here. Okay?"

"You're not even going to *try* to convince me I'm beautiful?" Her voice was better now. *Insouciant* was another word I used on her in my private world. But I was certain she wouldn't know what it meant.

"You're a nice package for the discriminating shopper. And you know it. More than the sum of your parts. You must've driven the boys in high school wild." I moved closer to her lamplit skin. "And we're not just fuck buddies. You know that."

She regarded that as a proposition and considered it. "No. We're not. But we're not going to be any more than we are now. I mean, we can't. *I* can't."

A model of dishonesty, I nodded my assent.

She gave me her crooked smile and maneuvered against me. "I'm sorry I gave you such a bad time last night. About Jessie. She's just such a total bitch. She probably made sure somebody was watching. Just to mess with us. And I was stupid and bought it. I'm sorry."

"I swear to you she'll never come between us. I mean, yuck. You have no idea how she repulses me."

Nikki propped herself up on an elbow. "Really?"

"Scout's honor."

"Well, I'm sorry. And I'm going to make it up to you."

"*That* sounds promising."

"Not that way. This weekend. I have a surprise for you."

8

Our romantic evening began in a junkyard in south Tucson. I found the place just before closing time. As I pulled up by the office, a German shepherd threatened to leap into the convertible.

"Now, you just git down," the proprietor told the dog. The barking subsided to a growl. "It's all right, you can git out. He won't do no harm, I don't tell him to."

I got out. Nikki did, too. Stretching after the drive.

With his straw cowboy hat, thick forearms, and thicker belly, the proprietor was a cartoon of a junkyard operator. He looked Nikki over, just long enough to price the merchandise.

She must have seemed a dream to him, although I preferred her without all the makeup. The brought-back-from-Mexico skirt, the camisole top, and the bright red beads were fine, but in honor of our special occasion, she'd put on big-girl makeup. She hadn't mastered the art, though. She looked like a schoolkid out to turn tricks. Lolita.

The sun polished her hair.

"I'm here about the radiator for the '68 Mustang."

He looked my car over and nodded. "Told the feller called she's a '67, but she'll fit fine and dandy. You ain't that feller, though."

"No, sir."

"Said you'd come on by." He called to a Mex kid and sent him running into the metal jungle. "How much you fixing to give me for her?"

"I'd like to see it."

"Pablito's gone after her, I had her put aside. If she's to your liking, what's your bid?"

I wanted to see the radiator. But I didn't want to piss him off. I stalled by turning toward Nikki, who had charmed the guard dog. She was wonderful with animals, fearless. She stroked the back of its neck. The dog closed its eyes, tongue lolling.

The proprietor looked at her, then at me. He offered a knowing smile.

The Mex kid lugged the radiator around the office shack. It was an effort for him. He put it down gently, against a line of old tires. I made a pretense of inspecting it, but couldn't tell much. It looked okay.

"Forty bucks," I said.

The proprietor pulled off his hat and patted his forehead with a ragged blue handkerchief.

"Now, I took you for a gentleman, you pulled up. Feller on the phone seemed like a gentleman. I couldn't make even a poor living, I sold a valley-bull part like that for forty dollars. No, sir." He looked at the radiator, almost as lustily as he'd looked at Nikki. "She's rare. I just couldn't do that. No, sir."

"How much?"

"Be a bargain, I was to say a hundred fifty."

I shook my head. "Well, sir, thank you for your time. I can't pay that." I waved my head back toward the Mustang. "Or I wouldn't be driving a thirteen-year-old car."

"Sometimes, those old ones have more spunk, though. Wouldn't take none of these new cars. Fall apart on you. But a car like that . . ."

"I can stretch to fifty-five. I think I have that much on me."

He spit. But not in an unfriendly way. The dog looked up at him. Nikki stopped playing friends.

"Hundred. Best I can do." He smiled. "But now a man can't help taking a shine to the little lady there. As a gentleman myself, I'll make it ninety. And I don't mean pesos."

"Sixty-five."

"Eighty."

"Seventy."

"Seventy-five. On account of the little lady. Rex took a shine to her, too. And Rex, he knows people."

"Seventy-two."

The counteroffer surprised him. "I swear, son . . . you must be part Jew and part coyote." But he was having fun. We grinned at each other. "I'm fixing to die in the poorhouse, and I hope you're going to think of me like that. Seventy-four."

"Seventy-three."

He was just about laughing. "You'll be wanting my trousers thrown in. Not that there's a thing in them. All right, son. Seventy-three, and don't you start arguing about the silver." He put his sweat-darkened hat back on and adjusted how it sat. "You bargain like a A-rab in a camel market."

"Well, I have my wife to think about," I said.

He caught the startled look on Nikki's face.

"That a fact?" he said.

I counted out the money, opened up the trunk, let the Mex kid put the radiator inside, and gave him a buck.

As Nikki walked away from the dog, it barked again. As if it didn't want her to go.

Major Dinwiddie had come through. Late on Friday afternoon, Staff Sergeant Munro, the female NCOIC from Gene's office, had delivered a note with the junkyard's address. All it said was, *He claims to have the radiator you need. Good luck. Major D.*

It was a kindness I had not expected.

As we drove up Kino boulevard, the desert mountains soared behind the city. Nikki spoke above the engine's throb and the wind.

"Where did you learn to bargain like that?"

"I wasn't even on my game."

"It really was like you were an Arab or something."

"I'm not."

We caught a yellow light. I accelerated.

"Why did you say that stuff about me being your wife?"

"It just came out."

"*Don't* say it. Please."

"Sorry."

"Just don't say it." We passed a lowrider pickup. Metallic blue. With a decal of the Virgin of Guadalupe on the rear window. Nikki decided that I'd been admonished sufficiently. Neither of us wanted to spoil the evening ahead. "Tell me again about this movie we're going to?"

"Wait and see."

Nikki's big surprise was that she was taking me out for dinner. To "this place that's really exotic, the kind of place you like." It was a very big deal. As generous as Nikki was sexually, she was a tightwad about money—not the kind of girl who showed up with a six-pack and a pizza. I told myself that I understood. She was saving every penny. For the house she and her husband planned to buy at Fort Lewis. I was just her last fling. It was taken for granted that I'd bear the costs.

I didn't care where we were going. It could've been a burger joint. All that mattered was that Nikki wanted to treat me to dinner. That said, I doubted that we were going to the Tack Room.

I wanted to make a long, memorable evening of it, though, so we were starting off with a French film at the art house near the university. Nikki's appetite ran to major Hollywood releases, but I wanted her to bite into something different. Even if she decided that she didn't like the taste. I was in full-throttle Pygmalion mode.

Playing a sexually frustrated wife, Isabelle Huppert dumped her hard-working husband for Gérard Depardieu as a jobless, drunken stud. In the final scene, tiny Mademoiselle Huppert supported a staggering Depardieu as they stumbled up an alley. I'd hoped for an Éric Rohmer knockoff, but got *Barf-Boy Among the Sluts*. The frogs were out of steam. 1981 was shaping up as a better year for the Aussies.

As we walked to the car, Nikki took my arm. The gesture made me conscious of how small she was.

"Why did they call it *Loulou*?" she asked. "When it wasn't about Loulou, but about her?"

"I don't know. Because it sounded better. Because they're French."

"It doesn't happen like that, you know."

"Like what?"

"She wouldn't really have gone off with him like that. She might've slept with him. But she would've stayed with her husband. No woman would've given up a husband like that for a man she couldn't count on."

I drove up Campbell to the block Nikki had specified. I wasn't allowed to know anything else; it was all a surprise. But I'd eaten at a Greek joint nearby. I figured that would be our destination.

I put up the top and we walked along a side street back to Campbell. Saturday night. Latino kids cruised, yelling from car to car. In a self-imposed apartheid, they avoided the university area. Spotting their dinner destinations, old folks in Buicks hit the brakes midblock.

"I hope you like this place," Nikki said. "It's new."

The Greek place wasn't new, so that was out. Japanese? Thai? For all I knew, Italian was exotic in Nikki's world. I knew very little about her, beyond the physical. And she knew less about me.

"I feel like I should blindfold you or something."

"Please don't. Listen, Nix. I know you're saving for the house. So I'll pay for the wine. Okay?"

"Okay," she agreed. I would have liked a moment's hesitation.

An unexpected name thrust from a storefront. It cut me. I knew, instantly, that it was our destination. Kismet. Fate. God's wicked sense of humor.

The lettering on the restaurant's sign read: ESFAHAN.

"Is something the matter?" Nikki asked as we sat down.

The waiter, slim and preening, left us with the menus.

"No. No, this is great."

"We can go somewhere else, if you want. I want this to be special for you." She looked genuinely concerned, on the verge of a great disappointment. I did not want her gift ruined for her.

"Nikki, this is terrific. I was just surprised that anybody would have the rocks to open an Iranian restaurant. Given the current mood."

She frowned. "I thought it was Persian?"

"Persians are the dominant group in Iran."

She looked down at her menu, but didn't open it. "I should know that. Right?"

"We all have a lot to learn. Come on. This is going to be great. Check out the menu, let's see what they've got."

I pretended to read the misspelled offerings. The place was exactly what I would have expected, had I known the identity of our destination: the handsome young waiter with oiled black hair, a white shirt, and tight black trousers; a harried-about-nothing proprietor by the register; and the invisible relative back in the kitchen listening to a Farsi version of Julie London. A photograph of the late shah, stern and brush-browed, hung behind the till. Posters of the spotlit mosques of Esfahan and of a ski resort in the Zagros Mountains just made the walls seem needier. The white tablecloths were starched but scarred. Hard chairs had replaced soft lives. The restaurant was a place of bitter exile.

The only other clients were a young couple who looked as if they had come in by mistake and a foursome of retirees. One of the old guys held forth about the great times he'd had as an oilman in Iran in "the old days." I tried to tune him out.

"What should I have?" Nikki asked. "I don't know any of these things."

"Kebabs," I said. "How about lamb?"

"I don't like lamb."

"Then chicken."

"What will it come with?"

"Oh . . . rice. Some *sabzi*. Vegetables, I mean. Spinach greens, something like that."

She made a little-kid face, but said, "Okay. I'll have the chicken kebab platter. Are you sure you're all right?"

"I'm great. I just wish it wasn't such a long drive home. That top is a brilliant piece of advertising."

She blushed. Surprising me. "Does it show too much?"

"No. But don't lean over when the waiter's around."

Her blush deepened. I reached across the table and took her wrist.

"Nikki. You look beautiful." She didn't. But she looked enticingly vulnerable. Which was better.

She sat up primly when the waiter approached. Sticking to their English names, I ordered *nan, mast-o khiar,* and some *adasi* to start, *jujeh kabab* for Nikki, *chenjeh kabab* for me. There was no wine list, just a choice of red, white, or rosé. I asked for a bottle of dry rosé.

"I hope this is good," Nikki said.

The two older couples got up, with the raconteur still rambling on about all-night parties and old friends in Tehran. "Hate to think of them all now," he said, "I just hate to think of them. My old pals. Those screwballs hanged two of them. Maybe more, for all I know. It's just one goddamned crying shame. You put your wallet away, Mickey. Tonight's on me. Trip down memory lane."

Belatedly noticing the poster, Nikki said, "I didn't know they had skiing in Iran."

I shrugged. "I doubt the slopes had a boom year." I pointed to the cherry red beads she wore. Struggling to keep away from certain subjects, to hold things together. "Is there a story behind that necklace?"

She lifted the thickest beads from the swell of her breasts. And she smiled. "A girlfriend gave it to me. At graduation. We were bad together. Two bad girls."

"I shudder to think."

Nikki's expression turned wistful. "I'm glad you never met her. You might've liked her better."

"I doubt it."

"No, really. She's more your type, the kind of woman I always picture you with."

"What kind's that?"

"Tall. Brunette. The kind who wears scarves and reads books." She smiled. "The nose-in-the-air type. Not that Samantha was like that. My friend, I mean."

"Jackie O's too old for me."

She brightened. "But that's the kind of woman I mean. Like that."

"I couldn't afford the upkeep."

The appetizers I'd order arrived. I had to ask again for the wine. The waiter clearly found his job an infernal humiliation.

"This is good," Nikki said, dipping the hot flatbread a second time. "What's it called?"

"I forget," I lied. "When I'm with you, I forget everything."

"You shouldn't have said I was your wife. It wasn't fair."

"No. It wasn't. Sorry."

"You don't know how it made me feel. It's all right now. But it upset me." She caught herself. We were both on edge. "Sorry for bringing it up again. I'm being stupid."

"You were thinking about it. It's better to say it."

"We'd never work. You know that. We have nothing in common. And we're both unreliable. We're not the faithful kind, neither of us."

"People change."

"I don't want to talk about it, Roy."

I almost said, *You brought it up.* Instead, I told her, "Try some of this."

Our nibbling slowed in anticipation of the main course. Nikki glanced around again and said, "They're not doing much business."

"Nothing Iranian—or Persian—is going to be very popular for a while."

"It doesn't seem fair. The food's good."

"Life's not fair."

The kebabs arrived. I slicked Nikki's meat off the skewer for her.

"You know how to do a lot of things," she said. "Weird stuff."

"A fox, not a hedgehog. Here, like this."

"You're not fooling me, you know."

"About what?"

"You haven't eaten very much."

"I was waiting for the kebabs. I don't have your manly appetite, Nix."

"But it's all right, isn't it?"

"It's terrific. Really."

She tucked in. I'd never known her to be without an appetite. But halfway through the meal, she stopped and said, "I meant a girl who looks like Jessie. Not Jessie, I wouldn't wish her on anybody. But a girl who looks like that."

"Jessie looks like trailer trash with a sugar daddy."

"You know what I mean."

Glad for the excuse to put down my fork, I said, "What do I have to do to convince you that I'd pass up a hundred Jessies for you?" I looked at her almost meanly. "For one fucking night with you."

She laughed again. "You mean for one night of fucking." She reached for the bottle and poured herself more wine.

In the background, the waiter snickered.

The stray young couple paid their bill and left.

Nikki had been drinking more than I had. Faster. And she was small. She raised her glass.

"Here's to the man who isn't my husband . . . ," she said. Her eyes grew wet, but she fought against the tears. "Here's to . . . to my fuck buddy. Excuse me. I have to go to the ladies' room."

As she rose, her chair nearly toppled backwards.

Huddling at the back counter, the waiter and the proprietor watched her go. They began to talk. Loudly. Speculating. By the time Nikki came back out, the commentary was gruesomely explicit.

Oblivious, she smiled at them.

The waiter remarked that he wasn't sure which hole he'd start with, but that they'd all be well greased.

Before Nikki could sit down, I was on my feet.

"Wait outside," I told her.

She had washed her face, and her makeup was almost gone. My tone bewildered her.

"What's the matter?"

I pushed her toward the door. Shoved her. "*Wait outside*. Don't come back in. *Go*."

As soon as I had her walking away, I turned to the waiter and his boss. And I lost it. Bellowing at them. Calling them cunts and impotent cowards.

I got poison breath close to the waiter. "Go ahead," I told him. "Tell me which hole you'd like to try first."

He made the mistake of smiling. I slammed him against the wall. The old guy stepped back and shouted toward the kitchen.

Pretty boy pulled out a switchblade. But he wasn't tough. He was the pampered kind of Iranian. Down on his luck now. No longer feeding at the big trough.

I broke his wrist over the counter. Both long bones snapped. The knife fell to the floor. I asked him again which hole would be his first choice.

The waiter looked at his dangling hand in shock. The proprietor wailed. Another Iranian, in dirty cook's whites, waddled through the kitchen door with a cleaver. He looked like he'd been a wrestler, but had long since let himself go.

"Kurds fuck your sisters in their asses," I told them. The switchblade was in my hand now. My bloody hand. I didn't know where the blood had come from, didn't care. "Arabs fuck your mothers in the mouth. And your mothers beg for more."

Shocked by the useless flipper dangling from his arm, the waiter cried to the boss. Who, predictably, was his father.

Halfway to me, the cook hesitated. I must have looked pure pscyho.

Everything stopped. The world went quiet. Breathing hugely, we stared at one another.

"Shit," I said in English. I threw the switchblade across the room and turned my back. Heading for the door. They were all cowards.

"You have to pay!" the proprietor called. "You have to pay!"

But no one came after me.

Outside, Nikki stood back from the window. In horror. She wasn't going to be much good in combat.

Two passersby stared at us, then corrected themselves and hurried on.

"You're bleeding," Nikki said.

"Fuck it. Come on." I looked down, though. I hadn't felt it, but the blade had cut into my palm. Between the thumb and the forefinger. As soon as I saw the wound, it started to hurt.

I pulled out my handkerchief, but kept walking. I wanted to put some distance between us and the restaurant. In case the shah's lost legion found its courage.

"Let me," she said. "Let me do it."

"*Just keep walking.* It's all right."

She stopped. Staring at me. Part horrified, part mystified. "What's going *on*? What was that all about? What language were you speaking in there?"

"I don't know what you're talking about."

"I *heard* you. You weren't speaking English."

I began to walk away. She could follow or not. "It sounds different when people are shouting. Voices distort. You were outside."

She hurried to catch up. "I *heard* you," she repeated. As we turned the corner toward the car. "What language was that? What were you saying to them?"

I reached out with my half-bandaged paw and seized her under the chin. Shoving her up against a wall. Between neon and darkness, her eyes lit with fear.

Instantly, I let her go. There was blood on her chin, her neck, the camisole top.

"Don't say a word," I told her. "Not one word."

9

"Come on in," I told Gene Massetto. "I was just reading."

I'd been going through *Dog Soldiers* again. Robert Stone got it. Others didn't.

Gene entered, glanced at the bandage on my paw, said nothing, and dropped onto the sofa. He looked glum. The bearer of bad news.

"Want a beer?" I asked him. "I'm out of everything else."

He shook his head. Looking for words. It was only the second time he'd been in my apartment. It was either work or a chow call with Marilyn that brought us together. Plus the occasional run. Gene could run.

"What's the matter?" I asked. "Am I in trouble?"

"It's not you. It's me."

"Something happen to Marilyn?"

He waved the thought away. "This is harder than I thought it was going to be."

I sat down. "Give me a clue."

He glanced at the book I'd been reading. It didn't register. "Do you ever get restless?" he asked. Not meeting my eyes.

"Only three or four times an hour. I'm ready to move on from the Great Map Exercise. To say the least."

"That's not what I mean. Maybe *restless* is the wrong word."

Gene was almost comically handsome. I filed him under "Italian prince," but his looks went well beyond that. He was from the Rudolph Valentino/Ramón Novarro School of Male Beauty. The female students adored him, ready with more than apples for the teacher.

"There are plenty of different flavors of restless," I said.

"I think I mean 'unhappy,' to be honest." He raised his eyes from a hard-worn rug. Meeting mine at last. Gene's eyes were the flaw in his perfection. Bassett hound brown, they played defense in the great game of existence.

"Unhappy comes in even more flavors than restless."

He nodded. Slowly. "Maybe I'll have that beer."

I rose.

"No, forget it. I don't want a beer. I'm just dragging this out." He fortified himself and looked straight at me. "It's Marilyn. Or me, to be precise. Roy, I just don't know. I just don't *know*."

I offered him a noncommittal shrug.

"Oh, I *love* her," he said. "That's not the point. It's . . . I don't know . . . it's that I don't love her the way I want to love her. I'm not excited. It's not even sex, I don't mean that. I mean, that's not the main problem. It's just that . . . I look around, I look at my life, and I ask myself, 'Is this it?' We have nothing in common, really. Nothing to talk about. Apart from all the how-was-your-day-honey stuff. We don't even want to go to the same place on vacations. I want a getaway, a beach, something far from the flagpole. For her, it's always back to visit the family, year after year. Have any bourbon?"

"Sorry."

"When I came back from Nam and went ROTC . . . man, there she was. Marilyn. This beautiful girl. I just went crazy. I thought I'd never need anything or anybody else. It was . . . absolute magic." He looked through the knotty pine wall that divided the living room from the bedroom. Looking back through the years. "Roy, you have no *idea* how beautiful she was."

"She still is. Marilyn's gorgeous."

"It's different now, it's not the same. I feel . . . I feel chained. Like I have to break out, do something to break the pattern. I don't know, volunteer for a solo assignment in Africa or something. I mean, if I have to face one more here-you-go-honey, white-bread-on-the-side lasagna dinner, I'll put my fist through the wall."

Silence plopped down between us. I pictured Gene punching one of the painted cinder block walls in his quarters. Gene was strong, but the wall was going to win.

At last, I said, "Don't you think this is normal? Wanting more? I mean, we all have fantasies of other lives. Restlessness . . . that's just the spirit of the pioneers corralled in suburbia."

"Are *you* unhappy, Roy? You have your freedom. And you seem to be enjoying it. Man-to-man: Wouldn't you say you're happy?"

"It comes and goes. I've had low expectations of happiness for a while now." The notion that Gene viewed me as happy jarred me. If he misread me that badly, how had I mistaken him?

"Well, for me, it just goes," he said. "I mean, *is* this it? Do I sleep with the same woman for the rest of my life, make the same how-was-your-day-honey small talk? Do I just throw myself into my career, focus on the next promotion, and wind up as one of those full birds who keep the staff working late because they don't want to go home? Is that *it?*"

I'd long since concluded that the real reason marriage has to be legally binding is that pussy wears out. But that didn't seem like a helpful direction for the conversation.

"What do you want, Gene? I mean, really? If you could take your pick of anything life has to offer? What would make you happy?"

The doorbell rang. I was relieved, to be honest. My repertoire of clichés had been exhausted.

Beyond the screen-door barricade, Jessie posed in the fan of light I'd released. She constructed a smile, then glanced past me to Gene.

"Are girls allowed at this party?" she asked.

It was almost eleven when I picked up Nikki from the BOQ. Our love-making was perfunctory. Her breasts were swollen and sensitive. Girl stuff. One of my stitches tore, and my hand left a crimson trail on her white flesh.

We got where we needed to go, but I found myself thinking of Marilyn along the way. Which was not good.

Nikki crashed hard. I lay awake. I would've liked to put on some mid-career Miles. *In a Silent Way.* But the rest of the world needed quiet.

Plenty to think about. Not much of it good. In the wake of our silent drive back from Tucson on Saturday, Nikki hadn't brought up the restaurant debacle. Nor had I. But it was there between us. Guilt and anger weren't a winning combination.

I almost left the bed to run in the darkness. But care-charmer sleep showed up with sudden force.

Gene's phone call woke me. My first thought upon hearing his voice was, *Shit. He's going to tell me he's leaving Marilyn.*

The notion wasn't far-fetched. The evening before, Jessie had abandoned my company before Gene could reach his Plymouth. Out in the lot, they'd struck up a conversation, which I tuned out. Bill Evans had gone on the turntable, with the volume notched up.

"What's up?" I glanced at the alarm clock. It would've gone off in five minutes.

"I just thought you'd want to know," Gene said. "Colonel Jacoby had a heart attack. Last night, at the gym. He's dead."

Pete Paulson should've been Infantry, in charge of ambush training. He had an unerring instinct for cornering people.

At the gym over the lunch hour, Jacoby's death had been the prevalent topic between the heaves and grunts. I was still thinking about him as I strolled down the stretch of scrub desert to the academic complex. By the time I recognized Pete hustling up the sidewalk, it was too late to flee.

He waved and grinned, then inflated his freckled cheeks. Which meant a tirade was coming.

I steeled myself.

"Roy, I'm *so* glad we ran into each other. It's . . . it's fortuitous."

"How are you, Pete?"

"Blessed. Each and every day."

A five-ton grumbled by. I wanted to jump in the back and pull down the canvas, but lacked the moral vigor.

I looked at my watch. Making the gesture unmistakable. "Pete, I've got a ton of work."

"Oh, sure. Of course. But what does such work profit a man, Roy?"

"It means I won't get court-martialed for dereliction of duty. For one thing."

It sounded as though he had learned to laugh from watching TV. "That's one of the great things about you, Roy. Your sense of humor. The members of our prayer group would love you as much as I do. I bet you'd be great teaching the children. I teach them martial arts, you know."

"The Church Militant. Pete, we've been through this a dozen—"

"No, no. Sorry, Roy. I didn't mean to sidetrack myself like that." The sonofabitch just gnawed away like a beaver. "I wanted to offer you an *opportunity*. You're always going down to Mexico, right? You love it down there, don't you?"

"I wouldn't say *always*. Or *love*. But I like Mexico. Yeah."

He beamed. "The weekend after next, we're making a missionary trip to Hermosillo. They're all Catholics, you know. The Mexicans. They've been held in their Babylonian Captivity for centuries. We're going to go down in a bus and expose the people to true Christian humility, to the unfiltered love of Jesus Christ, our Savior. We have picture Bibles in Spanish to hand out. And two dozen cases of Pepsi."

"Pete, I'm not the guy you need to be talking to." I'd had a wonderful inspiration. "You should talk to Jerry Purvis. His Spanish is just about fluent. He could be a real help."

Pete dismissed the idea. "He's a sinner. An *unrepentant* sinner. But you feel guilt, you'd like to change your ways. Anybody can see it. You're searching, Roy, you're a pilgrim on a journey. And Jesus Christ is the destination."

"Be that as it may, I'm not joining a mission trip to Hermosillo to bully a pack of hijacked *campesinos* into adult baptism. What on earth made you think I'd be interested?"

"Jessica's going. For one thing. Roy, she's absolutely . . . she's *fervent.* We're all going down on a bus, like I said. One big Christian family. The Mexicans are going to love her."

"Yeah. *La luz del mundo.* That's our Jessie. For Christ's sake, Pete. I have no interest in that woman. Or in your mission, to be frank. My best advice to you is to get separate rooms."

He ignored my wickedness. "But she's interested in *you,* Roy. Oh, I don't mean in the common way, the way people like you always take it. In a *virtuous* way, a Christian way. We've talked about you, prayed over you. She thinks you're crying out, that you need our help. She wants to *save* you."

That snapped the branch.

"Pete. Listen to me. Jessie's a calculating slut. She's using you. I don't know for what, or why, or how. But Jessie's *always* got an agenda. She is *not* Sister Jessica of the Old Wooden Cross. And this is *not* going to end well for you. Or for Jesus."

His conviction didn't waver. Pete had the shining eyes of the true believer, dead to reality.

Exasperated and late, I wrapped it up. "Would you just pay fucking attention, Pete? She's no more a religious believer than a python."

" 'Judge not, lest ye be judged.' "

"Oh, fucking shove it." I brushed past him and headed down to work.

"Jesus works miracles," Pete called after me. "You'll see!"

The spectacular landscape surrounding the burial party was like the Army: You could love it all you wanted, but it couldn't love you back. You simply had to live with the desert's laws, admiring it for what it was. And you had to stay alert to survive.

One of many mourners on Boot Hill, I paid more attention to the living than to the ceremony. Formalities rarely reached me. Even when I wanted them to punch through. So I stood there, empty-souled, amid a hundred officers and NCOs, all of us sweating through our dress-green uniforms. The wives stood their posts in Sunday outfits that grew darker under the armpits. Now and then, one sneaked a look to see how badly she'd scuffed her shoes on the walk up from the car. It was a school day, so there were few children by the grave, and those present looked sullen or bored.

Jacoby got the full treatment, an honor guard ready to fire blanks in his wake and a bugler standing by to finish him off. The post's mounted color guard had turned out in their old Cavalry getups. The riders maintained a respectful distance, but as the chaplain spoke, the horses pawed and whinnied. Down along the creek, a car drove by.

Head bowed for prayer, I watched ants hustling along. Mean little bastards you didn't want up your leg, they'd made their peace with the desert long ago. Mutual recognition, mutual respect. Hegelian *Anerkennung* meets Mother Nature. Ants seemed able to thrive in any environment. It was a talent I craved.

I longed to show more than perfunctory respect to Jacoby. But I didn't know how. I stood at attention as the rifle volleys fought a rear guard action with the silence of the grave. A child cried and was hushed. Taps sounded. The bugler had fine control and a flair for elegy. But it wasn't enough.

I wanted to reach Jacoby, to transmit beyond the grave, to tell him I understood. He *hadn't* loved the Army. It was more than that. The Army had been a passion. And passion devours the self that mere love strengthens. So he laced up his boots, marched forward in step, and gave the Green Machine everything he had. He never had a choice; it was predestined. There must have been times when he hated the tyranny of it.

Karma. In starched fatigues.

The last echo of taps faded into the canyons. The color guard wheeled about and took the trail back to the stables. The crowd broke up.

I let them go. Standing still beneath a sky so blue, it was unsettling.

After the rest of humanity had gone back to its air-conditioning and cold drinks, I took off my dress-green jacket and sat on the scrub grass. Away from the ants. Just me, the dead, and the desert. Breaking the eleventh commandment, I pulled off my cap. It left a crown of sweat.

I thought again of who had attended and who had not. Gene had shown up, of course, with Marilyn demure in a dark blue suit, auburn hair coiled. Major Dinwiddie had come alone, wincing at the sun and dabbing his eyes. The commanding general had been absent, but he was on the road a lot. Big crowd, though. More than respectable. None of the students had appeared, but they had classes and lived in their own world. In Nikki's daytime world. As for Jessie, she interested herself only in males who were still breathing. But Jerry had disappointed me. I had expected him to show.

What did it matter? Now? It wasn't as if Jacoby had been taking attendance. Still, I felt there should have been more to the day.

Light footsteps. On loose gravel.

The colonel's lady. Back for a personal good-bye. I rose and put my headgear back on.

She gave me a meaningless smile and stopped at the edge of the grave.

Just a casket with a dirty top, waiting for the front loader to cover it. Flowers that didn't belong in the high desert.

Mrs. Jacoby turned her attention to me. Reading my rank, my name tag. A nondescript Army wife, she'd mastered the frumpy-but-aloof look the wives of senior officers acquired. I'd seen her around the post, hadn't known who she was, hadn't cared.

She had no-nonsense eyes, though.

"Forgive me, Lieutenant Banks, but I don't believe we've met. Did you work for my husband?"

"Temporarily. On a special project."

She nodded. "So you didn't know him well?"

"No, ma'am. But I admired him."

Her next smile came more naturally. But it had an edge. "Ah, yes. The 'soldier's soldier.' Is that how Art seemed to you?"

"Yes, ma'am."

She looked at the grave. "He was, I suppose. A 'soldier's soldier.' All I know is that he was an interesting husband, a wonderfully interesting man." She cocked her head to one side, and gray hair brushed a shoulder. "Behind those gleaming boots and all those ribbons . . . in there, where others couldn't see . . . was the most fascinating man I've ever known. And a very good man. I wish our daughter . . ."

I felt awkward, *was* awkward. "She couldn't make it today?"

"No."

"I'm sorry."

"Jen was killed. Two years ago. By a drunk driver. It broke Arthur's heart."

I had nothing to offer.

Trained for the task at hand, Mrs. Jacoby bucked up. "I suppose I should have pretended to recognize your name, Lieutenant. And told you that my husband thought highly of you. But Art never had any patience with lies. Or fibs. Or whatever you want to call the deceits that let us survive contact with one another."

"I got that much. From knowing him."

Amused, she smiled. It was her first smile with unmistakable warmth. "A counseling session? Did he put you through one of his grillings? He used to tell me about those. We'd laugh and laugh. But I don't suppose you think of him as laughing, he wouldn't have let you see that. He was full of the joy of life, though, just bursting with it. He told me—more than once—that keeping a straight face was the hardest part of his job out here."

"I think I saw that, too."

She didn't hear me. Piercing a gap in the thermals, a hawk rushed toward the earth. On the way to inspect the dumpsters behind the mess hall.

"Do you know what his hobby was, Lieutenant Banks? Repairing old watches. Can you imagine that? With those enormous hands? He could be so amazingly delicate, astonishingly so." She shifted her position, as if a stone underfoot threatened to unbalance her. Fresh dust thickened the old dust on her shoes. "He said that he'd fixed so many watches that Father Time owed him a bonus. He seems to have been wrong about that."

"I'm sorry, ma'am."

She sighed. It would not have been audible in any place less still. "Forty-nine years old. I'll miss him terribly. But I never could picture Arthur retired from the Army, to tell you the truth. He would have felt like an exile." Her shoulders lost more of their discipline. "I wish he'd gotten a star, though. For his sake. Not for the vanity of it. For the acknowledgment, the recognition. But he was honest one too many times. More than one too many times." Her eyes challenged mine. "If you stay in the Army, Lieutenant, you'll have to learn to distinguish between honesty and the appearance of honesty. You'll find the latter better for your career." Her eyes sank to my hand. "And you need to change that bandage."

Eli Lemberger materialized at my apartment door. Wearing the most diffident expression I had ever seen on a lawyer. Or a jazz buff.

It was the first time he'd taken me up on my invitation, and he was unsure of himself. His long hair looked grayer. As if he'd worried the color out of it on the drive over from Bisbee.

I welcomed him. Not least because he carried several old LPs under one arm, with a vintage Blue Note cover showing.

"New stock," he said. "I thought you might like to hear a few of these."

"Sit down, make yourself as comfortable as the environment permits. Beer? Inexcusably cheap wine? I just stocked up."

He couldn't help looking around the room. With poorly concealed dismay. My place was clean. But the interior decorators had been absent without leave. What little money I had didn't go on antiques.

"Authentically bohemian," he decided.

"Early Junk Sale. I'm just passing through, Eli. Have a seat, for Christ's sake. It isn't museum quality, but it won't bite. Beer? Wine?"

"Beer. If you don't mind, Roy."

"Shiner Bock, imported straight from Texas? Or a Carta Blanca?"

"CB, please. Roy, you have *got* to hear this French Chet Baker pressing. He's at his absolute best."

"Put it on. The system's no Edith, but the cartridge is good. 'First do no harm.' Collector's rule number one."

We sipped our beers. Chet blew slow smack visions. Club-in-the-cellar stuff. Women with unfiltered cigarettes and Jean Seberg haircuts. Then Eli put on Maynard Ferguson for contrast.

We talked, in bits and pieces, during the lesser numbers. But Eli truly loved the music. He always went quiet at the right passages. Pushing his hair back behind his ear with his right hand and closing his eyes, he said, "Listen to this now . . . Max Roach was the *only* sticks man who knew how to tune his drums."

When the needle hit the dead zone, Eli went for the turntable. "Can you *believe* that last solo? I mean, you just *knew* Maynard was going to downshift into a lower register . . . and, bang, he takes it an octave higher!" He put the tonearm to rest as he swapped out albums. "He really is under-appreciated these days. Although a Mexican businessman who comes by has taken an interest. At first I pegged the poor man as *hopelessly* Herbie Mann. If not Herb Alpert. But he turned out to have a serious ear."

"Put on the Coltrane," I told him. "I haven't heard that one for years."

"You and your Trane. I was saving it. But here goes."

Then he thought better of it. "Actually, let's save it for a few moments. Shall we, Roy? Just for a minute or two. I'd like to talk. Confidentially."

"Sounds serious."

He sat down again, pushing his hair back with both hands this time. As if it would lend gravity to his words. "Maybe, maybe not. I doubt it has anything remotely to do with you. But then, I don't understand how these military things work, all the arcane relationships, who does what for whom."

"You know the ranks."

"Only because the police insignia are pretty much the same. I told you. Now, Roy, this really has to remain confidential. I'm absolutely not joking."

"Do I even want to hear it?"

"Maybe not. If that's the case, you can hear it and forget it."

"I'm listening."

He lifted the beer bottle to his lips, then lowered it without drinking. "In my other life . . . I mean, in my other life in Bisbee, my lawyer life . . . I hear things. Oh, I hear a great many things, of course. Although I make it a point not to *really* hear some of them. Dear me, I don't get the *least* thrill from it. Quite the contrary. I'm looking for calm, not some cheap border-town *frisson*. Perhaps I'll even move on from dear Bisbee at some point. If things become too enmeshing."

"You're talking drug stuff?"

He glanced around. Instinctively. "Roy, I overheard something a bit vague. But it had to do with drug smuggling and military people. People from Fort Huachuca. Ring any bells?"

"Nope. Eli, there are thousands of people on-post. I mean, I'm sure we've got the odd second lieutenant bringing back an ounce of smoke and a case of crabs from his Saturday night in Nogales. And the enlisted troops get into their share of trouble. But . . . beyond that . . . unless it's a couple of warrant officers flying down in a Mohawk to pad their pensions . . ."

"I'm glad to hear that. I mean, that you don't know anything about this. Not that I expected you to, I don't mean that. But this matter just sounded . . . serious. Very serious, Roy. Not just an ounce or two of pot. And I'd never heard about any sort of military connection before."

"Lot of federal and public land around here. You could pack stuff in, walk the spine of the Huachucas, use the fort as a buffer. It's pretty wild up in the mountains."

"No, no. It wasn't anything like that. These aren't two-bit people, Roy. They don't walk anywhere. They don't have to. But let's leave it, I've said enough. I just thought . . . I don't know . . . forewarned is forearmed. Something like that."

"Thanks. If I discover any opium dens underneath the barracks, I'll let you know."

He didn't smile along. Instead, his features took on an arctic sobriety. "It's not funny, Roy. Trust me. There's nothing funny about it. These are *bad* people."

"Well, I don't know anything about it. And I've already forgotten what you said."

"Good. Oh, let's wait on the Coltrane. Please, Roy. I have to play something absolutely *scrumptious* for you. . . ."

I let Eli turn up the volume higher than my usual weeknight level. The neighbors and I got along reasonably well. On one side, an old cowboy–cowgirl couple survived off Social Security and odd jobs. On the other, a hefty Air Force sergeant from the test range made lengthy, noisy love with his mammoth wife.

Von Freeman was wailing when Jerry knocked and let himself in.

"I know you aren't banging Nikki when you got this crap on . . ."

He registered Eli. *Genuinely* registered him. "Hey, if I'm crashing the party . . ."

"Get yourself a beer. And have a seat. And shut up."

Jerry started for the kitchen, but halted by the stereo. "Really, I just wanted to run something by you. Can I turn this crap down for a minute?" He reached for the volume knob before I could answer.

I introduced Eli and Jerry. Jerry didn't come close enough to put himself in danger of a handshake. He just smirked.

Eli let it slide. By L.A. standards, Jerry didn't even qualify as small-time.

"Speak your piece," I said.

Jerry dropped into a chair by the door. Across the room from Eli.

"Formal notification," he told me. "I am invoking a mandatory, all-hands meeting of the Officers' Club. This weekend. Destination: Puerto Peñasco. Departure time: 1800, Friday. Bring your sacrificial virgin, or an appropriate substitute, for the club rituals. How about it, man? You in? You and Nikki? I mean, I need you to be in on this one. I got a flaming hot date, but I need combat support. And maybe some medical attention. Who knows?"

"I'll ask Nikki. See if she's up for it."

"Tell her that, as a senior member of the Ladies' Auxiliary, her presence is mandatory."

"I'll tell her. But she's trying to pull her grades up. The finish line nears."

"Tell her she'll pass. I guarantee it. I'll pull some strings, if need be. Christ, I'd take the tests for her myself, just to get her scrawny ass gone and get you back to normal." He turned to Eli. Briefly. "Can you believe this guy used to be one happy-go-lucky, whore-fighting, bar-fucking in-dividual who was a constant delight to be around?"

"No whores," I corrected him.

"Better than being pussy-whipped by Jodie Foster. I mean, this is just like *Taxi Driver.*" He looked at Eli and grinned malevolently.

"Nikki's shorter," I said. "But she does like jam on her toast. I'll see what I can do. About the weekend."

That was enough for Jerry. He could go back to his trailer and Teilhard de Chardin. Sometimes I wondered if he understood a word of what he read.

Of course, he couldn't resist taking one last shot. Halfway out the door, he turned and said, "I'll just let you two girls get back to comparing recipes."

Out in the darkness, the Corvette rumbled to life. Annoyed, I got up to reload the turntable.

Before I could heal the atmosphere with a dose of Erroll Garner, Eli said, "What an insecure young man. What *do* you think he's hiding?"

10

Our fire had gone out. A crescent moon barely shone, but starlight paled the beach. The sea rasped. You could feel the hot weather coming by the lingering warmth in the sand. Jerry passed the bottle of tequila.

"I like it out here," Jessie said. "Away from the town." She drank and handed the booze to me. I skipped my turn, but held on to the bottle. Nikki was putting too much liquor away.

"It's quiet," I agreed.

"It isn't that," Jessie went on. "It's that it feels . . . dangerous. We could be murdered. Disappear without a trace."

"Unlikely," I said.

"I'd protect you," Jerry told her. "But *only* you. Those two can fend for themselves." Paleness and shadow shifted. "Man, you going to hog that bottle forever?"

I tried to route it directly back into Jerry's paws, but Nikki cried, "You forgot me!"

I gave her the bottle. She was small. And slugging it down. On top of all the day's beers. We were sunburned and dehydrated. I worried about her.

Jessie rummaged in her beach bag. "I have something better."

Star-combed hair framed an unlit face. The ambient light from the town behind the hill gave Jessie a halo. Before we hiked out to grill shrimp and drink, she had changed into a light sweater and pressed khaki shorts. Outclassing Nikki, who had just pulled on my old denim shirt over her bikini bottom.

Jessie's hand reemerged from her bag with a fat joint, white as a grub.

"Anybody got a light?" she asked.

Jerry was ready.

After a long, theatrical hit, Jessie exhaled then said, "Shotgun." She reversed the number, inserting the lighted end between her lips, and knelt before Jerry. He closed his eyes and drank in the blast of smoke.

Jessie extended the joint to Nikki, who took a big-girl toke and gave it to me. I just passed it on.

"You are such a stick-in-the-mud," Jessie told me. With a trill of laughter.

"He's a lifer," Jerry said. "Mr. Regulations."

"That's me," I agreed. "Mr. Moral Rigor."

"They're right, though," Nikki decided. "You *like* rules."

"You shouldn't drink any more of that."

"I can take care of myself, thank you."

Jerry took a power hit, then thrust the joint back at Nikki.

I shrugged. Nikki had been oddly distant all day, but not mad enough to fight. I had no idea what it was about. The night before, I would have understood. I'd been furious myself when Jerry's hot date turned out to be Jessie Lamoureaux. He'd lied to me. By omission. He knew that Nikki and I would not have signed up for a weekend in Mexico with Jessie. Then he hit me up for fifty bucks. Although he hadn't paid back the last hundred he owed me for the Corvette repairs.

In the small-miracles department, the long drive west through the rez, then the drop down to Puerto Peñasco, had gone better than expected. The only practical load plan crammed Nikki and Jessie into the Mustang's backseat. I expected a catfight, but they were giggling into their beer cans before we were a half hour out of Huachuca. I've never understood how women who hate each other can turn into instant pals.

By the time I rousted the crashed-out motel matron, my three passengers were singing oldies and I was feeling fine.

Nikki's goodwill deserted her by morning. We made love hard, as if she'd decided I was an enemy, then got through the day on the beach with a line between us.

"Man . . . that is some good shit," Jerry declared. "I feel like I'm back in Panama. You know what SF stands for, man? 'Smokin' Fools.'" He dropped back onto the sand with a faint thud, kicking out bare feet toward the fire's black remains.

"We're going to play a game," Jessie announced.

"What game?" Nikki asked. She sounded out of it.

"We're going to play Truth. Everybody gets a turn asking a question we all have to answer."

I looked at Nikki, then at Jessie. I was not a trusting soul.

"I'll start," Jessie said. "How old were you when you lost your virginity?"

"This is chickenshit," I said. As subtly as I could, I sidelined the tequila. The bottle was almost empty.

Nikki shifted her butt. Away from me.

"Okay, you first," Jerry told his date.

Jessie blew out a last cloud of marijuana smoke. Darkness visible. "I was sweet sixteen," she said. "I don't mind admitting it. Friend of my father's, but he was no gentleman. He took *advantage* of me." She was preening, performing. "He *was* handsome, though. And I just *loathed* his wife." She laughed and poked Jerry. "Your turn. Get up, you slug."

"Me? Man, I was, like, four years old. Friend of my mother's . . . but she was no lady."

"*No,*" Nikki told him. "You have to play right."

"Okay, okay. Seventeen," he said. "Sheila Bartlett shattered my illusions. Literally, at one blow. How about you, Lol?"

"I was twelve," Nikki told us.

Jessie found the abrupt silence intolerable. "*Your* turn," she told me.

"I'm not playing," I told her.

"You really are a stick-in-the-mud, you know that?" She giggled. Stoned, despite herself. "Well, we'll just play without you."

"He's a stick-in-the-mud, when he isn't hanging out with his faggot friends," Jerry said. "Hey, what happened to the tequila? What is this shit? Pass the fucking bottle, man."

I held it out by the neck. Nikki reached for it. "I want some, too."

On the verge of telling her she'd had enough, I held back the words and settled the bottle by the stain our fire had left. Jerry let Nikki drink first.

"My turn to ask a question," Jerry said. "What's everybody's secret fantasy? Me, I'm going to take over some nice, little country that needs a little discipline. Down in LatAm. Just a little one, you know? Something manageable. Maybe with a few of my SF buddies. And I am going to be, like, the fucking *caudillo*. The big man, *el jefe máximo*. And I'm going to have this harem . . . set up in the national library. . . ." He giggled. "In Panama did Jerry Purvis a pleasure dome decree . . . or maybe not Panama, too many gringos. Jeez, is anybody else this stoned?"

"If I could be anything at all," Jessie said, "I'd be mistress of one of those great, big houses in the Garden District. In New Orleans, of course."

"Not a plantation?" I asked.

"Plantations are overrated. Mr. Stick-in-the-Mud. I want society around me, glittering, gleaming, glorious, brilliant society. And it's not now, not today. It's before. Back when . . . people were kept in their places. I'd be the queen of everything, adored by all. With a mammy who knew how to work her John the Conqueror . . . and a handsome husband from an old family that hadn't lost its money. And I'd have a dashing young lover determined to fight a duel with my husband. Only I wouldn't let him. Because my young beau wouldn't have any money himself, of course. They never do."

Jessie had closed her eyes, but opened them again to look at Nikki. "What's *your* fantasy, Nicole?"

Nikki glanced at me, then looked away. I couldn't read her expression.

"There's . . . this poem we had to read. In high school. There's this woman. She's an innkeeper's daughter. And . . . and she's in love. Really, really in love. With a robber, a highwayman. Only the soldiers set a trap for him and they use her as bait. But she warns him. She dies to save him, she loves him so much. And he escapes. He rides away into the night. . . ."

"Alfred Noyes," Jerry said. He surprised me sometimes. "They made you read that shit?"

"Well, I think it's sweet," Jessie said. "Who would *you* die for, Nicole? Not Mr. Stick-in-the-Mud, there?"

"It's just a poem," Nikki said. She had confused herself.

"Now it's your turn," Jessie told her. "You get to pick the next question."

Nikki didn't hesitate. Fucked up, drunk, and stoned, she had her question ready: "Who do you all love most in the world?"

"You first," Jessie said. Gleefully.

"I love my husband," Nikki declared. "You all think it's funny. But it's true. I love him. I really do."

"That's nice," Jessie said.

"Who do *you* love?" Nikki asked her.

"My daddy, of course. All Southern girls love their fathers." She turned toward Jerry. "And you love *me*. Don't you?" she said.

"No. You're second, though. I love Nietzsche, man. That's who I love. I don't know how I missed him all these years."

"Nietzsche was a syphilitic twerp," I said. "Slobbering over his superman fantasies. Drooling spirochetes."

Jerry shook his head, dark on dark. "You just don't get it, man. The mundane details of his life and shit don't matter. Don't you get that? He was just the messenger. Of universal truths."

"He was a diseased little creep."

Jessie intervened. Leaving her spot in the sand to coil in front of me. Face swaying a foot from mine. Dark hair falling.

"I know what *you* love," she told me. "If you won't play, I'll play for you."

"What do I love?" I asked.

"The Army." She laughed and sat back.

Jerry laughed, too. "I told you he's a fucking lifer."

Nikki didn't laugh.

"Poor little Roy . . . loves the Army best of all," Jessie continued, her voice a singsong. "He loves the Army best of all . . . best of all . . . the girls at the ball . . ."

"You're all stoned," I said.

"And I can prove it," Jessie insisted. "Just answer one question, Mr. Shiny Boots. Tell the truth. Would you . . ." She brought her face so close to mine that her hair curtained off the starlight. Close enough for me to smell pot and alcohol. Almost close enough to taste her. "Would you give up the Army for a woman? If you really loved her? Would you give up your commission for love, Roy? Let's make it real: How about for Nicole? Would you do that? Leave the Army for Nicole. If she begged you to?"

"Nikki has other plans. What's your point?"

Triumphant, Jessie rocked back on her haunches, settling with her rump to the cold fire. She turned her attention to Nikki. "You know what I hate about men?"

Nikki shook her head. On time-delay. Way out of it now.

"What I truly *hate* . . . is the way they kiss. They're such slobs." She giggled, a stoned bitch. Nikki smiled along, utterly lost. "They're such . . . they're all such oafs. Don't you wish you'd meet just one man who knew how to kiss?"

"Hey, you weren't complaining last night," Jerry said.

"They have no delicacy, no charm," Jessie went on. "They're all pigs. Aren't they?"

Nikki nodded. Vacantly.

"Should we show them how they should kiss us?" Jessie asked.

Before Nikki could reply, Jessie knelt before her and took her face in both hands. Nikki closed her eyes. Passive. Jessie kissed her gently at first, then deeply.

"Knock it off," I said. "For Christ's sake. She's drunk."

Jessie broke the contact of their lips and turned her smile on me.

"I'm not . . . drunk . . . ," Nikki said.

Jerry slapped the sand. "More! More! *Encore!*"

Jessie kissed her again. Ferociously. As if tearing flesh from her. Then she stood up and dropped her shorts. "I'm going for a swim," she told us. Drawing her sweater over her head.

Jerry was already on his feet. Stripping off his own clothes.

"Come on, Nicole," Jessie said. "I'll help you."

Nikki tried to grasp the extended hand. But she couldn't hold on, couldn't rise.

I stood up. "That's *enough*."

Jessie pressed so close to me that I expected Jerry to respond.

"You really have no idea. Do you?" she asked me.

She brushed against me, then ran for the sea. Chased by Jerry, stumbling and hooting.

Nikki didn't watch them go, didn't even try. She wiped her mouth with the back of her hand, then slumped. Staring down at the sand.

"You can leave me here," she said. Then she mumbled to herself. "You should leave me here. I'm no good . . . I *can't* be good. . . ."

I helped her to her feet, but had to catch her when she tried to stand alone.

Her eyes would not stay open. I took her up in my arms. And began to carry her back toward town. She was so small.

"I'm a slut," she muttered. Cheek against my chest. "I'm just a dirty, filthy slut, a dirty slut. You don't know . . ."

"You're not. For Christ's sake."

I shifted her weight, wondering how far I could carry her that way. Bare feet registered. I had left her sandals behind. Her bag.

Maybe Jerry and Jessie would bring them. If not, I'd run out that way in the morning and police them up. Scavengers wouldn't come out too early on Sunday. And if her things were gone, I'd buy her new ones.

"I told her," Nikki said abruptly.

"What?"

She was fading in and out. Ripe with alcohol sweat and her own smell. My back began to ache, but my arms held out. Before she fell asleep in my arms, she cried a little.

"I'm sorry," she whispered. "So sorry . . ."

I found Nikki's sandals, but her bag was missing. I hoped that Jessie had brought it back for her.

The best thing about not having overdone the booze wasn't that I had been in control the night before. I hadn't been in control. The best thing was going off by myself, early in the morning, to run. Into the coolness that soon became not-quite-heat. The landscape was ugly, barren, dun colored. But the dirt road I followed led into a vast sky. Running purged the world's evils. For a little while.

I came back into town carrying the sandals and craving water. Slowing to a walk a few streets short of the motel, I was panting hard enough to wonder if I'd overdone it. There had been a lot to purge.

I was sure the other members of the Officers' Club, permanent and auxiliary, would still be sleeping things off. But before I could turn for the motel, I spotted Jessie. Down by the shrimp boats.

She was arguing. With two Mexicans. Neither of whom would have fit into her New Orleans fantasy.

Lot of arm waving. Shouting I couldn't quite hear. I shifted back into a jog. Expecting one of the thugs to smack her before I could get there.

A hand reached out and tore off Jessie's sunglasses, then flung them into the water between two boats.

They spotted me. Within seconds of each other. The thicker man tossed his hands up to shoulder level. His mouth moved. As if spitting. Then he and his *compadre* strutted off.

When I pulled up in front of Jessie, she looked sullen.

"What was that all about?" I demanded.

She shrugged. "They mistook me for somebody else. Thanks for rescuing me."

"What's going on? No bullshit."

"Nothing."

"Bullshit."

"And if there *was* anything going on? Why would it be any of your business?" She had come out without her makeup. Which was not Jessie's standard practice. There were bags underneath those merciless, matchless eyes.

"More bullshit. We're all down here together."

"I'm with Jerry. Who is, by the way, twice the man you could ever be."

"No doubt." I took her by the upper arm. "Let's go."

"You're hurting me."

"Call Jerry." I pulled her toward the motel.

"Aren't you worried," she asked, "about your child-bride?"

"No."

"Maybe you should be."

"Fuck you."

"You don't have a clue. Do you, Roy?"

I was pulling her along. Hard. Just the two of us, a dog across the street, and a few bored gulls. In hard light.

"Let me go," she said. "I'll be black and blue."

I released her arm. "Keep moving."

"Where are we going?"

"Your room. We'll see what Jerry has to say about this."

"He's not there."

"We'll go to your room, anyway."

She attempted a smile, but the smile didn't fill out. "Are you planning to take me by force?"

"Like your daddy's friend? In your bullshit story?"

"Roy, you don't know who your friends are."

"Just keep walking."

The bed was a shambles. They hadn't opened the windows, and the room stank of liquor, sweat, and fucking. Yesterday's swimsuits, last night's clothes, and a vibrator lay on the floor.

I almost made a crack about "twice the man." But I was too angry. I thought I knew what was going on.

"Where's your bag? That suitcase you brought?"

She pointed. The bag stood beside a tattered chair. I tossed it on the bed and clicked the latches.

"You're not very gentlemanly," Jessie told me.

"Shut up."

The only thing of interest in the suitcase was Nikki's shoulder bag. From the beach.

"I brought it back for her," Jessie said.

"Where's your purse?"

She drew it from a dresser drawer and held it out to me. "Why don't you just tell me what you're looking for? Maybe I could help."

"You know what I'm looking for."

Her purse was full of junk: car keys she didn't need for the trip, a fake-alligator wallet, two tampons in tattered paper, makeup, bills, breath mints.

I tossed the purse on the bed beside the suitcase and went through the drawers. Then I searched the closet.

Nothing.

Behind me, fabric tore. I turned. Jessie had ripped her top open from the neck down. Her lip was bleeding. Bitten.

"If you don't leave, I'll tell Jerry you tried to rape me."

"He'd never believe that."

"Shall we find out? You stupid motherfucker."

I shook my head. In disgust. And despair.

"You really should go see how Lolita's doing," she told me.

"She's worth ten of you," I said. Spiteful. Helpless. Heading for the door. With Nikki's bag in my hand.

"Don't forget the sandals."

Nikki was puking her guts out. I'd seen worse, but it wasn't pretty.

She was normally reserved about nonsexual bodily functions, but didn't even look up when I entered the bathroom. The defeated curve of her back declared she was hurting.

Another surge of retching shook her, splashing back on the T-shirt in which she'd slept. Bare and small, her backside looked pathetic. Her flesh seemed to whimper.

I knelt down and rested a hand on her back. She didn't react.

"You'll be all right," I told her. "It's just too much booze. Or a bad shrimp."

She wiped her chin, imperfectly, and showed me the face of an unfairly punished child. She had been weeping, too.

"It isn't that," she said.

11

"Why didn't you tell me you weren't using birth control?"

The simmering drive back from Mexico was over. We stood in Nikki's room in the bachelor officers' quarters, a too-public space I avoided as a rule. Shabby and gabby, the BOQ fell halfway between a barracks and a Motel 6. Most lieutenants gussied up their quarters with personal junk, but Nikki never bothered. Her room was neat, but the only items unmistakably her own were the short rank of pop cassettes on her desk, a framed photo of her husband—broad-shouldered and none-too-alert—and a dirty teddy bear centered on her pillow. She didn't really know who she was herself.

"I didn't think about it," she told me. She didn't seem chastened. Just weary.

"What's that supposed to mean? You didn't think about it? For God's sake, Nix . . ."

"I didn't think we'd get caught. I was being careful."

I shook my head in disbelief. "We've been fucking like monkeys."

I kept my voice down. I always kept my voice down. This was no one's business but ours.

Muffled laughter moved along the hallway. The decaying mood of a Sunday evening.

"You don't have to worry about it, anyway," Nikki told me. Slumping. She just wanted me to leave. But I wasn't ready to go.

"What's that supposed to mean?"

"I'm going to take care of it."

I looked away. Uncertain. Of everything. "Maybe I don't want you to take care of it."

She sat down on the edge of her bed. "Please don't make this worse." I expected her to do the girlie thing and take up the teddy bear. She didn't.

"Maybe . . . ," I began.

"We can't be stupid. Please, Roy."

"We've already been stupid. *I've* been stupid." I stared down at the institutional carpeting. "Jesus fucking Christ."

"I'm going to take care of it," she repeated.

"It's not that simple. For Christ'sake."

"I've already made the arrangements."

I found the gumption to look at her again. A worn-out kid. I was beating up a child. But I couldn't stop myself.

"How long have you known?"

"Two weeks. For sure."

"Jesus." My eyes faltered again. I didn't know what I wanted, what was possible. What Nikki wanted seemed all too clear. "Why didn't you tell me? Couldn't you at least have told me?"

"I was hoping something would happen."

I blew. Although I kept my voice low even then. Cowardice, not self-control. "Like what? Your husband dying in a training accident?"

"Don't say that."

"And then we'd live happily ever after?"

"We'd never live happily ever after. You know that. Why are you *doing* this? Why are you making me the bad one?" She sounded half a woman of the world and half a twelve-year-old.

"I'm not doing anything."

"Then stop."

"Nikki . . . don't do this. Please."

"I've already made the arrangements."

"Don't do it."

"I have no choice."

"You do."

"Don't pester me. Please, Roy. It's not that big a thing. I can deal with this. If you just don't pester me."

"You should've told me."

"I couldn't."

"Why?"

"Because I knew what you'd do. That you'd make a big thing of it. Like you're doing. I was stupid. I did something that was wrong. And I got caught. And I'm being punished."

"This isn't about punishment."

"Yes. It is. We're both being punished."

"That's nuts."

"It'll all be over on Saturday. I'm taking care of it. In Tucson. I've made an appointment." Now it was her turn to stare at the world's most uninteresting carpet. "I thought maybe—"

"Yeah," I told her. "I'll pay for it. And I'll drive you up." I couldn't resist being a smart-ass: "The wages of sin are outpatient surgery."

She ignored me. Pondering.

"What else?" I said. "Go ahead. Get it all out."

When she looked up, her face was pale. As if she would be sick again. I could feel her mustering her courage.

"You can pay for it. But I don't want you driving me to Tucson. I couldn't stand being pitied. You fussing over me."

"What are you going to do? Hitchhike?"

"Jessie's driving me up?"

"Her?"

Nikki bit her lower lip and nodded. As if that sealed the decision.

"Why her?" I demanded. "She's an absolute bitch. And you know it as well as I do. She's been trying to—"

Nikki waved me off. Feebly. It was true. I was being a pest.

"Because she won't pity me." Nikki looked straight into my eyes. "I know what you want, Roy. I do. You want me to cry now. You want me to be even more miserable than I am. You want to make it all romantic and dramatic. I'm not as smart as you, but I know some things. Better than you. You want everything to be all romantic and tragic. But it's not romantic. And I'm not going to let it be tragic."

"You're the one who blurted out that shit about the highwayman and the innkeeper's daughter. For fuck's sake."

"And you want me to say that I love you. So you can tell me you love me. And we can really mess things up."

To my boundless frustration, I felt tears in my eyes.

"I *do* love you. Okay? I love you. And you love me."

She left me there for a long time. Teetering on the edge.

"I did love you," she said at last. As if she had inspected the books and reached an accountant's decision. "I really did, I can admit it now. But it was wrong. And now it's over."

I declined Marilyn's offer of a second slice of lasagna. As she made her way around the table with the serving dish, the dependable scent of Shalimar trailed her. She always wore a little too much, but it suited her. Neither she nor I were happy campers, though.

The off-night, home-cooked meal had begun with a nasty surprise. I had grown accustomed to having Major Dinwiddie as our fourth at table, two strays gathered in by Gene's and Marilyn's sense of charity. But instead of Dinwiddie's Audi, I found Jessie's 280ZX parked in the driveway at Trattoria Massetto.

It was immediately apparent that Marilyn was at least as unhappy with the situation as I was. At the dinner table, Jessie chattered on, doing her Southern-belle shtick, overpraising Marilyn's barely edible cooking, then launching into tale after tale of how the female officers in the training courses adored Gene, how they just chased after him all the time, how they never stopped talking about him. She delighted in tormenting Marilyn, moving on to telling the wife effusively what a wonderful mentor the husband had been to little old her.

"Sure you don't want a glass of wine?" Gene asked Jessie.

"Oh, I don't really drink. Not to speak of. Roy here can tell you."

I shrugged. A book with seven seals. I didn't want any part of this particular episode.

When Marilyn rose to clear the plates, Jessie leapt to help. Smiling warmly. The innocent virgin, dedicated to serving others.

"You've done *wonders* with your quarters," she told Marilyn. The affected drawl was audible from the kitchen. "I wish I had taste like you."

When she and Marilyn brought in the bowls of ambrosia for dessert, the smiles they wore were as different as any two smiles in the pageant of human history.

All through that wretched meal I sat there remembering that Jessie knew. More than I could bear her knowing. More than I could bear anyone knowing. Nikki was present in spirit, abused and wronged.

"School night," I said, rising. I had hoped to speak privately with Gene. Colonel Jacoby's replacement had come by to inspect my work on the Advanced Course MAPEX. Just in from the Pentagon, Colonel Tobias G. Bullitt was short, with a bowling ball skull and a beach ball belly. I couldn't believe he met the Army's height-and-weight standards, but the word was that he was one of the Assistant Chief of Staff for Intelligence's golden boys.

Colonel Bullitt had listened to my briefing, nodded, and left without saying a word to me. I needed to know what he had told Gene afterwards. But I couldn't take any more of Jessie Lamoureaux. Or Gene. Who had basked in her praise. Glowing over Marilyn's born-dead lasagna. Oblivious of the change of complexion under his wife's makeup.

Marilyn hugged me good-bye more strongly than usual. Whenever our bodies met like that, I felt an urge to kiss her neck and drink in the perfume.

Instead, I waved to Gene and moved for the door.

Behind me, Jessie proclaimed, "I had no *idea* it was so late! I really, absolutely have to leave myself. And I suppose I need to leave you two lovebirds alone in your wonderful home. Thanks ever so much! It was all so delicious, Marilyn. . . ."

The bitch caught up to me between her car and mine, on the sidewalk in front of the house.

"Roy? Wait."

A brilliant evening faded toward night. Behind the rows of lamplit quarters, the mountains loomed high and dark.

"What?"

"You shouldn't be mad at me. Really."

"Who says I'm mad at you?" She really did walk in beauty, like the night. It wasn't fair. "Jessie, I'm tired."

She closed a hand over my biceps. I brushed it off. She stepped closer.

"I know you're mad, Roy. But it's what Nikki wants. Don't you think she's right, that it's for the best?"

"Look, I don't know what you want from me. But all I want from you is for you to leave me the fuck alone. All right?"

"We should be allies, Roy. Not enemies."

To my chagrin, I found myself battling back tears again. Thinking of Nikki. Of the whole mess. That burning in my eyes twice in three days did not fit my operational pattern.

"Couldn't you just leave Nikki alone?" I asked her. "For God's sake. Can't you just leave us alone? What do you get out of it? What do you want?"

"I want what's best. For you." She grasped my upper arm again.

I began to slap her hand away, but didn't complete the gesture.

"You are so full of shit," I said. "Why can't any of them see it? How do you do it, Jessie? Tell me. I really want to know. How do you con everybody like that?"

Her grip tightened. Fingers startlingly strong as they constricted.

"The truth is, Roy, that you really don't want to know much of anything," she said. "But I'm going to tell you, anyway. Because it hurts me to see you make such a fool of yourself."

"It's late. Let's save it. Okay?"

"She's not enigmatic, your little Nicole. She's just stupid, Roy. You're writing your romantic fantasies on a blank slate." She inched closer to me. I could smell the coffee on her breath, the day's sweat. "You think she has any genuine feelings for you? Any real feelings? If she did, how could she just kill your baby? It doesn't bother her at all—do you understand that, Roy? She's just annoyed by the inconvenience. And because she won't be able to fuck whoever happens to be around for the next few weeks. Before she flies back to the arms of her loving husband."

"You're such a snake."

Jessie came closer still. As if she meant to kiss me. Tongue darting out between her painted lips. "You thought she was safe, Roy. I understand. You're afraid, and you thought she'd be safe. Just a dumb little married lieutenant away from home, a target of opportunity. No risk. But she *wasn't* safe. Was she, Roy? Your little Lolita? Because you can't help falling in love." She laughed. Softly. "I know your kind, Roy. You're not hard. All that play-pretend of yours. You're not tough. You're the kind of fool who falls in love with a tramp *because* she's a tramp." She laughed again, but the sound had a bite this time. "You destroy things, Roy. You destroy people. You don't mean to. You're just selfish. And it happens." She sighed. "*Your* Nicole doesn't even exist. There's just a scared little girl who you got pregnant." She raised her mouth to complete the threatened kiss, but I pulled away. "You're just like me, Roy. We're both selfish people. That's why you're so afraid of me. We're soul mates, identical twins. If we slept together, we could be charged with incest."

I pushed her away. So roughly, she almost fell backwards.

Unsurprised, she laughed at that, too. "I noticed something else, Roy. You have a thing for Marilyn. Does Gene know?"

As I marched toward my car, I caught Gene watching us from a darkened window.

The next evening I drove to Bisbee. The Mustang's parking brake needed work, so I parked down in the gulch and hoofed it up the steep streets. Turning the corner into Eli's lane, the first thing that registered was a black Lincoln with tinted windows idling below the concrete steps that led to his house. Two Mexicans loitered on the sidewalk, watching everything. And everything came down to me. Wearing dark suits that looked cheap from a block away and wraparound sunglasses in the dusk, the two of them appeared as sinister as thugs in a comic book.

Eli had company. And it didn't look like a visit from Mr. Right.

I was about to do an about face, when Eli's front door opened. Smooth as baby oil, *el jefe* came down the steps. He looked like Ricardo Montalban with a mean streak. *Hombre número uno* yanked open the right-rear door of the Lincoln. Number two jabbed his right hand inside his jacket as if his armpit itched, swiveling his head to check out the universe. It was a crisp operation. The car disappeared in seconds, leaving me with the memory of a Sonora license plate.

I had no idea whether Eli would be up for more company after a visit from the Big Burrito, but I'd made the drive, so I decided to find out.

When I knocked, Eli called, "Oh, did you forget something?" Then he opened the screen door and smiled. "Why, Roy! This is my big evening for jazz fans. . . ."

"Bad time?"

"Not at all. Not in the least. Come in."

I warred against the idea of possessions, but Eli's place excited levels of envy I didn't know I could feel. Dark wood, old leather, good lamps, and fine books. And the music.

"I was just playing something for a friend of mine. You really should hear it, too."

"Michael Corleone with salsa?"

"You saw him?"

"Are you going to tell me to forget I saw him?"

Eli smiled. Bemused. "Not in the least. Remember him. Just don't mention him."

"Don't even know his name."

"That was Sammy Rodriguez."

"Rings no bells."

"If you lived in Bisbee, it would. Or Douglas. Or the right part of Phoenix, for that matter. Or the wrong part."

"Not Tucson?"

"Sammy's not welcome in Tucson. Different organization."

"A client of yours?"

"Started out that way. But it emerged that he's a complete jazz maniac. And my number one customer down at the Record Store of Doom." Eli held up an ancient shellacked album. "No offense, Roy. You're my *favorite* customer. But Sammy purchases in volume."

"Do I want to know any more?"

"I don't think so. Although Sammy's only trouble for those who trouble him. He's really a pussycat. With those of us who mind our own affairs. Roy, I have in my hand a Paul Whiteman recording that I guarantee you have neither heard nor heard of."

"I was afraid I was going to find you tied up and beaten."

"Oh, nothing that exciting. On the contrary, Sammy's something of a good luck charm. But won't you get yourself a beer? While I adjust our beloved Edith? No, a visit from Sammy does not go unnoticed in this neighborhood. It guarantees that my premises will remain inviolate for the next several months, at least. There is . . . a certain fear factor."

"Want a beer yourself?"

"I'd love one. But I have a medical exam in the morning. I'm condemned to water only. It's so cruel."

"Serious?"

"Just a checkup."

I fetched myself a Carta Blanca. From a refrigerator neatly provisioned with wine, bottled water, specialty cheeses, obscure condiments, and a .38-caliber revolver.

Back in the front room, I asked, "That pistol to scare away the cockroaches?"

Eli looked at me, put one hand on a hip, and rolled his eyes. "Really, Roy . . . I forget it's even there. Just a precaution, a habit from my days working Sunset and the Canyons. If you have an unwelcome guest, excusing yourself to go into a bedroom is just too suspicious. But you can always offer your intruder a cold beer."

"I'll bear that in mind. Eli? Before you drop the tonearm. I need to ask you something."

He smiled. "Sit. Drink. Ask."

"I've got a problem."

He sat down, settled his elbows on his knees, and interlocked his fingers under his chin. Longish hair fell forward.

"Nothing too serious, I hope. Legal?"

"No. I mean, I've got more than one problem, at the moment. But there's a strange one I thought . . ."

"That I might be able to help you with? Tell, tell!"

"There's this woman. A lieutenant over at the fort. Jessica Lamoureaux. Something's not right about her. She's too . . . too astute. Too sharp for who she is and where she is. And she's downright fucking evil."

"May I interpret that as impulsive fucking that resulted in a postcoital perception of evil?"

"No. I haven't touched her. And I don't intend to. But she's screwed a circle around me, one friend after another. There's something wrong about it, something pathological."

"She sounds energetic."

"She's evil."

He looked at me seriously. "Roy . . . I don't know what secrets you may have in your past." He brushed back a strand of hair and cocked an eyebrow. "You did promise to tell me your story, but you haven't kept your word, you know."

"I will. Just not—"

He held up a hand: *Peace.* "That wasn't my point. Just an observation. Dear, dear Roy. What I began to say was that I have no idea of the degree to which you're acquainted with authentic evil. I, on the other hand, have had all too close a relationship with genuine evil in more than one shape and sex. So, when you tell me this woman's evil . . ."

"She's evil, Eli."

"And?"

"I thought . . . that you might still have some connections. That you might be able to dig around in her background." I placed the empty beer bottle on a ceramic coaster. "Eli, she's a thunderhead booming over every friend I've got. Except you."

"Yes, I suppose I'd be immune."

"I'm asking a favor. And I have no right to. I couldn't pay you. Not your old rates, anyway."

He waved a hand to the side, as if shaking a cramp from his wrist. "Frankly, Roy, this sounds relatively minor. Although these things can take time—is time a factor?"

"I don't know."

"One thing I learned in my previous incarnation was to build up an account of favors due. I still have a few favors owed to me. Another beer? Tell me about her. What you know."

"That's part of the frustration. I get the feeling that everything about her is pure theater. Or impure theater. That it's all staged. I'm not sure I have many facts."

"But those facts are?"

"Jessica Lamoureaux. First lieutenant, U.S. Army. Formerly National Guard. Either in Mississippi or Louisiana, she's coy about it. According to her version of events, she went to Officer Candidate School as a Guard student, but convinced somebody somewhere to bring her on active duty. Now she's held up in temporary status because of something in her past; there's a delay in granting her a top-secret clearance. And I doubt it's just about smoking a few joints in high school. She claims the holdup has to do with her father's financial affairs, but that feels bogus. And her chronology has gaps. Born in Mississippi, or so she claims. Seems to have spent several years in New Orleans. Must've gotten in at least a few years of college, or she wouldn't have gotten a commission. Current abode an apartment somewhere in Sierra Vista. Sleeps around. With breathtaking nonchalance. For pleasure or power or both. New Nissan 280ZX, Arizona plates, KOS6699. Looks that bring traffic to a standstill. Mid to late twenties, raven hair, pale blue eyes that shade gray. Five-six or five-seven." I shook my head, trying to conjure other details. But I was dry. "That's about it. Should I write it all down?"

Eli lowered his hands from his chin without breaking the weave of his fingers. "No. I'm cursed with a very good memory, Roy. And it truly is a curse."

"Is that enough, though? To do anything?"

"Perhaps. If there was an L.A. tie-in, it would be easy enough. But the world's an amazingly interrelated place. Any idea if she's ever been married, if Lamoureaux's a married or maiden name?"

"That's not the kind of thing she'd tell anybody." Something occurred to me. "For all I know, something like that could be holding up her security clearance. A lie in the interview, an omission on a form. The investigators aren't geniuses, but they're dogged."

Eli nodded. Bouncing his joined hands up and down in front of his knees. Then he rose. "I always expected Army officers to be well scrubbed and annoyingly chipper. Naïve. Sincere. Upright. Strong. And unbearably dull. But you do have lively acquaintances, Roy. Take this woman, Miss Lamoureaux. If she's really both a miss and a Lamoureaux—frankly, the name's the first thing I'd check. Perhaps it's just my Hollywood background, but doesn't it smack a bit of the silent screen or the glamour days of the talkies? And then there's that rude friend of yours, the brash young fellow, the weight lifter. It sounds as though she's hiding something, while he's hiding *from* something." In his analytical mode, his expression was more a lawyer's than a friend's. "Really, the possibilities have screenplay potential; I'm tempted to scribble down a treatment."

He smiled again. "And you, Roy? When will you share *your* saga?"

"Soon," I told him.

Gene Massetto came by the closet where I worked. He shut the door behind him. Resolutely. His expression washed him out of the congeniality sweepstakes.

"Bad news?"

"Not yet," he told me. He tossed his baseball cap with the silver bars on my worktable. His starched fatigues were black under the armpits. The weather was burning toward the desert summer.

"So . . . what did Colonel Bullitt think?"

Gene perched his butt on the edge of my worktable. The space was as cramped as a U-boat's latrine.

"He thinks it's going to be too complicated for the captains."

I turned from the wall map to face him full-on. "It's supposed to be hard. That's what Colonel Jacoby wanted."

"There's a new general secretary heading up the politburo."

"So I'm supposed to dumb it down?"

"Cool it, Roy. I didn't say anything about dumbing anything down. I just said he thinks it's going to be too tough. And maybe it will be. But

I convinced him to give it a try, to let us run the exercise as is for the class that's wrapping up. Exactly as planned."

"Thanks. But they're going to whine. You know that."

"New regime in the Kremlin, comrade. I've done all I can. We'll just have to see how it goes."

"The current training's a joke."

"Am I being lectured to, Lieutenant Banks?"

"No, sir."

"Roy . . . I really have done all I can. Now do what you can. And— keep your temper for a minute—you might want to think about softening the exercise. Just a little. Around the edges. The point was never to humiliate the students."

"That an order, sir?"

"No. Advice."

"Noted."

He attempted a friendly smile. It flopped. "You'll be glad to get out of the Black Hole of Calcutta, anyway. There's that to look forward to."

"Gene . . . I've put my heart and soul into this."

"And you've done good work." He waved a hand at the map covering the long wall. "This is great stuff. But you're going to move on. One way or the other. Get your orders yet?"

"Sergeant Munro checked with Personnel just yesterday. She said they haven't heard anything. I think MILPERCEN's waiting for a green light."

"They already have one."

"I didn't know that."

"Folks are taking care of you, looking out for you. My advice is to wrap all this up before you dehydrate in this pit. It's just finishing touches now, right?"

"Right."

"Well, finish the touches during the morning hours. Wrap up by lunchtime from now on. Then come by the office, read the traffic. You've done good work. You've earned some downtime. This really is first-rate."

"Let's hope Bullitt thinks so."

Gene went phony on me. He moved as if he meant to leave. But the action telegraphed falsity.

Hand on the doorknob, he pretended a thought had struck him. "Roy . . . is there anything between you and Lieutenant Lamoureaux? A personal relationship?"

"None. Nothing."

"She makes it sound as though there is."

"There's nothing. I swear to God. And there won't be."

"Still seeing that little blonde?"

"The one you warned me off?"

"Just trying to look out for you. As a friend. You've been playing with fire. Regs are regs. But she should be leaving soon, right?"

"Soon. Yeah. I'm having trouble deciding whether to go Franciscan or full Carthusian."

"I suggest Jesuit. If you want to get ahead in Military Intelligence." He smiled. Halfheartedly. "There's really nothing . . . there hasn't been anything . . . between you and Jessie?"

"No." I stopped pitying myself long enough to look at him seriously. And I didn't like what I saw. "Don't go down that road, Gene. I beg you. Jessie's trouble. And nothing but."

"You don't know that," he said, picking up his hat.

12

Saturday sucked. The morning started off badly; then one wretched development piled atop another until, by the early hours of Sunday, the new life I had constructed lay in pieces. You can't escape the past. It's a cancer that tricks you with bouts of remission. A span of twenty hours turned me from an eager-beaver lieutenant struggling with his identity into a borderline killer.

And I wasn't the only one headed for a rendezvous with ghosts. I was just first in line.

The first hint of evil on Saturday morning came by telephone. My mother loved me dearly, pissed me off no end, and had superb tactical instincts. She'd learned to launch her raids early on weekend mornings, when I lacked the excuse of the call of duty and had not yet escaped into the day.

I nearly made it out the door, clutching my gym bag and dressed for a run up the canyon. The phone rang. I did an about-face. Hoping it was Nikki. Calling before her trip to Tucson.

"Roy, dear, you're *never* home," my mother began. Seize the initiative; then press the attack.

"Life's been busy, Mom. What's up?"

"I had a call. From that friend of yours, the one who can't make up his mind if his name's Al or Ali. I always thought—"

I returned the phone to its cradle. I didn't slam it down, but settled it decisively. The defense must be firm and uncompromising. I was determined to win our war of attrition. Of course, I felt guilty through every minute of my drive onto the post. Guilty and angry. When an arthritic coyote ambled into the brush, I beat back an urge to turn off the road and run him down.

So much for the old Zen spirit. The night before, alone and alternating between self-pity, concern for Nikki, and Trane's frustration at the saxophone's limits, I had tried to hide in a text by Shunryu Suzuki. Months before, I'd persuaded myself that the *roshi* was profound. Our capacity for self-deception knows no end.

Plagued by desire, I got to the bit that read "we do not care for excessive joy. So we have imperturbable composure." I felt sick. As if I'd eaten unwashed salad in Mexico. Instead of composure, I felt like scourging myself. I might have done so, had I owned a flail. God only knows what devils his saints were battling.

In the cool of the morning I ran. Hard. Harder than on the day when Jacoby and I had dueled. I tore off the bandage on my hand and scorned the sensible caution that keeps ankles from breaking, that shies from thorns and bayonets of grass. I wasn't one with the universe or with my body. I felt bound to break into pieces. Even the view from the ridge could not appease me. I felt only the pounding of my heart. A desert clown playing Lear on the heath, I bellowed.

The birds jabbered on. Intermittent pops reported early risers shooting skeet down at the gun club. Their reality annoyed me. How could life just go on?

Just as there are varieties of love, there are countless forms of self-pity. I called Nikki's name out loud.

If the run didn't do much for my soul, at least it punished my body. I was so self-absorbed that I drove over to the gym without realizing that my legs and arms were bleeding. Only the stares of the ever-present bodybuilders alerted me.

Ignoring the damage, I moved from the Universal to do bench presses. The bar gnawed the rotting stitches on my palm. I didn't ask anyone to spot for me, but a form loomed up after I'd done a half dozen reps. I smelled sweat and Old Spice. My muscles quivered; the strain contorted my face. I couldn't lift the weight a last time. Hands reached down to help me cradle the bar.

"You really should ask for a spotter," Major Dinwiddie told me. "Recklessness isn't manliness, you know."

"I thought I could handle it, sir." I sat up, flipped a leg over the bench, and turned my face toward him. Sucking down oxygen. "Thanks."

"We all need help sometimes. Every one of us, Lieutenant Banks. Yes, indeed. Every one of us needs help now and then. No shame in asking."

With his swollen belly torturing the waistband of his shorts, Dinwiddie looked like a minor Dickens character who'd blundered through a time warp into the gym. Even his thinning hair, glued down, had an early-Vic effect.

"Well, don't let me keep you from your workout," he said. "Not for a minute. 'Fit to fight,' that's what we all need to aim at." He smiled in embarrassed self-awareness, a melancholy fool. "Grows harder with the years, of course. Harder and harder. But we all must do our best. Every one of us."

"Yes, sir. Thanks again."

"Anytime, Lieutenant Banks. Anytime at all." He hesitated. "Of course, you know you've been bleeding. . . ."

"I was running up in the canyon. I tried to take a shortcut."

He nodded. Considering the thorn streaks on my thighs. Which had begun to itch. "We must respect the desert. Have to respect it. Nature, the wilds. Lesson learned, though, lesson learned. We do tend to learn the hard way, we soldiers."

"Yes, sir." The ill temper of the desert, when provoked, was the least of what I was learning. The hard way.

"Well, be sure to wash those . . . those wounds of yours thoroughly. Soap and water, plenty of it. Ounce of prevention, you know." And off he went to putter among the barbells.

I took a long shower, ignoring the locker room comings and goings. First, I scrubbed off the dried blood, punishing the scratches with soap and hot water. I forgot the world for a few minutes, standing, eyes closed, under the stream. Immobile. Then I turned on the cold water, full force, to numb the itching on my legs and arms. I was in no hurry to rejoin the world.

I wondered what kind of child it might have been.

Outside the gym, Major Dinwiddie waited under a faded picnic umbrella. He smiled when he saw me.

"Lieutenant Banks! Roy!" he called, huffing up alongside me. "I thought perhaps . . . that is, if you're not on a schedule . . . I thought you might join me for a cup of coffee. My treat. That is, if you don't mind. I'd like to speak with you."

We took our separate cars to the Dunkin' Donuts outside the main gate. I wasn't into the carbohydrate lifestyle. Black coffee, bitter, did it for me. Dinwiddie took a large coffee with cream and sugar to accompany his cruller. We stood outside in the retreating shade. The traffic gasped past on Fry Boulevard, adding fumes to the heat.

"I'm afraid I have a weakness for sweet things," Dinwiddie confided. "I deny myself, of course. Have to be mindful. But I allow myself a treat once in a while."

I shrugged.

He cleared his throat. "It seems, Roy . . . that my judgment has been flawed. Mistaken. Regarding a mutual acquaintance of ours."

I just looked at him. Too mean to help him out by speaking her name.

"Yes, mistaken . . . about Lieutenant Lamoureaux." He lifted both eyebrows. "I'm not saying she deceived me. Not exactly, not outright. Not her fault, not really. I mean, I may have deceived myself. I suspect that's what it was. I'm afraid I may have idealized her a bit."

They'd be in Tucson by now. At the clinic.

"Jessie's a bitch," I said.

That jarred him. "Well . . . I don't know if I'd . . . I mean, I suppose you'll think me an old fool, Roy, but I believe she led me on. Not that I didn't lead myself on, of course. I convinced myself that my intentions were all aboveboard, the rank difference and all that. But she can be a very appealing young woman. When she wants to be."

"She's a snake," I said. "There isn't an ounce of human blood in her veins."

He bit into his doughnut. As if to slow his speech. But he couldn't contain himself. "You . . . and she haven't . . ."

"No."

He nodded and took another bite of doughnut. "Do *you* think she's deceitful?"

"Christ, sir. That's the least of it. Jessie leads everybody on. She's just programmed to do it. She gets a buzz from the severed heads at her feet."

Two Mexicans brushed past us, headed inside for a gringo sugar high. They left the radio on in the cab of their pickup: yipping and yiking above a string bass, guitar, and accordion.

"She often talks about you, you know. Praises you to the skies. I believe she was using you to goad me, to tease me." Sweat beaded on his forehead, as if his flesh were weeping. "Jessica can be cruel, needlessly cruel." His doughnut, his life preserver, was gone, and the hand that held the paper cup was unsteady. "She implied things, hinted at comparisons. . . ."

"Honest to God, sir, I've never had a relationship with her. Not that way."

"Oh, I believe you. Now, I mean. But there were moments . . . moments of doubt. You always seemed a decent fellow, but how could I blame you? If you did have a secret relationship? After all, she is a beautiful woman, there's no denying it. And there were others. . . ."

"Well, I didn't. Zero interest. Look, sir, do yourself a favor. Write her off as sunk costs. And don't look back."

His closed lips contorted. As if a small animal fought to break free of his mouth. "It's not always as easy as it appears to the young and carefree. Not that I'm old, of course. In my prime, I like to say. But you're untested by life. . . ." He stepped closer, confiding. "Beauty has been my downfall, Roy. I've never been a good-looking fellow like you. Yet, I couldn't help being drawn to women who were . . . above my station, so to speak. Physically, I mean. In terms of attractiveness. I try not to be a superficial person. To be a good person, in fact. To be helpful. I've always wanted to be helpful, that's the thing. Boy Scout, I suppose. Eagle Scout, to be precise. But I get it all mixed up and use the helpfulness as an excuse to approach attractive people, appealing people. It's natural, I suppose. To be drawn to attractive people. We're all drawn to them, aren't we? But some of us are luckier than others. When it comes to our appeal to the fair sex. So those of us who aren't so lucky, we make ourselves useful. It's sneaky, really. Although we don't think of it that way. I mean, I never have. Until now. No, we're just being helpful. And then we fall in love with the person we're just there to help. . . ." He stared down into the remains of his coffee. "But it never quite works out. Does it? And there we are."

I just wanted to escape. But he wasn't ready to let me go. "I don't suppose you've ever been hopelessly in love, Roy. Hopelessly and helplessly. People are drawn to you. Even if you confuse them a bit. I suppose you've always been able to . . . that the women you wanted made themselves available. That you could pick and choose. Believe me, Roy, it isn't that easy for the rest of us. We're all out of balance, it isn't fair. Our capacity to love should only be commensurate with our ability to attract love in return, don't you think? But it doesn't work out that way. We love people . . . we love them unreservedly, devoutly . . . and it's a stunning thing, a terrible thing, to realize that they don't love us back, not even a little. That we're . . . that we're no more than a joke to them, that they're laughing at us." He summoned a smile, but it didn't come willingly. "I should've been an auto mechanic. That's one thing I really can do; a car is something I really can fix. A timing belt will never break your heart."

"Love's a curse," I said.

He chuckled. The sound evoked the frog word *triste*. "I suppose you read that in a book somewhere. You're a lucky man, Roy. Not that you won't have your little setbacks, of course. That's the human condition. But someone will always be there to pick you up, to back you up. Women will love you, and won't know why. And the Army will promote you. Not that you're undeserving, of course. I didn't mean that. On the contrary. But that's just it, you see. It all comes so easily to you."

I wore an old denim shirt with the sleeves torn off. He patted me on the upper arm, avoiding the long scratches. "Now and then, as you climb life's ladder . . . spare a thought for those of us who aren't so fortunate, what say?"

The Mexicans emerged again, each bearing a box of doughnuts. Rumbling, the pickup pulled out into the traffic, trailing a polka beat.

Dinwiddie withdrew his hand. "But I've been boring you to tears. You must think I'm a fool." He smiled, more easily this time. "And you'd be right, of course. But . . . in the end, I'm not sure I'd change it. The way I am, I mean. 'Better to have loved and lost.' Isn't that right? 'Once more into the breach!' 'Never give up the ship.' Well, off you go now. Enjoy the rest of your day. I'm sure you will. And I intend to have another doughnut."

Back at my place, I couldn't read. Or eat. I put on Gato Barbieri's soundtrack for *Last Tango in Paris,* but that was suicide music. On a whim, or maybe to scourge myself, I clicked in a cassette tape Nikki had left behind: The Cretones. New Wave stuff. Simple musicianship, but the songwriting engaged me. That morning, I understood the cut "Justine." It transcended the Marquis de Sade when it described love as "the cold wire edge of the whip" and claimed that "the face of Aphrodite is a blank when it looks at you. . . ."

I turned it off. I didn't know all the details about abortion. Talk about "suction" made me imagine a vacuum cleaner at work. I snickered and told myself it was no big thing, that I was just wallowing, being self-indulgent, posing for my own benefit.

But it was a big thing. I wasn't sure why. But it was a big thing.

I didn't want company. Other than Nikki. I could have tolerated seeing Eli, had he dropped by, and might have poured out the history he kept coaxing me to reveal. But when a car pulled up and the doorbell rang, it produced a less-welcome visitor.

"I heard music and thought you might be home."

"I'm not home."

That stopped him for a moment. But only for a moment.

"Roy, I really need to talk to you. Something happened."

"Just go away, Pete. Please. It's a bad day."

He brightened. "Would you like to pray together?"

I shut the door in his face and turned up the music. A half hour passed before I dared to peek out and see if God's terrier had gone.

I wasn't completely stupid. I understood that Nikki and I had no future, could not have had one. She was right. She was sensible. She was doing the right thing for both of us. A kid, she was the one behaving responsibly. I understood all that. But the heart is a mightier organ than the brain.

I put on my moccasins and dropped the top on the Mustang. Desperate to be in motion, I drove over to Tombstone, burying the speedometer's needle on the desert straightaway. Abused, the Mustang rattled. On the way back from the town too tough to die and too tacky to live, I pulled off above an arroyo, walked down into the khaki sand, and sat. Waiting. But it wasn't flash flood season.

My scratches itched in the heat.

Emotional coherence wasn't my strong suit. I looked back, again, over the Zen exercises I'd played at. I was as phony as a television prop. I didn't even get points for honest striving. I was a complete fraud. And the best I could say was that I'd concentrated mostly on fooling myself. Roy Banks, the Zen warrior. Right.

The Mustang developed a chinking sound from being driven so hard.

"You always hurt the one you love," I consoled the dashboard. I had glimmers of driving head-on into a wall. But the desert didn't have walls.

A stupid fraud. Laying waste to the lives around him. Nikki and I had less in common than a coyote and a sparrow. It was cross-species fucking. Fundamentally wrong. But I couldn't turn off my desire.

I lost track of time. When I finally returned to my apartment, Nikki and Jessie were back from Tucson, waiting.

Nikki looked like death's leftovers. Lying on my sofa. So small. Her jeans and tank top could have been play-clothes. I looked at her crotch for bloodstains. There were none.

Jessie, by contrast, was regal. My battered easy chair had become a throne, from which she gazed down upon the blundering peasants. With lipstick as red as geraniums and her sunglasses pushed back atop her thick black hair, she looked more like a charge-account wife than like an officer.

"I was worried about you," Nikki said. Her eyes didn't quite find me. She was fighting to keep them open.

"For Christ's sake, Nix. How are *you*?"

Her eyelids won the battle against her will. "I'm okay. It wasn't anything. Don't worry." She sounded ready to sink. Now that I was accounted for.

Jessie rose. "Well, I suppose you don't need little old me anymore," she said. In her sweet-as-Karo-syrup Southern mode. "Nicole, if there's *anything* you need, you just let me know, honey. And don't forget what we talked about."

Eyes clamped shut, Nikki nodded.

Passing me, Jessie paused. Her index finger traced the longest thorn scratch on my arm. She smiled, then turned away.

I listened as her car cranked up and backed out of the dirt strip that passed for a parking lot. Nikki's eyes remained closed. Quietly, I eased down on the floor between my junk-store coffee table and the sofa. I looked at her. Blond hair growing out a bit, thickened by the day's sweat upon her temples. Slightly turned-up nose, faint eyebrows. Lips too womanly for the rest of her. I wanted to touch her. In human solidarity, not sex. But I didn't dare.

She placed a hand atop my head, patted me like a dog, then stilled her hand again.

"Roy?"

"What is it, Nix?"

"Would you go get me a bag of Oreos and some milk?"

Foreign films had conditioned me to expect dramatic dialogue. Nikki came from another, more practical world.

"Sure. Of course." There was a 7-Eleven knockoff a couple of blocks down, out along the highway. "You okay alone?"

She nodded. Her small hand quit me and settled, palm up, on her forehead. "I just need to rest. I didn't want to go back to the BOQ. I didn't want anybody wondering about stuff. Or asking me questions."

"I'm glad you came here. Just rest. I'll be right back."

"You don't mind me being here? After everything?"

"I never minded you staying here. You know that."

"But it's different now."

"I'm glad you're here."

I ached for our eyes to meet. But nothing could force hers open.

"I just need to rest," she said. "But please don't pity me, Roy. Or I'll have to leave. And I don't want to leave, I'm just so tired."

"Oreos and milk. Anything else?"

Nothing else.

The late-afternoon streets were as empty as those in a Western before the gunfight. I walked down the middle of the road. The No-Bullets Kid in a showdown with the universe.

At the convenience store, I reached to the back of the refrigerated case to grab a carton of milk that hadn't passed its expiration date too catastrophically. Huachuca City wasn't famed for quality merchandise. There were no Oreos on the shelves, just a Keebler imitation with green filling between the chocolate wafers. A big-headed leprechaun grinned up from the wrapper.

I had a nodding acquaintance with the fat girl behind the register. She didn't like Mexicans or much else, but I was tolerable.

"Looks like somebody's got the munchies." She smiled slyly.

I walked fast on my way back to the apartment. To get the milk out of the heat.

Nikki was sitting up. A vampire had drained her veins.

I broke out the fake Oreos. "That's all they had."

"Those are good. I like those."

"Can I make you anything else?"

"No. I just want a glass of milk. With ice, please."

"Music?"

She shook her head.

Famished, she ate half the bag of cookies and drank three glasses of milk.

"I need a shower," she said. "But I'm too tired."

"Don't worry about it."

"Can I lie down? In the bedroom?"

"Sure."

She rose. A foal discovering its legs. I moved to help her, but she waved me away.

"No pity," she told me.

I followed her into the bedroom, tightened the blinds, and drew the ancient drapes.

"Go out while I undress. Please. I don't want you looking at me now."

I went back into the living room and sat. Listening. To the rasp of a zipper and cloth whispering over flesh. Bare feet tapped linoleum. The mattress squeaked.

"Roy?"

"Want me to come in?"

"Just for a minute."

She was deep under the covers. I began picking up her clothing, intending to fold it. Her jeans smelled of cunt and liniment.

"I'm cold," she told me. "Could you turn down the air conditioner?"

I cranked it down. The roar declined to a growl.

"Sit by me. For a minute. I have to ask you something."

I sat beside her, the way you'd sit beside an ailing child.

"I need you to do something for me."

"Sure. Anything."

"Don't say that. You haven't heard."

"Okay, what?"

"I need you to go to Tucson tonight."

"Why, for heaven's sake? You shouldn't be alone. What's up with Tucson?"

"I'm all right. But I need you to go to Tucson. With Jessie."

Before I could gather words to respond, Nikki told me, "She needs somebody to go with her. To some party. As her escort. So she can feel safe."

"What the fuck, Nix?"

"*Please,* Roy. She asked me to ask you. She did me a big favor today."

"Jessie doesn't do favors without a reason. Why can't she take Jerry?"

"They aren't getting along."

"They were getting along last weekend."

"Something changed. I don't know. He's making some kind of trouble for her or something. Please, Roy. I'm so tired."

"Nix, it doesn't make sense. So she gave you a ride to Tucson. Big deal. I'll reimburse her for the gas."

She drew an arm from her cotton-blanket cocoon and gripped my wrist. With remarkable strength. Her eyes flared. In the room's mid-afternoon shadows.

"Roy, she knows so much. About us, about everything. It's my fault. I've been stupid about everything, about every single thing since I got here, to Fort Huachuca. Think of what she could do to us . . . to me and my husband. With one phone call. Please, Roy. I thought I was doing the right thing when I asked her to give me a ride, I thought I was being all grown-up and smart and mature. And I just messed everything up even worse." Her eyes shone wet.

"I hate her fucking guts," I said.

Nikki loosened her grip, but maintained her touch. She tried to lift her head, wavering. Really seeing me now. "What happened to you? What did you *do* to yourself?"

"Nothing. I was just running up in the canyon. I got into some thorn-bushes."

She patted me again, then withdrew her hand. "You need somebody to take care of you. Like the woman we talked about. In the restaurant."

"Bullshit. That's not what this is about. And that goddamned Jessie. Goddamn her."

"Will you do it, though? Please, Roy? For me?"

"Yeah. Sure. Okay."

"Thank you."

"What about you? Here alone? If something happens?"

"Nothing's going to happen. I just need to rest. That's what the doctor said. He said everything went real smooth. So don't worry. There's a telephone by the bed, if I need it."

"I hate this."

She closed her eyes again. After a moment, she said, "Me, too. I'm sorry, Roy." One tear escaped.

I moved away to let her sleep. But Nikki spoke again: "I like knowing you'll be in the next room. For now, anyway."

Again, I moved to leave and shut the door. But she called me back a last time, the way a kid will.

When I turned, her eyes were open and wet in the bedroom twilight.

"I know this sounds stupid," she said. "But I'm not sorry. About us."

13

Pancho Villa in a cheap black suit, the guard told Jessie, "No more cars inside. You want, you park over there."

If Jessie hoped to impress me with her importance to Tucson society, she was off to a bad start. And that was after a drive up in which the loudest sound in the car was the roar of her perfume. Her attempts to cajole then to needle me fell flat. Determined to be stoic, I ended up sullen.

"Mike's parties are *so* popular," she said as she parked in front of a cactus sentinel, "you just have to get here early. Unfashionable though that may be."

It was also unfashionable to hoof it up a long driveway in high heels. But Jessie did her best to carry it off.

I walked behind her and couldn't help watching her ass. She had shown up at my apartment in a flesh-hugging lilac dress cut deep on top, high below, and slit on one side. The rag would have suited a top-shelf call girl. She hadn't even bothered to look in on Nikki.

Disco music poisoned the air. The 1970s had retired to the Tucson foothills. Ahead, a massive flat-roofed house sprawled over the crest of a hillock, Frank Lloyd Wright on a tequila jag. Big windows threw as much light as the floods on a car lot.

Better automobiles than I could afford crowded the driveway, nose to butt, and the garage tucked into the hillside below the house had six bays. I'd been in mansions in Cincinnati—owned by the men who controlled my father's life—but never anything quite this ostentatious. At least not in the U.S.

As we reached the turnaround below a busy patio, I realized that the music was live, not recorded. A white noise of voices fuzzed the aural landscape. Another bouncer stood before a sweeping flight of steps. Ignoring me, he checked out Jessie without turning his head.

Forelocks of bougainvillea fell over garden walls. On a side lawn, a woman in a bikini charged into my field of vision, then retreated.

"Let's be friends," Jessie told me. "Just for tonight, okay? It's important to me."

"Only friends?"

"Good friends. All right?"

"Best buddies," I assured her. I just wanted the hours to pass so I could return to Nikki. To be in the same room with her. For a few more hours.

Jessie smiled. Shifting into her glamour role for the evening. "I do appreciate you being here for me, Roy."

A huge terrace fronted the soaring windows. Couples and small groups admired the view. I did, too. Below us, the lights of Tucson stretched to a black horizon, the stars of a human galaxy. It wasn't a million-dollar view. A million wouldn't even get you close.

"Mike loves people," Jessie said. "His parties are famous."

"Not in my circles."

"Well, don't be a stick-in-the-mud. Okay?"

She led me inside. A vast hall held a chattering crowd. No blacks, but a good mix of well-off Latinos and purebred gringos. No trash from either side of the border. Not much long hair, not much gray hair, the party set looked like a gathering of the financial, legal, and business tribes of the rising generation. A fireplace with a copper hood as big as a ski jump framed two bartenders at work. The crowd kept them busy.

"Be a gentleman and get me a drink," Jessie said. She was scanning the crowd and showing cracks in her poise.

"I don't know if they serve human blood."

"Then I'll take a dry martini, thank you."

I excused my way past women who scorched you by sheer proximity. The also-ran gals eyed their glowing sisters with hatred. Great manes of hair, tanned legs, and jewelry so heavy, it almost passed for armor. A redhead on the payroll offered me mini tacos spilling shrimp. I waved her off and edged in to the bar.

"Yes, sir?"

"Dry martini." I peered past him. "Bourbon?"

"Jack or Wild Turkey."

"Turkey on the rocks."

"Coming right up, sir."

A white guy in a pale blue guayabera pushed up and called, loudly, for two margaritas. He was already drunk. A señorita trying to restrain him wore a mask of seething Aztec savagery.

I made my way back to the spot where I had last seen Jessie. She was gone. I strolled toward the music, which I figured came from a pool zone behind the house. Passing a side room, I glimpsed a knuckle-dragger cutting coke for a half dozen friends and making no effort to hide it. A girl sitting near him caught me looking, but grasped that I didn't count.

The music got louder, the islands of guests thickened. From a deck, I looked down on a pool party. Maybe a dozen swimmers, lit from under the water. The musicians used a big striped cabana as a band shell. Another bar thrived, this one with a bartender and a barmaid. Young women in cocktail outfits circulated with colorful trays of snacks. Waves of laughter broke over human shoals.

No Jessie.

A woman paused beside me. Faintly thick, but presentable. Thirty and dirty. Bejeweled.

"Can't find your date?"

"Always a bridesmaid, never a bride."

"Maybe you don't propose right. That a martini?"

"Dry."

"I was just thinking how I'd like a dry martini."

I handed it to her. She drank. "Tell me right out. You're not queer, are you?"

"Not that I know of. Is it my cape? Or the makeup?"

"Honey, only two kinds of men wear their hair that short, soldiers or sissies. You from down at the air base?"

"Farther afield." When I turned to face her, I realized three things: She had beautiful eyes; she was forty, not thirty; and she was stinking drunk. Time to go. But I asked her, "Tell me something. Are all those diamonds real?"

She laughed. Distillery breath. "Honey, if they were real, you think I'd still be here in fucking Tucson?"

The martini glass was already empty. I was stretching for a lifeline, when Jessie materialized. Seizing my arm, she kissed me on the cheek.

Diamond Lil looked her up and down with the purest hatred I had ever seen. Jessie was truly a presentation piece.

"Let me just steal you away from your new lady friend," she told me. And everyone nearby.

When we had put a few paces between us and the drunk with the splendid eyes, Jessie said, "Surely, Roy, you can do better than that."

"Victim of circumstances. She had nice eyes."

"Oh, please . . ."

"She enjoyed your martini."

"And a dozen more before that. Come on, I want you to meet Mike."

But the elusive Mike had slipped away again. We worked through a half dozen rooms and hallways, all of them crowded, including a bathroom where a splendid buffet of drugs stretched across a marble countertop.

"You've got some fast-living friends," I said.

"Don't pretend you're naïve, Roy."

"I've just never seen that much cocaine before. Or was it something else?"

"You should go back and ask them. Anyway, have you *ever* seen cocaine?"

I had. And a greater array of other poisons than I would ever reveal to Jessie. Or anyone else. I had been at parties that made this one look stingy, although the architecture had been different.

Previous incarnation. Left behind.

"I wouldn't know it from talcum powder," I told her. "Just jumping to conclusions."

She dropped my arm, smiled hugely, and scurried to hug a chubby man in a half-unbuttoned shirt. Multiple gold chains drooped into his chest hair. I couldn't tell if he was Mex or gringo. Tucson did a lot of blending.

"Ricardo, this is my friend Roy. Roy, Ricardo." He had a pulpy handshake. But his eyes were from a dark alley.

"Pleased to meet you. Hey, girl. I ever see that other boyfriend of yours, that fuck, me and him going to have a serious talk. You tell him that. No shit and pronto."

Jessie's smile didn't waver. "Have you seen Mike? I seem to have lost him."

"Mike'll be found when he wants to be found." Then he grinned. His teeth weren't great. "Did I forget my party manners? You two go and get another drink, looks like you're dry. Party hearty, right? I see Mike, I'll tell him you're looking for him, give him the shivers." He glanced at me again, confirming that I was irrelevant. "Now I got some business to do. Maybe I'll see you later, in the guest house."

"Probably not," Jessie said, pulling me along.

Back at the front-room bar, I told her, "I'm not even going to ask. Jessie, I came along because Nikki begged me. And I'm playing along. To the extent that I can figure out the rules. But I'm not going to be a patsy. Understand?"

She flashed her eyes. Flirting. As if we were on the verge of exchanging phone numbers. "You're not a patsy. Not tonight, anyway. You're my protection."

I made a show of looking around the room. "Me and my kung fu army. What am I supposed to protect you from?"

A lummox backed into her, thrusting her against me. Too much perfume. Too much of everything.

"Who knows?" she said. "Maybe just from myself."

Jessie disappeared again, which was fine by me. A prisoner of my Nikki-centric view of the universe, I didn't try to make new female friends. I just had another Wild Turkey on the rocks and wandered outside, into the magnificent night. The view from the terrace was worth a detour, if not a journey. I leaned on the railing, watching the city and letting the ice melt in my drink.

"Hey, brother! I call this meeting of the Officers' Club to order."

It was Jerry. Coming up behind me, bottle of beer in hand. Grinning. He startled me.

"What are *you* doing here?"

"Me? Shouldn't I be asking you that?" He tossed a look back over his shoulder. "This isn't exactly your usual parade-ground formation, General Banks."

"I'm confused, Jerry."

"You've been confused since the day we met. What's so special about tonight?" He was in great spirits. I wondered how much he knew. About anything and everything.

"You just get here?"

"No, man. I been out in the guest house." His grin changed to a you-don't-know-yet smile. "You might want to check it out. Live out some fantasies."

"Well, you may want to conduct a strategic withdrawal," I told him. "Sooner, rather than later."

"Why?"

"There's this character, Ricardo. He's seriously pissed at you. And he doesn't strike me as a choirboy."

"Ricardo? The fat guy?" Jerry looked baffled.

"Pleasingly plump. And fond of gold chains."

"What did he say?"

"Something about wanting to have a serious talk with Jessie's 'other boyfriend.' "

Jerry did the math and laughed out loud. "Oh, shit. You had me going for a minute. No, man. Ricardo's not talking about me, man. That was all about Major Dim-witted. The dumb fuck."

"Dinwiddie?"

"Jessie brought him up here a couple weeks ago. Ask the Baby Jesus why. I mean, I'm going to kill that bitch. But that's another story. Anyway, she drags old Dim-witted along, and the action's way too much for him. I wasn't present for duty, but I hear he went Puritan, Cotton Mather reincarnated." He shook his head in wonder. "What was Jessie *thinking*? I can't figure the angle."

"And now I'm here. Can you explain that angle?"

He looked at me oddly for a few seconds, then shrugged and sucked from his beer bottle. "Who knows? I've given up trying to figure the bitch out."

"She claimed she needed me to come along for protection. Long story, not worth telling. Did she mean protection from you?"

He laughed. The old Jerry again. "She's got bigger worries than me, kemo sabe. Hey, let me introduce you to some people."

"More of Mike's friends?"

"You met Mike?"

"No."

He considered that. "Maybe you want to keep it that way. But fuck Mike. I meant some serious squeeze. Loose on Tucson. I mean, have you surveyed the order of battle in there? This could be a massacre. We need to do our part in the gender wars, inflict some major casualties, before it's too late. To the barricades, man."

"I'll catch up."

He moved to go, then paused. "Best way to forget a woman is another woman."

"I'll catch up later."

He nodded and left me alone. He was right. About the last bit, anyway. But I didn't have it in me. I thought of Nikki. Picturing her in my bed. Hoping she was okay.

Maybe all this was a plot to get me out of there. So Nikki could rest. Without my pestering her. Maybe I was the melancholy clown, not Dinwiddie. Who I could barely imagine at a party where half the guests were nose-skiing.

I went back to admiring the view. But my hundred years of solitude were not going to start that night.

"I'm Mike."

I turned to face him and found his hand extended. On autopilot, I took it. He must have been waiting to pounce, letting Jerry clear off.

"Roy Banks," I said.

He smiled. "Yeah. I know. Jessie's friend. Is that girl amazing, or what?"

"She's a piece of work."

"Yeah, she is that. Actually, my name's Miguel. Miguel Cervantes. Like the *Don Quixote* guy. But Mike's just easier. More American."

He had no trace of an accent. Of medium height and not quite handsome, he sparkled with guy-magic, a compelling aura. Along with his evident wealth, it was bound to stand him in good stead with the female half of the species. Anyway, most women are afraid of men whose looks dominate their own. Mike had the advantage over the pretty boys.

"So, Roy—you don't mind if I call you Roy? Or is 'Lieutenant' better?"

"Roy's fine."

"Yeah. Roy. *El Rey*. The king."

I gestured toward the panorama below us. "Seems to me you're more of a king than I'll ever be."

He patted me on the shoulder. "Who knows? America's the land of opportunity. Nothing beats it, Roy, nothing on earth." He looked out over his domain. "When my parents came here from Colombia, during *La Violencia,* they had to start all over again. Like, they had nothing. And we're a proud family, we go way back. Spanish land grants, royal charters, family tree reaching all the way to Castile and Aragon. But we had to set out for another new world, just leave it all behind. And look around you now. One generation." He swept a hand toward the house behind us. "And just look."

"It's impressive."

"And you know what? Everybody deserves a piece of it. Every American. But people hold themselves back, they don't grasp the opportunities offered to them. I mean, some are just stupid, some are scared of even the least little risk. Some fools just like the harness they're accustomed to, they even get to like feeling the whip, they come to expect it. But for other people, smart people . . . Roy, for a go-getting guy, this country is heaven on earth. All you have to do is reach out and pluck the fruit that's waiting for you, that's just hanging there."

"I'll bear that in mind. The next time I pass by an orchard."

"Come on. Let's be friends. Any friend of Jessie's is a friend of mine. I want to show you something—Jessie tells me you're into vintage cars."

"Not by choice."

"You'll appreciate this, though. Anyway, I need a break from all the partying, I have to pace myself."

He snapped his fingers. Moments later, a serious *hombre*—another black suit—showed up. Mike gave him orders in rapid-fire Spanish. I got that he didn't want to be bothered by anybody for any reason, and that Benito was to deliver two Wild Turkeys on the rocks to the garage.

Smiling, Mike returned waves and nods as we crossed the terrace, then led me down a flight of steps that weren't meant to be noticed. Another dark-clad employee opened a door for us. As we stepped inside, bright lights came on. Sensors.

It doesn't take a car freak to recognize a prewar Mercedes roadster. It wasn't a mere automobile. It was a silver vision. And only the first in a line of revelations.

Mike read my awe.

"Tell me that isn't one beautiful piece of machinery. Nineteen thirty-eight Mercedes Benz 540 K. I ever meet a woman as good-looking as that, I'll marry her on the spot."

I walked around the front of the vehicle. The fenders were voluptuous, the high-mounted headlights insistent as bared nipples. For the first time in my life, I understood serious car junkies. I made a loop, admiring the lines, the coachwork. Forcing myself not to look at the next car prematurely.

Emiliano Zapata showed up with drinks, handed them over without a word, then disappeared. Mike raised his glass in my direction. "To good taste. In cars and women. The rest can take care of itself."

He walked to the next vehicle, shoes clicking on the linoleum. The garage was cleaner than a Quaker's conscience, its floor gleaming like the buffed and waxed hallways at Officer Candidate School. But everything else was merely the frame for the works of mechanical art.

"How about her, Roy? A '35 Bugatti Type 57. There's only one other '35 in the country, and this one's in better shape, all original parts." The car was red and as ripe as Sophia Loren in her prime.

After that came a 1932 Packard Model 904 Deluxe. Cream gray and a wealth of chrome. My Zen rejection of material possessions was history.

"Like I said," Mike told me. "This is the land of opportunity."

The last two bays held more recent models, a custom black Caddy with smoked windows and, as a finale, a brand-new Mercedes two-seater, a steel blue 380 SL.

"That one's not a car," Mike said. "That's a problem. Nice ride, but not really my bag. Fell into my hands in the course of some horse-trading. Now I'm looking for a friend to give it to, I got to get it out of here. I'm taking delivery of a 1934 Cadillac 452D V-16 on Tuesday. And I can't leave a car like that out in the sun."

"I'm sure you've got plenty of friends who'd love to have it."

He nodded. "Yeah, but there are friends, and there are friends. A man of the world like you understands that. Want to take her for a spin? Put the top down, enjoy the night air? I bet I could even find you a new friend to dress up the passenger seat."

I held up my glass. "I don't drink and drive."

After a second's delay, he said, "Smart man. I like that. I don't get behind the wheel myself, if I've had more than a couple." He looked back down the chorus line of cars. My eyes followed his. "Wouldn't want to wreck one of my babies. I lose my temper if I find even a speck of dust on them. And I got a bad temper, Roy, it's my downfall." He smiled. "Hey, you change your mind, you come back. Even if I'm not here. Doesn't matter. I'll leave word. You take that 380 out on the Interstate. Go to Phoenix, for all I care. Make a weekend of it. Hell, Roy, I'd even trust a sensible man like you with my Bugatti."

"How about the Thousand-Year-Reich Mercedes?"

He finished the last drops in his glass. "We'd have to get to know each other better." His smile became a friendly, vicious grin. "And maybe you'd let me drive that Mustang of yours? One of these days. If we get to know each other better?" He edged closer, growing confidential. "You know, Roy, I hear you live in a dump. And you drive a car that's about to give up the ghost. Now, why is that? Guy like you? You've got too much style for that, too much on the ball. You appreciate nice things, I can see that. So pardon me if I'm just trying to figure things out a little. The way Mike Cervantes sees the world, a reliable man like you should at least drive a reliable car. Something that suits him, that lets the world know who he is. Like that Mercedes 380 down on the end."

"The Mustang's going to be a classic," I told him.

By the time Mike deposited me back on the terrace, the crowd had dwindled to the dead-end party types. The view over Tucson had lost its popular appeal, and the action had shifted from the big representation room to the interior and the pool out back. The band had ceased its devastation as the witching hour passed, but somewhere music played on at a lower volume.

Along the hallways, more doors had been shut. Not all the noises behind the walls were family friendly. Headed for the pool area, I wedged past a weeping blonde whose eye makeup had melted down her cheeks. Her blouse was stained with red wine or dried blood. But I wasn't in the mood for charity work.

I was looking for Jessie. And I was not searching calmly. If I didn't find her out by the pool or in some other still-public area, I meant to start opening doors. If that didn't work, I'd check the fabled guest house. I hadn't been so furious in five years. The Persian-restaurant scene had been nothing.

Gaining the deck, I scouted the action below. A few of the women in the pool were topless now, and there were more spectators than swimmers. A cluster of wobbly humanity shifted and I spotted Jessie. Still fully clothed and chatting with the quality.

I navigated poolside and grabbed her by the arm, spilling her drink. Her male companions moved to interfere, but stopped as soon as they got a sense of me.

"You're hurting me," Jessie said.

"Call the cops."

"I'll call Mike."

"Go ahead. You're even more disposable to that guy than I am. Come on, we're going home."

"I'm not going anywhere. The party's just starting."

"Sorry to interrupt the orgy. But you either come with me now, or I walk out of here and you won't like the visitors you find waiting for you when you do get home."

"Jerry's around. He can drive you."

"I don't want Jerry to drive me. It's you and me, Jessie. The way you always claimed you wanted it. You and me. In your car. And I'm driving. Let's go."

She looked at me like a cobra longing to strike.

"You're such a coward," she told me.

14

"How fucking stupid do you think I am?" I asked Jessie. We were ripping down I-10, halfway to Benson. I didn't give a damn if I got a ticket.

"Fairly stupid," she told me.

"Well, I got it. I understand exactly what you and your cocaine sugar daddy were doing."

"Roy, I was just trying to open a door. The rest was up to you."

"Can the shit. Okay? You were just giving me the graduate-level version of what you laid on poor Dinwiddie. Christ."

She didn't answer. I could almost hear the machinery in her skull over the snarl of the sports car's engine.

"Oh, I realize you didn't pitch Dinwiddie. You just wanted him present and observant. Incriminated by proximity. And aware of it. So he wouldn't whisper a word even if someone tortured him. Poor Dinwiddie. Your pathetic knight-errant. You jerked that poor bastard around like . . . like I don't know what. . . ."

"Is Little Roy angry? Because his sandbox slut killed his little baby?"

"You knew there wasn't a chance in hell I'd go for Mike's offer. And he knew it. It was all just to set me up, so I had no good choices. Yeah,

I could do the right thing and turn you in to the CID. And drag Jerry down. And Dinwiddie. And God knows who else . . . Gene Massetto? Pete Paulson? Who else is wrapped up in your filth?"

"Nicole, for one," Jessie said.

"You're such an utter bitch." I slapped at the pine-tree air-freshener dangling from her rearview mirror. "Didn't anybody ever tell you that Southern girls who went to finishing school don't hang shit like that in their cars? What fucking trailer court did you crawl out of? Really?"

"Did Nicole ever tell you about the pictures she posed for? In college? So what are you going to do, Roy? Run to the CID? Or maybe the DEA?"

"And screw everybody I care about, or who's ever done me a favor? You really wired this. Didn't you?" I snorted. "You're wasted on MI. You should be a strategic planner."

"That's what's really making you angry, isn't it?" She laughed. "That I know you so well? Maybe better than you know yourself?"

"So I keep my mouth shut. And then I'm implicated, too. An accomplice by virtue of my silence. Dereliction of duty. To say the least."

Jessie had been shaken for the first half hour of our drive, but her confidence returned. It was a palpable presence in the darkness behind the dashboard lights.

"Is anything I've done worse than what *you've* done? Sleeping with another officer's wife? What does the UCMJ say about adultery, Roy? And you went along with an abortion, you just shrugged it off. Without any serious qualms. You think your displays of self-pity fool anybody? You *love* the pain, Roy. As long as it's somebody else's. Besides, you muled drugs in from Mexico."

"That's bullshit."

"Which part of it?"

I slowed, barely, for the exit ramp that led down to the long stretch of desert between the Interstate and Fort Huachuca. Jessie belonged in a ditch by the roadside. Dead.

"I never smuggled drugs. And you know it."

"You sure, Roy? I think you *did* smuggle drugs. Last weekend."

"You're lying. I checked your bags."

"You're thinking small, Roy. Real men check under their cars."

"I could kill you. I swear to God. I could stop this car right now and kill you."

"No, you couldn't. You know that. By the time you finished pulling over, you'd already have second thoughts." She snickered. "You're too weak to kill me, Roy. We both know it."

I raged and drove. Flooring the gas pedal. It didn't faze her. The road ran straight as a ramrod. Edward Hopper loneliness of headlights in the desert.

"Tell me something," she said after I backed off to eighty. "What are you running from, Roy? What is it that rough, tough Lieutenant Banks can't face? Was there another Lolita? Or was it a real woman that time? Or something else? A trust betrayed? A cheat that went bad for someone who depended on you? Someone who trusted you? Was it just stupidity, Roy? Clumsiness? With people like you, it's never calculation. You don't have the character for cruelty."

"You have no idea who I am." I nearly hit a roadrunner, a swift ghost in the headlights.

"I know the pattern; I just don't know the stitching."

"I really should pull over and snap your neck."

"Wouldn't you want to fuck me first? You know you want to. Right now, I mean. This minute. Even if you never did before. You want me now, Roy." She laughed again. "Why don't you pull over? I don't care if anybody drives by and sees us. Pull over. Anywhere. You can have me. Any way you want."

In the faint light, she drew up her dress up and slipped off her panties. She threw them, as hard as she could, at the side of my face.

"Give me your hand." She reached over and tried to pull it from the steering wheel.

I slapped her across the face. Backhanded. Registering her nose and lips under my knuckles.

It stunned her. Briefly.

"I know you so well," she said when she recovered. She spoke slowly, her voice stripped of emotion. She might have been a doctor discussing a dull case. "I know you very, very well. You borrow the tragedies of others. You're running from somebody *else's* misery, somebody *else's* disaster. You stole their pain. Didn't you? So you could keep it in a cage and take it out and pet it when you wanted. But you don't really know pain, Roy. Not the real thing. You're not marked enough." A serpent laughed in the darkness. "You could never be a killer. You're a born witness. That's all you'll ever be. You get all of the drama free. There's always somebody else to pay for your ticket. Like Nicole."

She pulled her panties back on. As businesslike as a hooker.

"How would you know anything about me?" I asked. Too late. Too weak.

I didn't have to look to see her smile.

"I told you," she said. "We're twins."

I didn't think my heart could sink any lower, but few of us are good judges of depth. It was after two in the morning when we reached Huachuca City. I just wanted to get shut of Jessie and assure myself that Nikki was all right. But before rounding the corner onto my block, I spotted a car in the side street shadows that didn't belong to the landscape. It looked like Pete Paulson's ride.

If Pete was spying on me, I intended to club the shit out of him. But I never made it back to the parked car. Leaving Pete a very lucky man.

The headlights caught a red Ferrari parked beside my Mustang. Inside my apartment, the lights were on.

My circle of friends did not include Ferrari owners. My first thought was that the car was tied to Mike Cervantes, that Jessie's friends intended to stay in my life. I even imagined, in a panic I struggled not to betray to Jessie, that harm had been done to Nikki. Logic was irrelevant.

I parked and turned off the engine. "Okay. We're quits. Get out of here."

"I just want to check on Nicole."

"Fuck off."

I got out of the car and marched for the apartment. Behind me, Jessie's car door slammed. Had I not been so freaked about Nikki, I would have turned and punched Jessie in the face.

The first thing I saw was Nikki. Sitting in the easy chair, alive, if not quite well. She was so worn out, she looked forty.

On the floor at her feet lay a pair of silk rugs, one fully unrolled, the other half revealed. A litter of too-familiar artifacts had been arranged on my ramshackle coffee table.

The bastard sat on my sofa. Ali. My old pal. He had updated his haircut and playboy clothes, but still had the familiar nose, too small for his strong cheekbones, thanks to an overeager plastic surgeon. Every member of Ali's family had a nose job done in London. Except his father, the minister of state, who had been too proud.

"Long time no see," he said. Not much of an accent left. He had always worked hard on his English. Harder than his brother. Not so hard as Fatima.

"What are you doing here?"

"Just bringing you your stuff, brother. I got it out of the country for you. I been trying to track you down, like, forever."

"I don't want it."

"Hey, come on, Roy. Let bygones be bygones. We were so tight, you and me. You and me and Mo. We *loved* you, man. You know that. Mistakes were made, I'm the first to admit it. But you know the Persian temper, how we get. You think I'm not sorry for what happened?"

Nikki knew me well enough to tense at the change in my posture. She shrank ever so slightly into her chair.

I turned to Jessie. As I spoke, I heard my own voice from a distance. It was unnaturally calm. "Get him out of here. Take him home with you. He's your dream date, baby. If his family read the tea leaves and got out in time, he's an order of magnitude richer than your buddy Mike. And take all of this shit with you. You can have it."

Ali tried Farsi on me. I didn't respond.

"Just get him out of here," I told Jessie.

Ali stood up. It was a bad idea. He spoke again. That was a worse idea.

"Roy, brother . . . is this the shits, or what? I just drove all the way from L.A., man. As soon as I found out where you were, I got in my car. Your mom, man . . . she wants you to reconnect with your old friends, too. Everybody does. Kiss and make up, you know? And I brought you all your stuff—doesn't that say something? That we were thinking about you, even with all that Khomeini shit going down?"

"I don't want any of it. Take it, and get out."

He looked at my wrist. I understood what he was looking at.

"You don't mean that. Hey, I'll come back tomorrow. All right?"

"Just take your shit and get out."

We were all tired. But it was the wrong kind of tired for the situation. Ali stopped being the Good Humor Man.

"You're talking crazy, you know that? I mean, you should be grateful. You don't want this?" He waved a hand toward the treasures the Ferrari caravan had carried through the desert. "You don't want any of this stuff? Nothing for old times' sake? Nothing at all? Even though you're lucky you got out alive? My father, man . . . you don't know. You came *this* close to buying it." He smirked. "If you don't want any reminders, why are you wearing that Rolex Fatty gave you? Because it's fucking platinum, you dick?"

Her name was enough. Fatty. The wildly inappropriate nickname she hated, perhaps the only thing she ever hated in her life. Fatima. The first punch I landed wasn't forceful enough to take him down, since I had to reach across the coffee table and that screwed up my stance. But Ali had never had much affection for pain. And his daddy, the grand wazoo high minister, couldn't save him now. He stumbled past Nikki, tripping over her feet, unsure of where he was going.

I grabbed him and slammed him into the nearest wall, knocking over a stereo speaker. He didn't fight back, just tried to shield his face. I pummeled him. He slipped sideways, bellowing, and lurched into the kitchen area.

The girls wailed. I heard them from a great distance. And didn't care. Catching up with Ali, I thumped him between the shoulder blades. The blow toppled him into the table. A chair went over sideways. I landed one on Ali's temple as he tried to right himself. Then I kicked his legs out from under him, hitting him wildly as he went down.

He was begging me to stop. The untouchable Ali was begging. It was wonderful. Beyond wonderful. He cried out in English and Farsi.

I kept hitting him. Lot of blood. He stopped talking. I grabbed him by the breast of his shirt, lifting his torso to slam it back down. Then I planted a knee just under his heart and concentrated on his face. He had loved to parade that face around the parties in Tehran.

Nikki was screaming. Ineffectual hands pawed me from behind, from the side. Jessie shouted for me to stop. She'd been wrong. I was capable of killing. Maybe she understood that now. She was luckier than she knew.

Ali tried to clutch me, to interrupt the locomotive rhythm of the blows. But he was as weak as a girl. Weaker. A far cry from Iran's famous body-builders. "A lover not a fighter" had been one of his favorite English phrases when we were friends.

Jessie tried to get a grip on my hair to make me stop. Nikki sought to catch my flailing hands. My bloody hands.

I elbowed Jessie off me. Brutally hard. Then, without thinking, I shoved Nikki away.

She fell backwards.

I retained just enough human feeling to look her way. She lay sideways by the bathroom door. With a stunned expression.

I remember thinking, with doomsday clarity, *What have I done?*

Abandoning Ali, I scrambled over to her. Horrified.

"Nix? Nix, you okay? I'm sorry, I'm so sorry."

She was crying. And struggling to catch her breath. I stroked her hair. Once. Twice.

"Bed," she said.

I knelt to pick her up.

Turning my head, I caught Jessie unawares. The expression on her face had lost every trace of confidence.

"Get him out of here," I told her. "Now."

I undressed Nikki, who remained lost in space long enough to have me truly worried. She had faded out, eyelids locked down. Leaving me to hope it was just exhaustion. I checked for blood on her panties, her thighs, but the few spots I found looked old. No crimson. No wet.

"Stop hitting him," she told me, opening her eyes. *"Stop it. You'll kill him."*

Thirdhand blood smeared one cheek and her hands.

I hushed her. "It's all right. They're gone. Everybody's gone now. It's all over." I pulled the covers up over her. Sick at myself. For a different reason every ten seconds.

The only good thing about living in Huachuca City was that I didn't have to worry about anyone calling the police. Gunshots might have done the trick, but even that was questionable. At most, the five minutes of shrieking and destruction had been entertainment for the neighborhood.

"Are you all right? Nix? Please. Tell me. Did I hurt you?"

She didn't know. She was elsewhere. I felt crumpled inside. My right hand hurt. But that was the least of it.

She came around enough to ask, "Why . . . did you do that? *Why?*" Eyes vast in the lamplight.

Sitting on the bed, I looked away. Shamed into answering.

"He killed his sister," I told her.

15

Fort Huachuca was an easygoing post, and our workdays didn't begin on Infantry time. But we did have one of our rare 0600 formations on Monday morning. To conduct a fitness test for the staff and students held over to do odd jobs.

The Army had just transitioned from a five-event PT test that demanded speed, strength, and skill to one that counted only push-ups, sit-ups, and a two-mile run. It became easier to cheat, which was a gift to the overweight and slothful. Run by staff NCOs who were not about to fail their superior officers, the test at Fort Huachuca was a joke.

I took it seriously. I took all the hardcore soldiering stuff seriously. With my personal life a shambles, I was doubly determined to shine professionally. The PT test, which I always maxed, was only a small part of it. This was also the week when the exercise scenario on which I'd been working for months would drop on the Advanced Course captains.

We assembled in sharp morning air on a field below the academic complex. The cadre NCOs dicked around in the growing light, waiting for someone in authority to take charge. As I stretched my hamstrings,

Jerry sauntered up. With muscles bursting out of his T-shirt and thighs like tree trunks sprouting down from his shorts, he looked like a cartoon.

"Roy, man. You missed the best part of the party."

"Get away from me."

He saw my right hand. I had skipped the clinic. I didn't want an X-ray machine telling me that I had broken bones. The knife wound across my palm had barely healed.

"Wow. Those knuckles are a work of art."

"Home repairs."

"Yeah. Jessie told me all about it. You're a more complex guy than you let on. I got the money I owe you, by the way. In the Vette."

"Keep it. Just get away from me."

"What's with you, man?"

"You know what's with me. I don't want any part of that Tucson shit you're into. The Officers' Club is formally dissolved. *No mas.* Just leave me alone."

I walked away and lined up in front of a female staff sergeant who flirted with me, within bounds, when I stopped by Gene's office. When my turn came, I handed her my score card and got down in position. As she bent to count my reps, our heads almost touched.

"You're going to be a show-off, aren't you, LT?" Sergeant Munro said. She had sharp hillbilly facial bones passed down from the poorest glens in the Scottish Highlands. Checking out my hands and bare arms, she added, "Interesting damage."

In the two minutes allowed me, I did ninety-seven perfect push-ups on pure mean. She refused to count the last one, just to devil me.

Milling around while the other officers were tested, I didn't see Jessie. I spotted Major Dinwiddie, though. The push-ups he did were pathetic, mere head bobs. Yet it was evident that he was giving it all he had. Most of the out-of-shape officers faked it all the way, knowing they were going to get a pass. Dinwiddie was a sweat volcano.

The sit-ups were harder to fake. But officers managed. We valued integrity. But selectively.

Two files down, Gene Massetto hit the test hard, a model officer when it came to fitness. As in so many respects. On the ground beside him, Jerry knocked out sit-ups as fast as the sergeant first class holding down his ankles could count them.

When my turn came, Sergeant Munro locked her hands over my ankles to anchor me.

"Press harder. Like you mean it."

She refused to smile at first, then broke into a grin. One of those just-more-than-plain girls with deeply coded charisma, Mary Jane Munro wore a stern face while in uniform. The admin NCOIC for the tactics teachers, she was efficient to the point of brusqueness. But I had made her laugh a couple of times over the months. I sometimes wondered what hid behind the starched armor of her uniform.

She counted off my sit-ups, staring at the scratches on my legs.

When Nikki said good-bye on Sunday, I had not even rated a farewell kiss. Just *Thanks for letting me stay here. I appreciate it.* She had asked no further questions about Saturday night's eruption.

It was over. Leaving in a couple of weeks, she said she was going to save herself for her husband. We were not even to see each other. Her tone during the drive to the BOQ had been as matter-of-fact as a menu discussion.

Sergeant Munro initialed my scorecard, glanced around to check the range of interested ears, then said, "You just think you're the biggest stud on earth. Don't you, LT?"

It was a false diagnosis at the moment.

The two-mile run was the biggest joke of all. The NCOs had marked out the course. Unsupervised. I completed it in barely eleven minutes, which was preposterous. I was a distance runner, not a speed demon. I broke twelve only on the rarest of days. The course was short by almost a quarter mile.

By the time the last runners stumbled up, with the quitters strewn along the street behind them, full daylight was upon us. Major Dinwiddie trotted toward the finish line, drenched monstrously. The guy was duking it out with his physiognomy, giving the contest all he had. Still, he wasn't stupid. He knew the whole thing was a cheat.

Most men caught in a con will skulk away. Dinwiddie didn't. He came straight for me. Gasping. On the heart attack express.

"Don't judge me too harshly, Roy," he said between gulps of air. Then he plodded toward the parking lot.

So began my week of disappointments.

I spent the morning in a modified classroom, training two order-of-battle techs and a quartet of NCOs to run the three-day exercise I'd designed. It was discouraging, to put it mildly. The pair of warrant officers seemed as befuddled as alchemists who woke up in Los Alamos, and the sergeants were utterly lost. Given that they were drawn from the faculty and specialized in Soviet military matters, it was not a good sign.

I was not about to relent, though. Patiently, I explained the master plan and went over the series of overlays that developed the offensive. I talked them through the hundreds of color-coded spot reports and intelligence summaries that would be fed to the captains at specific points in the exercise. I had paced them the way reports actually flowed, with a dearth of information followed by an overwhelming data dump to stress them under the rigid time constraints. To get other "bonus" reports, the students had to task the right collection systems and prioritize their information needs. It wasn't designed to be fun.

I had become obsessed with the exercise, my memorial to the late Colonel Jacoby. And to my vanity.

Allotted two days to train up the cadre, I told myself when we broke for lunch that the day and a half remaining would be plenty of time to bring them up to snuff. But my confidence was developing hairline cracks.

Avoiding the rest of humanity for an hour, I walked up to the commissary, where the rat-bite deli would make you a sandwich of all-unnatural ingredients. I had just emerged into the sunlight again, bearing my meal of processed meat, processed cheese, processed bread, and a withered rag of chemical-soaked lettuce, when I glimpsed Pete Paulson getting out of his car.

This time, I pursued him.

"Pete. Freeze."

He turned toward me with a surprised expression, but not in fear. Belief sabotages your defense mechanisms. And thus we have martyrs.

"If I *ever* catch you spying on me again, I'm going to beat the shit out of you. Take this seriously, Pete."

"I wasn't spying on you, Roy."

"I saw you, goddamn it. Your car. Saturday night. Make that Sunday morning."

"I wasn't spying on *you*."

I felt like grinding my sandwich into his face. In a futile effort to break through the reinforced-concrete ramparts of his consciousness.

"Then what were you doing?"

"It was her. I was watching her. You and Jessie were together. I saw you."

"Pete, that's sick. And I wasn't with her by choice, for what it's worth. But it's none of your business, anyway."

"It *is*. You don't know her. You don't know."

"I think I have a fair idea."

"She's a bad person, Roy."

"No fucking shit." I looked down at the parking-lot blacktop. Shaking my head. It was like coping with a little kid so pathetic, you just couldn't stay mad. Exasperated, yes. Mad, no. "Didn't I tell you to stay away from her? You had it coming, Pete. For not listening. 'Failure to follow instructions.' You are a no-go at this station."

"But she *lied* to me. She lied and lied."

"Welcome to the dating game. Just write off whatever happened as a lesson learned and forget her. Trust me, it's the best thing you could do. Concentrate on your prayer meetings, find some nice girl who'll read the Bible with you. Walk away. No, run. And don't look back."

He certainly looked chastened. His eyes reported a sleep deficit.

"I can't," he told me.

"Why not?"

It was his turn to inspect the gravel on the blacktop.

"That's what I wanted to talk to you about. When I stopped by your apartment."

"It was a bad time, Pete."

"I know. I understand. Your girlfriend, the adulteress, was having an abortion."

"Oh, great. Did you read that in the local paper, or did it make *The New York Times*?"

"Don't worry, Roy. Even that can be forgiven."

"Oh, piss off. Would you, Pete? Just cross Jessie Lamoureaux's name out of your little red book, huh? Tear out the whole page."

"I can't. I just can't, Roy. I *can't*."

"Pete, for Christ's sake. You don't want the enlisted kids to see you bawling your eyes out."

He drew out a hankie less spotless than his faith. "I'm *not*. The sun's just in my eyes, I'm not crying. I think about her, Roy. I can't stop thinking about her. I think bad thoughts."

"For heaven's sake, Pete. That's natural. Prayer doesn't make biology go away."

He looked up. "Not those kind of bad thoughts."

The afternoon session with the training cadre went better than the morning's torture round. It felt as though they had talked things out and decided to play the game. Or maybe they had complained to Gene and got yanked up by the short-hairs.

Gene put in an appearance toward the end of the duty day. Under his eyes, the OB warrants and NCOs renewed their interest, asking me more questions in thirty minutes than they had posed throughout the rest of the day.

He let them go a little before five, a mild reward.

When we were alone, he asked, "Well?"

"They're trying. I was surprised at how much they don't know. Especially the warrants. They're supposed to know all this stuff. Chief Laffer didn't know that East German and Soviet divisional tables of organization and equipment aren't identical, that they—"

"Are they going to be able to handle it?"

I gave him the polar bear salute, hands held up at shoulder level, palms out. "I think so. But if I could be in the control facility . . ."

"Absolutely not. I told you. You're to stay out of the building. For that matter, I want you to stay away from the entire academic complex for the duration. Go swimming, hang out at the gym, I don't care. But I don't want any of the captains suspecting that a second lieutenant's behind this. You understand me?"

I beat down a smile. Whenever he tried to be ultra-stern, Gene became the silent-screen heartthrob to which his looks condemned him, Valentino doing his male-vamp thing.

He must have sensed my amusement, since he zoomed back in for another strafing run. "I mean it, Roy. After you wrap it up with the red team tomorrow afternoon, clear out. And stay out. That's a direct order."

"Yes, sir."

He loosened up on the stick again. "By the way, I've got another order for you."

"My assignment come in?"

He frumped his chin. "Not yet. But this could be related."

"And?"

"Thursday evening, 1900 hours. Be at the DTIMS office. The Special Forces recruiter's staying late to fit you in."

That was news. I knew that an SF headhunter would be on post, but had not signed up for an interview.

"You put my name down?"

"No." He considered me. "You haven't been talking to anybody about going SF?

I shook my head. "More like the French Foreign Legion."

"Well, just be there. It's a command performance, not an option. An action message came down the chain. Somebody above my pay-grade thinks you might be snake-eater material."

He snatched up the green cap with the silver railroad tracks. "Note that I didn't ask about your right hand."

"Long story."

"Then save it. Just get the warrants and their crew up to speed on the exercise. We've both got a lot riding on this."

"Just tell me straight: What's the backup plan? If the captains can't cut it?"

"If they aren't getting it by noon on Thursday, I take over. And spoon-feed them. Colonel Bullitt's made it crystal clear, Roy. The captains are to be given confidence in their abilities, not discouraged."

"And when they get to the field?"

"They're on their own."

He moved as if to leave, but the action struck a false note. Sure enough, he turned around again.

"Almost forgot. I need you to do me a favor. It involves a trip to Tucson. On Wednesday evening."

"Tucson and I haven't been getting along very well."

"Well, maybe this will turn things around. I'd like you to do something for Marilyn, actually. She's been nagging me to take her up to see *Tess*. And you know how I hate that stuff. But I know you like it. I thought you could take her up on Wednesday night?"

"Gene . . . don't do this."

"Do what?"

"You know what. Jessie Lamoureaux. Don't."

His features tightened. Radiating isotopes of anger. But he had good self-control. "I need you to do this for me. As a favor. A personal favor. I've been flying top-cover for you for months, Roy. And Marilyn likes you. She'd love to go up to see it with you. It'll be a treat for her. I'll give you money for the movie. And dinner. If you're short."

"I'm not a gigolo. Accomplice is bad enough."

"But I should pay. After all—"

"I can pay for the damned movie. And dinner. Marilyn really doesn't suspect anything?"

He didn't answer the question. "Just tell me yes or no. It's the only favor I've ever asked of you. I need you to do this for me."

I could have pointed out that our professional lives and personal affairs fell into different categories of obligation, but the lines had long been blurred.

"Yes. But I beg you not to do this, Gene. Jessie's nothing but trouble, she'll ruin your marriage and laugh."

Gene's face closed down again. Tighter than before. His self-control had limits.

"You need to be quiet now," he told me.

I ate a bum's salad assembled from stray bits in the refrigerator, then tried to call Eli. No answer. I wasn't about to drive over to Bisbee on the chance that I might find him. I didn't need another disappointment.

I attempted to read the new Peter Matthiessen book, but my powers of concentration were kaput. And I didn't want to listen to jazz, either. Music led to uncontrolled thoughts and images.

The apartment's emptiness verged on the supernatural. It defied the laws of the Newtonian universe that a couple of small rooms could become as vast as an abandoned palace. I sat. The pretender to a worthless throne, deserted by all his courtiers. Helen of Troy? Anne Boleyn?

Nikki didn't even rate at the Christine Keeler level. Our Dumpster romance.

I hadn't used the phone book in months and found it, at last, in a cupboard above the fridge. I dialed the number.

"Hello?"

"Mary Jane . . . it's Roy Banks."

She hesitated. Then nudged things toward formality. "What's up, LT?"

"I . . . look, I'm sorry . . . I'm not even sure why I called."

"I think I am. Roy, I'm not anybody's Monday-nighter."

"That never crossed my mind. You have my word. Not only as an officer and poor excuse for a gentleman, but as a former NCO."

Her voice relaxed slightly. "So . . . you just called for me to tell you how much I admired your physical prowess on the PT test?"

"No. This is stupid. Sorry."

"Well, tell me about it. You're at least as interesting as the rerun of *Gilligan's Island* you interrupted. I'm all ears."

"Listen, Mary Jane . . . I'm not prowling for sex. Really."

"Should I be flattered? Or insulted? Hey, you don't sound like the brash and strutting Lieutenant Banks we all know and generally tolerate. What's wrong, LT?"

"Plenty."

"And you wanted to talk about it? To me?"

"No. I want to not talk about it."

She considered my reply. "Well, that's an interesting reason to call somebody you barely know and strike up a conversation. You sure it isn't a come-on line?"

"No. It's not a come-on line."

"And you called me just to tell me you don't want to talk about anything?"

"I was going to ask if I could buy you a beer."

"Bad idea. Officer and NCO. Out in the evening. In a small town."

"I know."

"No, you don't. I doubt you have any idea what it's like being a single female staff sergeant in this man's Army."

"My apologies. I was out of line."

We listened to each other's breathing. Then she said, "You know I've had this crush on you. Don't you? Is that why you called? Easy pickings?"

No. I hadn't known. Our office banter had meant nothing to me.

"Because nothing's going to happen," she continued. "Because I'm not going to let it. I need you to understand that. I'm not going to go there. I've learned the hard way not to mix up daydreams and reality."

"Honestly, this wasn't a come on."

"And you're sober? You sound sober."

"I'm sober."

She paused again, plotting her location in my universe with her woman's sextant and compass. At last, she said, "Then come over to my place. I'll buy you a beer, Roy."

We talked about nothing of consequence. We watched TV, which was something of a novelty, since I was too snotty to have a set in my apartment. Sipping beers, we maintained a cautious distance, but it was lovely to sit with someone in whom I had no bankrupting emotional investment and who didn't expect any more than was on the table. She didn't mention my banged-up hands again and ignored the scratches wherever my flesh was bared.

I wasn't alone, and Mary Jane got some second-rate entertainment. It was a useful trade.

She had a small place back in the wastes of paint-hungry apartment complexes and roughneck houses just south of Fry Boulevard. The furnishings veered too close to kitsch for me, the décor tyrannized by at least one tour in Germany, but her rooms had integrity. Everything felt earnest, from her collection of neatly ordered paperbacks to the dreadful china figurines under glass, a heartfelt attempt to construct a decent life. Staff Sergeant Mary Jane Munro did the best she could with what she had. It made me feel that I'd squandered a great deal.

The Army had been a guaranteed ticket out of eastern Kentucky. "I'll have you know I escaped with all my own teeth," she said with a laugh. It wasn't entirely a joke.

In civilian clothes, she had the slightly bowed legs of a girl who'd spent time on horseback and a look that was flinty and honest and fiercely alive. She had let down her brown hair and brushed it out, softening her cheekbones. Good company, she laughed well and often.

As the time neared for me to leave, she aimed the remote at the television and clicked off the rolling credits.

"Okay, what was this all about, Roy? What are you doing here?"

"You invited me."

"But you called. You were like a kid in ninth grade phoning a girl for the first time."

"The truth sounds like a bad line from a bad TV show."

"Try me. I know them all."

"I didn't want to be alone."

She cocked an eyebrow, a mountain girl who learned skepticism young. "And where did I fit in? Last seen, first dialed?"

"You were the only person I could think of."

"Well, that's some compliment. I thought you were the post playboy, line 'em up and knock 'em down. You and your ape-man buddy, Lieutenant Purvis. With your 'Officers' Club.' Oh, word gets around. What is it, some combination of a primitive orgy and white slave ring?"

"It was just a joke. A bad joke, as it turns out."

Her face grew serious. As if she spotted revenuers creeping up the hollow. "You shouldn't pal around with Purvis, Roy. If you want my opinion. He's a jerk. You're better than that. You always struck me as a decent guy, for all your strutting around. Find a better buddy."

"Our paths have diverged. And the Officers' Club has been permanently disbanded, by the way." I smiled halfway. The muscle movement was tentative, but it counted as my first smile of the evening. "He hit on you or something?"

"There isn't a woman of any rank on Fort Huachuca he hasn't hit on. Jerry Purvis is a joke."

"So he didn't get far with Staff Sergeant Munro?"

"Just as far as the other side of my desk. I've made mistakes, but never one that stupid."

"I've made a few of late. Maybe you've heard about some of those, too."

"Not so much. You're not our sole topic of conversation down in the lower depths. Anyway, my granddad always said that only the dead don't make mistakes, and he wasn't so sure about them, either. You get pretty good reviews, all in all. Although I suppose I shouldn't tell you. Some girls think you're stuck up; the rest think you just haven't been lassoed by the right cowgirl."

"What do you think?"

"I think you get big points for being the one male on Fort Huachuca who hasn't fallen head over heels for Lieutenant Lamoureaux. If the rumors of her failure aren't exaggerated."

"They're not. That's one mistake I haven't made."

"She's a first-class bitch."

"I wish I could convince a friend of that."

"Captain Massetto?"

That surprised me. So little remained hidden.

"I'd rather not discuss it."

"Massetto's a born sucker," she told me. "Nice guy, but a born sucker. Look at his eyes. They're weak. That's another thing my granddad told me. Always look at a man's eyes. Before you're taken in by anything else. Poor Captain Massetto. He's like a little dog when she comes by the office. And he's not the golden boy everybody thinks he is, Roy. He hit on me, too. I mean, it's a battlefield in that office. But at least he takes no for an answer."

"I can't talk about him."

"She'll wreck his marriage. Then she'll move right along, la-de-da. Somebody ought to put her out of her misery."

"Can we talk about something else?"

Tucking her legs in tighter, she said, "Sorry. Criticizing other people seemed safe. Safer than other topics that could come up."

"Such as?"

She twisted the lone ring she wore. Its stone was red and small. Looking up again, she met my eyes and held them.

"Such as it's time for you to go, because I've had this crush on you for months, and you're about the only guy who hasn't hit on me, and now you're here. And neither of us is going to do anything about it. And that's that." A look of wistful kindness and regret softened her face. "I was flattered when you called, though. It was good for my self-esteem. Even if you just dialed my number at random."

"I didn't."

We did not touch at all as we said good night. Not even a handshake.

"Thank you," I told her.

Nearing her door, we found ourselves unexpectedly close to each other. The moment had come, suddenly, when the course of our lives could change.

We let it pass.

Silhouetted in her doorframe, she watched me go and said, "Maybe in another lifetime, LT."

16

"Roy! It's been an absolute *lifetime*," Eli cried. **"Come in, come in. I** *must* get back to the stove."

I followed him. The household smelled acrid yet good. Count Basie crackled on the stereo.

"What a delight to see you," Eli said as he stirred a pot. "Help your-self to the wine, it's a decent Meursault. Glasses above the toaster. You're just in time to solve one of my eternal problems—what to do with the extra portion this recipe produces. It's only a clam sauce, but I add a few special touches."

After pouring myself a drink, I brought Eli's glass back up to a re-spectable level. He glanced across the counter at the motion. What he saw woke his attention.

"Your hand? Your arms?"

"I lost my temper."

The response raised one of his eyebrows, but he let it go. Tasting the sauce, he grimaced at the heat, then beamed over the flavor. "Be a help and get down an extra plate, would you? Just over there, the tall cabi-net."

I fetched. Gladly. The chow smelled great. Before trying the wine, I snared a floating nugget of cork with my finger.

Eli poured boiling water off pasta. "Forgive me if it's not perfectly *al dente*. Living alone, I find myself growing lax. But the wine? Isn't it lovely? I need an indulgence now and then. Not least, today. Someone tossed a brick through the window of the shop during the night. Nothing missing, either. Just the addition of the brick to my inventory."

"A case gone awry?"

He frowned, then brightened again. "I don't think so. But let's eat. Gobbling's permitted, even encouraged." Eli, who was usually prim, tucked his napkin into his collar like a mob boss in the movies. "And how was *your* day, Roy? Those worrisome knuckles aside."

"I spent it teaching people things they didn't want to learn."

Between twirls of spaghetti, Eli said, "I'm afraid I haven't heard anything back on the subject of our investigation, Miss Lamoureaux. Or Lieutenant Lamoureaux. But it hasn't been very long, we needn't despair. My requests don't receive the priority treatment they once did." He devoured another mouthful, then mused, "Los Angeles has a short memory, it's a form of protection. Otherwise, life simply couldn't go on. We forget yesterday's stars, it's true. But we also forget our sins. Nor does the City of Angels expect much penance. Although a bit of drama is always welcome."

"This is serious cooking, Eli."

"Dinner parties were my specialty. Once upon a time."

"Speaking of parties, I ended up at a major one in Tucson on Saturday. Know anything about Mike Cervantes? Miguel Cervantes? Definitely not the author."

Eli put down his fork and tablespoon. "I'm told he gives the grandest bashes Tucson has to offer. I've also heard that they're not always nice." I sensed him delaying what he really had to say.

"I didn't go of my own volition, for what it's worth. Escort duty. I'm not going back."

A shred of clam eluded his fork. "I think that's wise, Roy. Mike Cervantes couldn't do you any good, but he can do a great deal of harm."

"I got a hint of that. Mind if I top off my wine."

He snatched the bottle from the far side of the table and poured the pale gold treasure into my glass. "I've deteriorated *unforgivably* as a host. You like it, though?"

"It's sublime. To my peasant's palate."

"Ah, Roy, Roy! You shouldn't be disingenuous with me. You'll never be a peasant. Try as you may. Now file this away and don't repeat it. Mike Cervantes and Sammy Rodriguez—my client, the jazz fan—are competitors, they're rivals. And not especially friendly ones. I'm afraid it guarantees that I'll never be invited to one of Mr. Cervantes's parties. I'm irrevocably associated with Sammy. One just slips into these things, and there you are. Fate, not design."

"I could apply that formula to other matters," I said. "'Fate, not design.'"

"Such as?"

"Passion."

"Well, passion's always a matter of fate, isn't it? The great passions? Never planned, always accidental. But never incidental." He touched his glass to his lips, then caressed the wine in his mouth. "That little shoot-'em-up a few months ago? The one that began in Agua Prieta and ended down below the Copper Queen? A protégé of Mike's had appeared where he had no business appearing, and Sammy assumed a turf encroachment was being given a trial run. In the past, Mike and Sammy have been reasonably pacific neighbors. Mike owns the Nogales route and everything west to Yuma. Sammy has everything east of Nogales, as far as Franklin, New Mexico. The division's worked well enough in the past, but greed confuses people—I hope you don't have greedy friends, Roy."

"Acquaintances. Not friends."

"Of course, human beings are greedy for different things. I'm greedy for compliments about my cooking, for example. I'm terribly vain about it. Have I earned a good review?"

"Three Michelin stars."

"I knew you'd have a discriminating palate. But let's say two stars. I *despise* overrated chefs. A little more, then? Don't condemn me to all those calories myself."

"Gladly. Then maybe we can have a talk?"

He stopped in mid-kitchen and flipped a strand of hair behind his ear. "More details about Lieutenant Lamoureaux?"

"No. You wanted to hear my story."

His face lengthened in surprise.

"I think I shall open another bottle of the Meursault."

The parties. Whenever I think of Tehran, I think of the parties. I'm sure L.A. was kinkier—at least until you penetrated the Iranian inner sanctums—but it wasn't the libertine atmosphere that made me feel like a hick. It was the opulence. It was breathtaking. The goal was to be more wasteful than the guy in the next villa. You could eat yourself sick on caviar and not dent the black and gray mountains on the buffet tables. Don't like vintage champagne? Cut your reserve-label cognac with Coca-Cola. And the girls didn't mind if you ripped their designer dresses back at the ranch. They never wore the same thing twice.

You had only to get to one of those parties to understand why the revolution happened. Marie Antoinette was an amateur. The gulf between the haves and have-nots was intergalactic. Khomeini just whitewashed class hatred with religion. Of course, nobody took him seriously back then. There was some foreboding, sure. But it wasn't about the mullahs. Nobody dreamed that *they* were the biggest threat to the shah. There was just a vague sense that no party could last forever, a morning-after sort of thing that faded by the next evening's party. Maybe I sensed the storm coming before they did, since I was the product of an American campus in the early 1970s and intellectually primed to expect revolutions.

All it took was braving the traffic jam and driving from North Tehran to South Tehran to witness the desolation at the heart of the last Persian empire. Of course, the shah was strong. America was behind him. SAVAK, his secret police, would keep a lid on things. People fretted now and then, but they didn't truly worry. All you had to do to stay on the guest list for the endless party was to keep your mouth shut about politics. And stay connected, of course. If you weren't connected to the web of power relationships and wealth, you were stuck in the slums that grew bigger every day. And on the Peacock Throne sat a man who believed he could buy only those items he wanted from the modernity menu, the weapons and gadgets and luxuries he judged safe. He never understood it was all or nothing.

How did I get to Tehran? Check the job listings in the Sunday paper that require a bachelor's degree in Archaeology. I wanted to do field work. But the only field work for an archie with a BA was picking lettuce in California. An Iranian prof on the faculty had taken a liking to me, though. I'd done a paper on the legacy of the Zoroastrian era in Persia, the surviving monuments, the tangible stuff. He gave me an A, then told me, politely, that I didn't know what I was talking about, that the Zoroastrian centuries had never ended, that Shia Islam was just a wool cloak over the silks. But my choice of subjects flattered him. Ex-pat Persians can be uncontainably proud of their culture. He couldn't offer me a spot on any digs that year, but he connected me with a recruiter who was hiring English-language teachers on two-year contracts. It was bankers' pay, courtesy of the shah, and tax free. Plus I got a ticket to Iran, where my professional interests lay. Who knew what might come of it? Next year in Persepolis?

The Farsi I'd studied in college barely got me out of the airport. But it didn't matter. Everybody wanted to speak English. American English. As a young instructor who could talk pop culture, too, I was instantly in demand. I worked at Farsi in my off-time, but I could only use it in the streets. "Why do you want to talk that shit?" Ali would ask me. "You planning a pilgrimage to Qom or something?" He called me Haji Roy for a while. Until his father told him to knock it off.

Ali. My first, and best, friend in Iran. His father was a minister of state, a confidant of the shah. Ali had an engineering degree from an American college I'd never heard of. Rich Iranians bought American degrees back then the same way they bought American cars with big engines or blondes with big hair. Anyway, he had this degree, but he couldn't change the tire on a ten-speed. I had to do it for him.

I think he liked that. Having an American get his hands dirty while he watched.

We got on well, though. Ali was irrepressible, the life of every party. I'd met him through his girlfriend of the moment. She was taking an intermediate English class I taught and decided I'd make a good mascot for her set. Dumb as a rock, but her father was in charge of Evin Prison. Ali explained that it would be smart to grade her gently. And she was gorgeous, not one of the beak-and-whiskers type. One of those Persian women straight from a fifteenth-century miniature painting, but dressed in Italian fashions. The boys all wanted to be mistaken for Americans, but the girls wanted to pass as French or Italian. Nobody outside of the slums wanted to be Persian.

Ali slithered. But I liked the way he slithered. It was something new to me. And being taken up by the wealthy is seductive, I don't care how ethical or pure you think you are. And Ali's family was beyond wealthy. They had this monster of a marble-topped, gilt-legged table—Persian tastes make Louis XV furniture look Shaker. It stood just inside the vestibule of their Tehran place, near the door. There was a big silver bowl on it, filled to the brim with banknotes. If any members of the family needed pin money, they helped themselves on their way out, just grabbed a fistful of bills. No questions asked, no accountability. The largesse was the point. And the servants never helped themselves, believe it or not. They didn't dare.

James Bond was Ali's hero. The movie Bond, Sean Connery. I'm sure he never read the books. Reading for pleasure wasn't Ali's style. He had this riff he'd do. Cocking one of those black eyebrows, he'd hold up his fingers like a pistol and deadpan, "Montashemi. Al Montashemi." Naturally, he had an Aston Martin. We used to buzz donkey carts in it, out in the countryside.

I'll admit it. I liked the privileges and benefits that came with being his friend. But being his friend could be exhausting, too. He couldn't hold still, and he expected everyone around him to keep up. And to give him his way.

His older brother, Mohammed, went by Mo. He had a degree in architecture and couldn't draw a straight line. I don't know if he was smarter than Al—than Ali—or dumber. He was quieter, though. That said, I have never known a more prodigious drinker. His chosen poison was vodka, the Russian stuff. He was bigger than Ali, beefier. Manlier. But he lacked the social spark. Ali flitted about, finally landing on the prize girl of the evening. Mo just sat and drank. Or gambled. And they weren't penny bets.

Everybody in the family had had a nose job. From the same London surgeon, to maintain a family resemblance. Everybody but the old man, who was too proud. Or maybe he figured the shah wouldn't like it. But Mom and the kids all got Anglo-Saxon schnozzes. Even Fatima, the teenage daughter. Fatty, they called her. Which she hated, of course. She wasn't the least bit fat. She was small, with biology still adding the finishing touches. She was probably seventeen or eighteen when we first met, presentable, but no beauty. The international standard of the kid sister. Ali and Mo ribbed her about being a Goody Two-shoes, for dressing like a schoolgirl. Beyond that, I barely noticed her.

It was a giddy life, irresponsible. But a hell of a ride for a kid just out of college. There were women, too. Slumming, having a little adventure on the quiet. It wasn't done to be linked in public with an American male, but I couldn't have afforded serious relationships with them, anyway. I was more than happy to let things roll along.

Somehow, I made good progress in learning Farsi. Despite the party scene. I even took lessons from a cleric for a while. He was well spoken, cheap, and dependable. He used to badger me, playfully, about converting to Islam. I'd tell him I couldn't give up alcohol. So he'd quote these Sufis to me, all about wine and drunken visions of the divine, then he'd rock back and smile, a Shia mullah quoting Sunnis to persuade a Christian that Islam had room for Ernest and Julio Gallo. There was a lot of flex in things back then, but I doubt he's prospered under the new regime.

I wasn't just in Tehran, either. These people, they really were the jet set. They'd fly to London for the weekend or to New York for a week. Just on the spur of the moment. They could do that, they had houses everywhere. Or, if they didn't, they'd book the best suites in the top hotels. Paid for by the blood of the peasants and workers. Or by oil money, anyway.

Ali and Mo—and others—invited me along. I joined the gang now and then, but most of the time, it felt too much like charity. I didn't like playing the bought companion, the hired entertainment. Besides, I took my classroom duties seriously. Although it could be a battle. One time, they convinced the director of the language school to grant me an unscheduled long weekend. Without telling me about it. The director might have turned me down, but he knew who their father was. And off we went to London. First class seats, of course.

They had one of those posh row houses in Belgravia, straight out of the Forsyte Saga. And I don't mean the family had it. This one was just for the kids, their playhouse. It seemed crazy to me at the time, outrageously wasteful. Looking back, their father was a classic Persian chess master. Buying real estate everywhere, lots of it. He must've seen what was coming more clearly than he let on. The public line, of course, was that the Pahlavi dynasty would last a thousand years. But overseas real estate holdings were good insurance, just in case.

That weekend in London was a one-off for me. In more ways that one. It was the first, and last, time I had a prostitute. Not my style. But,

Jesus, this one was a dead-ringer for Julie Christie, only taller. Mine for the weekend. I didn't know how to handle it at first; it felt awkward. But Julie was hauling in a lot more than the girls working the registers at Harrods, and making life easy for customers was a specialty. She was happy, too, or so she claimed, that she'd drawn me, not one of the brothers. Iranians paid splendidly, she said, but they were abusive. She was being paid to flatter me, I understand that. But the next morning, Ali's date had blood running down her legs when he booted her out. At that point, I knew as much as I wanted to know.

Did I mention the bacon sandwiches? I think Al and Mo were into bacon just to be outrageous, to mortify the servants. Back in Tehran, we'd come in from a party, and Ali would lead the procession into the kitchen—there was always a cook on duty to satisfy the family's whims. Napping, maybe. But there. Ali would bellow for a bacon sandwich, sending the devout Muslim help into a panic. But Ali and Mo pushed the joke only so far. Once the butt of the routine had been sufficiently terrified by the prospect of pollution and damnation, Fatima would show up, awakened by the ruckus. Or maybe just waiting up for us. She'd take over, fetching the bacon from the "evil" Frigidaire that stood in a locked pantry and then frying it up herself—although I don't recall that she ever ate any. She'd make us hot, greasy, glorious sandwiches on a knockoff version of Wonder Bread—everything American was tops. She'd watch us eat and slowly close her eyes. I can still taste those sandwiches, hot in the mouth after a night of drinking and God knows what else—it was never my thing, not seriously, but there was even more cocaine around than caviar. And hashish, of course. You could've built houses out of the slabs. The usual assortment of chemicals rounded things out. Some of the would-be hipsters even did smack.

How could so many good memories end so badly? I didn't have a clue that Fatima had the least interest in me; I was utterly oblivious. I assumed I was just an adjunct to her brothers, as far as she was concerned. As far as I was concerned, she was just a kid.

One night when I was wrestling with the verses of Nizami and losing, she showed up at my door. I assumed she was looking for her brothers. She wasn't.

It took me a while to figure it out. I can be pretty slow, when developments don't fit the pattern. I really didn't get it, even when she asked me for a Johnnie Walker Black. I didn't have any around. I never drank it, rarely drank hard liquor. The joke was that I was a better "Muslim" than any of them. Fatima settled for a vodka and orange juice. The vodka belonged to Mo. I had to keep a couple of bottles in a cupboard for him. Emergency rations. Fatima had always struck me as diffident, to the extent I paid any attention to her, but the family's imperious streak was in her, too. When I couldn't figure things out, she stepped over and kissed me.

It was a child's kiss. Well-meant, unpracticed. She wasn't certain how far the tongues were supposed to go. She was so intent on that kiss that she just let her hands dangle at her sides. I had to break it off to get some air.

"Fatima," I said. "Your brothers."

She thought about that. "I want you for me, too. Not just for them."

"What would your father say, if he knew you were here?"

"He won't know. I won't tell him."

"Your driver might."

She glared. Hardly the kid sister now. "I'd have him killed."

That first evening, I got her out of there before any damage was done. But she came back. No one in that family was easily deterred. She brought me gifts, a practice I tried to discourage, at least at first. We kissed a little. It was playground stuff, though. I had no intention of being the villain in her postpuberty drama. All the while I wondered if her brothers knew and just weren't letting on. Not that she would have told them. The girl had her ways of being discreet, an innate ability to conceal things. All Persians do. They needed it, under the shah. But, then, they've probably always needed it. They certainly do these days. Without that gift for duplicity, there probably wouldn't be any Persians left.

The inevitable happened. Because I let it become inevitable. One night, Fatima wasn't there to make our bacon sandwiches. But Miss Oscar Meyer Sugar-Cured was in my bed when I got home. And I was drunk. As she knew I would be. That's how things got started.

I liked her. That's the damned thing about it. Beyond the occasional burst of rich-girl temperament, she was devastatingly tender, inexpressibly kind. Even in her most impassioned moments, there was a gentleness to her, a softness. A faint caravan of black hairs trekked down from her navel; that's the image that comes to mind when I think of her. I used to run my finger along it, tickling her.

I was careful, of course. Condoms, the whole works. Everything was under control. Everybody in the family got a different side of me. Even her father muttered now and then about finding something more worthy for me to do. I don't mean he regarded me as a prospective son-in-law; that would never have crossed his mind. But Persians can be wonderfully generous, impulsively so. Maybe he thought I'd be a good influence on Ali, as hopeless as that was. But Fatima . . . she'd be married off to a general's son, at the very least. There weren't a lot of poor generals under the shah. Everyone thought the military was indestructible. Safe.

I grew fond of Fatima, although I didn't take her entirely seriously. She remained a kid to me, if one with adult appetites in some things. I liked her, got used to her. But she wasn't a grand passion. The brutal truth is that she became a convenience. The kid was in love with me. And I let it happen. I even let her give me this watch. Which is something that I never should have done. I wondered how she came up with the money. By skimming a bit out of that bowl in the vestibule each day? It would've taken a while. I had no right to accept it, it was piggish. But I wanted it, once she put it on my wrist. She knew what I wanted better than I knew it myself. Stainless steel would have been beneath her family, of course. And men didn't wear gold in her world; gold's for women. So she gave me a platinum watch. And I took it.

Then one night—another drunken night—she didn't want any part of the condoms or foams. "I must feel you now," she said. It was half a plea, half a command.

Life was good. I was dating an Iowa girl who worked for the U.S. Information Service, but nobody, not even Fatima, gave that any weight. "Does she buy you your cornflakes at the embassy? I could buy you cornflakes. I would fly to America to get them for you, your cornflakes."

I was even approached by a CIA type I'd seen around the chancellery. Which made me wonder about the real line of work my corn-fed gal was in. It would be helpful, he explained, if I could report anything interesting I heard.

I assured him he'd be the first to know, then never dialed his number. I hadn't acquired a taste for betraying my friends. And I thought they were all my friends.

Life went on, the seasons changed, Fatima seemed to grow tired of me at last. She came less often. When she did, things were different, a veil of some sort had been lowered between us. I concluded that she'd found an Iranian boyfriend, somebody of her own class, and didn't have the heart to tell me outright. I missed her, the old Fatima. I certainly didn't love her, but I *liked* her. There really isn't a word for it in English. Or Farsi.

I was alone, correcting papers. It wasn't late, but it was almost winter and already dark outside. The CIA man showed up at my door. With two Iranians. Who looked and smelled and glowered like secret policemen.

"Pack a suitcase. One suitcase. You have fifteen minutes," he told me. "Take what you really want, because you're never coming back here. Give me your passport."

He didn't explain. Until we were at the airport. In a deserted lounge in an outbuilding. Amid the stench of old tobacco smoke.

"You really screwed this one up, Romeo. You're lucky you're not going home in a box. Or a couple of boxes." He offered me a look of such intense disgust that I might have been a traitor to my country. Perhaps, in his eyes, I was. "You know what they did to her? To that kid? Her brothers cut her throat like she was a sheep or a goat. Took her out in the boonies and cut her throat. To protect the family's honor. Because of you, Casanova. Jesus Christ. Knocking up the daughter of the shah's right-hand man. Did you think you could just do anything you wanted?" He glanced at the two SAVAK minders across the lounge. "These people still have a sense of shame. Forget what you saw at those parties. Scratch one of these boys, and he bleeds the Middle Ages. And now I've got to get your sorry ass on a plane before her daddy changes his mind and you disappear. You're one lucky sonofabitch, Mr. Banks."

"Are you sure you're okay to drive?" Eli asked me.

"I didn't drink that much."

"That's not what I asked you."

17

Marilyn showed up early. I was changing out of my uniform and had to scramble. She was overdressed for a movie. Her red dress clashed with her auburn hair, but looked great, anyway. Hard red on white skin. Marilyn stayed out of the sun.

As always, she wore too much Shalimar.

Before she even stepped inside, she said, "We can take my car."

"Afraid mine's going to break down?"

I was only kidding, but jocularity wasn't part of the program.

"I only meant . . . Gene's worried about the expense, the gas. He doesn't want you paying. For my night out. He gave me money."

"Well, I'm paying. It's the least I can do. After all those dinners."

She cringed. I read the interpretation on her face: The evening was an obligation to me. Onerous. Worse.

"I've been looking forward to this," I lied. "Alone with the most beautiful woman in southern Arizona. I'm amazed Gene trusts me."

I got that part wrong, too. Marilyn didn't reply. She looked first-date nervous. It wasn't a good situation. For either of us.

"Like a drink?" I asked. "Before we hit the road."

She didn't want a drink. Then she smiled and told me, yes, she'd love a drink. White wine?

I opened a bottle of chardonnay. It didn't rival Eli's Meursault. Marilyn bolted the contents of her glass like a sergeant major confronted with free whiskey.

"I want you to know," she announced, "that I'm not blind. I know what's going on. With Gene. I know what he's doing tonight. Don't think I don't. May I have another glass of wine before we go?"

I poured. She drank.

"You're a good friend, Roy. To both of us. I know that. And we've put you in a terrible position. But I don't know what to do. I don't want to lose him. We don't have to go to Tucson. You don't have to take me anywhere."

"I want to go." I manufactured a grin. To reinforce my second lie. "With you. My dream date."

A smile cut her face and bled out.

"I'm going to have a lovely evening, then." She staunched her eyes with the back of a hand. "I refuse to let them ruin everything. *Her*. We really are good friends, aren't we, Roy? And we're going to have a good time, a wonderful time. Just give me a minute to fix my makeup."

Despite her prophecy of an enchanted evening, Marilyn grew sullen and treated her plate of enchiladas as if they were contaminated. I had chosen El Charro, Tucson's check-the-block Mex joint, for a quick dinner. Gene had advised me that she loved Mexican food. But her platter cooled in front of her, barely tasted. I ate my burrito, drank my beer, and felt shitty.

If Marilyn wasn't hungry, she was thirsty. She downed three family-size margaritas, fast. Her cheeks flushed, competing with the color of her hair, and her eyes grew unsteady. She turned heads when she went searching for the ladies' room, weaving past the corny paintings and posters, but I was just glad she didn't fall down the stairs.

On the way back to the car, she seized my arm. I couldn't tell if she needed to steady herself or meant to signal closeness. Her nails caught on the remaining scabs from the thorn scratches, but she didn't notice. Snug against me, her forearm drew sweat through my shirt. I smelled perfume and alcohol.

The movie was beautiful and interminable, an endless fashion-shoot for Roman Polanski's nubile muse of the moment. Midway through, Marilyn reached over and took my hand. The rough feel of my knuckles seemed to jar her, as if she hadn't noticed my paw on the steering wheel during our drive or, later, across the table. She decided to trace and pet the damaged flesh, then settled our entwined hands on the cloth of her skirt.

Now and then, she renewed her grip, pressing my hand against her.

I told myself that she was going through hell and needed a friend. I imagined what she was imagining. How could Gene be so blatant, so shameless? How could she let him? We never know what goes on between two other human beings. Was Gene showing some brute Italian side that Marilyn secretly liked? Was she one of those women who need a dose of misery now and then? Why didn't she stand her ground, why give Jessie free access? Was she just reeling?

My thoughts veered between the immediacy of flesh beneath thin fabric, an all-too-absent Nikki, and mundane worries about my map exercise for the captains. The students had just gone through day one, but I hadn't heard a word about the results. Gene hadn't seen fit to get in touch with me.

As the film rolled on and on, I began to resent everything, ready to blame Gene for whatever might go wrong, with either the captains or his wife. As for Nikki, she had meant it when she said she wouldn't see me. But I wasn't going to turn into Pete Paulson, spying on a woman from a darkened car. And Jessie could rot in hell.

The movie gave me too much time to think. Marilyn's grip on my paw made the muddle worse.

At last, Tess died. By the glow of the credits, Marilyn read her watch. "I didn't know the movie was so long. Is it too late to get a drink before we go back?"

I took her to a bar near the university. She had two more margaritas. Her calf and knee rested against me, as though she were unaware. She smiled more and talked less, slouching toward me. I was relieved to get out on the Interstate without her suggesting a stop at a motel.

I had fantasized about Marilyn in the past. But the flesh-and-blood woman remained Gene's wife. And I wasn't going to be part of the havoc toward which they seemed headed.

It's a terrible thing, though, to know you could have a friend's wife.

As we headed down the last, long stretch of blacktop, she said, "I can't help thinking about them together. I can't help seeing them doing things. I can hear what they're saying."

I opened my mouth to answer, then shut it again. I'd been thinking about Nikki and her husband.

After I parked in front of my apartment, we sat in the car a bit longer. As if something remained to be done, but we didn't know what. I broke the spell by getting out and opening her door.

When Marilyn unclasped her purse to dig for her car keys, Shalimar fumes escaped. She must have lugged a bottle along. I thought, again, that her mother, or a nun, or maybe an idiotic early boyfriend must have made a remark about girls' smells. Or just her smell. The claws of the past go deep.

She paused before settling behind the wheel. I wasn't going to ask her if she felt too drunk to drive. I just wanted her to go.

"You're a good friend," she said. And she hugged me. Not as friends do.

"I'm not as nice as you think I am," she said.

Things came apart on Thursday, at the gym. I didn't hear it from Gene. I overheard two faculty majors talking in the locker room. The new exercise for the Advanced Course had been a disaster. Colonel Bullitt had gotten involved. They'd already gone back to the tried-and-true scenario.

"What could Massetto have been thinking? Springing shit like that on them at the end of the course?"

"Gene just does what he's told. Jacoby must've been behind it. Haunting us all from the dinosaur graveyard."

As I was hurrying out, Jerry waylaid me. Still in his workout duds.

"We need to talk, man."

"No. We don't."

"Cut me some slack, brother. I can explain things. Let's link up for a few beers after work. My treat."

I was about to push past without another word, but couldn't resist a cheap tease. "Couldn't do it, even if I wanted to. I've got an interview with the SF recruiter tonight."

Jerry. Standing there. Dumbfounded. I almost reached the front door before he caught up with me.

"*You?* Special Forces? You kidding me?"

Riled by his tone, I stopped. Despite all that had happened, I'd planned to make a pitch to the SF rep in Jerry's behalf. Calculating that, if SF took him back, it would get him out of Huachuca. Away from Jessie. And all the rest of it. I knew how badly he wanted back in. It might save him, even now.

But nobody likes being insulted by a friend. Or an ex-friend.

"I'm on the interview schedule. Nineteen hundred. Check it out, it's posted in the orderly room."

"Come off it, Roy. You're not SF material. And you know it."

"Somebody thinks I am. Anyway, it's none of your business."

"Hey, I'm just trying to spare you the embarrassment," he said. "I'm telling you, man, as a friend. You'd never cut it. You'd just ruin your career trying. No matter what they tell you, you flunk out of the Q course, you're toast." His scowl rearranged itself into a forced good-old-boy grin. "You can blow it off. Nobody's going to get on you about it. Come out and have a couple of beers. Come on, man. The Officers' Club is overdue for a grand reopening. Let's say it was a temporary closure for renovations."

Seething and oblivious, I walked away.

I didn't hear from Gene that afternoon, either. But he would have been drinking out of a fire hose, overwhelmed by the labors involved in swapping out the exercise protocols halfway through. Wounded in pride and spirit, I still had to sympathize with him. Professionally, at least. It seemed so clear now, so obvious. Jacoby had been wrong. I had been wrong. We expected far too much. Of officers conditioned to expect little of themselves. We weren't going to change Military Intelligence. That would take a war. And there was no war.

Craving the least good news, one good word, I disobeyed Gene's order to stay away from the academic complex. I gave the exercise building a wide berth, but stopped by the faculty offices.

When she saw me, Staff Sergeant Munro spoke in her polite, on-duty tone.

"Captain Massetto's not here," she said, "if that's who you're looking for, LT." When I didn't reply, she inspected me more closely. "I mean, I can find him for you. If it's important. I think he's over with the captains."

"Thanks. Forget it." At least my failure wasn't broadly known. Still, I couldn't help feeling as if the whole post was laughing at me. I meant to turn and leave, but didn't.

She checked the dead space around her desk. We were alone.

"You look like you need a beer, Roy," she said. "Or several."

As I headed back to my car, I hoped against hope I'd see Nikki. Who would soon be gone. It wasn't beer that I needed. I didn't even like beer, really.

. . .

Jerry had made me so angry that I began to fantasize about really going SF. But I wasn't interested, and I knew it. I wanted to do intelligence work. Nonetheless, I stopped by for a not-yet-needed haircut on the way home. And after spit-shining my jump boots to black glass, I put on a fresh set of starched fatigues for the interview.

I expected the SF rep to be a clone of Colonel Jacoby: tall, broad shouldered, and mighty. He wasn't. Lieutenant Colonel Furstenberg was a compact man, almost a bantam-weight, who looked old for an LTC. Weathered. Distilled down. But his eyes were hard and alert, and his movements were crisp. There was no sense of evening weariness about him. A green beret lay upside down on the desk.

Checking my name-tape against his list, he pulled a file from the top of a small stack. He let me stand at attention while he took his time.

"All right. At ease. Sit down," he said. "You speak Farsi, Banks?"

It wasn't recorded on my Officer Records Brief. I'd kept mum about it.

"Yes or no? Simple question, Banks."

"Yes, sir."

"Why isn't it on your ORB?"

"It's a long story, sir."

"Give me the one-sentence version."

"I didn't want it on my ORB, sir."

"You spent almost two years in Iran."

"Yes, sir. How—?"

"It's in your security-clearance paperwork."

"I thought that was restricted?"

"That depends on who's asking. You interested in going SF, Banks? We need Farsi speakers. We might even be able to figure out a use for an archaeologist. If that part of your bio's accurate, too. We're not just cavemen, you know."

"I'm not sure how welcome I'd feel in Iran."

"If we go back, we're not waiting for an invitation. Desert One wasn't the last chapter."

"Sir, the real reason I came here tonight was to ask a favor."

That pissed him off 100 percent. I was wasting his time.

"Why would I do you a favor, Banks?"

"It's for a friend of mine. He used to be SF. As an enlisted man. But he's been branched MI as an officer. And he's desperate to get back into Special Forces. He's tried everything."

The lieutenant colonel drew in his brows. Bunkering his eyes. "Doesn't ring any bells. What's your hotshot friend's name?"

"Jerry Purvis. Gerald Purvis, sir."

For the first time, the officer behind the desk revealed a hint of human frailty, of brief surprise. Then he tightened up again.

"That what Purvis told you? Is that what he tells people?"

"Yes, sir. He wants to get back into SF. He can't stand MI, he thinks it's for wimps. He wants to get back to Central America, to El Sal."

The SF rep ran a hand back over the bristles atop his skull. Two fingers were missing, and the flesh looked burned. He sighed in disgust.

"Save your breath. Your buddy was offered a chance to come back to SF. Only because we're so far understrength. Staying MI's his decision. And, for the record, he was never in LatAm. Purvis was in 10th Group, assigned to Bad Toelz, Germany, as a radio man." He stopped himself from offering further details. "So we've wasted each other's time."

"Sir, nothing against SF, but I was ordered to come here."

"Yes, I know. Major Dinwiddie thought you had possibilities."

"*He* signed me up? Dinwiddie?"

His face pinked at my tone.

In a lowered voice, he said, "Why are you so shocked, Lieutenant? Is the major a joke among you? Just among the students, or the cadre, too?" His anger crumbled down into disgust. "Get out of here, Banks. An officer with your lack of judgment isn't Special Forces material."

I stood up, came to attention, and saluted. He ignored me. But before I reached the door, he snapped, "Hold it right there. About-face, Lieutenant."

When he spoke, I grasped that it wasn't for my benefit. He'd written me off. He was speaking for a man who wasn't present.

"I'll bet Leon Dinwiddie's good for a laugh when you're out with your buddies. Or whispering behind his back when he goes past. But you'll never be a soldier of that man's quality, Banks. I've already seen and heard enough to know. You and your breed think you're heroes because you can pass a PT test. But let me set you straight, Lieutenant. Leon Dinwiddie may be the bravest man I've ever met. And I've met some goddamned brave men. He should be wearing the Medal of Honor around his neck, only Congress stopped giving them out for Vietnam. So he had to settle for a Distinguished Service Cross. And he probably hides that."

He scalped himself with his disfigured hand again. "Know how he got it, Banks? He was an ARVN adviser, as a brand-new captain. Way out in the boonies with a Vietnamese battalion. Up in the Highlands, beyond the end of the world. There wasn't much support left, America had given up. Nothing left but a dwindling number of decent men ashamed that we were breaking every promise we ever made to the South Vietnamese. He was on a firebase with two companies out of that battalion. Understrength, of course. The ARVN outfits were always understrength. A full-up NVA regiment hit them. There was no way they could hold. Sheer numbers. The ARVN division got a couple of Hueys in there to evacuate the officers and any U.S. advisers. But Leon refused to go. The sonofabitch stayed there, with a half dozen South Vietnamese lieutenants who couldn't fit on the choppers with their superiors and a couple of hundred ARVN enlisted men who hadn't eaten a full ration since the day they put on a uniform. They held off an entire regiment for two days. Toward the end, Leon was running the battle blind in one eye and with one lung shot to shit, a dink medic working on one side of his body and Leon firing his M16 one-handed when the NVA got inside the command bunker."

He paused to turn his head from left to right, surveying ghosts. "He may have been the only officer in history who led a counterattack holding an IV bag in one hand. It's a miracle he was still conscious, let alone leading a fucking bayonet charge. And one miracle led to another, because the NVA quit. They just left. An entire regiment, we confirmed it through intercepts. They just pulled out. Leaving Captain Dinwiddie and the thirty or so surviving ARVNs all shot up and barely alive."

Lieutenant Colonel Furstenberg rose to his feet behind the desk. He barely came up to my shoulders. "He should've been medically retired a long time ago. But he fought it. One lung functioning, reduced vision in one eye. He just won't quit."

He considered me one last time. "I wonder why he wasted his efforts on you, Lieutenant Banks."

Gene finally got in touch with me after the end of the duty day on Friday. I didn't merit a visit, just a phone call.

"Thanks for the Marilyn thing," he said. "She said she had a wonderful time."

"She would've had a better time with you."

He laughed. But not much. "I'm not so sure about that. Anyway, she said you were a perfect gentleman. That you even insisted on sitting a seat away from her at the theater, for heaven's sake. She wasn't sure if you thought she was contagious or something."

Marilyn wasn't what I wanted to talk about. But I said, "She's a splendid woman. You should think hard about things."

I don't believe he thought about it, but he did wait a few breaths before telling me, "She and I just need some space, some time on our own. Wednesday night was good for her. I wish you'd consider making it a regular date."

"I'm not dating your wife, Gene."

"That's not how I meant it. You know what I meant. As a friend."

"If she ever needs company, let her call me. But no more setups. Okay?"

"Sure. She'll call you."

"Gene?"

"What?"

"This sucks. Marilyn's five times the woman and at least fifty times the human being Jessie is."

More breaths. Then: "I don't know what you have against her. I feel like . . . I feel like she's saving my life, as though I've been dead for years and I'm alive again now. You don't understand, Roy."

I didn't want to argue. And I couldn't take any more of it, of them.

"I heard about the exercise," I told him.

"It was just too hard. They couldn't cut it. They were completely lost."

"Christ, Gene. It's their job. It's what the Army's paying them to do. And we wonder why MI's got a piss-poor reputation."

"Nobody's criticizing your effort."

"For God's sake. If you kill everything I worked on, that's criticism. To say the least."

"You win some, you lose some. That's the Army. Just take it for what it's worth. Lesson learned, move on. And don't worry. Your special efficiency report's already written and signed and submitted. Top block."

"Bullitt signed off? And gave me a top block? He hasn't been here long enough to senior-rate me."

"It wasn't Bullitt. Dinwiddie senior-rated you. He talked Bullitt into letting him do it. Special circumstances. With Jacoby's death and everything. And he made the ninety-day requirement."

"Thanks. For that, anyway."

"Thank Dinwiddie. He really went to bat for you. I'll tell you another thing, too. He wants you out of here. For some reason or another. He's been calling the Hoffman Building daily to get an assignment pushed through for you. So . . . moving on to the next subject. You have big plans for the evening? Find a new female victim yet?"

"Gene . . . salvage what you can. From the exercise. It can be dumbed down, okay? But it's still miles above and beyond the old exercise. Save what you can. I put my heart and soul into it. I could help you."

It was an evening for awkward silences on Gene's end of the line. At last, he said, "It's all been erased. Destroyed. All the paperwork's in burn-bags. I'm sorry, Roy. Colonel Bullitt's orders. He wants them to do everything on computers in the future, anyway. We're going to have to simplify things even more."

In yet another act of cowardice, I called Mary Jane Munro.

"Mary Jane? It's Roy."

"At least it's Friday night this time."

"Interested in driving up to Tucson? As friends. I know places where nobody'd know us."

"Sorry, LT. I'm planning a hot foursome. Me, ABC, NBC, and CBS."

It was a blow to my ego. Which thrived, despite everything. "Guess I can't compete with that."

"Oh, you could. But it's not going to happen. If I'm going to go sneaking around, it's not going to be just to be pals with somebody who bleeds all over and won't tell me who shot him. Anyway, I don't sneak around. I'm done with that kind of thing. I learned my lesson on that one."

"I didn't mean it the way you took it."

"Men never do. Roy, please. Don't you get it? We're not going to be lovers. Because we can't be. *Keine Zukunft,* as the Germans say. It's against the regs, you're leaving, and the truth is I'm not pretty enough to hold you. Be honest. To you, I'd only be a Monday-nighter. Even on Friday. And if I can't be your lover, I'm not going to be your sister, or your sidekick, or the shoulder you cry on. If I'm going to have my heart broken, I at least want to get something out of it."

"You've been thinking about it," I said.

"And I'm going to stop now. Please just leave me alone."

I finished the bottle of chardonnay I'd opened for Marilyn on Wednesday. I was tempted to pull another cork, but didn't. I didn't like to drink enough to drink alone. And I didn't like myself enough to drink alone.

I struggled to read, but a new work on the post-Schliemann excavations at Troy defeated me. After that, I tried a mick novel I'd picked up, Liam O'Flaherty, brogues and rogues. Words on a page. Just dead words on a page.

I put on a Lester Young album, then took it off again. Finally, I went to the bedroom closet and fetched the two silk rugs Ali had left behind. I rolled them out on the living room floor. And I stared at them.

A little after ten, the doorbell rang.

It was Mary Jane.

"I'm going to be the Monday-nighter you never forget," she told me.

18

"**Don't let him drink too much,**" **Mary Jane said. "Pull him up.**"

I drew back on the reins. My horse resisted. I yanked his head up. Mary Jane clucked her mount back into action, splashing across the brown-water stream. Above us, a porcelain dome had replaced the sky. No real sky could be so perfect.

My rent-a-horse knew the trails and tried to brush my leg against a cactus. I wasn't the world's finest horseman, but had taken lessons during my enlisted time at Fort Hood. I was skilled enough to bully the horse back onto the path.

Mary Jane was in a different class. She *fit* her horse. In the saddle, she became part of a greater whole. With a bandanna around her forehead, Apache-style, and old brown cowboy boots, she looked more like a born-and-bred cowgirl than a miner's daughter. She rode as confidently as she made love.

We trotted along, then walked the horses down through an arroyo, careful not to overheat the animals. Clattering up the far bank, we climbed a low ridge and paused, looking south toward Mexico. The vista followed a bowling alley of desert, with a chain of mountains for pins across the border. The late-morning world held still. You could hear yourself sweat.

"You ride like you've got Indian blood," I told her.

Her horse didn't rear, but Mary Jane did.

"That's not a joke to my kin," she snapped. Then she smiled like a she-devil and slapped her horse with the reins. Cawing at the animal, she took off down a fire road at a gallop.

My nag turned into a rocket. I barely stayed in the saddle. Lengthening the distance between us, Mary Jane whipped her horse, yelling and laughing. She stopped looking back and just rode.

I found myself clutching the saddle horn, breaking one of the basic rules of horsemanship. The reins scraped the last scabs off my knuckles. Knees tucked in tight, I got low and hoped for the best.

A clod of dirt or dried dung struck my shoulder, stinging my face and neck as it exploded. My sunglasses flew off. I gave up all hope of impressing Mary Jane as I struggled to get my horse under control. The heat, not my fumbling with the reins, broke his pace at last.

A rifle-shot ahead of me, Mary Jane eased her mount down to a trot, then to a walk, finally wheeling about to amble back to me. As we neared each other, I saw green foam drip from her horse's mouth.

She drew up beside me, patting the sweat-glossed animal.

"Cherokee, my mom says. My dad doesn't like it, though. His folks were Klan."

We turned northward toward the stable that hid on the dirt road down from Sonoita. There was something new between us now, something good. Her one-woman charge had equaled out the difference in our ranks, but it was more than that. She had revealed herself, a big step for a woman who lived under self-imposed guard. My sunglasses went forgotten. Later, I imagined them on a coyote.

Mary Jane was better at silence than I was. Despite all my playpen Zen. I needed to speak, but really had nothing to say.

"You ride here every week?"

"Beats sleeping with people you don't like for recreation."

The horses plodded homeward.

"I hope I'm not in that category," I told her.

She laughed. Wonderfully. "At least you stayed on."

Stinking of horse, we tumbled into my bed. We had agreed that showers were essential, but lust shattered nice intentions. There was a great deal more galloping, and this time I kept up. When at last we lay side by side, rancid and too weary to hold each other, it struck me that this was my best day in months. Since my first flaming brushes with Nikki.

And Nikki was the problem now. I should have been content, even delighted, with the turn of events in my personal life. Mary Jane was a better match for me in every meaningful way, even sexually. She was grown-up, serious, and wild within hard-learned boundaries. Every single moment with her was good. But I couldn't stop thinking of Nikki.

There was no logic to it. I didn't even like Nikki very much. I could count our serious conversations on one hand, with fingers to spare for a peace sign. Her carelessness, personally and professionally, annoyed me. She was dishonest and irresponsible, and pity went only so far. The sex had been intense but undistinguished. Nikki was selfish, hard, and blithe. Yet, she haunted me as I fled inside Mary Jane's body. Nor was it her slap to my vanity that kept Nikki between us. I was sickened to grasp how deeply I was in love with her. Love, not war, is the sleep of reason that gives birth to monsters.

Had Nikki phoned me as we lay in bed, I would have dressed and gone to her.

The phone did ring while Mary Jane was in the shower. But it wasn't Nikki.

"Roy? How are you?" Marilyn asked. The question was a pure formality.

"Exhausted. But good exhausted."

She thought about that, briefly, then thrust ahead. "Gene said I had to call you myself, if I wanted to see you. So I called you. Are you busy?"

"Telephone busy?"

"As in tonight. I thought that you and I—"

"Marilyn . . . please. I can't be part of this. This is between you and Gene."

"It's *not* just between me and Gene."

"Between the two of you and her, then."

"It's not just that, either. You know that."

No. I didn't know that. For once, I knew better. "Come on, Marilyn . . . you know you're not interested in me. Not in the least. I'm just a handy prop. You just have to wait this out. Jessie doesn't do stable relationships. She'll dump Gene, too. Unbelievable as that may seem to you right now."

"He told me he's in love with her."

I didn't want any part of this. "Well, I doubt she's in love with him. True love isn't her style. I give it a month, at the outside."

"I'm lonely. I'm afraid."

"Marilyn . . . I'd like to help you. But the two of us going off together . . . no matter what we tell ourselves, it's just asking for trouble."

Wrapped in one towel and drying her hair with another, Mary Jane stepped out of the bathroom to stand before me. Brown arms, white shoulders. A wry smile.

"I thought you liked me," Marilyn said over the line. Her voice was a pouting child's.

"I do. That's not the point. Anyway, I've got plans for the evening."

That startled Marilyn. In misery, we reduce the lives of others to our own needs.

"But I thought . . ."

"It's somebody new." I met Mary Jane's eyes. "Somebody great."

I wasn't sure that either the woman on the phone or the woman standing before me bought what I had to say.

When Marilyn said, "Please call me, Roy," tears deformed her voice. I didn't believe for an instant that she wanted me. She just *wanted*.

As I bedded the receiver, Mary Jane said, "Has my presence become inconvenient, LT?"

"No. And knock off the 'LT,' okay?"

Her eyes told of past disappointments. "I can't help wondering what I've let myself in for," she said.

"Drop the towel and find out."

She stepped back. But gently. "Just be straight wth me. I don't expect anything. I mean, nothing but that. Just be straight with me, huh? I don't mind being a piece of ass, but I hate being made a fool."

"That was Marilyn Massetto. She and Gene are going through a bad patch. Thanks to everybody's favorite lieutenant. Marilyn's distraught."

Mary Jane sat down on the arm of a chair. The towel parted over crossed legs. Wet hair gleamed. "I may be just a country girl studying-up at Cochise Community College, but I know that *distraught* is just another word for *unscrupulous*, when it comes to women. Anyway, I told you Massetto's a jerk, that all his rah-rah Army stuff's a fraud. Oh, he keeps his hands off the students who come running after him. But I think that's because he's afraid. Career first, cunt second."

The obscenity jarred me. She wasn't one of those female NCOs who thought cursing lent credibility.

Instead of pulling the bath towel away, I sat down in an opposing chair. "I have no interest in Marilyn Massetto. I thought she was a knock-out, back when she was safe, when she was just Gene's perfect wife. But fantasy and reality don't make happy bedfellows." I tapped the arm of the chair, impatient with my inability to capture matters in words. "Anyway, I'm coming off a thoroughly screwed-up relationship that I still haven't figured out."

"Do you really need to figure it out?"

I summoned my honest-Injun face to meet Mary Jane's stare. "I'm trying to get things right, to get a grip on things. I do *not* intend to jerk you around. But I can't promise you that I won't screw everything up. I can only promise that I don't want to screw things up. I've been stupid, I'm still stupid, but I'm trying not to go on being stupid. And I recognize your value, I'm smart enough for that." A light went off, and I laughed. "I'm so fucking self-absorbed. What if I'm *your* Monday-nighter?"

"You'd be the best Monday-nighter I ever had." The drapes weren't closed, but she rose and dropped the bath towel on one of the Persian rugs. "You really want to get a grip on things?"

Before I could reach her, the phone rang again.

"Get it," Mary Jane said. "Or she'll just keep calling." She picked up the towel again.

I grabbed the receiver, ready to rip into Marilyn.

"Roy, please, I need help," Jerry said. "Don't hang up."

His voice sounded damaged. I wanted to slam down the phone. But I didn't. Instead, I grabbed Mary Jane and pulled her against me, roughly. I wanted her to hear the male voice on the other end of the line.

"Your quarter," I said.

"Please, Roy. I'm in trouble, man. I'm in serious trouble. I need you to help me."

"What kind of trouble?"

"I . . . I can't tell you about it over the phone."

"If this is more bullshit to do with Jessie . . ."

"No, no. *Please.* This is serious." Jerry had acquired a lisp. And the catch in his voice transmitted authentic fear. "It's life and death, brother. I need help."

"Where are you?"

"Hold on. Please don't hang up, man."

I heard faint voices, as if Jerry's hand had not quite covered the mouthpiece.

"Roy? You still there? I'm in Mexico. Okay? And it's not good. It's really bad, man. I need you to help me out."

"What the fuck? What am I supposed to do?"

"I need you to go to my trailer and get the Corvette. And the title. I'll tell you where it is."

"I thought you still owed big bucks on the Vette?"

"I paid it off, it's all paid off, it's clean, man. But I need you to go to the trailer. There's a front-door key back under the propane tank. It's in a Baggie, under the bottom of the tank. There's a white stone. Just pull it out. The key's right there. Go inside, go into the bedroom. There's a strongbox in the closet, it's green. Bust it open. Use a hammer or something. Just get the title, okay? Then I need you to drive the Corvette over to Agua Prieta. You won't have any trouble crossing the border, you know how they are going south. Just park in front of the church on the main plaza, okay? Just park there and wait. Somebody will come. Then they'll let me go."

"Jerry, this is fucked. You need to tell me what's going on."

He was crying. Unmistakably. "I can't, man. Not now. Not on the phone."

"So I'm supposed to put my ass on the line? For old time's sake?"

"*Please,* Roy. *Please.* You won't get in any trouble, I swear. You got to help me, man."

"And if I don't?"

He paused long enough to flinch, then said, "They'll kill me."

"And I was planning a candlelight dinner for two," Mary Jane said after I hung up.

"How much did you hear?"

"Enough. Too much. It was Purvis, right? You're crazy if you go."

"And damned if I don't."

"He's heap bad medicine, Roy. Trust a girl who knows how to read the label. You could ruin your career, if he's mixed up in cross-border stuff. Or it might be worse than just your career."

I sat back down. Just for a moment. "I don't want to do this. I don't want any part of it."

"Then don't. Call the police."

I had already considered that. And rejected the option. There were too many other people caught in the chain.

"You said you were trying not to be stupid anymore," Mary Jane reminded me.

"You need to keep this to yourself. You understand that, right?"

She laughed. Not happily. "Like I'm supposed to be here? Screwing a lieutenant? Anyway, I'm a hillbilly gal. We don't tell the revenuers anything."

I saw her from yet another angle. She really was great, with more spunk than an entire Ranger battalion. A trustworthy woman who gave more than she took, Mary Jane deserved better.

"The truth is, I'm afraid," I told her.

"As afraid as I was? The first time you called on the phone?" She shook her head and told me, "We're born suckers, Roy."

Before I left to pick up the Corvette, I called Eli at the record shop. He was closing up after another slow day. They were all slow days. I told him I needed his advice about something serious and urgent. He didn't push me for details, just said he'd be at the house by the time I reached Bisbee.

Jerry's alarm proved contagious. I liked to picture myself as cool under fire, but driving across the valley, I felt wired. I didn't know what I might be getting into, except that it was all bad. I hoped Eli would offer me wise counsel, but beyond that, I was so edgy, I nearly drove the Corvette right up to his door. Which would have tied him to the problem, had there been any surveillance checking license plates.

A block from his house, I realized how careless I had become. Fear doesn't always inspire caution. I turned around and parked down in the gulch. Walking back up the hillside, I tried to impose a semblance of discipline on myself, to organize my thoughts.

Eli greeted me by saying, "I suppose this visit doesn't call for charming background jazz?"

I shook my head. We sat down. I told him what I knew.

"This isn't good," he told me. "Give me a minute. Let me think."

"I'm not trying to get you involved. I can just leave."

He hushed me. "Just be quiet now, Roy. I really do need to think. And you do believe drug trafficking's involved, that's not just a wild guess?"

"More than a guess, less than an established fact."

He held up his hand: *Be quiet.* An air conditioner grumbled. Two flies air-danced. The evening thrust shafts of gold between amber shadows, enriching the perfect room. Eli had two things that rarely come in one package, money and taste.

"Okay," he said at last. "Let me make a phone call."

"Sammy Rodriguez?"

"I wouldn't dare call Sammy directly. Not on a matter like this. Roy? Would you mind waiting out on the porch? This is all a bit tricky."

I went out on the porch. And down the steps. At the bottom, I sat on a crumbling ledge of concrete. A terminal hippie shambled along, alerting just short of tripping over my shoes. He recoiled at my haircut, which must have screamed *Law enforcement!* But I wasn't on the right side of the law.

Trailing primitive scents, he loped off, mumbling.

Residual heat singed the air. A dog trotted about, sniffing. Cooking smells thickened.

Up on the porch, a door opened.

I stood. Eli waved me back inside.

"This is not good," he began.

"Your comrade-in-arms did something very foolish," Eli explained. "He trespassed. Apparently, he's a mule for the Tucson organization, for Mike Cervantes. He went down to Cananea to make a pickup in one of Mike's fleet cars, which was madness to begin with, then he tried to bring the load in through Agua Prieta. Which is not a part of Mike's allotted territory." Eli's expression was hard. The legal savage he had been in L.A. had taken possession. "This is all getting overheated. Cervantes isn't using good judgment. Unless he wanted to get rid of your friend, which is a possibility I've learned not to discount. Either way, somebody's going to end up dead. Sooner, rather than later. Probably more than one somebody."

"I don't want it to be Jerry. He's an asshole. But I don't want anything to happen to him."

"Something already has happened to him. These people play rough, Roy. I'm told that he's been taught a significant lesson."

"Can I get him back?"

Eli shrugged. "They say you can. Assuming that you yourself have no connections with Mike Cervantes you haven't told me about."

"I don't. Only that party."

"Then let's hope Sammy's people aren't holding the guest list. Look, I can't guarantee anything, you have to understand that. These are not gentle people. And you can't count on honor among thieves, that's a complete myth. But I've been assured, for what it's worth, that if you deliver this fellow's Corvette as instructed, things will work out. At least, you'll be able to drag what's left of your friend back across the border into Douglas."

"But they won't kill him?"

"They say they won't. Behavior can be erratic."

"Eli, I owe you. A lot."

"As a matter of fact, you don't. But it would be too hard to explain right now. Anyway, I put in a good word for you. And they know Sammy trusts me. They don't appear to have any interest in you. But be careful. You may find yourself in the presence of unstable temperaments. Don't overreact, don't complain, don't ask questions, and don't look into anyone's eyes for more than a few seconds. If you're asked any questions, keep your answers short. Be respectful but not craven. Most of these people are businesslike. But not all of them."

"I guess I'd better get going."

"What do you plan to do with your friend? If he's in bad shape. For that matter, how do you plan to get home? Afterward?"

"I haven't thought that far ahead."

"Wait a moment." He disappeared into a back room, reemerging with a scrap of paper. "Here. The Mexican police won't be a problem, but if our border-agent friends get curious, tell them he was in a fight. There are always fights on Saturday. Then take your friend to this address. Three blocks in from the border, you'll turn right. The address is a couple of streets down, he'll have to walk that far. It's an in-home doctor's office. I'll call ahead. Leave your friend with Dr. Lewis, he's used to this sort of thing. And your friend is going to need some serious repairs, I think you'll want to leave him overnight. I'll wait for you in the coffee shop of the Gadsden Hotel—you know it?"

"You don't have to get any more involved."

He sighed. "I've already crossed the line. It doesn't take much, Roy. And you're going to need a ride home. But I want you to promise me something."

"Such as?"

"That you'll cut all ties you have to any people who might be involved in this. Friends or not. The Cavalry doesn't always ride to the rescue, I'm afraid. In fact, it rarely does. I have yet to see a positive outcome among these people. So promise me."

"You didn't even have to ask. Believe me. I didn't intend to get this involved. And I damned well hate it."

"It's not about intentions, Roy. It's about choices. The road to Agua Prieta is paved with good intentions." He smiled. "See you at the coffee shop. I suspect you'll be hungry."

I rose to go. Changing the subject, I asked, "So what's with the long-sleeve shirts these days? Should I be reading the style mags in the barber shop more closely?"

His eyes grew troubled in the dying light. "It's a little skin problem, some spots. They embarrass my aesthetic sense."

19

The drug gang's chosen meeting place was anything but furtive.
Driving into the main plaza, with the Corvette's engine rumbling, I had
to slow to a pedestrian's pace. The citizens of Agua Prieta and their
country neighbors had gathered for the Saturday-night *paseo,* strolling
about to look each other over, waiting for surprises that never came.
Families paraded, young males strutted, and lazy, giggling girls flirted
and pouted. Kids hawked dirty candy, and *ranchero* music blasted from
tin speakers. Sagging strings of multicolored lights adorned the square,
an endless rehearsal for Christmas.

As directed, I parked in front of the church. The parking spot was
open, despite the slow-poke congestion of dusty sedans and chrome-
piped pickups. I sat in the heat with the windows down and waited. The
Corvette was a hit. Teenagers of both sexes were entranced, although the
family fathers pulled their daughters away, sizing me up as another
gringo on the prowl for prostitutes or poor girls full of dreams.

A kid with a filthy squeegee begged to wash my windows. Another kid
tried to sell me lottery tickets. Boys catcalled, while girls in overgrown
confirmation dresses preened. From the corner, a cop in military tan kept

an eye on me. I'd had enough experience with his brethren to assume he was trying to concoct an infraction that I could repair with five bucks. He watched me as if I were the most fascinating human being in Sonora.

A massive belt buckle dividing a dark shirt from blue jeans blocked my window. The guy had slipped up beside the automobile.

A voice said, "Get out."

I got out. Noting that the cop had disappeared.

My contact had a knife scar that began just below his hairline, crossed the bridge of his nose, and curved into his cheek. The original bad *hombre*. Doused with aftershave, he wore gorgeous cowboy boots with turquoise insets.

"Get in." He pointed to the passenger's side. "Over there."

He gunned the engine. Unnecessarily. Showing off. The local drug-sters didn't care much about anonymity.

"Donde esta mi amigo?" I asked.

"Shut the fuck up."

That settled that.

At least he didn't plow through the throng of moving flesh. He let the Vette throb low until we cleared the square and covered a couple of blocks. Then he hit the gas.

I had prepared myself to be blindfolded. But my new pal just stared straight ahead. I wondered if not being blindfolded might be a bad sign, an indicator that Jerry and I were both slated to disappear.

The driver pulled up before a typical neighborhood compound of the sort I'd seen on past forays across *la frontera*. Cinder block walls topped with cemented shards of glass hid all but the roofline of the house. A dented metal gate stood open.

"*Ándale,* fuck-face."

I got out and followed him. Another bad boy, fatter, lurked behind the gate. Scratching for lice or fingering a pistol under his armpit. The front door of the house opened.

The interior wasn't the squalid lair or torture chamber I expected.

The furnishings evoked Mexican middle-class respectability. The sofa and chairs wore prim lace bibs as protection against hair oil, antimacassars of the sort that had disappeared with Grandma's death north of the border. The only oddity was a Hawaiian hula-girl lamp.

Left to myself while Mexicans jabbered in another room, I tried to construct a confident facade. But the calm I mustered was fragile. It's easy enough to be brave when you're armed and flanked by buddies, but we're not all made of the stuff of Daniel when thrown into the lions' den alone.

I smelled ghosts of fried meat.

Another thug appeared, tall and wearing a spotless guayabera shirt. He checked me out, then motioned for me to follow him.

A half dozen men lounged in the kitchen, waiting for the additional Saturday-night entertainment. They had grown bored with Jerry.

He hunched on the floor in front of the sink, Quasimodo after fifteen rounds with Muhammad Ali. I had seen men beaten that badly only in movies. And that was all makeup.

Jerry looked up at me with the eye he still could open. Torn lips separated, but he didn't speak. There was space where teeth should have been. His shirt was ripped and stained, and he had blood-pissed his filthy khakis. I wasn't sure if his one-eyed stare was a plea or just stunned vacancy.

More rapid-fire Spanish, too quick for me. A silver-haired gent in an open-collared white shirt and black jacket asked, "You got the title?"

I nodded. "It's in the dashboard pocket."

He told an underling to go get it, then said to me, "You recognize this *maricón,* this piece of shit?"

"Yes."

He grinned. "Then I guess we didn't do our jobs." He translated that into Spanish. They all laughed.

Bad *hombre X* came back in with the title and handed it over. Silver-hair read it. Or pretended to.

He looked up. "Okay. *Muy* fucking *bueno*." He turned to a pair of his happy helpers and told them to get Jerry out of his sight. Addressing me again, he said, "Okay, Mr. Lucky. Take that piece of shit, if you want him. But I ever see him again, he's dead. You, too, for that matter. You tell Eli he just used up a lot of credit. He should know better."

The boys lifted Jerry, who had difficulty unfolding his arms and legs. He was a hefty load. They dragged him. I followed them outside.

A Ford pickup had backed halfway into the compound. With the help of the gate guard, they got Jerry into its bed. They motioned for me to climb in after him.

Gold tooth sucking light from a streetlamp, one of the peasants and workers smirked and asked me, "Hey, maybe you and your buddy want to stop for some tacos, huh? Or you looking for girls, maybe?"

Bantering in Spanish as his friends laughed, he and the other thug on the work detail climbed into the cab.

"Can you talk, man?" I asked Jerry.

He didn't answer. Instead, he shut the eye that still worked. Squeezing out the pain. He looked bad.

Riveted by his smashed face, I hadn't noticed back in the kitchen that all the fingers on his right hand had been broken.

He grunted, then said, "Water." I think that was the word. His enunciation was less than perfect.

"You have to wait. First, I need to get you across the border. Then you can have all the water you want."

Two blocks short of the border crossing, the pickup turned off and parked out of the line of sight of any officials. Our escorts left the motor running while they leapt from the cab and came back to yank Jerry to the ground. He hit the sidewalk hard.

My watch caught the joker's interest. He grabbed my wrist to take a better look. I jerked free.

"I think maybe you should leave that here, man. Donate it to the poor. I'll give it to the priest for you."

"No," I said.

His buddy looked on in silence.

"What shit's that, telling me no? You cocksucking *maricón*."

"*No* means 'no.'"

I wasn't going to give up the watch—Fatima's watch—without a fight. But I felt like an idiot for not leaving it at home. I'd had other things on my mind. And the watch had become part of me.

Jerry groaned. He wasn't going to be much help in a slugfest. I didn't think that I could take the two of them. Probably not even one. They were serious *hombres*. But I intended to fight. And that meant I had to knock down the one closest to me fast.

Just as I tensed, the driver said, "Carlos. *Vámonos*. It's probably a fake, man."

Carlos stepped back. Smoldering. He gave Jerry a last kick below a shoulder blade.

As soon as the pickup disappeared, I knelt beside Jerry. Resting a hand on his forearm. His own watch was missing.

"Jerry? I need you to walk. It isn't far. But you've got to walk now."

His eye opened again. "Ssshh . . ."

"What are you trying to say, man?"

"She . . . Jessie . . ."

"Jessie's not here. I need you to get up. I'll help you, but you've got to walk across the border."

"She set me up."

Jerry was enough of a soldier to struggle to his feet. But he needed to lean on me to shuffle along. Heavy with muscle, he was the human equivalent of a duffel bag filled with wet sand.

Up ahead, the lights of the twin border stations shone brighter than the towns on either side of the line. Jerry grunted in pain. We stopped to rest. I felt anger, not sympathy. I had broken plenty of Army regs in the battle of the sexes, but had never knowingly broken a single law that didn't have to do with posted speed limits. I *believed* in the law. And I meant to do better regarding the regulations. For all my self-dramatization as an untamed spirit, I was an organization man at heart, a born cog in the machine. As my father had been in his machine. And I didn't want anything to spoil it.

My fury didn't stem so much from the prospect of being arrested. I was outraged at being set up myself. If Jessie had pulled some stunt on Jerry, what had he done to me?

And he'd lied to me. About the great soldier he'd been in Central America. When he'd spent his Special Forces years at *Oktoberfest*. He'd duped me into admiring him, into wanting to be the soldier I thought he was. He'd duped me almost as badly as I'd duped myself.

"Get your shit together," I told him. "If there's any explaining required, let me handle it."

Bloody-mouthed, he mumbled.

"Buck up. Straighten up," I told him.

Jerry was struggling. Hurting. And that was fine with me. I should have felt some pity, some human solidarity, despite everything. But it was all I could do not to shove him into the gutter and walk back across the border by myself.

Glad to repatriate trouble, the smirking Mexican border cops let us pass. In the hours of darkness, you had to walk through an enclosed turnstile. Metal bars divided it into pie slices. I loaded Jerry into the first space and shoved him along. On the other side, he clung to a pole until I could work myself under his arm again.

I realized that I'd forgotten a basic question.

"Jesus. You have any ID? They take your wallet?"

He didn't seem to understand. Then he said, "Uhhh."

"What?"

He crimped his battered head toward his right side.

Alone behind a chest-high counter, a U.S. Border Patrol agent watched us through a window. He seemed to be pulling duty for his Customs counterpart, too.

I worked to keep Jerry upright while reaching to search his pockets. The Mexican glee club had not been interested in his wallet. Or, more likely, they'd put it back. After going through it and taking anything of interest.

He still had his military ID and a driver's license.

Inside the glass door, air-conditioning hit us. Jerry twitched, as if splashed with cold water.

The Border Patrol officer had no interest in our IDs. He'd seen it all before. Shaking his head, he asked, "When will you boys ever learn? What the hell happened this time?" He sounded mildly annoyed, not deeply curious.

"Bar fight," I told him. "I wasn't there when it happened."

"Well, I hope you were wearing a rubber when you weren't there. He need an ambulance?"

"No. Thanks. I've got him."

"Get that eye of his checked. Tonight."

"Yes, sir."

And that was all there was to it. We made it out into the lukewarm night. Back in the Land of the Big PX.

"Keep it together now," I told Jerry. "We have a couple more blocks to go. I've got a doctor set up for you. Private practice. Discretion for dollars."

He grunted. It might have meant "thanks."

The urge to dump him on the sidewalk and leave struck me again. I wanted to shout at him, to tell him I knew he was a fraud, bullshit from top to bottom. But I was determined to do my duty. Right to the end.

"Kill her," he said.

"What?"

"*Kill her*. I'm . . . going to kill her. Bitch. Dirty bitch."

"Yeah, well, you're not going to kill anybody for a while, hero."

A stumpy Mex gal bearing two brown grocery bags got a danger-close glimpse of Jerry and scurried toward the border. Headlights slashed us. The drivers and their passengers were duly cautioned: It ain't all señoritas and margaritas south of the line. They should have put Jerry's face on a warning billboard.

I wanted to tell him he'd betrayed me. That he was worthless. And a criminal. Who'd made me an accomplice. I would have liked to let him drop, then to punch him and kick him myself. But I didn't do it. Not because I was too good a human being. Because I just wanted to escape as cleanly as possible.

The doc's home office was in a frontier Victorian. The porch lights were on. It didn't appear that the medicine man enjoyed a booming practice. His shrubs were dead or dying, and the porch needed paint.

I shifted Jerry onto a rusty glider. The metal shrieked. He looked horrific under the overhead light. I rang the bell.

As soon as I heard footsteps, I turned away.

"You're on your own now," I said to Jerry. "We're quits."

When I entered the hotel coffee shop, Eli smiled. Relieved to see me. But concern rumpled his forehead as I approached his booth. He pushed a strand of hair behind an ear.

"You have blood on your shirt."

I looked down. He was right. I shrugged. "It's from Jerry. He's a mess."

"But alive?"

"More or less. I left him on the doc's porch."

Eli nodded, sighed. "Well, I suspect the locals are accustomed to a few bloodstains on Saturday night. Have a seat."

I was starting to come down from the ordeal. And I ached. My neck and shoulders had congealed into cement after lugging Jerry. I closed my eyes, then opened them again, renewing the universe.

Still-life of a half-eaten cheeseburger and an untouched portion of fries.

Eli followed my stare. "My appetite's been off lately. So unlike me. And I do *so* like the cheeseburgers here. I mean, I like to *order* them. It makes me feel so American. Not that they're very tasty. But you must be *starved.*"

A waitress appeared. Young. Not bad. A little plump. Trapped.

I ordered two cheeseburgers and an iced tea.

The waitress swayed off. I said, "Thank you."

Eli waved it away. Embarrassed by gratitude. "You know this hotel?"

"I've been here."

"How grand it must have seemed in its golden years! The Gadsden was the finest hotel between Tucson and El Paso—did you know that? When the West was adolescent and railroads mattered. I *do* wish someone would rescue the lovely old girl, I really do. Have you seen the stained-glass windows above the staircase, Roy? I've fantasized about fixing her up myself. But the money wouldn't stretch, and I'd lose interest. Besides, I'm not the hotelier sort. I've spent quite enough of my life cleaning up other people's messes."

"Again tonight."

"That was a pleasure. To do a good deed for someone I like. I should have done more good deeds. They're very satisfying, you know."

"The people on the other side aren't happy with you. An old guy with silver hair laid it on pretty thick."

"Oh, that was just Reynaldo. He dislikes my inclinations so vocally that it makes me wonder about his own desires."

"He sounded serious."

"He *is* serious, Roy. But I'm not concerned. I've made a decision, actually. I'm leaving Bisbee. Paradise has been a disappointment. The serpents just follow you around, there's no escaping them."

"I'm sorry."

He brightened. "For what?"

The waitress dropped off my burgers. They looked classically bad. But I was cowboy hungry. I reached for the ketchup.

"I'm sorry it didn't work out."

"Oh, but it *did*. It allowed me to think. And we became friends, didn't we? Isn't *that* worth something?"

It had been worth more to me than it had been to Eli.

"So you're going back to L.A.?"

"It seems I may have to. I've developed a health problem that baffles the Tucson medicos. My spots." He lifted a long-sleeved arm slightly off the table, hinting but not revealing. "And I seem to have less energy. Which . . . brings me to a selfish request, Roy."

"Something I can do?" The burgers were bad, indeed. I gobbled them. As the waitress paraded by, I resisted the temptation to reach out and tug open the big bow atop her ass. Surviving danger, real or imagined, moves us in complex ways.

"Perhaps." Eli looked down at his own dead food. "I don't know how these things work in the Army, taking days off. Or even if you'd be willing—you *must* be honest with me. But I'm scheduled for a series of tests up in Scottsdale. Next Thursday. It's a long drive and . . . well, driving back, after the tests . . . I thought perhaps . . ."

"You need a lift? That's all?"

"It would help me, Roy."

"It shouldn't be a problem. I've finished my project for the schoolhouse—which is another story—and they're looking for busywork for me while I wait for my orders to come through. I'm pretty sure I can take a day or so of leave. I'll check first thing Monday morning."

"It's good of you." To my surprise, his eyes glistened. He really was a lonely soul.

"It's nothing. *De nada*. After tonight. And I don't mean that I'm just paying a debt, Eli. Glad if I can help. I hope the medics sort out whatever's wrong."

He laughed. "Oh, physically, I'll manage. That should be the easy part. Thank God for modern medicine, Roy. But I do think that I'll need to go back to L.A. The care's *so* much better. And I've had a letter, terrible news. When it rains, it pours. My old flame, my little Kurt. The love of my life, to be honest. It appears that he's dying, of some odd form of cancer." Eli smiled, wistful, damaged. "I wonder if my own little aches and pains aren't a sympathy offering? What a terrible force love is, the way it possesses us and just *rampages* over us. I've had to accept that I'll never stop loving him, that there's no running away from it, no exile sufficiently far removed from wherever Kurt may be." He attempted a smile. "If I sound sentimental, forgive me. But I *am* sentimental."

"I thought he treated you badly?"

"He *did,* Roy. Shamefully badly. But he's alone now, our old friends seem to have deserted him. He must be in a bad way. So I think I shall be welcomed. Instead of a hard-hearted lawyer, I'll be a nurse. Once I'm back in shape myself." He mused on that. "It's selfish of me, really."

"Love eats shit."

He sucked in his cheeks, then laughed out loud. "Well, *that* rather takes the romance out it." We sat for a moment, staring into our different worlds. Then he said, "I've been thinking a great deal, Roy. About your story. And mine. The difference between us is that I deserve to be punished, but you don't. Wait a moment. Listen. Please. He who pays for the cheeseburgers—as I shall—delivers the sermon."

"You gents like coffee? Pie?"

Two coffees.

"During my years as a henchman for the famous, I did evil. Not inadvertent evil. *Knowing* evil. Evil for hire. That's a terrible sin, Roy. Even if there's no god, there's still sin. I see that now. And it has nothing to do with what passes for morality among the pharisees. I'm speaking of the man or woman who knowingly does evil, the man or woman who has a choice, but chooses evil . . . we're the damned, the souls beyond all hope." His smile warmed. "Kurt hurt me. Quite badly. At times, he took a mischievous pleasure in it, too. But he had a child's mind. And children do harm, not evil."

The coffee appeared. It was worse than the cheeseburgers. How the West was lost.

"For a very different example, look at yourself and that Iranian girl," Eli continued. "You didn't voluntarily and knowingly do evil to her. You didn't even do inadvertent evil. You did her thoughtless harm. You were callous, careless . . . self-centered, to be sure. But you did not intend to do evil, did you? And intent matters, you see, in our sins as much as in the crimes we try in court. Of course, intent's not the only factor . . . but premeditated murder is a very different thing from involuntary manslaughter. That's why they have different sentences."

He paused to think, perhaps remembering a particular case. His silence forbade interruption. "What that girl's brothers did to her was evil. Even if done in anger, in passion. It was unnatural . . . evil of the most fundamental kind . . . the evil that lurks behind the hedges of love, the evil wrapped in piety, the evil gleaming in Abraham's raised knife." He sighed. The sound was a prematurely old wheeze. "What you did, on the other hand, was foolish. Now, foolishness may create the opportunity for evil to be done . . . but it strikes me that you were simply young, with all that youth implies—not least, obliviousness of the price that others might have to pay for your transgressions. The girl's tragedy—what was her name? Fatima? Yes, Fatty. I remember. Well, her fate was certainly a tragedy for her, but for you it was no more than a misfortune. You must accept that. The weight isn't evenly distributed in life. The scales are always rigged, one way or the other."

He sat back, closing his hands on the lip of the table. As if steadying himself. "Why do I bring all this up? Because we both have regrets. But only I can claim authentic sins. You made a serious mistake. But that's what it was, a *mistake*. And there's nothing you can do to rectify it, is there? Has your self-mortification helped your Fatima in the least? Do you imagine you could ever pay her back? Or bring her back? It's up to God to raise the dead, if he's up to the trick. Meanwhile, it's simply morbid to live with corpses. You've done your penance . . . and even that had no value to her, only to you." He leaned toward me, as earnest a man as I have ever known. "Don't make a cult out of a mistake, Roy. It's self-indulgent. And ugly. And useless."

Eli reached across the table and closed a hand over my fist. His grip was alarmingly weak. "Accept the gift of life. And live."

He eased back into the booth, exhausted. As bleak as her border town, the waitress came by again.

"Everything okay with you two gents?"

20

Mary Jane postponed the dinner she'd planned until Sunday evening. That day, I ran up the canyon in the morning, then extended my route to trot past the BOQ where Nikki holed up. I didn't see her.

Later in the day, I found an excuse to drive by the BOQ. Hoping, like a smitten teenager, just to catch a glimpse of her. I didn't.

Her graduation ceremony was on Tuesday. After that, she'd be gone. Perhaps on the same day.

I didn't phone her. It wasn't that I was too proud. I was afraid.

It couldn't end like this. With less than a whimper.

But it would. I masked my distraction when I showed up at Mary Jane's apartment. I was good at dissembling in matters of the heart when my own heart wasn't engaged. Perhaps I had learned too much back in Iran.

I expected Southern cooking, mountain-style. Maybe fried chicken. Or a pot roast.

Mary Jane made steaks she couldn't afford.

. . .

On Monday morning, I went to the faculty building to ask Gene to initial off on my leave request for Thursday. Guarding access to the offices as always, Mary Jane sat at her desk. Prim and proper from a distance, she looked distressed up close. And seeing me didn't help.

Glancing around to see if we were reasonably alone, she said, "Morning, LT."

"Howdy, Sarge."

She shifted a file from the center of her desk to her out-box. "Lieutenant Purvis is in the post hospital."

"I don't care. It's none of my business."

"Broken facial bones, broken collarbone, broken fingers."

"You forgot the missing teeth."

"They weren't in the report. His story is that he got jumped in Mexico."

"Like I said. None of my business."

"Just thought you might want to know how things stand." She looked beaten down. Utterly different from the woman whose bed I had left just hours before. She had pulled her hair back so severely into its duty-day knot that it strained the flesh on her temples. When last I saw it, that hair had been a lovely catastrophe on her pillow.

I checked for unwanted eyes and ears, then bent over her desk.

"What's wrong?"

She looked away. "I'm being stupid. I knew it was coming. What was I thinking?" She straightened her posture, growing businesslike. Or struggling to. Pulling a stapled sheaf of official papers from a folder, she thrust the packet toward me. "They came over from the orderly room this morning."

My orders. I scanned past the symbols and codes to get to the heart of things. I was being assigned to the Field Station Sinop, our strategic listening post in Turkey, up on the Black Sea. Sinop worked the Soviet problem. And now the Iranian one. I had a reporting date less than three weeks away.

"I've never seen them do that," Mary Jane said. "They always give you at least a week or so to out-process and time for a month's leave before you head overseas."

I was stunned. It was not the assignment I had expected. SIGINT wasn't my military specialty. And I wanted to go back to the dirty-boots Army. To Germany. Or Korea. My dream-sheet hadn't listed any field stations or other strategic assignments. I wanted to be a soldier, not a paper-pusher.

"Either they want you pretty bad, or somebody wants to get you out of here pretty bad," Mary Jane said. She thought for a moment. "Or *you* want to get out of here pretty bad."

Gene signed my leave request. He didn't even ask what it was for. He had seemed harried by work when I walked in, but as I turned to go, he grabbed his cap and walked outside with me. Which gave me no time to assure Mary Jane that Turkey had not been my idea.

She put on her stern NCO face as we walked past. I must have looked glum myself. I didn't want to hear any more of Gene's lovelorn bullshit.

We huddled in the shade on the side of the building. He started off mildly enough. Bait-and-switch.

"What's the story on Purvis?"

I shrugged. "I hear he got beat up in Mexico."

"You with him? When he got beat up?"

"No." That was an honest answer. Technically.

"What was he up to?"

I lifted my shoulders and dropped them. "We've had a parting of the ways."

"I thought you were conjoined twins?"

"You thought wrong, sir."

"He's in bad shape."

"That's his problem."

Gene folded his arms and considered me. At last, he said, "Well, you might be better off staying away from him for a while. This doesn't feel right. Although the chain of command finds his story convenient."

"That all, sir?" I knew it wasn't.

He glanced at the manila folder in my hand. "I hear you got your orders."

"Sinop."

"Plenty of officers would love that assignment."

"I'm not a SIGINT type." I shrugged again. "I'll make the best of things. It was just a surprise. I was thinking S-2 in a line battalion."

"Those your orders?"

I offered him the folder. Gene studied the arcane codes. And looked up. "Your position's coded for a Farsi speaker."

"It's not on my ORB. Somebody figured it out."

"Where'd you learn Farsi? You never told me about that."

"In another lifetime."

He opened his mouth to ask another question, then decided to get to the point. Even in the shade, the heat crowded against our bodies. Sweat-stained, Gene was even handsomer than in cool repose. It was obvious why the female officers swooned. But I saw him differently now.

"Break, break," he said. "I need to ask you one more favor."

"I can't."

"You don't know what it is."

"I have an idea."

"I need somebody to look after Marilyn for a bit. You're the only one she trusts. The only one *I* trust."

"Gene, please. I can't do this. And it's not just me. You're putting her in a horrible situation. I mean, she knows. About you and Jessie. She's not blind."

"I know she knows. I told her. But that's not the point. I need time. I need to work some things out. I need . . . look, couldn't you just take her to Tucson one more time? Just one more time? Get her out of here for a few hours? There's a concert, at the university."

"Gene, for Christ's sake. This isn't just playing with fire. It's playing with nuclear weapons. You're ruining a good marriage. She's still crazy in love with you. You're throwing both your lives away. And for what?"

"What would *you* know about a marriage? What does anybody know about anybody else's marriage? I told you how unhappy I've been. Don't you understand anything that I told you?"

"I know what you have is in danger of being destroyed by the most dishonest and worthless woman I've ever met. Gene, you're soiling yourself."

He reddened. With hints of purple. "I don't want to hear that kind of talk. From you, or from anyone else." Battling his temper, he continued: "So you won't do me this last favor?"

"No."

He looked ready to throw a punch. Instead, he pivoted as sharply as a sergeant major on parade. "That's 'No, *sir*.'"

Pete Paulson had parked his car beside my Mustang. He got out from behind the wheel as I walked up. Smiling the smile of the Saved.

"Roy! I hope you're having a blessed day. I heard your friend was beaten up. Lieutenant Purvis, I mean."

"That's what I hear, too. And he's not my friend, for what it's worth."

He folded his arms across his chest, but smiled as if presented with something delicious. "Mexico's a bad place."

"So I hear."

"They're all oppressed by Rome. That's why they're so violent. And downtrodden. And uneducated. The Church of Rome likes keeping them that way. Damned in this life *and* the next."

"But you've been saving them, right?" The heat was massive, more August than May.

"That's right. They long for the unfiltered love of Jesus Christ."

"Sounds like a cigarette."

He tut-tutted. "Roy, I don't know why you always have to play the devil. When you do so much good for other people."

"Of that, Pete, I am blissfully unaware. Although it's a nice thought."

He took off his baseball cap just long enough to wipe the sweat from his forehead back into his crew cut. "Well, you set me straight, for one thing. Not about faith, of course. The things of this world. I needed that talking-to. To see the difference between that which I desire and that which I require, between selfishness and duty."

I tried to recall which talking-to he could have meant.

"Anyway," he said, "congratulate me!"

"Congratulations, Pete. For what?"

"I'm getting married."

I must have done a Three Stooges double-take. The last time I'd tuned in, Pete had been stalking Jessie Lamoureaux.

"To a wonderful girl," he went on.

"Do I know her?" I asked. Warily.

"Oh, I don't think so. I mean, I'd be surprised. She's Mexican, she's really sweet. She's from Hermosillo and she wants to convert, to abandon the graven images of Rome for the redeeming light of Jesus Christ, our Lord and Savior."

"Well, that's great. Love at first taco. I hope you're very happy together." I didn't want or need to know any further details. But Pete stood there, five feet six of quivering expectation: Share the joy.

I dredged up what conversation I could. "So . . . how did you two meet? On one of your evangelizing trips?"

"Jessie introduced us," he told me.

I didn't go to the hospital. I really was finished with Jerry. As a friend and as a comrade. I was angry at myself, but not about neglecting him. On the contrary. According to Army regulations and the law, I was obliged to rat him out. But I still couldn't see myself doing that. The old enlisted code of not telling the officers anything you could avoid telling them still had a grip on me. Even though I had been transformed into an officer myself.

I told myself that Jerry already had gotten the punishment he deserved, between the beating, the loss of the Corvette, and his missing Rolex. I hoped it would be a lesson to him, that he'd be scared or sobered enough to turn his back on everything to do with Mexico. Or with Jessie.

As for her, I couldn't help being curious about Jerry's insistence that she had set him up. It was human nature to wonder about the details. But I wasn't going to pursue it. I was done. With all their tawdry crap.

And it was too grim to game out her motives for delivering a bride to Pete. I wrote off his Mexican betrothed as a hustler in on the game. Big brown eyes, full lips, and a freebie Bible. Poor Pete.

But the situation was funny, too. I couldn't help smiling.

And I needed something to smile about, with Nikki about to leave. I tried to force myself to think exclusively about Mary Jane, who was so right for me in so many ways. But it just didn't work. I recalled Nikki's flesh against mine and shuddered as I drove over to the orderly room to turn in my paperwork for the day of leave and pick up my out-processing checklist.

Outside the company headquarters shack, a contingent of newly arrived lieutenants stood loosely in formation, answering to the first sergeant's roll call. One class out, another on the way in. Despite all our little dramas, the Army went on.

Merrily voracious, Mary Jane gasped, "I'm going to get my money's worth before you leave. *There. Like that.*"

The phone rang. I let it go. I wasn't convinced that Alexander Graham Bell had done humanity such a great favor.

After a clumsy, laugh-addled, mixed-ranks shower, I made us a pride-of-Cincinnati omelette for our dinner. The phone rang again.

I ignored it again. A proper omelette demands attention. And Mary Jane deserved every attention. She sat at the table in my old robe, drinking a beer from the bottle. Hair streaming, she had undergone her regular fairy-tale metamorphosis from a no-nonsense NCO into a woman who bore no stamp of the U.S. Army.

We didn't get to the dirty dishes immediately. Mary Jane really did want her money's worth. Later, I cleaned up while she dressed. She had to go home to study for her class the next evening at the community college. Practical in most ways, she had chosen to study business administration.

"You're going to have to change those sheets," she said. "They're soaked."

She kissed me, sweetly, and left.

The phone rang again. I picked it up, figuring the alternative was a succession of calls through the night. And I could hear my mother's voice warning, *It might be important.*

It wasn't important. At least, not to me. It was Marilyn Massetto. If she wasn't hysterical, she was close.

"He's going to leave me. He's going to leave me for her. I can't stand this." She rambled on in that vein, punctuating her soliloquy with sobs. She claimed she needed a friend, but she didn't need a conversational partner. Just an ear.

I let her cry herself out, failed to soothe her, and told her, after an hour with the phone biting my ear, that I needed to go to bed.

I watched Nikki cross the stage to receive her graduation certificate. She looked like a kid playing dress-up. Her Class A uniform didn't fit her, and she hadn't spent the money to have it tailored. Nor did she look particularly attractive.

But I could taste her. And feel her. And smell her.

I stood in the back of the small auditorium, along with stray faculty officers, and watched the handover of the certificate and the handshake. Nikki smiled vacantly at the colonel doing the honors. None of the faculty crowd commented on her. She had not made an impression. On anyone but me.

She saw me and didn't try to pretend she didn't. She met my eyes, then calmly looked away.

I didn't know her. I began to grasp that now. I had thought her simple. But none of us are simple. She slept with me and held fast to her husband. She wanted to give her life for a poetic highwayman, but wouldn't part with a quarter. Confounding the old maxim that the Army doesn't care about you, she cared less about the Army. She was slight, selfish, and untrustworthy. And I loved her.

Intellectually, I understood her unwillingness to stage a grand goodbye. She had to leave me behind. And everything that went with me. The abortion was bound to be rippling down deep in her being. Or was it? Did she feel much of anything beyond the immediate pleasure of getting fucked? I couldn't say with certainty. I didn't know her.

Too proud, or perhaps too afraid, to be a pest, I didn't try to force a last encounter. I milled around long enough to give her the opportunity to talk to me, if she wanted to. She didn't.

She chatted with her peers, one among many, all of them young and shining and about to meet the real Army at last.

My last glimpse of Nikki was blocked by one of her classmates.

After the ceremony, I drove up to the finance office to continue out-processing. I spotted Jerry limping down the sidewalk by the PX parking lot. He looked like the Hunchback of Notre Dame. I was surprised that the Army doctors had shoved him out of his hospital bed so soon.

He saw my car. I didn't stop to offer him a ride.

· · ·

My lunchtime workout didn't help. Reason didn't help, either. I thought of Nikki through the afternoon into the evening, imagining her already headed to Tucson and the flight back to her husband. It was useless to tell myself what a poor sap the guy was, with his new wife an easy mark for casual sex. I couldn't see a grand future before them, that was certain. The marriage was doomed.

But soon she would be in his bed, not in mine.

I wouldn't see Mary Jane, either. On Tuesday and Thursday evenings, she had her classes at Cochise Community College. A woman with a plan, she was determined not to end up back in eastern Kentucky. She joked about her escape, hamming up her accent to tell me, "Never even been romanced by close-up kin." But when it came to constructing her new life, she had a side harder than the coal her father and granddad had mined. She had her future mapped out for years ahead. I was just a detour.

I changed into a pair of cut-off jeans, made myself a salad with canned tuna, then tried to read. *Fire in the Minds of Men* was a brilliant book, although James Billington didn't convince me that Saint Just was a "just saint." Not terribly comforting stuff, of course. And not nearly so powerful as Nikki's ghost.

I wished that I had taken more photos of her.

It was almost ten, and I hadn't read fifty pages. But I wasn't ready to sleep, either. I closed the book and stared down at the silk rugs I'd been too lazy to roll back up. Mine, and not mine. I recalled how, in my apartment in Tehran, I'd look at them and wonder about the fingers that had tied all the microscopic knots. Children were put to the work early, because their fingers were small and nimble. But these rugs had not been made by children. They were masterpieces, valuable. Ali must have had a lot of unwanted baggage in his soul to track me down and return them. But what could he have expected from me? The mullah who had given me Farsi lessons was fond of saying "We all make our own devils in our lives." But he was wrong. We *are* devils.

The doorbell rang, followed by a woman's knock.

It was Marilyn Massetto. In a short skirt and gripping tank top. Her face was puffy from weeping, but her makeup was fresh. Despite the heat, her red hair hung down on her shoulders.

"Please let me come in," she said.

I made way for her. She passed close by me, trailing her usual Shalimar cloud and brushing hands over her skirt. As if drying them on the fabric.

I didn't want to see her. In fact, I dreaded it. She was unwelcome in my apartment. She and Gene had made themselves unwelcome in my life. I had problems of my own.

"You shouldn't have come."

She clasped her hands before her waist. Shackling her fingers together. Squeezing the blood from her knuckles.

"I want you to make love to me," she said. Her voice was frightened and petulant.

We stood, apart, looking at each other.

"I wanted you to make love to me the night we came back from Tucson," she insisted.

I shook my head. "Come on. You don't want me, Marilyn. You want Gene. And we both know it."

"I want *you*. And you want me. You've wanted me for years. I could always tell. No woman on earth could've missed it. And I wanted you. But I was afraid. Now I want to feel you inside me, to take you in my mouth. I've always wanted it, too. I'll do anything you want. Anything . . ."

It was a bizarre conversation to have without touching each other. We just stood there. Our voices could have been disembodied.

At last, I said, "Revenge-fucking's never a good idea."

She stepped toward me. I held up my hands. I didn't want to feel her touch, didn't want things to start. It was all bad enough.

"That's not what this is," she told me.

"Yes, it is. And you know it. You want Gene. Not me. I'm not even in the game."

She raised her arms for an embrace, then lowered them again.

"I could make you," she said.

"And where would that get us, exactly?" I had to look away from her. "Don't do this to Gene. Don't demean yourself. He'll come around. I swear it. Jessie does sprints, not marathons."

Tears bunched in her eyes. But her expression spoke more of frustration than of sorrow.

A fist hammered on the front door. It wasn't a woman this time.

Marilyn alerted. "That's Gene. Don't let him know I'm here."

I stood there bewildered. How could she know it was Gene?

The fist thumped the cheap wood again. Gene's voice called, "Open up, you sonofabitch."

I opened the door. Gene looked volcanic.

He pushed in. I backed up.

Looking around my living room and beyond into the kitchen, he said, "Tell my slut of a wife to get out here. *Now.*"

"Gene—"

He pushed the flat of his hand into my chest, attempting to thrust me aside. I stood my ground, but said nothing.

"I know she's here!" Gene shouted. "How stupid do you think I am? Her car's out front." He decided to speak to Marilyn through the walls. "You slut. Get out here. Or I'll drag you out by the hair."

"Gene, calm down. Listen to me."

Flaring, he looked me up and down. Then his eyes shifted over my shoulder and focused hard.

I turned to see what he saw. Marilyn had come out of the bedroom. She was naked above the waist.

Gene sucker-punched me, and I went out.

I'm not sure how long I remained unconscious. There was a blurry transition between utter incapability and the moment I felt together enough to attempt to rise from the floor. My thoughts were incoherent, to the extent that the images swarming in my brain qualified as thoughts. Lying flat, I felt rigid and nauseated. Pinned down. Unable. Overwhelmed. Later, sitting up, I wondered if I had a concussion. If I didn't, I had Ali to thank. My head had landed on one of the Persian rugs. There wasn't any blood. Just bad-hangover dizziness.

When I finally dragged myself into the bedroom, I found Marilyn's top and bra lying on the floor. Gene had dragged her outside the way he found her.

21

Eli showed up at my door a half hour early for the trip to the hospital.
Just as I let him inside, Mary Jane emerged from the bathroom, naked after her shower.

It was an interesting moment.

Instead of shrieking and fleeing, Mary Jane stood still, as if the world's pieces weren't fitting together properly. A bit slowly, she covered herself with her hands and wrists in the classic pose of Venus. Then she stepped into the bedroom and out of sight.

She didn't run. Or even frown. She merely had looked confused.

"My timing seems inopportune," Eli said. He flapped the manila envelope under his arm, as if that explained everything. I assumed it was his medical records, but he added, "We can go over this stuff in the car."

"Coffee?"

"Best not. But go ahead. Please. Would it be better if I waited outside?"

Around the corner, in the bedroom, Mary Jane laughed. The sound bounced between a cackle and a hoot.

"I guess I'm already as compromised as I'm going to get," she said. "Now Mr. Lemberger knows *all* my secrets."

I turned to Eli. I was the one who wasn't clued in.

"Attorney–client relationship," Eli explained. "I leave it to the client to discuss things further."

We waited.

Black boots gleaming, Mary Jane marched forth in her fatigues, laughing again.

"Mr. Lemberger handled my divorce," she said.

Divorce? I hadn't pried into Mary Jane's past. And she hadn't volunteered much. But every soldier was entitled to at least one trial marriage. In Special Forces, you were allocated three or four.

"He left my husband happy as a hoedown," Mary Jane went on. "Grinning at his good luck in getting rid of me. And grinning wasn't my ex's style."

"Uncontested," Eli explained. "There was no reason for nastiness."

"Well, ya done good," Mary Jane told him.

"Miss Munro may be my only client in recent memory who paid her bill in full. Ahead of schedule, I might add."

"My debt to society," Mary Jane said. "So you're the friend who needs a ride to Scottsdale. Small world."

"Indeed," Eli agreed. He looked at me, then back toward Mary Jane. "I think I shall lurk outside, after all. Even the briefest farewells are best said in private."

When he stepped outside and pulled the door shut behind him, Mary Jane grabbed me. Her kiss took charge of the heavens and the earth.

"It's still pretty fresh, the divorce thing," she said as we caught our breath. "I didn't feel like going into it."

"No need."

"He's a good guy. Lemberger, not my husband. Although my husband wasn't a bad guy, either. Not particularly bad. I just got tired of being alone even when I was with him. If that makes any sense."

"No need to explain. Have some coffee, make yourself some breakfast. Just turn the lock when you leave. See you tonight? If it's not too late?"

"I have class. But call me. Somebody might have an itch."

I touched her inappropriately through her starched fatigues.

"Oh, that's all I need," she said, pulling away. Her face grew serious and her eyes drifted away from me. "I suppose I wanted you to think I was some virgin damsel in a tower or something." Her eyes, warm and brown, found their way back to mine. She was a wonderfully brave girl. "I really have it bad for you, Roy. It's a good thing you're leaving."

"Virgin damsels are overrated."

Eli insisted that we take his car, a reasonably new Audi. That made sense, given the Mustang's fickle mechanical state. He also insisted on driving the first leg. That part didn't make sense. He was shaky even before he released the emergency brake.

He tossed the manila envelope in my lap, cranked up the engine, and began to back out of the parking lot.

"I had planned to go over all this in your apartment. Thus my farcical arrival." He turned us toward the highway.

"What is it?"

"Open it. Check the photos first."

Eli had turned back his sleeves nearly to his elbows. Liver-colored spots showed on his forearms. One rose above his collar, as well.

I undid the clasp of the envelope and eased the contents partway into my lap. The mug shots raced ahead of the photocopied paperwork.

A hard-faced teenage girl with bleached-blond hair stared right, left, and toward me. The name below the shots was Joanne Lampert. She could have been Jessie Lamoureaux's white trash cousin. Or her sister. But I knew she wasn't.

"That was her first prostitution bust. Procurement, too. Even as a teenager, she was running other girls. Six-month sentence, which was light by the standards of Jackson, Mississippi. And that was quietly suspended. Either the girl had friends with plenty of pull, or her better clients were frightened by what she knew. The newspapers dropped it, probably after some down-home persuasion. Cops don't forget, though."

"So your contacts came through."

"When the right plug finally went into the right socket, a great many lights just couldn't wait to come on. The Jackson bust was just the start. Joanne Lampert, convicted felon, executed a legal name-change in the state of Louisiana. And became Jessica Beauharnais Lamoureaux." Eli clicked his tongue in disgust. "I mean, how *could* she expect to pull off such a preposterous name?"

"She did, though."

"I suppose it's the tastelessness that offends me. 'Lamoureaux' is the-atrical enough, but 'Beauharnais'? The girl's aesthetically impossible." The morning sun struck a silver mobile home out in the desert. A wooden windmill held still. "By the way, Roy. Before Miss Munro emerged like Aphrodite in her glory, I meant to ask *you* something."

"Ask," I said. Although I was impatient to dive deeper into the history of Joanne Lampert, aka First Lieutenant Jessica Lamoureaux.

"I don't want to seem . . . condescending. If I do, you *must* forgive me. But those two rugs you have on your floor? They're not doormats, you know."

"I meant to roll them back up."

"They should be displayed on a wall. And somewhere safe. Not in—forgive me—a slum like Huachuca City, Arizona. Good Lord, Roy . . . do you have any *idea* what they're worth?"

"Yes."

"To the eye of one who's done battle with the fiercest carpet-mongers in Los Angeles, they look like museum pieces."

"They may have been. For all I know. Iran was complicated."

"Roy . . . whatever history may be involved here, whatever emotional entanglements there may be . . . you mustn't be irresponsible." He clearly was exasperated with me. "Didn't our talk last Saturday night make any impression on you?"

"It did. Things have just been a mess. I've been derelict in my duties."

"You *must* give me your word that you'll roll those rugs up the *instant* you return home. And that you'll hide them away. Until you decide on a safe place to store them."

"You have my word."

The morning shadows suffered lingering deaths. Exposed, the landscape grew ugly.

"Can we get back to the ace detective stuff?" I asked. "If I promise to be a good Scout?"

He thought about it. "How much do you really want to know, Roy? Or need to know? It isn't pretty."

"I don't want it to be pretty."

We drove in silence for a stretch. Eli was heavier on the gas pedal than I would have been. And I didn't drive slowly. We had almost reached the interchange at Benson, the first checkpoint on the convoy route to Scottsdale, before he found the wherewithal to speak again.

"Her second bust was in New Orleans. That one was a stinking mess. The prosecutor wanted her declared a threat to public health. She apparently gave her clients a lot more than they paid for. The mayor's office was involved, society names, Garden District addresses . . ."

"And?"

"She walked. One can only speculate as to how much incriminating evidence she had stockpiled. Knowledge is a whore's only insurance, Roy. Whether it's New Orleans or L.A. On the other hand, it's a wonder she wasn't found dead 'of undetermined causes,' given the scope of the scandal. Even then, someone protected her."

"She's good at enlisting protectors. Christ, though. It's no wonder her security clearance has been held up."

"She's a tough customer. What I meant to say earlier, when I asked how much you really wanted to know, is that you might want to be careful. The girl has a knack for outliving the catastrophes she creates." He kept his eyes on the straight black road that stretched ahead of us. "Of course, sooner or later . . ."

"I'm not interested in inflicting damage on her. I just want to stop her from inflicting damage on others."

He raised an eyebrow. "Is it really your business?"

"It's a matter of friendship. Even if the friendship's over."

"Well, you'll find plenty of ammunition in those files. But as a creature well-versed in legal viciousness, I advise you to aim carefully before you pull the trigger. Purloined evidence won't hold up in court. For one thing."

"I'm not planning to take her to court. It's not about her. Not that way."

"Well, her next home of record was Baton Rouge. Presumably, after some medical attention. Back and forth between there and Natchez for about three years. Ultimately, she shows up back in New Orleans for special appearances. On the arm of some muckety-muck in the National Guard. Very public. There are even tattletale newspaper photos. With Miss Lamoureaux looking alluring and adroit. Which is more than one could say of her startled escort. Either this general's wife didn't know, or outright refused to know. Of course, Louisiana seems to have its own rather complicated social rules."

"Any mention of her joining the National Guard, the circumstances?"

"A little over a year ago, she received a direct commission. Out of the blue. Is that how these things usually work?"

"No. And she told me she was commissioned through OCS, for what it's worth. A lot of things are beginning to make sense."

Eli pondered matters. "I have little experience with Southern belles outside of the Gothic *oeuvre* of Tennessee Williams . . . but it's my impression that they operate on the principle that a lie is *always* better than the truth. If they've been out to dinner and you see them walk out of the restaurant, they'll *still* insist that they were at the movies all evening. Apparently, the Southern boys believe them."

"What could she have been thinking?" I asked. The question was more for myself than for Eli. "How could she think she could bluff the entire U.S. Army? And get a top secret clearance? With police records in two states?"

Eli shifted his thin shoulders. "She's been able to bluff her way this far. You said as much yourself."

Eli pulled off the highway into a truck stop lot. "There's plenty more in the file. It's yours, keep it. Frankly, it made me feel dirty just reading it. And I know 'dirty,' Roy. Would you mind driving from here?"

"Sure. No problem."

He paused before getting out from behind the wheel. Despite the air-conditioning, sweat gleamed on his forehead.

"Would you go inside and get me a Coke? With plenty of ice? I'm feeling a bit dizzy."

At the end of a long afternoon of waiting and nearly memorizing Jessie's files, a nurse tracked me down in the dead-zone of the lobby.

"Lieutenant Banks?"

I looked up. She was not the glamorous nurse on the welcoming billboard.

"Yes, ma'am."

"Your friend's asking to see you. I'm afraid he won't be going home today."

I followed her. To the infectious diseases ward. I had to sign in.

"Just a precaution," she told me. "Your friend's symptoms are just a little confusing."

I put on the booties, a paper overgarment, and a face mask.

Shrunken under a sheet drawn up to his shoulders, Eli smiled when he saw me. "I've always had a fondness for fancy-dress parties."

"Is it all right to sit down?" I asked the nurse. I was, indeed, a creature of rules.

She nodded. "Don't stay too long. He's tired. And make sure you sign out at the desk."

Clearly unnerved, Eli tried to put a confident face on things. He sang, " 'Is it plague or . . . is it cholera . . . now that Eli's . . . back in town . . . ' " Then he dropped the tune and admitted, "This is discouraging."

He began to weep. At first, I thought they were tears of fright or self-pity. I didn't know what to say. Sickrooms turned me mute.

"Oh, Roy! When it rains, it *truly* pours. I've tried to be . . . to be *manly* about all this. But I received some dreadful news last night, on the very eve of this *hejira*."

I sat and let him speak.

"A friend called. It's Kurt, my Kurt. He *died*, Roy. Just like that. He's dead. So young, so golden . . . so perfectly golden . . ."

"Cancer, you said?"

"I suppose. I don't know if they ever quite figured it out, to be honest. I wonder, is the same thing happening to me? I mean, 'cancer' is something of a catch-all, when the medicine men are baffled. You know, I simply can't grasp that he's no longer there. He *can't* be dead. Not Kurt. But he is. It bewilders me. I don't know, Roy . . . maybe I seem laughable to you, a pathetic old queen. But I had my heyday."

"You don't. You don't seem pathetic."

"We love who we *must* love, that's the awful thing of it. I don't believe I would have *chosen* him. Frivolity can be carried to an excess, even among the golden creatures. Nor was it only his beauty, not just that. I didn't choose. I was chosen. To love him. Everything in my life pointed me toward him, I think."

He let his face turn partway into the pillow. "Should I be grateful, after all the pain? And now this? Knowing that I shall never see him again? I think that I *should* be grateful, more fool me. Poor Kurt. I doubt that any man who ever lived gave less thought to death."

"I'm sorry."

"I'm growing maudlin. Forgive me. My world must be difficult for you to grasp. Unpleasant. Repellent, even. But the thing of it is that I refuse to regret loving him. There's so little love, so little. And I had a great big slice of it."

"More to come. When you get better. You still going back to L.A.?"

He nodded. Weakly. Changing the soft contours of the pillow. "That decision's been made for me, I think. I befuddle the good doctors here on the Wild Frontier. And I've used up Bisbee's social and business opportunities." He smiled. "Do you have any idea, by the way, how glad I am that we met? It's an odd friendship, really. But not a bad one, I think."

"Listen, Eli . . . I'm slated to leave Fort Huachuca next Friday, a week from tomorrow. Drive to Ohio, kiss Mom good-bye again, drive to Delaware to ship my car . . . and it's off to the ruins of the Ottoman Empire. But if you're released before then, call me. Promise me that you'll call. If you want me to roll up those rugs and hide them. I'd be glad to pick you up and drive you home. I've got plenty of leave days stacked up."

"That's very good of you, Roy. And I think I'll take you up on it. If the medical establishment doesn't deem me too great a curiosity to let go." He chuckled. "Not sure what else I could do, to tell you the truth. I'm not quite up to the rigors of Trailways or Greyhound." He tried to shift his body in the bed. I couldn't judge if he succeeded to his satisfaction. "If I'm still here when you leave . . . if we don't see each other . . ."

"I'll drop by, anyway. Just to shoot the breeze. On my way east. Saves me the most boring drive in the universe, through southern New Mexico and west Texas."

". . . what I wanted to say is that you can leave the Audi at my place. Anna, the woman who lives next door, can hold the keys for me. If it comes to that. And there's a stray cat who comes to my back door in the mornings. Would you take a twenty from my wallet in the drawer there and ask her to keep it fed? I've already let down enough creatures in my life."

A different nurse popped in. Younger eyes above the surgical mask. "Mr. Lemberger, I'm going to have to ask your guest to leave now."

I stood up. Selfishly. Hospitals made me uncomfortable and impatient.

"Poor Kurt," Eli said. "My golden child. If I could only have music here, things wouldn't be so bad. I'd like to listen to Trane, 'A Love Supreme.' As a requiem Mass. There's a box of cassettes behind the driver's seat, Roy. It may be in there. Listen to it on the way home. For me."

It was after midnight when I reached my apartment, so I didn't call Mary Jane. As much as I would have liked to take advantage of her yet again. I phoned her in the morning, though, to explain. We agreed that she'd come over after work, after she had changed out of her fatigues and taken a shower. I mentioned going to the Steak-Out, over in Sonoita, for dinner, but she shot that down as too risky.

"I'm just your back-street girl," she said. "You can't break ranks, LT."

"Knock off the 'LT,' huh?"

She laughed. Then she stripped the mirth from her voice and said, "You probably haven't heard. Lieutenant Purvis got busted yesterday."

I went cold. Drugs. The whole mess. We'd all go down. Because of his bullshit.

"What happened?"

"The dumb jerk was shoplifting," she said. "With a cast on his hand. They got him walking out of the commissary with a pack of ham and some cheese slices in his sling."

When I failed to respond, she continued. "Can you imagine being so stupid? Throwing away your career? For lunch meat and cheese?"

After we said good-bye, I called information. For Jessie Lamoureaux's, aka Joanne Lampert's, phone number. I had never had a reason to call her before this.

She was still at home, but seemed in a hurry. The call of duty. We both were running late.

"It's Roy."

"Why, Roy! How delightful!"

"It's not delightful. Trust me. I need to talk to you."

"Your place, or mine?"

I told her to meet me in the parking lot on Reservoir Hill. At high noon.

22

Jessie got there first. She waited in her air-conditioned car. Not a girl to perspire without a purpose.

Shadows are nature's makeup. Noon strips off the paint. The earth looked dead.

I parked across the lot. It sat on a spur above the fort. At dawn, rattlesnakes down from the mountains lay stretched over the paving, doped by the leftover heat. Now Jessie and I were the only living things on the scene.

She didn't get out to meet me. I walked over to her car and stood by her window. She lowered it and smiled.

"What an interesting setting for our date."

"It's not a date," I said. "Get out. We need to talk."

She looked up at me. With a perfected mask of innocence. "Why don't you get in?"

"This needs to be out in the open. In every respect."

"We're the only ones here. And it's hot. Get in, and don't be silly, Roy."

"I'll wait down by the picnic tables. I won't wait long."

I headed down the path that led to the sand-colored water tank. Splintering tables baked in the sun, worthless without umbrellas.

A lizard shot across the trail. We weren't the only living things. You were never alone in the desert. Its natives hid until ready to lash out.

The vehicles down in the streets below us seemed burdened by the heat. On the southern horizon, Mexico quivered. A lone cloud rose from the copper smelter hidden behind the mountains.

I heard Jessie's footsteps and turned. The Army's fatigue uniform deformed female bodies. Jessie looked seductive in it.

With her dark hair drawn back and tucked under her cap, her face was classical in its proportions and lines. Even the brutal light of noon adored her. Uncertain why it didn't work on me, I grasped her appeal. She was the seductress of all the myths. Even the beauties of Tehran hadn't come close.

Discarding her innocent pose, Jessie grew hard.

"All right, Mr. Important," she said. "Talk."

"I want you to leave Gene and Marilyn Massetto alone. And Dinwiddie, for that matter. I don't care what else you do. But I want you out of their lives. That clear enough?"

Her face tightened under the visor of her cap. Her jaw led. "Who the fuck do you think you are?"

"Wrong question. Who do you think *you* are?"

"Oh, that's rich. Coming from you. Your friend Ali told me all about you, you know. How you seduced his baby sister and dumped her. How she killed herself over you." She inched closer. "Did you get off on that, Roy? A little girl killing herself for you? Do you come in your underwear just thinking about it?"

"That's not what happened."

Misjudging the force ratio between us, she attacked. "You're a big fraud, Roy. It's always little girls, it's never women. They ought to keep you away from playgrounds, you know that? And you want to tell me how to run *my* life? You think you can give *me* an ultimatum?"

"I'm not the topic of today's seminar."

She smirked. "Isn't that your favorite subject?"

"I need you to stay away from Gene. And Marilyn. Let them have their lives, for God's sake. Give them both a break. You can have anybody you want."

"Anybody?"

"Yes or no. Will you agree to get out of their lives and stay out?"

She brushed away a fly. "Why should I? You asshole. Why the fuck should I do anything you say?" The fly returned, and she backhanded it again. "Little girls? You can't even manage them." She edged closer still. Looking into my face as if ready to strike. "Nicole dumped you. Your little Nikki. She killed your baby and dumped you. You didn't even rate a good-bye fuck."

"She was going back to her husband. That was the deal all along. And it's none of your business."

"But it *is* my business, Roy." She smiled triumphantly. "I didn't want to have to tell you this . . . but your ex-girlfriend likes some kinky things. I mean, she's game for anything, isn't she? Or didn't you get that far?"

"How would you know?"

Still smiling, she said, "I'm not pure and holy like you, Roy. I like the things I like. And I just *loved* having a threesome with your little Nikki before she left. Just last week. Me, Nicole, and Jerry. I mean, she's into things that just plain embarrassed me. And I'm hard to embarrass, once the bedroom door closes." She cocked her head, evaluating my reaction. "And so soon after the abortion. I wasn't sure it was safe. But she didn't have any problems. On the contrary. She wore poor Jerry out. Me, too. I wish I'd taken pictures for you."

"You're most vicious human being I've ever met."

"Then you haven't lived."

"Hold out your hand."

"Are you going to slap me, Roy? Did you bring a ruler?"

"Hold out your hand."

She did as I asked. Giggling. "There. Are you going to read my fortune?"

"You don't have one," I told her. "You should've done your intelligence work. Before you attacked."

"Why, are those tears in your poor little eyes? For your absent sweetheart?"

"I know what a liar you are."

"Ask her. Call her. She's honest, I'll give her that. Ask her what she begged us both to do to her."

The fly decided I was a safer target than Jessie. I slapped it away with an overwrought gesture. Then I unbuttoned my left breast pocket and fished for the single photo I'd brought along.

About to withdraw her hand, Jessie told me, "Come on. I have places to go and things to do."

I dropped one of the mug shots into her palm.

"You take a sweet picture, Joanne."

Jessie attacked me. It wasn't girlie stuff. She came at me with her fists. And it wasn't her first fight.

I was quick enough to fend off the blows she aimed at my face, but she landed several elsewhere. I avoided the jerked-up knee, but not the boot tip into my ankle. It hurt, even through boot leather.

She tried again to land one on my face. I sidestepped and tripped her while she was off balance.

Jessie crashed down. Hard. She landed full-length and flat, hat flying off. Dust gripped her body, raven hair came loose.

Face hidden from me, she shrieked, "You motherfucker! You cocksucker!"

"That must be Joanne Lampert speaking," I told her. "Lieutenant Lamoureaux just told me she's hard to embarrass."

Twisting away from the earth and bleeding from the nose, she glared up at me with hatred that thickened the air. Her right hand was badly scraped, and she clutched it as if the wrist might have a problem. She was the one crying, not me. The sight of tears streaking Jessie's face was jarring.

"Fuck you," she said.

I stood over her. "How in the name of Christ did you think you'd get away with it? Did you really think they'd give you a security clearance? Do you think they're that stupid?"

"Yeah. They're that stupid. Like you. Fuck yourself."

"You're not displaying a constructive attitude, Joanne. You must've been a lot nicer to those judges."

"*You're* in no position to judge me."

"I don't have to. Others already did. I mean, so far I only know about the two prostitution busts. Oh, and the procurement charge. And the Typhoid Mary stuff. Have you told Gene all about that?"

Uncoiling like a snake, she came at me again. It was instinctive, irrational. There was no design. She just launched herself at my legs. Hands clawing. Mouth open to bite.

I kicked her away. I wasn't in a gentlemanly mood.

Attempting to wipe the blood from her face, she smeared it. The fly returned. She ignored it.

"What do you want?"

I let her worry. Without taking her eyes off me, she climbed back to her feet. But she kept her distance now.

"What do you want?" she repeated. "I have money, I can pay you."

"You know better."

"A *lot* of money, Roy. You don't know."

"I told you what I want. I want you to extract yourself from Gene's life. And Marilyn's. And Dinwiddie's, if you haven't already finished with the poor guy. But start with Gene."

"I can't." Her uniform was torn and bloody at the knees. She had become a creature of tears, blood, and dust. A smeared thing. Her loosened hair looked crazed.

"Why?"

"Because . . . we're getting married. Gene asked me to marry him."

"He's already married."

"He's going to divorce her. He loves me."

"Ah, true love."

"And I love him."

"And after he hears you were a teenage hooker with multiple busts? And that seems to be the least of it."

She raised her fist again, then thought better of it.

"Why should you care?" she demanded. "It's none of your business."

"You made it my business." I stared at her, seeing and not seeing. Maybe it was the sight of her blood, how blood calls for more blood, but I wanted to hammer her back to the ground with my fists. And to keep at it, to hurt her, to mark her. Restraining myself was one of the hardest things I had ever had to do. Maybe the hardest. "What you said. About Nikki . . ."

"She's a slut. You want me to lie? To make you feel good? I could've used her back when I was working. She's game for anything." Jessie tried out a smile. White teeth through drying blood. "I finally got what you saw in her, though." She edged closer to me again. Entering the sexual radius. "Roy . . . can't we work something out?"

"You break it off with Gene—completely—or everything I have on you goes to the investigators. It's my duty as an officer and a taxpayer. To save Uncle Sam an expensive investigation."

"I don't really think you'd do that to me. You're not that cruel, Roy. You don't take pleasure in hurting people."

"I thought I got my kicks from little girls killing themselves over me? Which didn't happen, for what it's worth."

"That was said in anger. I spoke in anger."

"And you didn't really mean it. Come off it, Joanne."

"Don't call me that. Please."

I looked at my wrist, at my memento of a girl who didn't kill herself. Who never would have killed herself. "I've got an out-processing appointment. One last chance, Jessie. Will you break things off with Gene and leave them alone?"

She raised both fists, but the fight instantly drained out of her. She sagged. "I'm going to marry him. I'm going to *marry* him."

"No. You're not."

"*Please.* Please let me be happy. *Please.* Can't you believe that I can love somebody? I've been caught, Roy. Cupid's arrow. All of it. Really and truly. *Please.* I beseech you, I'll get down on my knees and beg. If you want, I'll get out of the Army. I can make that happen, if that's what's bothering you. I can find an excuse, I'll find a way. But don't cut me off from him." She was crying again. Bawling. But I no longer knew what was real and what was an act.

"Your choice. Make it now."

"*Please.* I just want to be happy. Everybody else can be happy. Why not me? I'm entitled to a life. Even if I've made mistakes."

"It was more than just mistakes. And what about Marilyn's happiness?"

She really did drop to her knees. Hanging her head. It only made me flash on Pete Paulson. Which didn't help her cause.

"Tell me what you want me to do, Roy. Only not that, not Gene. Don't try to make me give him up, because I *can't*." She lifted her face, her eyes, to plead. If it was theater, it was good theater. "Do you have any idea, any real idea, what my life has been like? You think I'm trailer trash? I wish. A trailer had class, it had appliances that worked, plumbing, you could clean it out. Do you have any idea what it's like when your own mother puts you out to sell it and tells you not to come home without twenty dollars? And you haven't even had your first period? You have no idea how . . . how *filthy* this world is. And all I've wanted, all these years, was a chance. And now I have a chance."

She reached out, as if to clutch my leg. In the eternal posture of female supplication. "I've changed. It's been hard. But I've changed. I buried my past, I killed it. It was dead and gone. Until you interfered."

"The past never dies. It just takes naps."

She wept, and bowed down, and touched the dust on the toes of my boots with her fingertips.

I applauded. Slowly. Sadistically. "By the way, why did you set Jerry up? With the Mexicans? And right after your fantastic threesome?"

She gave up. It had been an act, after all. She scrambled to her feet, spitting venom.

"He's a fucking loser," she said. "The asshole set himself up."

"Maybe he just made some mistakes. Maybe you have no idea. Maybe all he wanted was a chance."

I thought she was bending to pick up her cap. But she picked up a rock. It was big enough to hurt.

"Not a good idea," I told her.

"I could go down to the MP station and tell them you lured me up here and tried to rape me."

"You're dirty in all the wrong places. And you'd have to explain why there's no blood on me. Moot point, though, since I'll be at the MP station before you get there. Turning over photocopies of your police records from Jackson and New Orleans. Enjoy the polygraph. And the court-martial."

She held the rock suspended in the air. Burning with fury.

"I could have you killed," she said.

I walked away. Offering her my back. Headed to my car.

She didn't throw the stone.

I didn't go straight to the MP shack. I wanted to give her time to think, to make the only sane decision. I told myself that I'd give her until the evening, then wondered if I should grant her the entire weekend. Even given all that had passed between us, the idea of ratting her out unsettled me. I told myself that I wanted results, not revenge.

Distracted, to say the least, I sleepwalked through my afternoon appointments. Confronted with forms, I just signed them.

I wrapped things up at the travel office a little after four, then drove over to the convenience shop that doubled as the post's Class VI store. I bought a bottle of tequila and got back in the Mustang. Then I went back in and bought a second bottle. I didn't bother with margarita mix and didn't stop at the commissary for limes.

At home, I stripped off my boots and uniform, then discarded my socks and underwear. I meant to take a shower, but sidetracked myself by drinking tequila out of the bottle. I pulled on a pair of cut-offs, put on *Filles de Kilimanjaro,* and planted myself on the sofa, bottle in hand.

I forgot that Mary Jane was coming over, forgot about all my ambitions, great or small. The things that should have mattered disappeared.

I hate tequila. That was part of my punishment.

The phone rang. I grabbed it, expecting to hear Jessie's voice. Telling me that she was ready to meet my terms.

Hysterical, Marilyn wailed on the other end.

"He's leaving me, he's leaving me. I'm sorry, so sorry. It didn't work. I'm so sorry, Roy . . . so sorry for what I did. He's *leaving* me, it didn't work. I'm so sorry. . . ."

I didn't hang up. I just laid the receiver beside the phone and let her rant to the music. I'd moved on from Miles to Charles Lloyd. The near-cacophony suited the situation.

I spilled tequila on my bare chest. The only possible response was to drink more. I forgot about the phone, didn't hear the "Please hang up" message, if and when it came. The I lost the last of my self-control.

I hung up the phone, then took up the receiver again and dialed for information. Working through the layers, I reached the operator responsible for the Fort Lewis area. I requested the listing for Nikki's husband. Yes, I was willing to pay the charge for the operator to connect me.

I told myself that if anyone but Nikki answered, I'd hang up.

Nikki answered.

"It's me, it's Roy. Please don't hang up."

She didn't hang up.

"Nikki . . . I have to ask you something. Did you—?"

"Yes."

"Why?"

"Because I wanted you to know it was over."

She ended the call.

At some point during the evening, Mary Jane arrived at my door. I knew her knock, but didn't get up. I wasn't certain I could.

Letting herself in, Mary Jane scoped things out and asked, "Have I stepped into the wrong movie?"

I didn't look straight at her, couldn't face her. But the girl wasn't a quitter. She scrounged up some scraps for dinner, eating without me when I failed to answer her summons to the table. When I stumbled and fell in an attempt to change the album on the turntable, she let me pick myself up. She'd dealt with male drunks before.

At some point, we tumbled into bed. I recall things working better than they should have. We even woke up and went at it in the middle of the night. After which, I cold-sweated my way into the bathroom and vomited.

I woke up back in bed, suffering a five hundred-kiloton alcohol concussion. The blinds and drapes were drawn, but the daylight that cut through was savage.

Mary Jane was gone.

When I finally got it together to stumble out and make coffee, I found a note on the kitchen table:

It's been a treat, LT, but my name's not Nicky.

I attempted a run in the proving ground that began a few blocks from my place, but it wasn't exactly a triumph of the will. I walked back.

Reeling. Two fat Mexican brats mocked me. The tiny house that had expelled them bulged with people whose pickups and rust-buckets were staging a *reconquista* of the street. My hangover congealed into bristling bigotry.

I needed water, but drank coffee and ate aspirin like breath mints. It wasn't that I couldn't hold my liquor, but that the liquor held me.

I found the second bottle of tequila with a third of its contents missing. I poured the remains down the kitchen drain and gagged over the fumes. For a chaser, I made a can of Campbell's chicken-noodle soup.

The phone didn't just ring; it attacked. Conjuring a lust to break things that I barely restrained.

I answered. In case it was Jessie, contrite and acquiescent. Or Eli, calling from the hospital for a ride. Or an angel from on high. Offering hope, consolation, tidings of comfort and joy, transfiguration, sex.

At first, I couldn't identify the creature shrieking at the other end of the line.

Marilyn. Utterly maddened.

I put the phone down. Gently. Wary of myself.

Moving to disconnect the line, I stopped. I called my mother, telling her, belatedly, that I'd be passing through in a week or so. Her delight made my head hurt worse. Then I called City Hospital in Scottsdale. The operator connected me to Eli.

He had to wait for the A-team docs to come back to work on Monday and scrutinize his test results. He expected, or at least hoped, to be released shortly thereafter. He was feeling better, he insisted. But the hospital was a torment.

"There's no music," Eli complained. "None. Not even a radio. Just this dreadful television, perched up there like the eye of a wicked god. Do you have any idea, Roy, how *insipid* television has become, how . . . how dehumanizing? One begins to understand the surge in domestic violence. . . ."

I assured him that I'd do everything possible to get there to pick him up. The only day I had blacked out was Monday, when I had to wait for the movers to show up and box my few possessions so I could get out of town by the end of the week. If worse came to worst, if he wasn't released from the hospital in time, I'd make the promised detour to see him on my drive east.

"Don't even *say* that, Roy. Don't *think* it. I can't bear much more of this place. And it's not just the absence of music. It's that everyone seems so *satisfied* with themselves. They come into my room and they're positively *chipper*. I'd never realized that nurses embody the banality of evil." He paused. "Do you think watching television does that to them?"

He didn't mention Kurt, his dead lover. I understood. The man or woman who can dissect the love they knew in words did not know love.

As soon as I put down the receiver, the phone trilled again.

Marilyn. Howling. Screaming.

This time, I unplugged the telephone. I knew I should call Mary Jane, to apologize, to explain. But any bearable explanation would have been a lie. And any apology would have been inadequate. I told myself that I needed to give her some time. That was a lie, too.

Apart from a drive in for a few last groceries, it was a day of being and nothingness. Music didn't work. I couldn't read. So I scrubbed the place down, prepping it for the landlady's inspection. My life's ambition had shrunk to the hope of getting back my security deposit.

I was on my knees in the bedroom, grinding out ghosts, when a car pulled in. A door slammed, and a woman's footsteps hurried across the dirt to the concrete walk. My doorbell rang. A light fist banged. A hand tried the door. Marilyn began howling.

I dropped the scrub brush and hid in a corner, waiting for her to go away. It took a long time. Had I lived in a more civilized place, the police would have shown up to put an end to the scene.

Her sobbing penetrated the cinder block walls.

When the Marilyn Show finally ended, I plugged the phone back in and dialed Mary Jane's number. But I hung up before it could ring.

Worthless, I lay on the sofa as the light quit. Then I lay on in the darkness. I'm not sure how late it was when I went to bed, but I lay awake for hours, bleeding with memories.

I woke up late on Sunday morning and went for a punitive run out in the proving grounds. I ran farther and harder than I should have done. But it exorcised any last trace of the hangover.

Back at my apartment, I put on some music, cracked open a can of Tecate, and took a long, mindless shower. As I was toweling off, the doorbell rang, followed by heavy knocking.

That wasn't Marilyn. Or Mary Jane, for that matter. And if it was Gene, he wasn't going to get the drop on me this time.

I pulled on a pair of cut-offs. Beer in hand, I headed to the door.

It was Special Agent Tompkins, with his questions.

23

―――――――

"I want to know what happened," I insisted. "It wasn't suicide, was it?"

His deadpan expression wavered. "Not likely. She was hacked to bits. With a cleaver or a hatchet." He canted his head, evaluating me. "What made you think it might be suicide?"

"No particular reason," I lied.

"Did she seem depressed? The last time you saw her? Was she upset about something? Did she seem afraid? Of anything?"

I thought of her blood-smeared face up on Reservoir Hill.

"She wasn't fearful by nature," I told him. Hoping the answer would suffice. I had already decided not to turn over the background information Eli had produced. It would only lead to questions about why I had wanted it, which would lead to Gene and Marilyn, to Jerry and even to Major Dinwiddie, who didn't deserve to be mixed up in this. Let the ace detectives figure things out.

"Then she's the sort of woman who wouldn't be afraid to open the door? Even if it was late?"

"I suppose it would depend on the circumstances. If it was someone she knew . . ."

"Who do you think she would've opened the door for in the middle of the night?"

"Jessie knew a lot of people."

"Mutual acquaintances?"

"Some of them."

"Any of them ever make any threats against her?"

Several of them had. I said, "No."

I just wanted him to leave. There were things to sort out. And I wasn't sure I'd ever sort them out.

"Did you ever sleep with her?"

"I told you the answer. Twice. No. That's three times."

"Remember the green lamp on her nightstand?"

I rolled my eyes. "Get off it. No, I don't remember it. Impossible though it may seem to you, I've never even been in her apartment." It did seem nearly impossible. Even to me. There had been so much between us, and yet so little.

"Then how do you know she lived in an apartment? And not a house? Or a trailer?"

I shrugged. "Take your pick. Most lieutenants here for training live in the BOQ or in an apartment downtown. I knew Jessie didn't live in the BOQ." I decided to take the offensive. "Look, this is sick. You know it wasn't me. So why are you out here wasting my time and yours?" Then I got it. And I couldn't help smiling, if grimly. "Man, you're desperate. Aren't you? The chain of command must be going ballistic. You're grasping at straws."

"And why don't you want to aid the investigation, Lieutenant Banks? It's apparent that you don't."

He had a good, steady stare.

I lowered my eyes, dropped onto the sofa. "Glad to help out, if I can." It was true, and it wasn't. "This is all a shock. I mean, I wasn't Jessie's biggest fan. We hadn't been getting along for some time. And my opinion of her hadn't been getting any higher. But . . . Jesus . . . she was *alive.* I'll give her that. Incredibly alive, just burning with life." My mouth grew a crooked smile. "Funny, the things you realize at a time like this."

"That sounds almost affectionate."

"No. It's not. The last adjective you'd apply to our relationship was *affectionate.*"

He chewed on that for a moment, then said, "So why did she have a framed picture of you in her nightstand drawer?"

"Mind if I use your phone?" Tompkins asked.

"Go ahead."

He picked it up and fixed the receiver against his ear. His face pinched in.

I crossed the room and plugged the phone back into the wall.

"Disturbs my beauty sleep," I told him.

"Mind waiting outside? While I call in?"

I stepped outside my own apartment while he used my phone. With the sun on the other side of the building, the morning air was pleasant. A dark green Army sedan stood beside my Mustang. The sleuth's ride. I tried to connect the jumble of facts in my mind, to decide on a proper course of truth, justice, and the American way that also protected the people I cared about. Despite everything.

Tompkins stayed on the phone for a good ten minutes. Then he opened the screen door and motioned me back inside.

"Okay," he said. "I'll level with you. The commanding general's going ape-shit. He's not having the Sunday morning he had planned. So neither is anybody else. There's a lot of heat coming down to get this solved fast." His solemn expression had turned grumpy, as if he bore me a personal grudge. But his voice had become less antagonistic and more resigned. He sounded tired too early in the day. "Her apartment's in Sierra Vista, so we've got the town cops and the sheriff's department and everybody but Wyatt Earp and Doc Holliday getting in each other's way." He fortified himself with a good, strong breath. "The CG would like us to police up any dirty laundry ourselves. Keep it in-house, to the extent possible. We'd like that, too."

"Go Army," I said. "Good luck."

He looked at me as if he hated me now. "We'd like you to help out the team, Lieutenant. Listen, I don't give a damn if you fucked her or not—"

"I didn't."

"—but how about getting on the right side of Jesus and doing us all a favor?"

"Such as?"

He looked me up and down. The cut-offs were all I wore.

"Such as getting dressed so you look semi-official. For that matter, put on your uniform. That'll cut down on the questions. Then you can come with me."

"Under arrest?"

"Being a smart-ass won't get you anywhere. But for the record, no. You're not a suspect. We're trying every line of investigation we can think of. And you were filed under 'Everything.' I'd just like you to take a ride with me. To Lieutenant Lamoureaux's apartment. All you have to do is keep your mouth shut, look around, and tell me if anything jumps out at you—you're supposed to be an intelligence hotshot, right?"

"I told you. I've never even been in her apartment. Glad to go for a Sunday drive, Agent Tompkins, but I don't really see what I bring to the party."

He considered that. "I guess it depends on which party we're talking about." His look of spite turned wistful until his expression matched his wearied voice. "You know how I know you didn't kill her?"

"My unmistakable aura of innocence?"

"Mary Jane called me."

Suddenly, I couldn't connect the dots.

"She was upset," he went on. "Which is unusual for her. She called early, about an hour before I got pulled in on all this. I don't think I've ever known her to be so distraught. I had her come by for coffee—which she needed—and she was bawling her eyes out. Over you, Lieutenant. She'd been sitting outside your apartment in her car all night, trying to get up the nerve or whatever she needed to knock on your door. It wounds my pride, but there it is. Thank her for scratching you off the list of suspects. *She* knew where you were."

I was seriously confused. "You've lost me. Why would Mary Jane go to you?"

"She's my ex. It wasn't a great marriage, but we all need someone to turn to when we get shit on."

I was wrong, and Special Agent Tompkins was right. I was more help than I ever wanted to be.

We pulled up in the Army sedan. Jessie had lived—and died—in one of Sierra Vista's interchangeable, this-place-sucks apartment complexes. Cops and unshaven newspaper types loitered in the parking lot, with curious neighbors ranged on its outer perimeter. Nothing seemed to be happening fast, but what little was going down centered on a second-story unit.

Before we got out of the car, Tompkins told me, "The body's already gone, so you won't have to deal with that. Assuming they got all the parts. The interior's pretty bad, though. If you have to barf, go outside. Don't puke on the crime scene, all right?" The heat had begun to build inside the sedan the moment he turned off the engine. He pushed open his door and I mimicked him. "We're going to put on booties and gloves before we go in. But I still don't want you touching anything. If something catches your interest, call me over and I'll deal with it. Beyond that . . . just don't say anything to the local boys. Try to look official, like you're on the team."

We walked past Jessie's sports car. The windshield had been smashed. The maroon smears on the white paint job looked like dried blood.

There was more old blood on the concrete stairs that led up to her apartment.

"She fought back," Tompkins explained. "Somebody's hurting out there. They'll have to go to a hospital, at some point. We've put out an alert."

Outside the apartment, we dressed for success. Transparent booties, surgical gloves.

I expected the drill to be useless, but I was curious, too. Crime-scene pornography.

The apartment was a wreck. As if it had hosted a riot, not just a murder. And it stank. Old blood and chopped-up bowels aren't aromatic.

I wish that had been all that I smelled. But there was another, unmistakable odor that struck me like a fist.

Shalimar lingered in the tiny rooms. As if a perfume bottle had been smashed.

We weren't the first to find Marilyn's body. Gene had been bunking with a buddy, but had gone home to fetch more clothes. He found her in their living room, bled out in an easy chair, with her left hand held to her wrist by a strip of skin and a couple of tendons.

Gene didn't recognize me, didn't seem to see anything. He wore a post-combat stare and a dreadful smile.

I noticed that his hands and clothes were clean. He had found Marilyn, but had not touched her. It was none of my business. But it made me angry. I suppose I was looking for something to be angry about.

I wasn't needed any longer. So I left. I walked over to the pay phone by the shoppette and called a cab to take me home.

The story got even grimmer, when the details emerged. Marilyn had been cut up badly in her combat with Jessie. She got herself home, but must have realized that everything was bound to come out, that she couldn't explain her wounds, the blood. First, she tried to hang herself from a ceiling fan, but only managed to pull it down on top of her.

The textbook way to bleed yourself to death is to slit your wrists in a warm tub and go gently into oblivion. Marilyn was beyond that. She had done her best to hack off her left hand with a butcher knife. She splattered the house with blood before settling into the easy chair to die.

As for Jessie, the primary murder weapon used against her had been Gene's Boy Scout hatchet.

I didn't have much of a backyard at the apartment. Just a strip of dirt with a few tufts of grass and a rusting charcoal grill for a luxury touch.

The grill earned its keep. I burned all the papers and photos Eli had given me. I saw no point in adding to the misery. The cops could do their cop thing. I wasn't one of them.

I phoned Mary Jane and she came over. We slept together. But it wasn't the same.

"When are you leaving?" she asked.

"Friday."

She thought about that, then said, "I did this to myself."

On Tuesday, I drove up to Scottsdale to take Eli home. They brought him downstairs in a wheelchair. On principle, I suppose. Or because it let them tack on one last fee. He could walk perfectly well, even seemed rejuvenated. He smiled to see me.

"I hope you brought all the tapes?" he said. "I *crave* music."

I had. And something else, as well.

We stopped in Tucson for an early dinner. Eli rolled down his sleeves to hide the blemishes on his skin, but he ate with gusto.

"The hospital food . . . ," he said. ". . . you have *no* idea . . ."

He really did seem on the road to recovery. Almost magically so. We had a long talk in the car. He was far less surprised than I had been by Jessie's murder.

"Just another day in L.A.," he commented.

"This isn't L.A."

He shrugged. "She would've ended up there eventually. Her kind always does."

Eli hoped to attend a memorial service for Kurt the following week. "His parents are the sweetest people," he told me. "They must be devastated. Only son. At first, they hoped he was just going through a phase. Later, they saw me as his only hope—isn't that sad? We used to have lunch and commiserate. Over *our* Kurt . . ."

Just short of Bisbee, as we climbed the mountain pass, Eli said, "Love is so much grander than our vocabulary."

I was prepared to help him up the steps that led to his porch. They were steep. But Eli got up them just fine. I went back to the car, got my farewell gift out of the trunk, and followed him inside.

After my presentation, he said, "Roy . . . I can't *possibly* accept that."

"Well, you have to. I can't take it with me to Turkey. Now that we have a ban on the importation of Iranian rugs and carpets. Customs would seize it when I tried to bring it back again. I have no documenta-tion."

"You could leave it with your mother. In Cincinnati, right?"

I shook my head. "Mom pledges allegiance to wall-to-wall carpet."

"She sounds delicious," Eli said. "But, really, Roy . . ."

He wanted the rug. That was the beauty of it. I could give him one thing he coveted. Eli appreciated the beautiful things of this earth. Compared to him, I was an aesthetic piker. The rug wanted to be with him.

"Well, I'm leaving it here. If you want to throw it out with the trash, or donate it to the Salvation Army . . ."

A shimmer of horror passed over his features. He clutched the rolled-up silk rug against his chest.

"Just kidding," I assured him.

A lawyerly look crossed his face and left again. "Tell you what, Roy.

I'll take this as a *loan*. I shall guard it for you, until your safe return from the ends of the earth. At which point, you *must* take it back."

"We'll settle up later."

I put a Lester Young album on Edith, his beloved stereo system, and Eli opened his last bottle of Meursault. We drank to friendship and the future.

It's a strange world. Once, I would have written that it's a "queer" world, but that word has been hopelessly debased. I was leaving Fort Huachuca and a lot of personal history behind. And the best friendship I'd made had been with a runaway gay lawyer from Hollywood.

I like to remember him the way he appeared that night, briefly healthy again and holding a glass of splendid wine in his hand, surrounded by the fine things with which he adorned his life. He had *become* a good man. That was the lesson I needed to take with me.

The rug went perfectly under a Glasgow side table he cherished.

On Wednesday, I called Special Agent Tompkins to ask if there was any reason why I couldn't leave on Friday, as scheduled.

"The best advice I can give you," he said, "is to get out of here. If you don't, you'll be dragged into the investigation. Lieutenant Lamoureaux seems to have had some history. But you're not important enough to haul back here, once you're gone."

I called on Major Dinwiddie at his office, to thank him for everything he'd done for me. And to apologize. If I could find the right words.

He wouldn't hear of it. "Self-interest, Roy, self-interest! Just taking care of my Army. Go forth, young knight, and don't hesitate to tilt at the occasional windmill. Good for the soul, my boy, good for the soul. Don't worry, you'll do fine. . . ."

. . .

Instead of bunking at a cheap motel, I stayed with Mary Jane for the last few nights before I hit the road. I could have listed a hundred things I liked about her and valued in her. But I knew I would never love her. The Newtonian universe doesn't seek justice, only equilibrium.

I felt something toward her, though. Eli was right. Our vocabulary didn't reach. Perhaps it was one of the odd forms of love that glow briefly amid the ashes and cinders of gratitude. Or maybe I just liked the way she fucked me. Analysis gets you only so far.

On the morning of my departure, I skipped my run to have a final bout with her. She was perfect for me, yet wrong. Maybe it was only that the timing was off. And Army regulations.

Before I pulled out and headed for the Interstate, I brought the other silk rug up from the trunk of the Mustang.

"This is for you," I told her. Before she could speak, I continued: "But you need to listen to me. If you're ever in a serious financial hole, take this to at least two of the fanciest rug dealers you can find and ask them for estimates of its value. Offer to sell it to whoever gives you the highest estimate. For fifty percent above the price they quote you. They'll jump at it."

She clutched the rug against her breasts, as Eli had held his. A tough girl from the hills, she had avoided tears until that moment.

"Do you really believe I'd ever sell this?" she asked.

24: Epilogue

Mary Jane sold the rug. She held on to it for almost twenty years, though, before her hour of need struck. We never saw each other again, but remained loosely in touch by mail and then, in a new world, by e-mail before her death.

She married, happily, and had two children. She and her husband, a Navy man, settled in a suburb of San Diego, as far away from eastern Kentucky as Mary Jane could go and still remain within the continental United States. After retiring from the Army at the twenty-year mark, she managed a Home Depot. Just after the turn of the millennium, I received a long handwritten letter from her. It had been posted by her husband, who seemed to be a good man. The letter said good-bye. Mary Jane had written it when the cancer had already advanced through much of her body. I hadn't known about the cancer, since she wasn't a woman who ever looked for pity. The letter explained that she had sold the rug to pay for an experimental treatment in Mexico—her military-retiree health care wouldn't cover it, and the family couldn't afford it. She thanked me again and said she remembered me fondly.

Major Leon Dinwiddie did fine. Someone on his promotion board must have known his story, since its members bent the height-and-weight rules and selected him to pin on silver oak leaves. He got his full career in the Army he loved. We also corresponded over the years, if erratically. He, too, married and had two children. When last I heard from him, he was teaching high school in Philadelphia and spending his summers doing inner-city volunteer work with his wife. His elder son had just entered West Point.

I lost track of Nikki, but heard, thirdhand, that a scandal at Fort Lewis ended her marriage and her military career. I never tried to contact her again. I owed her, though. She had done me a good turn, if a harsh one. We had no future, no matter what either one of us might have desired. She knew it. I knew it, too, but had refused to accept it. She saved me from my fit of madness.

My connection with Gene Massetto broke off, too. Understandably. He remained visible in outline, though.

Much in the Army is luck. Gene was lucky to have a chain of command that felt he was worth protecting. He popped up now and again in conversations over the years. Each time, a higher rank preceded his name. I always pictured him young and dashingly handsome. Memory freezes those whom we leave behind.

Then I met him again in 2009. In a restaurant, at lunchtime, in Washington, D.C. I was in town to beg Congress for funds for an international archaeology project in Iraq, and I was preoccupied with the pitch I had to deliver. So I didn't recognize Gene until he introduced himself. I might not have spotted him, anyway. He had grown fat. Instead of a matinee idol, he looked like an aging, exasperated mobster. Since retiring from the Army, he had become a vice-president at a major defense-industry firm. He lived in Potomac, Maryland, with his family. He, too, was giving a pitch on Capitol Hill that afternoon. The figure he was chasing seemed astronomical, and he was proud of the number, if mildly evasive about the utility of the system he was selling. We agreed to get together for drinks, but never did. He got his funding, but I didn't get mine.

Jerry left the Army and disappeared. I sometimes wondered what became of him, but didn't care enough to try to find out.

Eli Lemberger didn't sell the rug I had given him. I had been at my duty station in Turkey for less than a year when my mother forwarded two documents I needed to sign for a law firm in Pasadena. Eli's will had specified that the rug was my property, on loan, and was to be returned to me. He also left me his personal collection of jazz recordings. There was no note or message.

He was a good soldier.